Praise for *The Spinoza Problem*

"[A]s an accessible introduction to Spinoza's complex philosophy, Yalom's method has much to recommend it. . . . The conversations he creates give a lovely sense of the philosopher's character and provide a lucid explanation of the man's major ideas about nature, free will, and re... n." —*Washington Post*

"[A] daring novel. . . . Be... y written, remarkably ambitious, filled with vivid descriptions of place, a ... ting with brilliant insights, *The Spinoza Problem* carefully develops its p ... ities and issues so that they come alive in a highly original and absorbing ... y.' —*Jewish Book World*

"What links renowned 17th-century Jewish philosopher Baruch Spinoza with the Nazi party ideologue whose 'master race' theory led to Hitler's 'final solution? That question is brilliantly explored in the new novel *The Spinoza Problem*." —*San Jose Mercury News*

"In this highly intriguing novel, Irvin D. Yalom . . . builds a plot around the obsession that the infamously anti-Semitic Rosenberg had with Spinoza, a Jew. Yalom seamlessly parallels the intellectual and personal lives of these two very different men in this engaging, erudite tale." —*Tucson Citizen*

"Yalom connects these stories in a powerful mash of what it means to be human." —*San Francisco Book Review*

"Another example of how a psychiatrist's stock in trade—the secrets spoken only in the therapist's office—can be spun into gold by a gifted storyteller." —*Jewish Journal*

"Yalom delivers a powerful philosophical and psychological novel." —*City Book Review*

"Gripping and informative, a brilliant work of psychological fiction." —*Baltimore Jewish Times*

"Inspiring." —*Haaretz.com*

"*The Spinoza Problem* covers a vast amount of extraordinary historical territory."
—*San Francisco Chronicle*

"[Yalom] translates Spinoza's ideas into clear, accessible language. . . . [A]s an introduction to a notoriously difficult philosopher, [*The Spinoza Problem*] is very good indeed."
—*Jewish Chronicle* (UK)

"Yalom has written another intriguing novel that sheds light on what it means to be human. . . . Yalom weaves psychoanalytical knowledge with brilliant story-telling ability. The result is a warmly intelligent novel of ideas which is utterly absorbing."
—*Courier Mail* (Australia)

"This is a book that is fascinating in its detail, as it is in its reimagining of such iconic moments in Western history. Yalom recreates the atmosphere of 17th century Amsterdam beautifully, and he depicts Rosenberg's psychological state and the Nazi rise to power with incredible insight. If you like your historical fiction to be peopled with vividly drawn characters, do read this."   —*Readings* (Australia)

"Yalom has artfully pulled off a feat that could easily backfire in the hands of a less-gifted novelist. . . . Dramatically pleasing, and wonderfully crafted. . . . [Yalom] seeks to plumb the depths of the human mind and its myriad workings."
—*Philosophical Practice: Journal of the APPA*

"Any reader familiar with Spinoza's philosophy will find this book to be a treasure which complements the rationalist's works. Readers unfamiliar with Spinoza will find themselves amidst an enthralling tale of faith, reason, identity and community. However, both readers will leave the book enlightened and eager to make sure the questions they ask in their day to day lives are the right ones."
—Metapsychology Online Reviews

"Imaginative and erudite."   —*Kirkus Reviews*, starred review

"[Yalom] is the perfect author to bring together Spinoza and Rosenberg in a novel. . . . *The Spinoza Problem* informs the reader of the passionate ideas of Spinoza and the disturbing mindset and writings of Rosenberg. . . . A highly intriguing exploration of the connections between a Jewish philosopher and a Nazi ideologue."
—*Shelf Awareness*

"Irvin Yalom does a masterful job in bringing to life Spinoza and his philosophy and connecting it to the apocalyptic history of Nazi Germany and the persona of Alfred Rosenberg. It's the sort of temporal alchemy and alchemy of science and fiction that Yalom does so well. *The Spinoza Problem* is engrossing, enlightening, disturbing and ultimately deeply satisfying."

—Abraham Verghese, author of *Cutting for Stone*

"Spinoza had no 'real life' outside his reading and writing: he lived in his brilliant mind. So how do you write about a philosopher—a writer beloved of Goethe, Schopenhauer, and so many other thinkers—who spent most of his time in thought? And how do you regard Spinoza—a Jew whose work helped to usher in the Enlightenment—if, indeed, you're a Nazi? Irvin Yalom is just the writer to take on such a problem, and he solves it, with his own novelistic brilliance, in this vibrant book. In my view, Yalom is one of the most eclectic, wide-ranging, and dazzling writers of our time."

—Jay Parini, author of *The Last Station* and *The Passages of H.M.*

"The great-souled psychiatrist has written a novel about the great-souled philosopher. Ambitious, erudite, and engaging, *The Spinoza Problem*'s interweaving tale forces a reader to confront the fundamental question: can reason exert its force for good?"   —Rebecca Newberger Goldstein, author of *Betraying Spinoza*

"This is the most intriguing novel I've read in many a year. Irvin Yalom has created a taut, deeply informative page turner. I enthusiastically recommend *The Spinoza Problem*."   —Sir Anthony Hopkins, actor

"*The Spinoza Problem* is a ringing endorsement for an authentically philosophical life, wherein a toweringly heroic philosopher is persecuted in two eras: one governed by medieval superstition; the other, by totalitarian racism. The novel is a masterpiece, depicting the ultimate triumph of clear and compassionate reason over religious dogma and political pathology alike. I think it's Yalom's greatest yet."

—Lou Marinoff, Professor of Philosophy, City College of New York,
and President, American Philosophical Practitioners Association

"In *The Spinoza Problem*, Irvin Yalom has given us a suspenseful and meaningful novel spanning nearly three centuries and depicting how philosophy and wisdom can spur evil counter-responses that can continue for centuries. This book is another tour de force from a leading psychiatrist psychotherapist who has truly created a genre of fiction and whose novels engross and enlighten us as we anticipate turning the next page. *The Spinoza Problem* is another not to be missed work from one of the great contributors to the scientific and fictional literature of psychotherapy."
—Alan F. Schatzberg, M.D., Kenneth T. Norris, Jr. Professor
of Psychiatry and Behavioral Sciences, Stanford University,
and Past-President, American Psychiatric Association

"Irvin Yalom is the most significant writer of psychological fiction in the world today. I didn't think he could top *When Nietzsche Wept* or *The Schopenhauer Cure*, but he has. *The Spinoza Problem* is a masterpiece."
—Martin E. P. Seligman, Past President,
American Psychological Association, and author of *Flourish*

"Irvin Yalom's *The Spinoza Problem* is an amazing novel that combines fact and fiction in a spell-binding manner. Little is known about the psyche of either Baruch Spinoza or Alfred Rosenberg, yet using his extraordinary ability to peer into the minds of his patients, Dr. Yalom has produced a rare gem in existing literature. Only an incomparably gifted author could write such a fascinating and thought-provoking novel. A real page-turner."
—Dilip V. Jeste, M.D., Past President,
American Psychiatric Association

"A thrilling philosophical narrative."   —*Humanité* (France)

"Plausible and fascinating."   —*Liberté Hebdo* (France)

"Clear, well documented, and nuanced."   —*CLES* (France)

The Spinoza Problem

A Novel

IRVIN D. YALOM

BASIC BOOKS
A MEMBER OF THE PERSEUS BOOKS GROUP
New York

Hardcover first published in 2012 by Basic Books,
A Member of the Perseus Books Group
Paperback first published in 2013 by Basic Books

Books published by Basic Books are available at special discounts for bulk purchases in
the United States by corporations, institutions, and other organizations. For more information, please contact the Special Markets Department at the Perseus Books Group,
2300 Chestnut Street, Suite 200, Philadelphia, PA 19103, or call (800) 810-4145,
ext. 5000, or e-mail special.markets@perseusbooks.com.

Typeset in 11 point Minion Pro by the Perseus Books Group

The Library of Congress has catalogued the hardcover as follows:

Yalom, Irvin D., 1931–
    The Spinoza problem: a novel / Irvin D. Yalom
       p.   cm.
    ISBN 978-0-465-02963-1 (alk. paper)—ISBN 978-0-465-02965-5 (e-book) 1. Spinoza,
Benedictus de, 1632–1677—Fiction. I. Title.
    PS3575.A39S65 2012
    813'.54—dc23

                                                                               2011038770

ISBN 978-0-465-06185-3 (paperback)

10 9 8 7 6 5 4 3 2

To Marilyn

CONTENTS

PROLOGUE

Spinoza has long intrigued me, and for years I've wanted to write about this valiant seventeenth-century thinker, so alone in the world—without a family, without a community—who authored books that truly changed the world. He anticipated secularization, the liberal democratic political state, and the rise of natural science, and he paved the way for the Enlightenment. The fact that he was excommunicated by the Jews at the age of twenty-three and censored for the rest of his life by the Christians had always fascinated me, perhaps because of my own iconoclastic proclivities. And this strange sense of kinship with Spinoza was strengthened by the knowledge that Einstein, one of my first heroes, was a Spinozist. When Einstein spoke of God, he spoke of Spinoza's God—a God entirely equivalent to nature, a God that includes all substance, and a God "that doesn't play dice with the universe"—by which he means that everything that happens, without exception, follows the orderly laws of nature.

I also believe that Spinoza, like Nietzsche and Schopenhauer, on whose lives and philosophy I have based two earlier novels, wrote much that is highly relevant to my field of psychiatry and psychotherapy—for example, that ideas, thoughts, and feelings are caused by previous experiences, that passions may be studied dispassionately, that understanding leads to transcendence—and I wished to celebrate his contributions through a novel of ideas.

But how to write about a man who lived such a contemplative life marked by so few striking external events? He was extraordinarily private, and he kept his own person invisible in his writing. I had none of the material that ordinarily lends itself to narrative—no family dramas, no love affairs, jealousies, curious anecdotes, feuds, spats, or reunions. He had a large correspondence, but after his death his colleagues followed his instructions and removed almost all personal comments from his letters. No, not much external drama in his life: most scholars regard Spinoza as a placid and gentle soul—some compare his life to that of Christian saints, some even to Jesus.

So I resolved to write a novel about his *inner* life. That was where my personal expertise might help in telling Spinoza's story. After all, he was a human being and therefore *must* have struggled with the same basic human conflicts that troubled me and the many patients I've worked with over the decades. He must have had a strong emotional response to being excommunicated, at the age of twenty-three, by the Jewish community in Amsterdam—an irreversible edict that ordered every Jew, including his own family, to shun him forever. No Jew would ever again speak to him, have commerce with him, read his words, or come within six feet of his physical presence. And of course no one lives without an inner life of fantasies, dreams, passions, and a yearning for love. About a fourth of Spinoza's major work, *Ethics*, is devoted to "overcoming the bondage of the passions." As a psychiatrist, I felt convinced that he could not have written this section unless he had experienced a conscious struggle with his own passions.

Yet I was stumped for years because I could not find the story that a novel requires—until a visit to Holland five years ago changed everything. I had come to lecture and, as part of my compensation, requested and was granted a "Spinoza day." The secretary of the Dutch Spinoza Association and a leading Spinoza philosopher agreed to spend a day with me visiting all the important Spinoza sites—his dwellings, his burial place, and, the main attraction, the Spinoza Museum in Rijnsburg. It was there I had an epiphany.

I entered the Spinoza Museum in Rijnsburg, about a forty-five-minute drive from Amsterdam, with keen anticipation, looking for—what? Perhaps an encounter with the spirit of Spinoza. Perhaps a story. But entering the museum, I was immediately disappointed. I doubted that this small, sparse museum could bring me closer to Spinoza. The only remotely personal items were the 159 volumes of Spinoza's own library, and I turned immediately to them. My hosts permitted me free access, and I picked up one seventeenth-century book after another, smelling and holding them, thrilled to touch objects that had once been touched by Spinoza's hands.

But my reverie was soon interrupted by my host: "Of course, Dr. Yalom, his possessions—bed, clothes, shoes, pens and books—were auctioned off after his death to pay funeral expenses. The books were sold and scattered far and wide, but fortunately, the notary made a complete list of those books prior to the auction, and over two hundred years later a Jewish philanthropist reassembled most of the same titles, the same editions from the same years and cities of publication. So we call it Spinoza's library, but it's really a replica. His fingers never touched these books."

I turned away from the library and gazed at the portrait of Spinoza hanging on the wall and soon felt myself melting into those huge, sad, oval, heavy-lidded eyes, almost a mystical experience—a rare thing for me. But then my host said, "You may not know this, but that's not *really* Spinoza's likeness. It's merely an image from some artist's imagination, derived from a few lines of written description. If there were drawings of Spinoza made during his lifetime, none have survived."

Maybe a story about sheer elusiveness, I wondered.

While I was examining the lens-grinding apparatus in the second room—also not his own equipment, the museum placard stated, but equipment similar to it—I heard one of my hosts in the library room mention the Nazis.

I stepped back into the library. "What? The Nazis were here? In this museum?"

"Yes—several months after the blitzkrieg of Holland, the ERR troops drove up in their big limousines and stole everything—the books, a bust, and a portrait of Spinoza—everything. They carted it all away, then sealed and expropriated the museum."

"ERR? What do the letters stand for?"

"Einsatzstab Reichsleiter Rosenberg. The taskforce of Reich leader Rosenberg—that's Alfred Rosenberg, the major Nazi anti-Semitic ideologue. He was in charge of looting for the Third Reich, and under Rosenberg's orders, the ERR plundered all of Europe—first, just the Jewish things and then, later in the war, anything of value."

"So then these books are *twice* removed from Spinoza?" I asked. "You mean that books had to be purchased again and the library reassembled a second time?"

"No—miraculously these books survived and were returned here after the war with just a few missing copies."

"Amazing!" *There's a story here*, I thought. "But why did Rosenberg even bother with these books in the first place? I know they have some modest value—being seventeenth-century and older—but why didn't they just march into the Amsterdam Rijksmuseum and pluck a single Rembrandt worth fifty times this whole collection?"

"No, that's not the point. The money had nothing to do with it. The ERR had some mysterious interest in Spinoza. In his official report, Rosenberg's officer, the Nazi who did the hands-on looting of the library, added a significant sentence: 'They contain valuable early works of great importance for the exploration of the Spinoza problem.' You can see the report on the web, if you like—it's in the official Nuremberg documents."

I felt stunned. "'Exploration of the Nazis' Spinoza problem'? I don't understand. What did he mean? What was the Nazi Spinoza problem?"

Like a mime duo, my hosts hunched their shoulders and turned up their palms.

I pressed on. "You're saying that because of this Spinoza problem, they protected these books rather than burn them, as they burned so much of Europe?"

They nodded.

"And where was the library kept during the war?"

"No one knows. The books just vanished for five years and turned up again in 1946 in a German salt mine."

"A salt mine? Amazing!" I picked up one of the books—a sixteenth-century copy of the *Iliad*—and said, as I caressed it, "So this old storybook has its own story to tell."

My hosts took me to look at the rest of the house. I had come at a fortunate time—few visitors had ever seen the other half of the building, for it had been occupied for centuries by a working-class family. But the last family member had recently died, and the Spinoza Society had promptly purchased the property and was just now beginning reconstruction to incorporate it into the museum. I wandered amid the construction debris through the modest kitchen and living room and then climbed the narrow, steep stairway to the small, unremarkable bedroom. I scanned the simple room quickly and began to descend, when my eye caught sight of a thin, two-by-two-foot crease in a corner of the ceiling.

"What's that?"

The old caretaker climbed up a few stairs to look and told me it was a trap door that led to a tiny attic space where two Jews, an elderly mother and her daughter, were hidden from the Nazis for the duration of the war. "We fed them and took good care of them."

A firestorm outside! Four out of five Dutch Jews murdered by the Nazis! Yet upstairs in the Spinozahuis, hidden in the attic, two Jewish women were tenderly cared for throughout the war. And downstairs, the tiny Spinoza Museum was looted, sealed, and expropriated by an officer of the Rosenberg task force, who believed that its library could help the Nazis solve their "Spinoza problem." And what was their Spinoza problem? I wondered if this Nazi, Alfred Rosenberg, had also, in his own way, for his own reasons, been looking for Spinoza. I had entered the museum with one mystery and now left it with two.

Shortly thereafter, I began writing.

CHAPTER ONE

AMSTERDAM—APRIL 1656

As the final rays of light glance off the water of the Zwanenburgwal, Amsterdam closes down. The dyers gather up their magenta and crimson fabrics drying on the stone banks of the canal. Merchants roll up their awnings and shutter their outdoor market stalls. A few workers plodding home stop for a snack with Dutch gin at the herring stands on the canal and then continue on their way. Amsterdam moves slowly: the city mourns, still recovering from the plague that, only a few months earlier, killed one person in nine.

A few meters from the canal, at Breestraat No. 4, the bankrupt and slightly tipsy Rembrandt van Rijn applies a last brushstroke to his painting *Jacob Blessing the Sons of Joseph*, signs his name in the lower right corner, tosses his palette to the floor, and turns to descend his narrow winding staircase. The house, destined three centuries later to become his museum and memorial, is on this day witness to his shame. It swarms with bidders anticipating the auction of all of the artist's possessions. Gruffly pushing aside the gawkers on the staircase, he steps outside the front door, inhales the salty air, and stumbles toward the corner tavern.

In Delft, seventy kilometers south, another artist begins his ascent. The twenty-three-year-old Johannes Vermeer takes a final look at his new painting, *The Procuress*. He scans from right to left. First, the prostitute in a gloriously yellow jacket. Good. Good. The yellow gleams like polished sunlight. And the group of men surrounding her. Excellent—each could easily stroll off the canvas and begin a conversation. He bends closer to catch the tiny but piercing gaze of the leering young man with the foppish hat. Vermeer nods to his miniature self. Greatly pleased, he signs his name with a flourish in the lower right corner.

Back in Amsterdam at Breestraat No. 57, only two blocks from the auction preparations at Rembrandt's home, a twenty-three-year-old merchant (born only a few days earlier than Vermeer, whom he would admire but never meet) prepares to close his import-export shop. He appears too delicate and beautiful to be a shopkeeper. His features are perfect, his olive skin unblemished, his dark eyes large, and soulful.

He takes a last look around: many shelves are as empty as his pockets. Pirates intercepted his last shipment from Bahia, and there is no coffee, sugar, or cocoa. For a generation, the Spinoza family operated a prosperous import-export wholesale business, but now the brothers Spinoza—Gabriel and Bento—are reduced to running a small retail shop. Inhaling the dusty air, Bento de Spinoza identifies, with resignation, the fetid rat droppings accompanying the odor of dried figs, raisins, candied ginger, almonds, and chickpeas and the fumes of acrid Spanish wine. He walks outside and commences his daily duel with the rusted padlock on the shop door. An unfamiliar voice speaking in stilted Portuguese startles him.

"Are you Bento de Spinoza?"

Spinoza turns to face two strangers, young weary men who seem to have traveled far. One is tall, with a massive, burly head that hangs forward as though it were too heavy to be held erect. His clothes are of good quality but soiled and wrinkled. The other, dressed in tattered peasant's clothes, stands behind his companion. He has long, matted hair, dark eyes, a strong chin and forceful nose. He holds himself stiffly. Only his eyes move, darting like frightened tadpoles.

Spinoza offers a wary nod.

"I am Jacob Mendoza," says the taller of the two. "We must see you. We must talk to you. This is my cousin, Franco Benitez, whom I've just brought from Portugal. My cousin," Jacob clasps Franco's shoulder, "is in crisis."

"Yes," Spinoza answers. "And?"

"In severe crisis."

"Yes. And why seek me?"

"We've been told that you're the one to render help. Perhaps the only one."

"Help?"

"Franco has lost his faith. He doubts everything. All religious ritual. Prayer. Even the presence of God. He is frightened all the time. He doesn't sleep. He talks of killing himself."

"And who has misled you by sending you here? I am only a merchant who operates a small business. And not very profitably, as you see." Spinoza points at the dusty window through which the half-empty shelves are visible. "Rabbi Mortera is our spiritual leader. You must go to him."

"We arrived yesterday, and this morning we set out to do exactly that. But our landlord, a distant cousin, advised against it. 'Franco needs a helper, not a judge,' he said. He told us that Rabbi Mortera is severe with doubters, that he believes all Jews in Portugal who converted to Christianity face eternal damnation, even if they were forced to choose between conversion and death. 'Rabbi Mortera,' he said, 'will only make Franco feel worse. Go see Bento de Spinoza. He is wise in such matters.'"

"What talk is this? I am but a merchant—"

"He claims that if you had not been forced into business because of the death of your older brother and your father, you would have been the next great rabbi of Amsterdam."

"I must go. I have a meeting I must attend."

"You're going to the Sabbath service at the synagogue? Yes? We too. I am taking Franco, for he must return to his faith. Can we walk with you?"

"No, I go to another kind of meeting."

"What other kind?" says Jacob, but then immediately reverses himself. "Sorry. It's not my affair. Can we meet tomorrow? Would you be willing to help us on the Sabbath? It is permitted, since it is a mitzvah. We need you. My cousin is in danger."

"Strange." Spinoza shakes his head. "Never have I heard such a request. I'm sorry, but you are mistaken. I can offer nothing."

Franco, who had been staring at the ground as Jacob spoke, now lifts his eyes and utters his first words: "I ask for little, for only a few words with you. Do you refuse a fellow Jew? It is your duty to a traveler. I had to flee Portugal just as your father and your family had to flee, to escape the Inquisition."

"But what can I—"

"My father was burned at the stake just a year ago. His crime? They found pages of the Torah buried in the soil behind our home. My father's brother, Jacob's father, was murdered soon after. I have a question. Consider this world where a son smells the odor of his father's burning flesh. Where is the God that created this kind of world? Why does He permit such things? Do you blame me for asking that?" Franco looks deeply into Spinoza's eyes for several moments and then continues. "Surely a man named 'blessed'— Bento in Portuguese and Baruch in Hebrew—will not refuse to speak to me?"

Spinoza nods solemnly. "I will speak to you, Franco. Tomorrow midday?"

"At the synagogue?" Franco asks.

"No, here. Meet me here at the shop. It will be open."

"The shop? Open?" Jacob interjects. "But the Sabbath?"

"My younger brother, Gabriel, represents the Spinoza family at the synagogue."

"But the holy Torah," Jacob insists, ignoring Franco's tugging at his sleeve, "states God's wish that we not work on the Sabbath, that we must spend that holy day offering prayers to Him and performing mitzvahs."

Spinoza turns and speaks gently, as a teacher to a young student, "Tell me, Jacob, do you believe that God is all powerful?"

Jacob nods.

"That God is perfect? Complete unto Himself."

Again Jacob agrees.

"Then surely you would agree that, by definition, a perfect and complete being has no needs, no insufficiencies, no wants, no wishes. Is that not so?"

Jacob thinks, hesitates, and then nods warily. Spinoza notes the beginnings of a smile on Franco's lips.

"Then," Spinoza continues, "I submit that God has no wishes about *how*, or even *if*, we glorify Him. Allow me, then, Jacob, to love God in my own fashion."

Franco's eyes widen. He turns toward Jacob as though to say, "You see, you see? This is the man I seek."

CHAPTER TWO

REVAL, ESTONIA—MAY 3, 1910

Time: 4 PM
Place: A bench in the main corridor outside Headmaster Epstein's office in the Petri-Realschule

Upon the bench fidgets the sixteen-year-old Alfred Rosenberg, who is uncertain why he has been summoned to the headmaster's office. Alfred's torso is wiry, his eyes grey-blue, his Teutonic face well-proportioned; a lock of chestnut hair hangs in just the desired angle over his forehead. No dark circles surround his eyes—they will come later. He holds his chin high. Perhaps he is defiant, but his fists, clenching and relaxing, signal apprehension.

He looks like everyone and no one. He is a near-man with a whole life ahead of him. In eight years he will travel from Reval to Munich and become a prolific anti-Bolshevik and anti-Semitic journalist. In nine years he will hear a stirring speech at a meeting of the German Workers' Party by a new prospect, a veteran of World War I named Adolf Hitler, and Alfred will join the party shortly after Hitler. In twenty years he will lay down his pen and grin triumphantly as he finishes the last page of his book, *The Myth of the Twentieth Century*. Destined to become a million-copy best seller, it will provide much of the ideological foundation of the Nazi party and offer a justification for the destruction of European Jews. In thirty years his troops will storm into a small Dutch museum in Rijnsburg and confiscate Spinoza's personal library of one hundred and fifty-one volumes. And in thirty-six years his dark-circled eyes will appear bewildered and he will shake his head no when asked by the American hangman at Nuremberg, "Do you have any last words?"

Young Alfred hears the echoing sound of approaching footsteps in the corridor, and spotting Herr Schäfer, his advisor and German teacher, he bolts to his feet to greet him. Herr Schäfer merely frowns and shakes his head slowly as he passes and opens the headmaster's door. But just before entering, he hesitates, turns back to Alfred, and in a not unkind voice whispers, "Rosenberg, you disappointed me, all of us, with your poor judgment in your speech last night. This poor judgment is not erased by having being elected class representative. Even so, I continue to believe you are not without promise. You graduate in only a few weeks. Don't be a fool now."

Last night's election speech! *Oh, so that's it.* Alfred hits the side of his head with his palm. *Of course*—that *is why I am ordered here.* Though almost all forty members of his senior class had been there—mostly Baltic Germans with a sprinkling of Russians, Estonians, Poles, and Jews—Alfred had pointedly directed his campaign comments entirely to the German majority and stirred their spirits by speaking of their mission as keepers of the noble German culture. "Keep our race pure," he had told them. "Do not weaken it by forgetting our noble traditions, by accepting inferior ideas, by mixing with inferior races." Perhaps he should have stopped there. But he got carried away. Perhaps he had gone too far.

His reverie is interrupted by the opening of the massive ten-foot-high door and Headmaster Epstein's booming voice, "*Herr Rosenberg, bitte, herein.*"

Alfred enters to see his headmaster and his German teacher seated at one end of a long, dark, heavy wood table. Alfred always feels small in the presence of Headmaster Epstein, over six feet tall, whose stately bearing, piercing eyes, and heavy, well-tailored beard embody his authority.

Headmaster Epstein motions to Alfred to sit in a chair at the end of the table. It is noticeably smaller than the two tall-backed chairs at the other end. The headmaster wastes no time getting to the point. "So, Rosenberg, I'm of Jewish ancestry, am I? And my wife, too, is Jewish, is she? And Jews are an inferior race and should not teach Germans? And, I gather, certainly not be elevated to headmaster?"

No response. Alfred exhales, tries to shrink further into his chair, and hangs his head.

"Rosenberg, do I state your position correctly?"

"Sir . . . uh, sir, I spoke too hastily. I meant these remarks only in a general way. It was an election speech, and I spoke that way because that is what they wanted to hear." Out of the corner of his eye, Alfred sees Herr Schäfer slump in his chair, take off his glasses, and rub his eyes.

"Oh, I see. You spoke in a general way? But now here I am before you, not in general but in particular."

"Sir, I say only what all Germans think. That we must preserve our race and our culture."

"And as for me and the Jews?"

Alfred silently hangs his head again. He wants to gaze out the window, midway down the table, but looks up apprehensively at the headmaster.

"Yes, of course you can't answer. Perhaps it will loosen your tongue if I tell you that my lineage and that of my wife are pure German, and our ancestors came to the Baltics in the fourteenth century. What's more, we are devout Lutherans."

Alfred nods slowly.

"And yet you called me and my wife Jews," the headmaster continues.

"I did not say that. I only said there were rumors—"

"Rumors you were glad to spread, to your own personal advantage in the election. And tell me, Rosenberg, the rumors are grounded in what facts? Or are they suspended in thin air?"

"Facts?" Alfred shakes his head. "Uh. Perhaps your name?"

"So, Epstein is a Jewish name? All Epsteins are Jews, is that it? Or 50 percent? Or just some? Or perhaps only one in a thousand? What have your scholarly investigations shown you?"

No answer. Alfred shakes his head.

"You mean that despite your education in science and philosophy in our school you never think about how you know what you know. Isn't that one of the major lessons of the Enlightenment? Have we failed you? Or you, us?"

Alfred looks dumbfounded. Herr Epstein drums his fingers on the long table, then continues.

"And your name, Rosenberg? Is your name a Jewish name also?"

"I'm sure it is not."

"I'm not so sure. Let me give you some facts about names. In the course of the Enlightenment in Germany . . ." Headmaster Epstein pauses and then barks, "Rosenberg, do you know when and what the Enlightenment was?"

Glancing at Herr Schäfer and with a prayer in his voice, Alfred answers meekly, "Eighteenth century and . . . and it was the age . . . the age of reason and science?"

"Yes, correct. Good. Herr Schäfer's instruction has not been entirely lost on you. Late in that century, measures were passed in Germany to transform Jews into German citizens, and they were compelled to choose and pay for German names. If they refused to pay, then they might receive ridiculous names, such as Schmutzfinger or Drecklecker. Most of the Jews agreed to pay for a prettier or more elegant name, perhaps a flower—like Rosenblum—or names associated with nature in some way, like Greenbaum. Even more popular were the names of noble castles. For example, the castle of Epstein had noble connotations and belonged to a great family of the Holy Roman Empire, and its name was often selected by Jews living in its vicinity in the eighteenth century. Some Jews paid lesser sums for traditional Jewish names like Levy or Cohen.

"Now your name, Rosenberg, is a very old name also. But for over a hundred years it has had a new life. It has become a common Jewish name in the Fatherland, and I assure you that if, or when, you make the trip to the Fatherland, you will see glances and smirks, and you will hear rumors about Jewish ancestors in your bloodline. Tell me, Rosenberg, when that happens, how will you answer them?"

"I will follow your example, sir, and speak of my ancestry."

"I have personally done my family's genealogical research back for several centuries. Have you?"

Alfred shakes his head.

"Do you know how to do such research?"

Another headshake.

"Then one of your required pregraduation research projects shall be to learn the details of genealogical research and then carry out a search of your own ancestry."

"One of my projects, sir?"

"Yes, there will be two required assignments in order to remove any of my doubts about your fitness for graduation as well as your fitness to enter the Polytechnic Institute. After our discussion today, Herr Schäfer and I will decide upon another edifying project."

"Yes sir." Alfred is now growing aware of the precariousness of his situation.

"Tell me, Rosenberg," Headmaster Epstein continues, "did you know there were Jewish students at the rally last night?"

A faint nod from Alfred. Headmaster Epstein asks, "And did you consider their feelings and their response to your words about Jews being unworthy for this school?"

"I believe my first duty is to the Fatherland and to protect the purity of our great Aryan race, the creative force in all civilization."

"Rosenberg, the election is over. Spare me the speeches. Address my question. I asked about feelings of the Jews in your audience."

"I believe that if we are not careful, the Jewish race will bring us down. They are weak. They are parasitic. The eternal enemy. The anti-race to Aryan values and culture."

Surprised by Alfred's vehemence, Headmaster Epstein and Herr Schäfer exchange concerned glances. Headmaster Epstein probes more deeply.

"It appears you wish to avoid that question I asked. Let me try another line of discussion. The Jews are a weak, parasitic, inferior little race?"

Alfred nods.

"So tell me, Rosenberg, how can such a weak race threaten our all-powerful Aryan race?"

As Alfred tries to formulate an answer, Herr Epstein continues, "Tell me, Rosenberg, have you studied Darwin in Herr Schäfer's classes?"

"Yes," Alfred responds, "in Herr Schäfer's history course and also in Herr Werner's biology course."

"And what do you know of Darwin?"

"I know about evolution of the species and about the survival of the fittest."

"Ah, yes, the fittest survive. Now of course you've thoroughly read the Old Testament in your religion course, have you not?"

"Yes, in Herr Müller's course."

"So, Rosenberg, let's consider the fact that almost all of the peoples and cultures—dozens of them—described in the Bible have become extinct. Right?"

Alfred nods.

"Can you name some of these extinct people?"

Alfred gulps: "Phoenicians, Moabites . . . and Edomites." Alfred glances at the nodding head of Herr Schäfer.

"Excellent. But all of them dead and gone. Except the Jews. The Jews survive. Would not Darwin claim that the Jews are the fittest of all? Do you follow me?"

Alfred responds in lightning quick fashion, "But not through their own strength. They have been parasites and have held back the Aryan race from even greater fitness. They survive only by sucking the strength and the gold and wealth from us."

"Ah, they don't play fair," Headmaster Epstein says. "You're suggesting there is a place for fairness in nature's grand scheme. In other words, the noble animal in its struggle for survival should not use camouflage or hunting stealth? Strange, I don't remember anything in Darwin's work about fairness."

Alfred, puzzled, sits silently.

"Well, never mind about that," says the headmaster. "Let's consider another point. Surely, Rosenberg, you'd agree that the Jewish race has produced great men. Consider the Lord, Jesus, who was Jewish-born."

Again Alfred answers quickly, "I have read that Jesus was born in Galilee, not in Judea, where the Jews were. Even though some Galileans eventually came to practice Judaism, they had not a drop of true Israelite blood in them."

"What?" Headmaster Epstein throws up his hands and turns toward Herr Schäfer and asks, "Where do these notions come from, Herr Schäfer? If he were an adult, I would ask what he had been drinking. Is this what you are teaching in your history course?"

Herr Schäfer shakes his head and turns to Alfred. "Where are you getting these ideas? You say you read them but not in my class. What are you reading, Rosenberg?"

"A noble book, sir. *Foundations of the Nineteenth Century.*"

Herr Schäfer claps his hand to his forehead and slumps in his chair.

"What's that?" Headmaster Epstein asks.

"Houston Stewart Chamberlain's book," says Herr Schäfer. "He's an Englishman, now Wagner's son-in-law. He writes imaginative history: that is, history that he invents as he goes along." He turns back toward Alfred. "How did you come upon Chamberlain's book?"

"I read some of it at my uncle's home and then went to buy it at the bookstore across the street. They didn't have it but ordered it for me. I've been reading it this last month."

"Such enthusiasm! I only wish you had been so enthusiastic about your class texts," says Herr Shäfer, gesturing with a sweep of his arm to the shelves of leather-bound books lining the wall of the headmaster's office. "Even one class text!"

"Herr Schäfer," asks the headmaster, "you're familiar with this work, this Chamberlain?"

"As much as I'd wish to be with any pseudo-historian. He is a popularizer of Arthur Gobineau, the French racist whose writings about the basic superiority of the Aryan races influenced Wagner. Both Gobineau and Chamberlain make extravagant claims about Aryan leadership in the great Greek and Roman civilizations."

"They *were* great!" Alfred suddenly interjects. "Until they mixed with inferior races—the poisonous Jews, the Blacks, the Asians. Then each civilization declined."

Both Headmaster Epstein and Herr Schäfer are startled by a student daring to interrupt their conversation. The headmaster glances at Herr Schäfer as though it were his responsibility.

Herr Schäfer shifts the blame to his student: "If only he had such fervor in the classroom." He turns to Alfred. "How many times did I say that to you, Rosenberg? You seemed so uninterested in your own education. How many times did I try to incite your participation in our readings? And yet suddenly today here you are, set on fire by a book. How can we understand this?"

"Perhaps it is because I never read such a book before—a book that tells the truth about the nobility of our race, about how scholars have mistakenly written about history as the progress of humanity, when the truth is that our race created civilization in all the great empires! Not only in Greece and Rome, but also Egypt, Persia, even India. Each of these empires crumbled only when our race was polluted by surrounding inferior races."

Alfred looks toward Headmaster Epstein and says as respectfully as possible, "If I may, sir, this is the answer to your earlier question. This is why I do not worry about the hurt feelings of a couple of Jewish students, or about the Slavs, who are also inferior but not so organized as the Jews."

Headmaster Epstein and Herr Schäfer again exchange glances, both of them now, finally, appreciative of the seriousness of the problem. This is no mere prankish or impulsive teenager.

Headmaster Epstein says, "Rosenberg, please wait outside. We shall confer privately."

CHAPTER THREE

AMSTERDAM—1656

J odenbreestraat at dusk on the Sabbath teemed with Jews. Each carried
    a prayer book and a small velvet bag containing a prayer shawl. Every
    Sephardic Jew in Amsterdam headed in the direction of the synagogue,
save one. After locking his shop, Bento stood on the doorstep, took a long
look at the stream of fellow Jews, inhaled deeply, and plunged into the crowd,
heading in the opposite direction. He avoided meeting the gaze of anyone
and whispered reassurances to diminish his self-consciousness. *No one no-
tices, no one cares. It is a good conscience, not a bad reputation, that matters.
I've done this many times.* But his racing heart was impervious to the feeble
weapons of rationality. Then he tried to shut out the outside world, sink inward, and distract himself by marveling at this curious duel between reason
and emotion, a duel in which reason was always overmatched.

When the crowds thinned, he strolled with more ease and turned left
on the street bordering the Koningsgracht Canal toward the home and
classroom of Franciscus van den Enden, teacher extraordinaire of Latin
and classics.

Though the encounter with Jacob and Franco had been remarkable, an
even more memorable meeting had taken place in the Spinoza export shop
several months earlier, when Franciscus van den Enden first entered the store.
As he walked, Bento amused himself by recalling that encounter. The details
remained in his mind with perfect clarity.

*It is nearly dusk, on the eve of the Sabbath, and a portly, formally attired,
middle-aged man of courtly bearing enters his import shop to inspect the
wares. Bento is too absorbed with scribbling an entry into his journal to notice*

12

his customer's arrival. Finally, van den Enden politely coughs to indicate his presence and then remarks, in a forceful but not unkindly manner, "Young man, we're not too busy to attend to a customer, are we?"

Dropping his pen in mid-word, Bento bolts to his feet. "Too busy? Hardly, sir. You're the first customer of the entire day. Please pardon my inattention. How may I help you?"

"I'd like a liter of wine and perhaps, depending upon the price, a kilogram of those scrawny raisins in the lower bin."

As Bento places a lead weight on one plate of his scale and uses a worn wooden scoop to add the raisins to the other plate until they balance, van den Enden adds, "But I disturb your writing. What a refreshing and uncommon— no, more than uncommon, let me say singular—experience, to enter a shop and come upon a young clerk so absorbed in writing that he is unaware of customers. Being a teacher, I generally have quite the opposite experience. I come upon my students not writing, and not thinking, when they should be."

"Business is bad," replies Bento. "So I sit here hour after hour with nothing to do other than think and write."

The customer points toward Spinoza's journal, still open at the page on which he had been writing. "Let me hazard a guess about your writing. Business being bad, no doubt you worry about the fate of your inventory. You chart expenses and income in your journal, make a budget, and list possible solutions? Correct?"

Bento, face reddened, turns his journal face down.

"Nothing to hide from me, young man. I am a master spy, and I keep confidences. And I, too, think forbidden thoughts. Moreover, I am by profession a teacher of rhetoric and most assuredly could improve your writing."

Spinoza holds up his journal for viewing and asks, with a hint of a grin, "How is your Portuguese, sir?"

"Portuguese! There you have me, young man. Yes to Dutch. Yes to French, English, German. Yes to Latin and Greek. Yes even to some Spanish, and a smattering of Hebrew and Aramaic. But no to Portuguese. Your spoken Dutch is excellent. Why not write in Dutch? Surely you are native here?"

"Yes. My father emigrated from Portugal when he was a child. Though I use Dutch in my commercial dealings, I am not entirely at home in written Dutch. Sometimes I also write in Spanish. And I have been steeped in Hebrew studies."

"I've always yearned to read the Scriptures in their original language. Sadly the Jesuits gave me only meager training in Hebrew. But you still have not yet responded about your writing."

"Your conclusion that I write about budgets and improving sales is based, I assume, upon my comment about business being slow. A reasonable deduction, but in this particular case, entirely incorrect. My mind rarely dwells upon business, and I never write about it."

"I stand corrected. But before pursuing further the focus of your writing, please permit me one small digression—a pedagogical comment, a habit hard to break. Your use of the word 'deduction' is incorrect. The process of building upon particular observations to construct a rational conclusion, in other words building upward to theory from discrete observations, is induction, whereas deduction starts with a priori theory and reasons downwards to a collection of conclusions."

Noting Spinoza's thoughtful, perhaps grateful, nod, van den Enden continues. "If not about business, young man, then what do you write?"

"Simply what I see outside my shop window."

Van den Enden turns to follow Bento's gaze out to the street.

"Look. Everyone is on the move. Scurrying back and forth all day, all their lives. To what end? Riches? Fame? Pleasures of the appetites? Surely these ends represent wrong turns."

"Why?"

Bento has said all he wished to say but, emboldened by his customer's question, continues, "Such goals are breeders. Each time a goal is attained, it merely breeds additional needs. Thus more scurrying, more seeking, ad infinitum. It must be that the true path toward imperishable happiness lies elsewhere. That's what I think and scribble about." Bento blushes deeply. Never before has he shared such thoughts.

The customer's face registers great interest. He puts down his shopping bag, draws nearer, and gazes at Bento's face.

That was the moment—the moment of moments. Bento loved that moment, that look of surprise, that new and greater interest and regard on the stranger's face. And what a stranger! An emissary from the great, outside, non-Jewish world. A man of obvious consequence. He found it impossible to review that moment only a single time. Instead he reimagined the scene a second and then, sometimes, a third and fourth time. And each time he visualized it, tears filled his eyes. A teacher, an elegant man of the world taking interest in him, taking him seriously, perhaps thinking, "This is an extraordinary young man."

With effort Bento ripped himself away from this moment of moments and continued his recollection of their first meeting.

The customer persists, "You say that imperishable happiness lies elsewhere. Tell me about this 'elsewhere.'"

"I only know that it does not lie in perishable objects. It lies not outside but within. It is the mind that determines what is fearful, worthless, desirable, or priceless, and therefore it is the mind, and only the mind, that must be altered."

"What is your name, young man?"

"Bento de Spinoza. In Hebrew I am called Baruch."

"And in Latin your name is Benedictus. A fine, blessed name. I am Franciscus van den Enden. I conduct an Academy in classics. Spinoza, you say . . . hmm, from the Latin spina *and* spinosus, *meaning respectively 'thorn' and 'full of thorns.'"*

"D'espinhosa in Portuguese," says Bento, nodding. "'From a thorny place.'"

"Your kinds of questions may prove thorny to orthodox, doctrinaire instructors." Van den Enden's lips curl into a mischievous grin. "Tell me, young man, have you been a thorn in the side of your teachers?"

Bento grins too. "Yes, once that was true. But now I have removed myself from my teachers. I confine my thorniness to my journal. My kinds of questions are not welcome in a superstitious community."

"Superstition and reason have never been close comrades. But perhaps I can introduce you to like-minded companions. Here, for example, is a man you should meet." Van den Enden reaches into his bag and extracts an old volume, which he hands to Bento. "The man is Aristotle, and this book contains his exploration into your kinds of questions. He, too, regarded the mind and the pursuit of perfecting our powers of reason as the supreme and unique human project. Aristotle's Nichomachean Ethics *should be one of your next lessons."*

Bento raises the book to his nostrils and inhales its aroma before opening the pages. "I know of this man and would like to meet him. But we could never converse. I know no Greek."

"Then Greek should be part of your education, too. After you have mastered Latin, of course. What a pity that your learned rabbis know so little of

*the classics. So narrow is their landscape they often forget that non-Jews also
engage in the search for wisdom."*

*Bento answers instantaneously, reverting as always to being Jewish when
Jews were attacked. "That is not true. Both Rabbi Menassch and Rabbi Mortera
have read Aristotle in Latin translation. And Maimonides thought Aristotle
to be the greatest of philosophers."*

*Van den Enden draws himself up. "Well said, young man, well said. With
that answer you've now passed my entrance examination. Such loyalty toward
old teachers prompts me now to issue you a formal invitation to study in my
academy. The time has come for you not only to know of Aristotle but to know
him yourself. I can place him within your understanding along with the world
of his comrades, such as Socrates and Plato and many others."*

"Ah, but there is the matter of tuition? As I have said, business is bad."

*"We shall reach an accommodation. For one thing, we shall see what type
of Hebrew teacher you are. Both my daughter and I wish to improve our Hebrew. And we may yet discover other forms of barter. For the present, I suggest
you add a kilogram of almonds to my wine and raisins—and not the scrawny
raisins—let's try those plump ones on the upper shelf."*

———

So compelling was this remembrance of the genesis of his new life that
Bento, lost in reverie, walked blocks past his destination. He came to with
a start, oriented himself quickly, and retraced his steps to the van den Enden
house, a narrow, four-story home facing the Singel. As he climbed to the
top floor, where classes were held, Bento, as always, halted at each landing
and peeked into the living areas. He took little interest in the intricately
tiled floor margined by a row of blue and white Delft windmill tiles on the
first landing.

At the second story the aroma of both sauerkraut and pungent curry reminded him that he had, once again, forgotten to eat lunch or supper.

At the third story he did not linger to admire the gleaming harp and
hanging tapestries but, as always, savored the many oil paintings filling every
wall. For several minutes Bento gazed at a small painting of a boat beached
on the shore and took careful note of the perspective provided by the large
figures on the shore and the two smaller figures in the boat—one standing

in the prow and the other, even smaller, sitting in the bow—and committed it to memory in order to make a charcoal copy later that evening.

On the fourth level he was greeted by van den Enden and six young academy students, one studying Latin and five who had progressed to Greek. Van den Enden began the evening, as always, with a Latin dictation exercise that students were to translate into either Dutch or Greek. Hoping to inject passion into the mastery of new languages, van den Enden taught from texts meant to interest and amuse. Ovid had been the text for the past three weeks, and tonight van den Enden read a portion from the story of Narcissus.

Unlike the other students, Spinoza displayed minimal interest in magical tales of fantastical metamorphoses. It was soon apparent that he needed no amusements. Instead, he had a passion for learning and a breathtaking aptitude for language. Though van den Enden had known immediately that Bento was to be an extraordinary student, he continued to be astounded as the young man grasped and retained every concept, every generality, and every grammatical singularity before the explanations had left his teacher's lips.

The quotidian task of Latin language drill was overseen by van den Enden's daughter, Clara Maria, a long-necked, gangly thirteen-year-old with a beguiling smile and crooked spine. Clara was herself a prodigy in languages and shamelessly demonstrated her facility to the other students by switching back and forth from tongue to tongue as she and her father discussed each student's lessons for the day. At first, Bento was shocked: one of the Jewish tenets he never challenged was the inferiority of women—inferior rights and inferior intellects. Though he was stunned by Clara Maria, he came to regard her as an oddity, a freak, an exception to the rule that women's minds were not equal to men's.

Once van den Enden left the room with the five students working on Greek, Clara Maria commenced, with a gravity almost comical in a thirteen-year-old, to drill Bento and a German student, Dirk Kerckrinck, on their vocabulary and declension homework. Dirk was studying Latin as a prerequisite to entering medical school in Hamburg. After the vocabulary drill Clara Maria asked Bento and Dirk to translate into Latin a popular Dutch poem by Jacob Cats on the proper behavior of young unmarried women, which she read aloud in a charming manner. She beamed, stood, and curtsied when Dirk, joined quickly by Bento, applauded her performance.

The final segment of the evening was always the highlight for Bento. All the students convened in the larger classroom, the only one with windows, to listen to van den Enden discourse on the ancient world. His topic for this evening was the Greek idea of democracy, in his opinion the most perfect form of government, even though—here he glanced at his daughter, who attended all his sessions—he admitted, "Greek democracy excluded over 50 percent of the population, namely women and slaves." He continued, "Consider the paradoxical position of women in Greek drama. On the one hand, Greek women were either forbidden to attend performances or, in later, more enlightened centuries, were permitted into the amphitheaters but could sit only in the areas with the poorest view of the stage. And, yet, consider the heroic women in the drama—women of steel who were protagonists of the greatest tragedies of Sophocles and Euripides. Let me describe briefly three of the most formidable characters in all of literature: Antigone, Phaedra, and Medea."

After his presentation, during which he asked Clara Maria to read several of Antigone's most powerful passages in both Greek and Dutch, he asked Bento to stay for a few minutes after the others had left.

"I have a couple of issues to discuss with you, Bento. First, you remember my offer at our initial meeting in your shop? My offer to introduce you to kindred thinkers?" Bento nodded, and van den Enden continued, "I haven't forgotten, and I shall begin to fulfill that promise. Your progress in Latin has been superb, and we shall now turn to the language of Sophocles and Homer. Next week Clara Maria will begin instruction in the Greek alphabet. Moreover, I've chosen texts that should be of special interest to you. We'll work on passages from Aristotle and Epicurus that pertain to the very issues in which you expressed interest during our first encounter."

"You refer to my journal entries about perishable and imperishable goals?"

"Precisely. As a step toward perfecting your Latin, I suggest you now begin writing your entries in that language."

Bento nodded.

"And one more matter," van den Enden continued. "Clara Maria and I are ready to commence our Hebrew training under your tutelage. Are you agreeable to beginning next week?"

"Gladly," responded Bento. "It would give me much pleasure and also allow me to repay my great debt to you."

"Perhaps, then, it is time to think about pedagogical methods. Have you teaching experience?"

"Three years ago Rabbi Mortera asked me to assist him in teaching Hebrew to the younger students. I have jotted down a great many thoughts about the intricacies of Hebrew and hope, someday, to write a Hebrew grammar."

"Excellent. Rest assured you will have eager and attentive students."

"By coincidence," Bento added, "I had an odd request for pedagogy this afternoon. Two distraught men sought me out a few hours ago and attempted to engage me as an advisor of sorts." Bento proceeded to relate the details of the encounter with Jacob and Franco.

Van den Enden listened intently and, when Bento finished, said, "I'm going to add one more word to your Latin vocabulary homework tonight. Please write down *caute*. You can guess the meaning from the Spanish *cautela*."

"Yes, 'caution'—*cuidado* in Portuguese. But why *caute*?"

"Latin, please."

"*Quad cur caute?*"

"I have a spy who tells me that your Jewish friends are not pleased that you study with me. Not pleased at all. And they are not pleased with your growing distance from your community. *Caute*, my boy. Take care to give them no further grievances. Trust no strangers with your deeper thoughts and doubts. Next week we will see if Epicurus may offer useful counsel to you."

CHAPTER FOUR

ESTONIA—MAY 3, 1910

After Alfred left, the two old friends stood and stretched while Headmaster Epstein's secretary laid a plate of apple and walnut strudel on the table. They sat down and quietly nibbled at it as she prepared their tea.

"So, Hermann, this is the face of the future?" said Headmaster Epstein.

"Not a future I want to see. I'm glad for the hot tea—it's chilling to be with him."

"How worried should we be about this boy, about his influence upon his classmates?"

A shadow passed by—a student walking by in the hallway—and Herr Shäfer stood to close the door, which had been left ajar.

"I've been his adviser since he started, and he's been in a number of my classes. Strangely, I don't know him at all. As you see, there's something mechanical and remote about him. I see the boys engaged in animated conversations, but Alfred never joins in. He keeps himself well hidden."

"Hardly hidden the last few minutes, Hermann."

"That was entirely new. That jolted me. I saw a different Alfred Rosenberg. Reading Chamberlain has emboldened him."

"Maybe that has its bright side. Perhaps other books may yet come along to inflame him in a different way. In general, though, you say he is not a lover of books?"

"Oddly, it's hard to answer that. Sometimes I think he loves the idea of books, or the aura, or perhaps only the covers of books. He often parades around school with a stack of books under his arm—Hauptman, Heine, Nietzsche, Hegel, Goethe. At times his posturing is almost comical. It's a way of showing off his superior intellect, of bragging that he chooses books over popularity. I've often doubted he really reads the books. Today I don't know what to think."

"Such passion for Chamberlain," remarked the Headmaster. "Has he shown passion for other things?"

"That's the question. He has always kept his feelings very much in check, but I do remember a flash of excitement in local prehistory. On a few occasions I've taken small groups of students to participate in archeological digs just north of the church of St. Olai. Rosenberg always volunteered for such expeditions. On one trip he helped uncover some Stone Age tools and a prehistoric hearth, and he was thrilled."

"Strange," said the headmaster as he rifled through Alfred's file. "He elected to come to our school rather than the gymnasium, where he could have studied the classics and then been able to enter the university for literature or philosophy, which seems to be where his interests lie. Why is he going to the Politechnikum?"

"I think there are financial reasons. His mother died when he was an infant, and his father has consumption and works only sporadically as a bank clerk. The new art teacher, Herr Purvit, considers him a reasonably good draftsman and encourages him to pursue a career as an architect."

"So he keeps his distance from the others," said the headmaster closing Alfred's file, "and yet he won the election. And wasn't he also president of the class a couple of years ago?"

"That has little to do with popularity, I think. The students don't respect the office, and the popular boys generally avoid being class president because of the chores involved and preparation required to be the graduation speaker. I don't think the boys take Rosenberg seriously. I've never seen him in the midst of a group or joking around with others. More often he is the butt of pranks. He's a loner, always walking by himself around Reval with his sketchbook. So I wouldn't be too concerned about his spreading these extremist ideas here."

Headmaster Epstein stood and walked to the window. Outside were broad-leafed trees with fresh spring foliage and, further off, stately white buildings with red-brick roofs.

"Tell me more about this Chamberlain. My reading interests lie else-where. What's the extent of his influence in Germany?"

"Growing fast. Alarmingly fast. His book was published about ten years ago, and its popularity continues to soar. I have heard it has sold over a hun-dred thousand copies."

"Have you read it?"

"I started but grew impatient and scanned the rest of it. Many of my friends have read it. The trained historians share my reaction—as does the church and, of course, the Jewish press. Yet many prominent men praise it—Kaiser Wilhelm, the American Theodore Roosevelt—and many leading foreign newspapers have reviewed it positively, some even ecstatically. Chamberlain uses lofty language and pretends to speak to our nobler im-pulses. But I think he encourages our basest ones."

"How do you explain his popularity?"

"He writes persuasively. And he impresses the uneducated. On any page you may find profound-sounding quotations from Tertullian or St. Augus-tine, or maybe Plato or some eighth-century Indian mystic. But it's just the appearance of erudition. In fact he has simply plucked unrelated quotations from the ages to support his preconceived ideas. His popularity is helped, no doubt, by his recent marriage to Wagner's daughter. Many regard him as the successor to Wagner's racist legacy."

"Crowned by Wagner?"

"No, they never met. Wagner died before Chamberlain courted his daughter. But Cosima has given him her blessing."

The headmaster poured more tea. "Well, our young Rosenberg seems so thoroughly taken in by Chamberlain's racism that it may not be easy to peel him away from it. But when you think about it, what unpopular, lonely, somewhat inept adolescent would not purr with pleasure to learn that he is of superior stock? That his ancestors founded the great civilizations? Es-pecially a boy who never had a mother to admire him, whose father is on death's doorstep, whose older brother is sickly, who—"

"Ah, Karl, I hear the echoes of *your* visionary, that Viennese doctor Freud, who also writes persuasively and also dives into the classics, never failing to surface without a tasty quote clenched between his teeth."

"*Mea culpa.* I confess that his ideas seem ever more sensible to me. For instance, you just said a hundred thousand copies of Chamberlain's anti-

Semitic book have been sold. Of the legions of readers, how many dismiss him like you do? And how many are electrified by him like Rosenberg? Why does the same book elicit such a range of responses? There must be something in the particular reader that leaps out to embrace the book. His life, his psychology, his image of himself. There must be something lurking deep in the mind—or, as this Freud says, the unconscious—that causes a particular reader to fall in love with a particular writer."

"A pithy topic for our next dinner discussion! Meanwhile my little student, Rosenberg, is, I suspect, fretting and sweating out there. What shall we do with him?"

"Yes, we're avoiding that. We promised him assignments and need to come up with some. Maybe we're overreaching. Is it even remotely possible to assign a task that could exert a positive influence in just the few more weeks we have? I see so much bitterness in him, so much hatred for anyone but the phantasm of the 'true German.' I think we need to get him away from ideas onto something tangible, something that he can touch."

"I agree. It's harder to hate an individual than a race," said Herr Schäfer. "I have a thought. I know one Jew he must care about. Let's call him back in, and I'll start with that."

Headmaster Epstein's secretary removed the tea dishes and fetched Alfred, who resumed his seat at the end of the table.

Herr Schäfer slowly filled his pipe, lit it, drew in and exhaled a cloud of smoke, and began, "Rosenberg, we have a few more questions. I am aware of your sentiments about Jews in broad racial terms but surely you have crossed the paths of fine Jews. I happen to know that you and I have had the same personal doctor, Herr Apfelbaum. I have heard he delivered you."

"Yes," Alfred said. "He has been my doctor all my life."

"And he has also been my close friend all these years. Tell me, is he poisonous? Is he a parasite? No one in Reval works harder. When you were an infant, I saw with my own eyes how he worked day and night trying to save your mother from tuberculosis. And I have been told that he wept at her funeral."

"Dr. Apfelbaum is a good man. He always gives us good care. And we always pay him, by the way. But there can be good Jews. I know that. I speak no ill of him as a person, only of the Jewish seed. It is undeniable that all Jews carry the seeds of a hateful race, and that—"

"Ah, that word again, 'hateful,'" Headmaster Epstein interrupted, trying hard to restrain himself. "I hear a great deal about hate, Rosenberg, but I hear nothing about love. Do not forget that love is the center of Jesus's message. Not only loving God but loving your neighbor as yourself. Don't you see some contradiction between what you read in Chamberlain and what you hear about Christian love in church every week?"

"Sir, I am not in church every week. I've stopped going."

"How does you father feel about that? How would Chamberlain feel?"

"My father says he has never set foot in a church. And I read that both Chamberlain and Wagner claim that the teaching of the church more often weakens, than strengthens, us."

"You do not love the Lord Jesus?"

Alfred paused; he sensed traps everywhere. This was treacherous ground: the headmaster had already referred to himself as a devout Lutheran. Safety lay in staying with Chamberlain, and Alfred struggled to recall the words in his book. "Like Chamberlain, I admire Jesus greatly. Chamberlain calls him a moral genius. He had great power and courage, but unfortunately his teachings were Jewified by Paul, who turned Jesus into a suffering, meek man. Every Christian church shows paintings or stained glass of Jesus being crucified. None show images of the powerful and the courageous Jesus—the Jesus who dared to challenge corrupt rabbis, the Jesus who single-handedly flung moneychangers out of the temple!"

"So Chamberlain sees Jesus the lion, not Jesus the lamb?"

"Yes," said Rosenberg, emboldened. "Chamberlain says that it was a tragedy that Jesus appeared in the place and time he did. If Jesus had preached to Germanic people or, say, to Indian people, his words would have had quite a different influence."

"Let us return to my earlier question," said the headmaster, who realized he had taken the wrong trail. "I have a simple question: whom do you love? Who is your hero? The one whom you admire above all others? Besides this Chamberlain, I mean."

Alfred had no immediate answer. He deliberated long before answering. "Goethe."

Both Headmaster Epstein and Herr Schäfer straightened a bit in their seats. "Interesting choice, Rosenberg," said the headmaster. "Your choice or Chamberlain's?"

"Both. And I think Herr Schäfer's choice too. He praised Goethe in our class more than any other." Alfred looked at Herr Schäfer for confirmation and received an affirming nod.

"And tell me, why Goethe?" asked the headmaster.

"He is the eternal German genius. The greatest of Germans. A genius of writing, and science, and art and philosophy. He is a genius in more fields than anyone."

"An excellent answer," said Headmaster Epstein, suddenly energized. "And I believe I now have come upon the perfect pregraduation project for you."

The two teachers conferred privately, whispering softly to one another. Headmaster Epstein left the room and returned shortly carrying a large book. He and Schäfer bent over the book together and flipped through the pages for several minutes scanning the text. After the headmaster jotted down some page numbers, he turned to Alfred.

"Here is your project. You are to read, very carefully, two chapters—fourteen and sixteen—in Goethe's autobiography, and you are to write down every line that he writes about his own personal hero, a man who lived a long time ago named Spinoza. Surely, you will welcome this assignment. It will be a joy to read some of your hero's autobiography. Goethe is the man you love, and I imagine it will be of interest to you to learn what he says about the man *he* loves and admires. Right?"

Alfred nodded, warily. Baffled by the headmaster's good spirits, he sensed a trap.

"So," the headmaster continued, "let us be very clear about the assignment, Rosenberg. You are to read chapters fourteen and sixteen in Goethe's autobiography, and you are to copy every sentence he writes about Benedict Spinoza. You are to make three copies, one for you and one for each of us. If we find you miss any of his comments about Spinoza in your written assignment, you will be required to do the whole assignment over again until you have it right. We will see you in two weeks to read your written assignment and to discuss all aspects of your reading assignment. Is that clear?"

Another nod. "Sir, may I ask a question? Before, you said two assignments. I have to do genealogical research; I have to read two chapters. And I have to write three copies of the material on Benedict Spinoza."

"That's correct," said the headmaster. "And your question?"

"Sir, isn't that three assignments rather than two?"

"Rosenberg," interjected Herr Schäfer, "twenty assignments would be lenient. Calling your headmaster unfit for his position because he is Jewish is sufficient grounds for expulsion from any school in Estonia or in the Fatherland."

"Yes, sir."

"Wait, Herr Schäfer, perhaps the boy has a point. The Goethe assignment is so important that I want him to do it with great thoroughness." Headmaster Epstein turned to Alfred. "You're excused from the genealogy project. Concentrate fully on Goethe's words. Meeting adjourned. We will see you here in two weeks exactly. Same time. And be sure to turn in your copies of the written assignment to me the day before."

CHAPTER FIVE

AMSTERDAM—1656

Good morning, Gabriel," called Bento as he heard his brother washing in preparation for the Sabbath services. Gabriel merely grunted in response but reentered their bedroom and sat down heavily on the imposing four-poster bed that they shared. The bed, which filled most of the room, was the one familiar remnant of their past.

Their father, Michael, had left all the family possessions to Bento, the elder son, but Bento's two sisters protested their father's will on the grounds that he had chosen not to be a true member of the Jewish community. Though the Jewish court had decided in favor of Bento, he then startled everyone by immediately turning over all the family property to his siblings, keeping for himself only one thing—his parents' four-poster bed. After the marriage of his two sisters, he and Gabriel were left alone in the fine three-story white house that the Spinoza family had rented for decades. Their home fronted the Houtgracht, near the busiest intersections in the Jewish section of Amsterdam, just a block from the small Beth Jacob Synagogue and the adjoining classrooms.

Bento and Gabriel had, with regret, decided to move. With their sisters gone, the old house was too large and too haunted by images of the dead. And too expensive as well—the 1652 Dutch-English war and pirate raids of ships from Brazil had been disastrous for the Spinoza import business, obliging the brothers to rent a small house only a five-minute walk from the store.

Bento took a long look at his brother. When Gabriel was a child, people often called him "little Bento," for they had the same long, oval face, the same piercing owl eyes, the same powerful nose. Now, however, the fully formed Gabriel was forty pounds heavier than his older brother, five inches taller, and far stronger. And his eyes no longer seemed to peer far into the distance.

In silence, the brothers sat side by side. Ordinarily, Bento cherished silence and felt at ease sharing meals with Gabriel or working together in the shop without exchanging a word. But this silence was oppressive and begat dark thoughts. Bento thought about his sister, Rebekah, who in the past had always been loquacious and bubbly. Now she, too, offered him silence and averted her glance whenever she saw him.

And silent, too, were all the dead, all those who had died cradled by this very bed: his mother, Hanna, who had died seventeen years ago, when he was barely six; his older brother, Isaac, six years ago; his stepmother, Esther, three years ago; and both his father and his sister Miriam, only two years ago. Of his siblings—that noisy, high-spirited, band who played and quarreled and made up and sorrowed for their mother and slowly grew to love their stepmother—there remained only Rebekah and Gabriel, both quickly receding from him.

Glancing at Gabriel's puffy, pallid face, Bento broke the silence. "You slept poorly again, Gabriel? I felt you thrashing about."

"Yes, again. Bento, how can I sleep? Nothing is good now. What's to be done? What's to be done? I hate the trouble between us. Here, this morning, I dress for the Sabbath. The sun shines for the first time this week, there is some blue sky above, and I should feel joy, like everyone else, like our neighbors on every side. Instead, because of my own brother—forgive me, Bento, but I will burst if I do not speak. Because of *you* my life is miserable. There is no joy in going to my own synagogue to join my own people to pray to my own God."

"I am grieved to know that, Gabriel. I yearn for your happiness."

"Words are one thing. Actions are another."

"What actions?"

"What actions?" exclaimed Gabriel. "And to think that for so long, for my whole life, I used to believe you knew everything. To someone else asking such a question, I'd say, 'You're joking,' but I know you never joke. Yet surely you *know* what actions I mean."

Bento sighed.

"Well, let's start with the action of rejecting Jewish customs, and rejecting even the community. And then the action of dishonoring the Sabbath. And turning away from the synagogue and donating practically nothing this year—those are the kinds of actions I mean."

Gabriel looked at Bento, who remained silent.

"I'll give you more actions, Bento. Only last night the action of saying no to Sabbath dinner at Sarah's home. You know I'm going to marry Sarah, yet you will not link the two families by joining us for the Sabbath. Can you imagine how it feels for me? For our sister, Rebekah? What excuse can we offer? Can we say that our brother prefers Latin lessons with his Jesuit?"

"Gabriel, it is better for everyone's digestion that I do not come. You know that. You know that Sarah's father is superstitious."

"Superstitious?"

"I mean extreme-orthodox. You've seen how my presence incites him into religious disputation. You've seen how any response I offer merely sows more discord and more pain for you and for Rebekah. My absence serves the cause of peace—of that I have no doubt. My absence equals peace for you and for Rebekah. More and more I think of that equation."

Gabriel shook his head, "Bento, remember when I was a child, I sometimes got scared because I imagined the world disappeared when I closed my eyes? You corrected my thinking. You reassured me about reality and the eternal laws of Nature. Yet now you make the same mistake. You imagine that discord about Bento de Spinoza vanishes when he is not present to witness it?

"Last night was painful," Gabriel continued. "Sarah's father began the meal by talking about you. Once again he was furious that you bypassed our local Jewish court and turned your lawsuit over to the Dutch civil court. No one else in memory, he said, has ever insulted the rabbinical court in that fashion. It's almost basis for an excommunication. Is that what you want? A *cherem*? Bento, our father is dead; our older brother is dead. You're the head of the family. Yet you insult us all by turning to the Dutch court. And your timing! Could you at least have waited till after the wedding?"

"Gabriel, I have explained again and again, but you have not heard me. Listen again, so that you may know all the facts. And, above all, please try to understand that I take my responsibility to you and Rebekah seriously.

Consider my dilemma. Our father, blessed be he, was generous. But he erred in judgment when he guaranteed a note held by that greedy usurer, Duarte Rodriguez, for the grieving widow Henriques. Her husband, Pedro, had been a mere acquaintance of our father, not even a relative nor, as far as I know, a close friend. None of us have ever met him or her, and it is a mystery why our father undertook to guarantee that note. But you know Father—when he saw people in pain, he reached out to help with both hands without thinking of the consequences. When the widow and her only child died last year in the plague leaving the debt unpaid, Duarte Rodriguez—that pious Jew who sits on the bimah of the synagogue and already owns half the houses on Jodenbreestraat—attempted to transfer his loss to us by pressuring the rabbinical court to demand that the poor Spinoza family pay the debt of someone whom none of us ever knew."

Bento paused, "You know this, Gabriel? Do you not?"

"Yes, but—"

"Let me finish, Gabriel. It is important that you fully know this. You may one day be head of the family. So Rodriguez presented it to the Jewish court, a court containing many members who seek favors from Rodriguez, as he is the synagogue's major donor. Tell me, Gabriel: Would they want to displease him? Almost immediately the court ruled that the Spinoza family must take on the entire debt. And it is a debt that will drain our family's resources for the rest of our lives. And even worse, they also ruled that the inheritance our mother left us should go to pay the debt to Rodriguez. Do you follow all this, Gabriel?"

After a reluctant nod from his brother, Spinoza continued. "So three months ago I turned to the Dutch law because it is more reasonable. For one thing, the name Duarte Rodriguez has no sway over them. And the Dutch law states that the head of the family must be twenty-*five*, to bear responsibility for such a debt. Since I am not yet twenty-five, our family may be saved. We do not have to accept the debts of our father's estate, and, what's more, we can receive the money that our mother meant for us. And by us, I mean you and Rebekah—I intend to turn my entire share over to you. I have no family and no need of money.

"And one last thing," he went on. "About the timing. Since my twenty-fifth birthday falls *before* your wedding, I had to act *now*. Now tell me, can you not see that I *do* act responsibly for the family? Do you not value freedom? If I take no action, we shall be in servitude for our entire life. Do you want that?"

"I prefer to leave the matter in God's hands. You have no right to challenge the law of our religious community. And as for servitude, I prefer it to ostracism. Besides, Sarah's father spoke of more than the lawsuit. Do you want to hear what else he said?"

"I think you want to tell me."

"He said that the 'Spinoza problem,' as he calls it, could be traced back many years, back to your impertinence during your bar mitzvah preparation. He remembered that Rabbi Mortera favored you above all other students. That he thought of you as his possible successor. And then you called the biblical story of Adam and Eve a 'fable.' Sarah's father said that when the rabbi rebuked you for denying the word of God, you responded, 'The Torah is confused, for if Adam was the first man, who exactly did his son, Cain, marry?' Did you say that, Bento? Is it true you called the Torah 'confused'?"

"It is true that the Torah calls Adam the first man. And it is true that it says that his son, Cain, married. Surely we have the right to ask the obvious question: if Adam was the first man, then how could there have been anyone for Cain to marry? This point—it's called the 'pre-adamites question'—has been discussed in biblical studies for over a thousand years. So if you ask me whether it is a fable I must answer yes—obviously the story is but a metaphor."

"You say that because you don't understand it. Does your wisdom surpass that of God? Don't you know that there are reasons why we cannot know and we must trust our rabbis to interpret and clarify the scriptures?"

"That conclusion is wonderfully convenient for the rabbis, Gabriel. Religious professionals throughout the ages have always sought to be the sole interpreters of mysteries. It serves them well."

"Sarah's father said that this insolence in questioning the Bible and our religious leaders is offensive and dangerous not only to the Jews but to the Christian community also. The Bible is sacred to them as well."

"Gabriel, you believe we should forsake logic, forsake our right to question?"

"I don't argue *your* personal right to logic and *your* right to question rabbinical law. I'm not questioning *your* right to doubt the holiness of the Bible. In fact, I don't even question your right to anger God. That's your affair. Perhaps it is your sickness. But you injure me and your sister by your refusal to keep your views to yourself."

"Gabriel, that conversation about Adam and Eve with Rabbi Mortera took place more than ten years ago. After that I kept my opinions to myself. But two years ago I made a vow to conduct my life in a holy manner, which includes never again lying. Thus, if I am asked for my opinion, I will offer it truthfully—and *that* is why I declined to have dinner with Sarah's father. But, most of all, Gabriel, remember that we are separate souls. Others here do not mistake you for me. They do not hold you responsible for your older brother's aberrations."

Gabriel walked out of the room shaking his head and muttering, "My older brother speaks like a child."

CHAPTER SIX

ESTONIA—1910

Three days later a pale and agitated Alfred sought a conference with Herr Schäfer.

"I have a problem, sir," Alfred began as he opened his school bag and extracted Goethe's seven-hundred-page autobiography with several raggedly torn bits of paper jutting from the pages. He opened to the first bookmark and pointed to the text.

"Sir, Goethe mentions Spinoza here in this line. And then again here, a couple of lines later. But then there are several paragraphs where the name does not appear, and I can't figure out if it's about him or not. Actually, I can't understand most of this. It is very hard." He turns the pages and points to another section, "Here, it's the same thing. He mentions Spinoza two or three times, then four pages without mentioning him. As far as I can tell, it is not clear if he is speaking about Spinoza or not. He is also talking about somebody named Jacobi. And this happens in four other places. I understood *Faust* when we read it in your class, and I understood *The Sorrows of Young Werther*, but here in this book I can't understand page after page."

"Much easier to read Chamberlain, is it not?" Instantaneously, Herr Schäfer regretted his sarcasm and hastened to add, in a kinder voice, "I know that you may not grasp all of Goethe's words, Rosenberg, but you have to realize this is not a tightly organized work but a series of reflections on his life. Have you ever kept a diary yourself or written about your own life?"

Alfred nodded. "A couple of years ago, but I only did it a few months."

"Well, consider this something like a diary. Goethe wrote it as much for himself as for the reader. Trust me, when you get older and know more about Goethe's ideas, you'll understand and appreciate his words more. Let me have the book."

After scanning the pages that Alfred had marked, Herr Schäfer said, "I see the problem. You're raising a legitimate question, and I'll need to revise the assignment. Let's go over these two chapters together." Their heads close together, Herr Schäfer and Alfred pored at length over the text, and on a notepad Herr Schäfer jotted down a series of page and line numbers.

Handing Alfred the notepad, he said, "Here is what you have to copy. Remember, three copies legibly written. But there is a problem. This is only twenty or twenty-five lines, so much shorter a task than the headmaster originally assigned that I doubt it will satisfy him. So you must do something additional: memorize this shortened version, and recite it at our meeting with Headmaster Epstein. I think this will be acceptable to him."

A few seconds later, noting a trace of a scowl on Alfred's face, Herr Schäfer added, "Alfred, even though I don't like this change in you—this race superiority nonsense—I'm still on your side. Over the past four years you've been a good and obedient student—though, as I've often told you, you could have been more diligent. It would be tragic for you to ruin your chances for the future by not graduating." He let that sink in. "Put your whole heart into this assignment. Headmaster Epstein will want more than just copying and reciting. He will expect you to understand the reading. So, apply yourself, Rosenberg. I myself wish to see you graduate."

"Do I still hand my copy to you before I make the two other copies?"

Herr Schäfer's heart dropped at Alfred's mechanical response, but he only said, "If you follow my instructions on the note pad, it will not be necessary."

As Alfred walked away, Herr Schäfer called him back. "Rosenberg, a minute ago, I just reached out to you and said that your were a good student and that I wished you to graduate. Did you not have some response? I have been your teacher for four years, after all."

"Yes sir."

"'Yes sir?'"

"I don't know what to say."

"All right, Alfred, you can go."

Herr Schäfer packed his briefcase with student papers yet to read, brushed Alfred from his mind, and, instead, thought of his two children, his wife, and the spaetzle and verivorst dinner she had promised for that night.

Alfred left in a state of confusion about his assignment. Had he made things worse? Or had he gotten a break? After all, memorization was easy for him. He liked memorizing passages for drama presentations and speeches.

———

Two weeks later Alfred stood at one end of Herr Epstein's long table looking for instructions from the headmaster, who, today, looked larger and fiercer than ever. Herr Schäfer, much smaller, his face grave, gestured for Alfred to begin his recitation. Taking a last look at his copy of Goethe's words, Alfred stood and announced, "From the autobiography of Goethe," and began:

"'The mind which worked so decisively upon me and had so great an influence on my whole manner of thinking was Spinoza. After I had looked about throughout the world in vain for a means of cultivating my strange nature, I came at last upon the Ethics of this man. I here found a sedative for my passions; there seemed to open for me a wide and free view over the material and mortal world.'"

"So, Rosenberg," interrupted the headmaster. "What is it that Goethe got from Spinoza?"

"Uh, was it his ethics?"

"No, no. Good Lord, didn't you understand that the *Ethics* is the name of Spinoza's book? What is Goethe saying he got from Spinoza's book? What do you think he means by 'a sedative for my passions'?"

"Something that calmed him down?"

"Yes, that's part of it. But continue now—that idea will come up again very shortly."

Albert recited to himself for a moment to recapture his spot and began:

"'But what especially fastened me to Spinoza was the boundless interest which shone—'"

"Disinterest—not interest," barked Headmaster Epstein, who was following every word of the recitation closely in the notes. "'Disinterest' means not being attached emotionally."

Alfred nodded and continued:

"'But what especially fastened me to Spinoza was the boundless disinterest which shone forth from every sentence. That marvelous expression: 'He who loves God rightly must not desire God to love him in return,' with all the premises on which it rests and all the consequences which follow from it, filled my whole power of thought.'"

"That's a difficult passage," said the headmaster. "Let me explain. Goethe is saying that Spinoza taught him to free his mind from the influence of others. To find his own feelings and his own conclusions and then act upon them. In other words, let your love flow, and do not let it be influenced by the idea of the love you may get in return. We could apply that very idea to election speeches. Would Goethe make a speech based on the admiration he would get from others? Of course not! Nor would he say what others want him to say. You understand? You get that point?"

Alfred nodded. What he truly understood was that Headmaster Epstein had a deep resentment toward him. He waited until the headmaster gestured for him to continue:

"'Further, it must not be denied that the closest unions follow from opposites. The all-composing calmness of Spinoza was in strong contrast with my all-disturbing activity. His mathematical method was the opposite of my poetic feelings. His disciplined way of thought made me his impassioned disciple, his most decided worshipper. Mind and heart, understanding and feeling, sought each other with a necessary affinity, and hence came the union of the most different natures.'"

"Do you know what he means here by the two different natures, Rosenberg?" Headmaster Epstein asked.

"I think he means mind and heart?"

"Exactly. And which is Goethe and which Spinoza?"

Alfred looked puzzled.

"This is not just an exercise in memory, Rosenberg! I want you to understand these words. Goethe is a poet. So which is he, mind or heart?"

"He is heart. But he also had a great mind."

"Ah, yes. Now I understand your confusion. But here he is saying that Spinoza offers him balance that allows him to reconcile his passion and bursting imagination with the necessary calmness and reason. And *that* is why Goethe says he is Spinoza's 'most decided worshipper.' You understand?"

"Yes sir."

"Now continue."

Alfred hesitated, signs of panic in his eyes. "I've lost my place. I'm not sure where we are."

"You're doing fine," interjected Herr Schäfer, in an effort to calm him down. "We know it's hard to recite with so many interruptions. You may check your notes to find your place."

Alfred took a deep breath, scanned his notes briefly, and continued:

"'Some have represented the man as an atheist and considered him reprehensible, but then they also admitted he was a quiet, reflective man, a good citizen, a sympathetic person. So Spinoza's critics seem to have forgotten the words of the Gospel, 'By their fruits, you shall know them'; for how can a life pleasing to men and God spring from corrupt principles? I still remember what calm and clearness came over me when I first turned over the pages of the Ethics of that remarkable man. I therefore hastened to the work again to which I had been so much indebted, and again the same air of peace floated over me. I gave myself up to the reading and thought, when I looked into myself, that I had never beheld the world so clearly.'"

Alfred exhaled deeply as he finished the last line. The headmaster signaled him to take his seat and commented, "Your recitation was satisfactory. You have a good memory. Now let's examine your understanding of this last section. Tell me, does Goethe think Spinoza is an atheist?"

Alfred shook his head.

"I didn't hear your answer."

"No sir." Alfred spoke loudly. "Goethe did not think he was an atheist. But others thought he was."

"And why did Goethe disagree with them?"

"Because of his ethics?"

"No, no. Have you already forgotten that *Ethics* is the name of Spinoza's book? Again, why did Goethe disagree with Spinoza's critics?"

Alfred trembled and remained silent.

"Good Lord, Rosenberg, look at your notes," said the headmaster.

Alfred scanned the final paragraph and ventured. "Because he was good and lived a life pleasing to God?"

"Exactly. In other words it is not what you believe or say you believe, it is how you live that matters. Now, Rosenberg, a last question about this passage. Tell us again, what did Goethe get from Spinoza?"

"He said he got an air of peace and calmness. He also says he beheld the world more clearly. Those were the two main things."

"Exactly. We know that the great Goethe carried a copy of Spinoza's *Ethics* in his pocket for a year. Imagine that—an entire year! And not only Goethe but many other great Germans. Lessing and Heine reported a clarity and calmness that came from reading this book. Who knows, there may come a time in your life when you, too, will need the calmness and clarity that Spinoza's *Ethics* offers. I shan't ask you to read that book now. You're too young to grasp its meaning. But I want you to promise that before your twenty-first birthday you will read it. Or perhaps I should say, read it by the time you're fully grown. Do I have your word as a good German?"

"Yes sir, you have my word." Alfred would have promised to read the entire encyclopedia in Chinese to get out of this inquisition.

"Now, let's move to the heart of this assignment. Are you fully clear why we assigned you this reading assignment?"

"Uh, no, sir. I thought it was just because I said I admired Goethe above all others."

"Certainly that is part of it. But surely you understood what my real question was?"

Alfred looked blank.

"I'm asking you, what does it mean to you that the man *you* admire above all others chooses a Jew as the man *he* admires above all others?"

"A Jew?"

"Did you not know that Spinoza was a Jew?"

Silence.

"You have found out nothing about him these last two weeks?"

"Sir, I know nothing about this Spinoza. That was not part of my assignment."

"And so, thank God, you avoided the dreaded step of learning something extra? Is that it, Rosenberg?"

"Let me put it this way," interjected Herr Schäfer. "Think of Goethe. What would he have done in this situation? If Goethe had been required to read the autobiography of someone unknown to him, what would Goethe have done?"

"He would have educated himself about this person."

"Exactly. This is important. If you admire someone, emulate him. Use him as your guide."

"Thank you, sir."

"Still, let us proceed with my question," said Headmaster Epstein. "How do you explain Goethe's boundless admiration and gratitude to a Jew?"

"Did Goethe know he was a Jew?"

"Good God. Of course he knew."

"But, Rosenberg," said Herr Schäfer, who was now also growing impatient, "think about your question. What does it matter if he knew Spinoza was a Jew? Why would you even ask that question? Do you think a man of Goethe's stature—you yourself called him the universal genius—would not embrace great ideas regardless of their source?"

Alfred looked staggered. Never had he been exposed to such a blizzard of ideas. Headmaster Epstein, putting his hand on Herr Schäfer's arm to quiet him, did not relent.

"My major question to you is still unanswered: how do you explain that the universal German genius is so very much helped by the ideas of a member of an inferior race?"

"Perhaps it is what I answered about Dr. Apfelbaum. Maybe because of a mutation there can be a good Jew, even though the race is corrupt and inferior."

"That's not an acceptable answer," said the headmaster. "It is one thing to speak of a doctor who is kind and plies his chosen profession well and quite another thing to speak in this way of a genius who may have changed the course of history. And there are many other Jews whose genius is well-known. Think about them. Let me remind you of those you know yourself but maybe did not know were Jews. Herr Schäfer tells me that in class you've recited the poetry of Heinrich Heine. He tells me, too, that you like music, and I imagine you have listened to the music of Gustav Mahler and Felix Mendelssohn. Right?"

"They're Jews, sir?"

"Yes, and you must know that Disraeli, the great prime minister of England, was a Jew?"

"I did not know that, sir."

"Yes. And right now in Riga they are doing the opera of *Tales of Hoffmann* composed by Jacob Offenbach, another born of the Jewish race. So many geniuses. What is your explanation?"

"I can't answer the question. I will have to think about it. Please may I go, sir? I'm not feeling well. I promise to think about it."

"Yes, you may go," said the headmaster. "And I want very much for you to think. Thinking is good. Think about our talk today. Think about Goethe and the Jew, Spinoza."

———

After Alfred's departure, Headmaster Epstein and Herr Schäfer looked at one another for a few moments before the headmaster spoke. "He says he's going to think, Hermann. What's the chance of his thinking?"

"Next to zero, I would guess," said Herr Schäfer. "Let's graduate him and be rid of him. He has a lack of curiosity that is, most likely, incurable. Excavate anywhere in his mind, and we run into the bedrock of unfounded convictions."

"I agree. I have no doubt that Goethe and Spinoza are, at this very moment, fast receding from his thoughts and will never trouble him again. Nonetheless I feel relieved by what has just happened. My fears are quelled. This young man has neither the intelligence nor fortitude to cause mischief by swaying others to his way of thinking."

CHAPTER SEVEN

AMSTERDAM—1656

B ento stared out the window, watching his brother walk toward the synagogue. *Gabriel is right; I do injury to those closest to me. My choices are horrendous—either I must shrink myself by giving up my innermost nature and hobbling my curiosity, or I must harm those closest to me.* Gabriel's account of the rage toward him expressed at the Sabbath dinner brought to mind van den Enden's paternal warning about the growing dangers Bento faced in the Jewish community. He meditated escape strategies from his trap for almost an hour before rising, dressing, making himself coffee, and walking out the back door, cup in hand, to the Spinoza Import and Export Shop.

There he dusted and swept litter through the front door into the street, and emptied a large sack of fragrant dried figs, a new shipment from Spain, into a bin. Sitting at his usual window seat, Bento sipped his coffee, nibbled on the figs, and focused on the daydreams coasting through his mind. He had lately been practicing a meditation wherein he disconnected himself from his flow of thought and viewed his mind as a theater and himself as a member of the audience watching the passing show. Gabriel's face in all its sadness and confusion immediately appeared on stage, but Bento had learned how to lower the curtain and pass on to the next act. Soon van den Enden materialized. He praised Bento's progress in Latin while lightly grasping his shoulder in a fatherly manner. That touch—he liked the feel of it. *But, now,* Bento thought, *with Rebekah and now Gabriel turning away, who will ever touch me again?*

Bento's mind then drifted to an image of himself teaching Hebrew to his teacher and to Clara Maria. He smiled as he drilled his two students, like children, in the *aleph, bet, gimmel* and smiled even more at the vision of little Clara Maria in turn drilling *him* on the Greek *alpha, beta, gamma.* He noticed the bright, almost luminous quality of Clara Maria's image— Clara Maria, that thirteen-year-old wraith with the crooked back, that woman-child whose impish smile belied her pretense of a grown-up severe teacher. A stray thought floated by: *If only she were older. . .*

By midday, his long meditation was interrupted by movement outside the window. In the distance he saw Jacob and Franco conversing as they headed toward his shop. Bento had vowed to conduct himself in a holy manner and knew that it was not virtuous to observe others surreptitiously, especially others who might be discussing him. Yet he could not shift his attention from the strange scene unfolding before his eyes.

Franco lagged three or four steps behind Jacob, whereupon Jacob turned, seized his hand, and tried to tug him. Franco pulled away and shook his head vigorously. Jacob replied and, after looking about to ensure that there were no witnesses in view, placed his huge hands on Franco's shoulders, shook him gruffly, and pushed him along in front of him until they arrived at the shop.

For a moment Bento leaned forward, riveted to this drama, but soon reentered a meditative state and considered the riddle of Franco's and Jacob's odd behavior. In a few minutes he was pulled out of his reverie by the sound of his shop door opening and footsteps inside.

He bolted to his feet, greeted his visitors, and pulled over two chairs for them while he himself sat on a huge crate of dried figs. "You arrive from the Sabbath services?"

"Yes," said Jacob, "one of us refreshed and one of us more agitated than before."

"Interesting. The identical event launches two different reactions. And the explanation for that curious phenomenon?" asked Bento.

Jacob hastened to respond. "The matter is not so interesting, and the explanation is obvious. Unlike Franco, who has no Jewish education, I am schooled in the Jewish tradition and the Hebrew language and—"

"Allow me to interrupt," Bento said. "But even at the onset your explanation requires explanation. Every child raised in Portugal in a Marrano family is unschooled in Hebrew and Jewish ritual. That includes my father, who learned his Hebrew only after he left Portugal. He told me that when he was a boy in Portugal, great punishment would be meted out to any family educating children in the Hebrew language or Jewish tradition. In fact," Spinoza turned to Franco, "did I not yesterday hear of a beloved father killed because the Inquisition found a buried Torah?"

Franco, nervously running his fingers through his long hair, said nothing but nodded slightly.

Turning back to Jacob, Bento continued, "So my question, Jacob, is whence your knowledge of Hebrew?"

"My family became New Christians three generations ago," Jacob said quickly, "but they have remained crypto-Jews, determined to keep the faith alive. My father sent me to Rotterdam to work in his trading business as a youth of eleven, and for the next eight years I spent every night studying Hebrew with my uncle, a rabbi. He prepared me for bar mitzvah in the Rotterdam synagogue and then continued my Jewish education until his death. I've spent most of the last twelve years in Rotterdam and returned recently to Portugal only to rescue Franco."

"And you," Bento turned toward Franco, whose eyes had interest only in the poorly swept floor of the Spinoza import store, "you have no Hebrew?"

But Jacob answered, "Of course not. There is, as you just said, no Hebrew permitted in Portugal. We are all taught to read the scriptures in Latin."

"So, Franco, you have no Hebrew?"

Once again Jacob interposed, "In Portugal no one dares to teach Hebrew. Not only would they face instant death, but their whole family would be hunted down. At this very moment Franco's mother and two sisters are in hiding."

"Franco"—Bento bent down to peer directly into his eyes—"Jacob continues to answer for you. Why do you choose not to respond?"

"He tries only to help me," responded Franco in a whisper.

"And you are helped by remaining silent?"

"I am too upset to trust my words," said Franco, speaking more loudly. "Jacob speaks rightly, my family is endangered, and, as he says, I have no Jewish education aside from the *aleph, bet, gimmel* he taught me by drawing the letters in the sand. And even these he had to erase by grinding his feet on them."

Bento turned his body entirely to Franco, pointedly facing away from Jacob. "Is it your view also that, though he was refreshed by the service, you were agitated by it?"

Franco nodded.

"And your agitation was because . . ."

"Because of doubt and feelings." Franco cast a furtive look at Jacob. "Feelings so strong that I fear to describe them. Even to you."

"Trust me to understand your feelings and not to judge them."

Franco looked down, his head trembling.

"Such great fear," Bento continued. "Let me attempt to calm you. First, please let's consider if your fear is rational."

Franco grimaced and stared at Spinoza, puzzled.

"Let us see if your fear makes sense. Consider these two facts: *first*, I represent no threat. I give you my promise I will never repeat your words. Furthermore I, too, doubt many things. I may even share some of your feelings. And, *second*, there is no danger in Holland; there is no Inquisition here. Not in this shop nor this community nor this city nor even this country. Amsterdam has been independent of Iberia for many years. You know this, do you not?"

"Yes," Franco replied softly.

"Yet even so, some part of your mind, not under your control, continues to behave as though there is great immediate danger. Is it not remarkable how our minds are divided? How our reason, the highest part of our mind, is subdued by our emotions?"

Franco showed no interest in these remarkable events.

Bento hesitated. He felt both a growing impatience and a sense of mission, almost of duty. But how to proceed? Was he expecting too much too soon from Franco? He recalled many occasions when reason failed to quell his own fears. It had happened just last evening while walking against the crowd heading toward the synagogue Sabbath service.

Finally he decided to use his only available leverage and in his most gentle voice said, "You begged me to help you. I agreed to do so. But if you want my help, you must trust me today. You must help me help you. Do you understand?"

"Yes," said Franco, sighing.

"Well, then, your next step is to enunciate your fears."

Franco shook his head, "I cannot. They are terrifying. And they are dangerous."

"Not too terrifying to withstand the light of reason. And I've just shown you they are not dangerous if there is nothing to fear. Courage! Now is the time to face them. If not, I say to you again"—here Bento spoke firmly— "there is no purpose in our continuing to meet."

Franco inhaled deeply and began, "In the synagogue today I heard the scriptures chanted in a strange language. I understood nothing—"

"But Franco," interrupted Jacob, "*of course* you understood nothing. Over and over I tell you this problem is temporary. The rabbi has Hebrew classes. Patience, patience."

"And over and over," Franco shot back, anger now flooding into his voice, "I tell you it's more than the language. *Listen* to me sometime! It is the whole spectacle. In the synagogue this morning, I looked around and saw everyone with their fancy embroidered skull caps, with their fringed blue and white prayer shawls, their heads bobbing back and forth like parrots at their feed pan, eyes lifted to the heavens. I heard it, I saw it, and I thought—no, I cannot say what I thought."

"Say it, Franco," said Jacob. "You told me only yesterday that this is the teacher you seek."

Franco closed his eyes. "I thought what is the difference between this and the spectacle—no, let me speak my mind—the *nonsense* that went on in the Catholic Mass we New Christians had to attend? After Mass, when we were children, Jacob, do you remember how you and I used to ridicule the Catholics? We ridiculed the outlandish costumes of the priests, the endless gory pictures of the crucifixion, the genuflecting to the bits of bones of the saints, the wafer and wine and eating the flesh and drinking the blood." Franco's voice rose. "Jewish or Catholic . . . there is no difference . . . It is madness. It is all madness."

Jacob put his skullcap on his head, placed his hand upon it, and softly chanted a prayer in Hebrew. Bento, too, was shaken and searched carefully for the correct, the most serene, words. "To think such thoughts and to believe that you are the only one. To feel alone in your doubt. That must be terrifying."

Franco hastened on. "There is something more, another more terrible thought. I keep thinking that for this madness my father sacrificed his life.

For this madness he endangered all of us—me, his own parents, my mother, my brother, my sisters."

Jacob could not restrain himself. Stepping closer and bending his huge head to Franco's ear, he said, not unkindly, "Perhaps the father knows more than the son."

Franco shook his head, opened his mouth, but then said nothing.

"And think, too," Jacob went on, "of how your words make your father's death meaningless. To think such thoughts truly makes his death a wasted death. He died to keep the faith sacred for you."

Franco appeared beaten and bowed his head.

Bento knew he had to intervene. First, he turned to Jacob and said softly, "Only a moment ago you pleaded with Franco to speak his mind. Now that he finally does as you ask, is it not better to encourage him rather than to silence him?"

Jacob took a half step backward. Bento continued addressing Franco in the same serene voice, "What a dilemma for you, Franco: Jacob claims that if you don't believe things you find unbelievable, then you've made your father's martyrdom a wasted death. And who would want to harm his own father? So many obstacles to thinking for yourself. So many obstacles to perfecting ourselves by using our God-given ability to reason."

Jacob shook his head. "Wait, wait—that last part about God-given ability to reason? That's *not* what I said. You're twisting things. You talk about reason? I'll show you reason. Use your common sense. Open your eyes. I want you to compare! Look at Franco. He suffers, he weeps, he grovels, he despairs. You see him?"

Bento nodded.

"And now look at me. I am strong. I love life. I take care of him. I rescued him from the Inquisition. I am sustained by my faith and by the embrace of my fellow Jews. I am comforted by the knowledge that our people and our tradition continue. Compare the two of us with your precious reason, and tell me, *wise man*, what reason concludes."

False ideas offer false and fragile comfort, thought Bento. But he held his tongue.

Jacob pressed harder. "And apply that to yourself, as well, scholar. What are we, what are you, without our community, without our tradition? Can you live wandering the earth alone? I hear you take no wife. What kind of life can you have without people? Without family? Without God?"

Bento, who always avoided conflict, felt shaken by Jacob's invective.

Jacob turned to Franco and gentled his voice. "You will feel sustained as I do when you know the words and the prayers, when you understand what things mean."

"With that statement I agree," said Bento, attempting to placate Jacob, who had been glowering at him. "Bewilderment adds to your state of shock, Franco. Every Marrano who leaves Portugal is disoriented, has to be newly educated to become a Jew again, has to start like a child and learn the *aleph, bet, gimmel*. For three years I assisted the rabbi in Hebrew courses for Marranos, and I assure you that you will learn quickly."

"No," insisted Franco, now resembling the resistant Franco whom Bento had seen through the window. "Neither *you*, Jacob Mendoza, nor *you*, Bento de Spinoza, listen to me. Once again I tell you, *It is not the language.* I know no Hebrew, but this morning at the synagogue, all through the service, I read the Spanish translation of the holy Torah. It is full of miracles. God divides the Red Sea; He assails the Egyptians with afflictions; He speaks disguised as a burning bush. Why do all the miracles happen *then*, in the age of the Torah? Tell me, both of you, why is the miracle season over? Has the mighty, all-powerful God gone to sleep? Where was that God when my father was burned at the stake? And for what reason? For protecting the sacred book of that very God? Wasn't God powerful enough to save my father, who revered Him so? If so, who needs such a weak God? Or didn't God know my father revered Him? If so, who needs such an unknowing God? Was God powerful enough to protect him but chose not to? If so, who needs such an unloving God? You, Bento de Spinoza, the one they call 'blessed,' you know about God; you are a scholar. Explain that to me."

"Why were you afraid to speak?" Bento asked. "You pose important questions, questions that have puzzled the pious throughout the centuries. I believe the problem has its root in a fundamental and massive error, the error of assuming that God is a living, thinking being, a being in our image, a being who thinks *like* us, a being who thinks *about* us.

"The ancient Greeks understood this error. Two thousand years ago, a wise man named Xenophanes wrote that if oxen, lions, and horses had hands with which to carve images, they would fashion God after their own shapes and give him bodies like their own. I believe that if triangles could think they would create a God with the appearance and attributes of a triangle, or circles would create circular—"

Jacob interrupted Bento, outraged. "You speak as though we Jews know nothing of the nature of God. Do not forget that we have the Torah containing his words. And, Franco, do not think that God is without power. Do not forget that the Jews persist, that no matter what they do to us, we persist. Where are all those vanished people—the Phoenicians, Moabites, Edomites—and so many others whose names I do not know? Do not forget that we must be guided by the law that God Himself gave to the Jews, gave to us, His chosen people."

Franco gave Spinoza a glance as though to say, *You see what I have to face?* and turned to Jacob. "Everyone believes God chose them—the Christians, the Muslims—"

"No! What does it matter what others believe? What matters is what is written in the Bible." Jacob turned to Spinoza, "Admit it, Baruch, admit it, scholar: does not the word of God say that the Jews are the chosen people? Can you deny that?"

"I have spent years studying that question, Jacob, and if you wish, I will share the results of my research." Bento spoke gently, as a teacher might address an inquisitive student. "To answer your questions about the specialness of the Jews we must go back to the source. Will you accompany me in exploring the very words of the Torah? My copy is only a few minutes away."

Both nodded, exchanging glances, and rose to follow Bento, who carefully put the chairs back in place and locked the shop door before escorting them to his home.

CHAPTER EIGHT

REVAL, ESTONIA—1917-1918

Headmaster Epstein's prediction that Rosenberg's limited curiosity and intelligence would render him harmless proved entirely wrong. And wrong, too, was the headmaster's prediction that Goethe and Spinoza would instantaneously vanish from Alfred's thoughts. Far from it: Alfred was never able to cleanse his mind of the image of the great Goethe genuflecting before the Jew Spinoza. Whenever thoughts of Goethe and Spinoza (now forever melded) appeared, he held the dissonance only briefly and then swept it away with every ideational broom at hand. Sometimes he was persuaded by Houston Stewart Chamberlain's argument that Spinoza, like Jesus, was of the Jewish culture but did not possess one drop of Jewish blood. Or perhaps Spinoza was a Jew who stole thoughts from Aryan thinkers. Or perhaps Goethe had been under a spell, mesmerized by the Jewish conspiracy. Many times Alfred contemplated pursuing these ideas in depth through library research but never followed through. Thinking, really thinking, was such hard work, like moving heavy trunks about in the attic. Instead, Alfred grew more adept at suppression. He diverted himself. He plunged into many activities. Most of all, he persuaded himself that the strength of convictions obviates the need for inquiry.

A true and noble German honors an oath, and as his twenty-first birthday approached, Alfred remembered his pledge to the headmaster to read Spinoza's *Ethics*. He intended to keep his word, bought a used copy of the book, and launched into it only to be greeted on the first page by a long list of incomprehensible definitions:

I.   By that which is Self-Caused, I mean that of which the essence in-
     volves existence, or that of which the nature is only conceivable
     as existent.

II. A thing is called *Finite After Its Kind* when it can be limited by an-
     other thing of the same nature; for instance, a body is called finite
     because we always conceive another greater body. So, also, a
     thought is limited by another thought, but a body is not limited
     by thought, nor a thought by body.

III. BY SUBSTANCE, I mean that which is in itself, and is conceived
     Theologically through itself; in other words, that of which a con-
     ception can be formed independently of any other conception.

IV. BY ATTRIBUTE, I mean that which the intellect perceives as con-
     stituting the essence of substance.

V.   BY MODE, I mean the modifications ["Affectiones"] of substance,
     or that which exists in, and is conceived through, something other
     than itself.

VI. BY GOD, I mean a being absolutely infinite—that is, a substance
     consisting in infinite attributes, of which each expresses eternal
     and infinite essentiality.

Who could understand this Jewish stuff? Alfred flung the book across
the room. A week later he tried again, skipping the definitions and moving
to the next section of Axioms:

I.   Everything which exists, exists either in itself or in something else.

II. That which cannot be conceived through anything else must be
     conceived through itself.

III. From a given definite cause an effect necessarily follows; and, on
     the other hand, if no definite cause be granted, it is impossible
     that an effect can follow.

IV. The knowledge of an effect depends on and involves the knowledge
     of a cause.

V.   Things which have nothing in common cannot be understood,
     the one by means of the other; the conception of one does not in-
     volve the conception of the other.

These were equally indecipherable, and again the book took flight. Later he sampled the next section, the propositions, which were also inaccessible. Finally it dawned on him that each successive part depended logically upon the preceding definitions and axioms, and nothing would come of further sampling. From time to time he picked up the time-worn volume, turned to the portrait of Spinoza facing the title page, and was transfixed by that long oval face and those gigantic, soulful, heavy-lidded Jewish eyes (which stared directly into his own eyes regardless of how he rotated the book). Get rid of this cursed book, he told himself—sell it (but it would fetch nothing, being much the worse for wear after several aerial excursions). Or just give it away, or throw it away. He knew he should do this, but, strangely, Alfred could not part with the *Ethics*.

Why? Well, the oath, of course, was a factor but not the compelling one. Had not the headmaster said that one had to be fully grown to understand *Ethics*? And did he not have years of education still ahead of him before he was fully grown?

No, no, it was not the oath that vexed him: it was the Goethe problem. He worshipped Goethe. And Goethe worshipped Spinoza. Alfred could not rid himself of this cursed book because Goethe loved it enough to carry it in his pocket for an entire year. This obscure Jewish nonsense had calmed Goethe's unruly passions and made him see the world more clearly than ever before. How could that be? Goethe saw something in it that he could not discern. Perhaps, someday, he would find the teacher who could explain this.

The tumultuous events of the First World War soon pushed this conundrum out of consciousness. After graduating from the Reval Oberschule and saying farewell to Headmaster Epstein, Herr Schäfer, and his art teacher, Herr Purvit, Alfred began his studies in the Polytechnic Institute in Riga, Latvia, about two hundred miles from his home in Reval. But in 1915, as the German troops threatened both Estonia and Latvia, the entire Polytechnic Institute was moved to Moscow, where Alfred lived until 1918, when he handed in his final project—an architectural design for a crematorium— and received his degree in architecture and engineering.

Though his academic work was superior, Alfred never felt at home in engineering and preferred, instead, to spend his time reading mythology and fiction. He was fascinated by the tales of Norse mythology contained in the Edda as well as the intricately plotted novels of Dickens and the monumental works of Tolstoy (which he read in Russian). He dabbled in philosophy, skimming the essential ideas of Kant, Schopenhauer, Fichte, Nietzsche, and Hegel and, as before, shamelessly took pleasure in reading philosophical works in conspicuous public places.

During the chaos of the 1917 Russian Revolution Alfred was appalled by the sight of hundreds of thousands of frenzied protestors taking to the streets, demanding the overthrow of the established order. He had come to believe, on the basis of Chamberlain's work, that Russia owed everything to Aryan influence through the Vikings, the Hanseatic League, and German immigrants like himself. The collapse of the Russian civilization meant only one thing: the Nordic foundations were being overthrown by the inferior races—the Mongols, Jews, Slavs, and Chinese—and the soul of the real Russia would soon be lost. Was this to be the fate, too, of the Fatherland? Would racial chaos and degradation come to Germany itself?

The sight of the surging crowds repulsed him. The Bolsheviks were animals whose mission was to destroy civilization. He scrutinized their leaders and grew convinced that at least 90 percent were Jews. From 1918 forward, Alfred rarely spoke of the Bolsheviks: it was always the "Jewish Bolsheviks," and that double epithet was destined to work its way into Nazi propaganda. After graduation in 1918 Alfred was thrilled to board the train taking him across Russia back to his home in Reval. As the train chugged westward, he sat day after day staring at the endless Russian expanse. Transfixed by the space—ah, the space—he thought of Houston Stewart Chamberlain's wish for more Lebensraum for the Fatherland. Here, outside his second-class train window, was the Lebensraum that Germany so desperately needed, and yet the sheer vastness of Russia made it unconquerable unless . . . unless an army of Russian collaborators was to fight side by side with the Fatherland. Another germ of an idea took hold: this forbidding open space—what to do with all of it? Why not put the Jews there, all the Jews of Europe?

The train whistle and the clenching and squealing of the brakes signaled that he had arrived home. Reval was as cold as Russia. He donned all the sweaters he owned, knotted his scarf tightly around his neck, and with bags in hand and diploma in briefcase, exhaling clouds of mist, he walked the familiar streets and arrived at the door of his childhood home, the dwelling of Aunt Cäcilie—his father's sister. His knock was welcomed with shrieks of "Alfred," broad smiles, male handshakes, and female embraces, and he was ushered quickly into the warm fragrant kitchen for coffee and streusel while a young nephew was sent galloping to fetch Aunt Lydia living a few doors down the street. Soon she arrived laden with food for a celebratory dinner.

Home was much as he recalled it, and such persistence of the past offered Alfred a rare respite from his tormented sense of rootlessness. The sight of his own room, virtually unchanged after so many years, brought an expression of childlike glee to his face. He sank into his old reading chair and basked in the familiar sight of his aunt noisily beating the pillow and fluffing the down coverlet into place on his bed. Alfred scanned the room: there was the handkerchief-sized scarlet prayer rug on which, for a few months, years ago (when his antireligious father was out of earshot), Alfred said his bedtime prayers: "Bless Mother in heaven, bless Father and make him well again, and heal my brother, Eugen, and bless Aunt Ericka and Aunt Marlene, and bless all our family."

There on the wall, still glaring and powerful and blissfully unaware of the faltering fortunes of the German army, was the huge poster of Kaiser Wilhelm. And on the shelf under the poster were his lead figures of Viking warriors and Roman soldiers, which he now picked up tenderly. Bending down to examine the small bookcase crammed with his favorite books, Alfred beamed to see them still aligned in the same order he had left them in so many years ago—his favorite, *Young Werther*, first, then *David Copperfield*, followed by all the others in order of descending merit.

Alfred continued to feel at home during dinner with aunts, uncles, nephews, and nieces. But when everyone had left and silence descended, and he lay under his down coverlet, his familiar anomie returned. "Home" began to pale. Even the image of his two aunts, still grinning, waving, and nodding, slowly receded into the distance, leaving only chilly darkness. Where was home? Where did he belong?

The next day he roamed the streets of Reval searching for familiar faces, even though all his childhood playmates were grown and scattered, and, besides, he knew deep in his heart that he was searching for phantoms— the friends he *wished* he had had. He strolled to the Oberschule, where the halls and open classrooms looked both familiar and uninviting. He waited outside the classroom of the art teacher, Herr Purvit, who had once been so kind to him. When the bell rang, he entered to speak to his old teacher between classes. Herr Purvit searched Alfred's face, uttered a sound of recognition, and inquired about his life in such general terms that Alfred, walking away as the students for the next class scampered into their seats, doubted he had been truly recognized. Next he searched in vain for the room of Herr Schäfer but noted the room of Herr Epstein, no longer headmaster but once again a history teacher, and slipped by quickly with his face turned away. He did not wish to be asked about keeping his Spinoza vow or learn that the vow of Alfred Rosenberg had long ago evaporated from Herr Epstein's mind.

Outside again he headed toward the town square, where he saw the German army headquarters, and impulsively made a decision that might change his entire life. He told the guard on duty, in German, that he wished to enlist, and was directed to Sergeant Goldberg, a hulking figure with a large nose, bushy mustache, and "Jew" writ large on his face. Without looking up from his paperwork, the sergeant briefly listened to Alfred and then gruffly dismissed his request. "We are at war. The German army is for Germans, not for citizens of combatant occupied countries."

Disconsolate, and stung by the sergeant's manner, Alfred took refuge in a beer hall a few doors away, ordered a stein of ale, and sat at one end of a long table. As he raised his stein for his first sip, he noted a man in civilian dress staring at him. Their eyes met briefly, and the stranger raised his stein and nodded to Alfred. Alfred hesitantly reciprocated, then sank back into himself. A few minutes later, when he again looked up, he saw the stranger, tall, thin, attractive, with a long German skull and deep blue eyes, still staring at him. Finally, the man arose and, stein in hand, walked toward Alfred and introduced himself.

CHAPTER NINE

AMSTERDAM—1656

Bento led Jacob and Franco to the house he shared with Gabriel and directed them to his study, passing first through a small living room furnished with no trace of a woman's hand—only a rude wooden bench and chair, a straw broom in the corner, and a fireplace with bellows. Bento's study contained a rough-hewn writing table, a high stool, and a rickety wooden chair. Three of his own charcoal sketches of Amsterdam canal scenes were pinned to the wall above two shelves bending under the weight of a dozen sturdily bound books. Jacob immediately headed to the shelves to peer at the book titles, but Bento beckoned for him and Franco to sit while he hastily fetched another chair from the adjoining room.

"Now to work," he said as he lifted his well-worn copy of the Hebrew Bible, set it down heavily in the center of the table, and opened it for Jacob and Franco's inspection. Suddenly he thought better of it and stopped, letting the pages fall back into place.

"I shall keep my promise to show you precisely what our Torah says, or doesn't say, about the Jews being the chosen people. But I prefer to begin with my major conclusions resulting from years of Bible study."

With Jacob and Franco's approval, Bento began. "The Bible's central message about God, I believe, is that He is perfect, complete, and possesses absolute wisdom. God is everything and from Himself created the world and everything in it. You agree?"

Franco nodded quickly. Jacob thought it over, stuck out his lower lip, opened his right fist to show his palm, and offered a slow, cautious nod.

"Since God, by definition, is perfect and has no needs, then it follows that He did not create the world for Himself but for us."

He received a nod from Franco and a bewildered look and outstretched palms from Jacob that indicated, "What does this have to do with anything?"

Bento calmly continued, "And since He created us out of his own substance, His purpose for all of us—who, again, are part of God's substance—is to find happiness and blessedness."

Jacob nodded heartily as though he had finally heard something he could agree with. "Yes, I've heard my uncle speak of the God-spark in each of us."

"Exactly. Your uncle and I are entirely in agreement," said Spinoza and, noting a slight frown on Jacob's face, resolved to refrain from such remarks in the future—Jacob was too intelligent and suspicious to be patronized. He opened the Bible and searched the pages. "Here, let's begin with some verses from the Psalms." Bento began reading the Hebrew slowly while pointing with his finger to each word that, for Franco's sake, he translated into Portuguese. After only a couple of minutes Jacob interrupted, shaking his head and saying, "No, no, no."

"No what?" asked Bento. "You don't care for my translation? I assure you that—"

"It's not your words," interrupted Jacob. "It's your manner. As a Jew, I am offended by the way you handle our holy book. You don't kiss it or honor it. You practically threw it on the table; you point with an unwashed finger. And you read with no chanting, no inflection of any sort. You read in the same voice as you might read a purchase agreement for your raisins. That type of reading offends God."

"Offends God? Jacob, I beg you to follow the path of reason. Have we not just agreed that God is full, has no needs, and is not a being like us? Could such a God possibly be offended by such trivia as my reading style?"

Jacob shook his head in silence, while Franco nodded in agreement and moved his chair closer to Bento.

Bento continued to read the psalm aloud in Hebrew and translate into Portuguese for Franco. "The Lord is good to all, and His tender mercies are over all His works." Bento skipped ahead in the same psalm and read, "'The Lord is near unto all them that call upon Him.' Trust me," he said, "I can find a host of such passages clearly stating that God has granted to *all* men the same intellect and has fashioned their hearts alike."

Bento turned his attention to Jacob, who again shook his head. "You disagree with my translation, Jacob? I can assure you it says 'all men'; it does *not* say 'all Jews.'"

"I cannot disagree: the words are the words. What the Bible says the Bible says. But the Bible has many words, and there are many readings, and many interpretations by many holy men. Do you ignore or not even know the great commentaries of Rashi and of Abarbanel?"

Bento was unflustered. "I was weaned on the commentaries and the super-commentaries. I read them from sunup till sundown. I have spent years studying the holy books, and as you yourself have told me, many in our community respect me as a scholar. Several years ago I struck out on my own, acquired a mastery of ancient Hebrew and Aramaic, put the commentaries of others aside, and studied the actual words of the Bible afresh. To truly understand the words of the Bible, one must know the ancient language and read it in a fresh, unfettered spirit. I want us to read and understand the exact words of the Bible, not what some rabbi thought they meant, not some imagined metaphors that scholars pretend to see, and not some secret message that Kabbalists see in certain patterns of words and numerical values of letters. I want to go back to read what the Bible actually says. That is my method. Do you wish me to continue?"

Franco said, "Yes, please go on," but Jacob hesitated. His agitation was evident, for as soon as he heard Bento emphasize the phrase "all men," he sensed where Bento's argument was heading—he could smell the trap ahead. He tried a preemptive maneuver: "You haven't yet answered my pressing and simple question, 'Do you deny that the Jews are the chosen people?'"

"Jacob, your questions are the wrong questions. Obviously I'm not being clear enough. What I want to do is challenge *your whole attitude toward authority*. It is not a question of whether I deny it, or some rabbi or other scholar claims it. Let us not look upward to some grand authority but instead look to the words of our holy book, which tell us that our true happiness and blessedness consist solely in the enjoyment of what is good. The Bible does not tell us to take pride in the fact that we Jews alone are blessed or that we have more enjoyment because others are ignorant of true happiness."

Jacob gave no sign he was persuaded, so Bento tried another tactic. "Let me give you an example from our own experience today. Earlier, when we were in the shop, I learned that Franco knows no Hebrew. Right?"

"Yes."

"Then tell me this: should I therefore rejoice that I know more Hebrew than he? Does his ignorance of Hebrew make me more learned than I was an hour ago? Joy of our superiority over others is not blessed. It is childish or malicious. Is that not true?"

Jacob conveyed skepticism by hunching his shoulders, but Bento felt energized. Burdened by his years of necessary silence, he now relished the opportunity to express aloud many of the arguments he had been construct-ing. He addressed Jacob. "Surely you must agree that blessedness resides in love. It is the paramount, the core message of the entire Scriptures—and of the Christian Testament as well. We must make a distinction between what the Bible says and what the religious professionals say that it says. Too often rabbis and priests promote their own self-interest by biased readings, readings that claim that only they hold the key to truth."

Out of the corner of his eye, Bento saw Jacob and Franco exchanging astonished glances; he nonetheless persisted. "Here, look, at this section in Kings 3:12." Spinoza opened the Bible to a place he had marked with a red thread. "Listen to the words God offers Solomon: 'No one shall be as wise as you in time to come.' Think now, both of you, for a moment about that comment by God to the world's wisest man. Surely this is evidence that the words of the Torah can not be taken literally. They must be understood in the context of the times—"

"Context?" interrupted Franco.

"I mean the language and the historical events of the day. We cannot understand the Bible from the language of today: we must read it with knowledge of the language conventions of the time it was written and com-piled, and that is about two thousand years ago."

"What?" exclaimed Jacob. "Moses wrote the Torah, the first five books, far more than two thousand years ago!"

"That's a big topic. I'll come back to that in a couple of minutes. For now, let me continue with Solomon. The point I want to make is that God's comment to Solomon is simply an expression used to convey great, sur-passing wisdom and is meant to increase Solomon's happiness. Can you possibly believe God would expect Solomon, the wisest of all men, to rejoice that others would always be less intelligent than He? Surely God, in his wis-dom, would have wished that everyone be gifted with the same faculties."

Jacob protested. "I don't understand what you're talking about. You pick out a few words or sentences, but you ignore the clear fact that we are chosen by God. The Holy Book says this again and again."

"Here, look at Job," said Bento, entirely undeterred. He flipped the pages to Job 28 and read, "'All men should avoid evil and do good.' In such passages," Bento continued, "it is plain that God had in mind the entire human race. And then keep in mind too that Job was a Gentile, yet, of all men, he was most acceptable to God. Here are these lines—read for yourself."

Jacob refused to look. "The Bible may have some of those words. But there are thousands of opposite words. We Jews are different, and you know it. Franco has just escaped the Inquisition. Tell me, Bento, when have the Jews held Inquisitions? Others slaughter Jews. Have we ever slaughtered others?"

Bento calmly turned the pages, this time to Joshua 10:37 and read: "'And they took Eglon, and smote it with the edge of the sword, and the king thereof, and all the cities thereof, and all the souls that were therein; he left none remaining. He destroyed it utterly.' Or Joshua 11:11 about the city of Hazor," Bento continued, "'and the Hebrews smote all the souls that were therein with the edge of the sword, utterly destroying them: there was not any left to breathe: and He burnt Hazor with fire.'

"Or here again, Samuel 18:6–7, 'When David returned from the slaughter of the Philistine the women came out of all the cities of Israel, singing and dancing, to meet King Saul, with tambourines, with joy, and with instruments of music . . . The women sang one to another as they played, *Saul has slain his thousands, David his ten thousands.*'

"Sadly there is much evidence in the Torah that when the Israelites had power, they were as cruel and as pitiless as any other nation. They were not morally superior, more righteous, or more intelligent than other ancient nations. They were superior only in that they had a well-ordered society and a superior government that allowed them to persist for a very long time. But that ancient Hebrew nation has long ceased to exist, and ever since they have been on a par with their fellow peoples. I see nothing in the Torah that suggests that Jews are superior to other peoples. God is equally gracious to all."

With a look of disbelief on his face Jacob said, "You are saying there is nothing that distinguishes Jews from Gentiles?"

"Exactly, but it is not I saying this, but the Holy Bible."

"How can you be called 'Baruch' and speak thusly? Are you actually denying that God chose the Jews, favored them, helped the Jews, expected much from them?"

"Again, Jacob, reflect upon what you say. Once again I remind you: human beings choose, favor, help, value, expect. But God? Does God have these human attributes? Remember what I said about the fallacy of imagining God to be in our image. Remember what I said about triangles and a triangular God."

"We *were* made in His image," said Jacob. "Turn to Genesis. Let me show you those words—"

Bento recited from memory, "'Then God said, "Let us make man in our image, in our likeness, and let them rule over the fish of the sea and the birds of the air, over the livestock, over all the earth, and over all the creatures that move along the ground." So God created man in His own image, in the image of God He created him; male and female He created them.'"

"Exactly, Baruch, those are the words," said Jacob. "Would that your piety were as great as your memory. If those are God's words, then who are you to question that we are made in His image?"

"Jacob, use your God-given reason. We cannot take such words literally. They are metaphors. Do you truly believe that we mortals, some of us deaf or crooked or constipated or wretched, are made in God's image? Think of those like my mother who died in their twenties, those born blind or deformed or demented with huge cavernous water heads, those with scrofula, those whose lungs fail them and who spit blood, those who are avaricious or murderous—are they, too, in God's image? You think God has a mentality like ours and wishes to be flattered and grows jealous and vindictive if we disobey His rules? Could such flawed, mutilated modes of thought be present in a perfect being? This is merely the manner of talking of those who wrote the Bible."

"Of those who wrote the Bible? You speak disparagingly of Moses and Joshua and the Prophets and Judges? You deny the Bible is the word of God?" Jacob's voice grew louder with each sentence, and Franco, who was intent on every word Bento uttered, put his hand on his arm to still him.

"I disparage no one," Bento said. "That conclusion comes from your mind. But I do say that the words and ideas of the Bible come from the human mind, from the men who wrote these passages and imagined—no,

I should better say *wished*—that they resembled God, that they were made in God's image."

"So you do deny that God speaks through the voices of the Prophets?"

"It's obvious that any words in the Bible referred to as 'God's words' originate only in the imagination of the various prophets."

"Imagination! You say 'imagination'?" Jacob placed his hand before his mouth open with horror, while Franco tried to suppress a smile.

Bento knew that each utterance from his lips shocked Jacob, yet he could not still himself. He felt exhilarated to burst his shackles of silence and express aloud all the ideas he had pondered in secret or shared with the rabbi only in heavily veiled form. Van den Enden's warning of "*caute, caute*" came to mind, but for once he ignored reason and plunged ahead.

"Yes, it's obviously imagination, Jacob, and don't be so shocked: we know this from the very words of the Torah." Out of the corner of his eye Bento noted Franco's grin. Bento continued, "Here, Jacob, read this with me in Deuteronomy 34:10: 'And there arose not a prophet since in Israel like unto Moses whom the Lord knew face to face.' Now, Jacob, consider what that means. You know, of course, that the Torah tells us not even Moses saw the Lord's face, right?"

Jacob nodded. "Yes, the Torah says so."

"So, Jacob, we've eliminated vision, and it must mean that Moses heard God's real voice, and that no prophet following Moses heard His real voice."

Jacob had no reply.

"Explain to me," said Franco, who had been listening carefully to Bento's every word. "If none of the other prophets heard the voice of God, then what is the source of prophecies?"

Welcoming Franco's participation, Bento answered readily: "I believe that the prophets were men endowed with unusually vivid imaginations, but not necessarily highly developed reasoning power."

"Then, Bento," said Franco, "you believe that miraculous prophecies are nothing more than the imagined notions of prophets?"

"Exactly."

Franco continued, "It is as though there is nothing supernatural. You make it appear that everything is explainable."

"That is precisely what I believe. Everything, and I mean *everything*, has a natural cause."

"To me," said Jacob, who had been glaring at Bento as he spoke about the prophets, "there are things known only to God, things caused only by God's will."

"I believe that the more we can know, the fewer will be the things known only to God. In other words, the greater our ignorance, the more we attribute to God."

"How can you dare to—"

"Jacob," Bento interrupted. "Let us review why we three are meeting. You came to me because Franco was in a spiritual crisis and needed help. I did not seek you out—in fact I advised you to see the rabbi instead. You said that you had been told the rabbi would only make Franco feel worse. Remember?"

"Yes, that is true," said Jacob.

"Then what end is served for you and me to enter into such dispute? Instead there is only one real question." Bento turned to Franco. "Tell me, am I being of help to you? Has anything I've said been of aid?"

"*Everything* you've said has provided comfort," said Franco. "You help my sanity. I was losing my bearings, and your clear thought, the way you take nothing on the basis of authority, is—is like nothing I have ever heard. I hear Jacob's anger, and I apologize for him, but for me—yes, you have helped me."

"In that case," said Jacob suddenly rising to his feet, "we have gotten what we came for, and our business here is finished." Franco appeared shocked and remained seated, but Jacob grabbed his elbow and guided him toward the door.

"Thank you, Bento," said Franco, as he stood in the doorway. "Please, tell me, are you available for further meetings?"

"I am always available for a reasoned discussion—just come by the shop. But," Bento turned toward Jacob, "I am not available for a disputation that excludes reason."

Once out of sight of Bento's house, Jacob smiled broadly, put his arm around Franco, and grasped his shoulder, "We've got all we need now. We worked well together. You played your part well—almost too well, if you ask me—but I'm not even going to discuss that, because we have now finished what we had to do. Look at what we have. The Jews are not chosen by God; they differ in no way from other peoples. God has no feelings about us. The prophets merely imagine things. The Holy Scriptures are not holy but entirely the work of humans. God's word and God's will are nonexistent. Genesis and the rest of the Torah are fables or metaphors. The rabbis, even the greatest of them, have no special knowledge but instead act in their self-interest."

Franco shook his head. "We don't have all we need, not yet. I want to see him again."

"I've just recited all his abominations: his words are pure heresy. This is what Uncle Duarte requested of us, and we have done as he wished. The evidence is overwhelming: Bento de Spinoza is not a Jew; he is an anti-Jew."

"No," repeated Franco, "we do *not* have enough. I need to hear more. I'm not testifying until I have more."

"We have more than enough. Your family is in danger. We made a bargain with Uncle Duarte—and no one wiggles out of a bargain with him. That is exactly what this fool Spinoza tried to do—to swindle him by bypassing the Jewish court. It was only through Uncle's contacts, Uncle's bribes, and Uncle's ship that you are not still cowering in a cave in Portugal. And in only two weeks, his ship goes back for your mother and sister and my sister. Do you want them to be murdered like our fathers? If you don't go with me to the synagogue and testify to the governing committee, then you'll be the one lighting their pyres."

"I'm not a fool, and I'm not going to be ordered around like a sheep," said Franco. "We have time, and I need more information before I testify to the synagogue committee. Another day makes no difference, and you know it. And what's more, Uncle is obligated to take care of his family even if we do nothing."

"Uncle does what Uncle wants. I know him better than you. He follows no rules but his own, and he is not generous by nature. I don't ever want to visit your Spinoza again. He slanders our whole people."

"That man has more intelligence than the whole congregation put together. And if you don't want to go, I'll speak to him alone."

"No, if you go, I go. I won't let you go alone. The man is too persuasive. I feel unsettled myself. If you go alone, the next thing I'll see is a *cherem* for you as well as for him." Noting Franco's puzzled look, Jacob added, "*Cherem* is excommunication—another Hebrew word you'd better learn."

CHAPTER TEN

REVAL, ESTONIA—NOVEMBER 1918

*G*uten Tag," the stranger said, extending his hand, "I'm Friedrich Pfister. Do I know you? You look familiar."

"Rosenberg, Alfred Rosenberg. Grew up here. Just returned from Moscow. Got my degree from the Polytechnic just last week."

"Rosenberg? Ah, yes, yes—that's it. You're Eugen's baby brother. I see his eyes in you. May I join you?"

"Of course."

Friedrich set his stein of ale on the table and sat down facing Alfred. "Your brother and I were the closest of friends, and we still stay in touch. I saw you often at your home—even gave you piggyback rides. You're what— six, seven years younger than Eugen?"

"Six. You look familiar, but I can't quite remember you. I don't know why, but I have little memory of my early life—it is all blotted out. You know, I was only nine or ten when Eugen left home to study in Brussels. I've hardly seen him since. You say you're in touch with him now?"

"Yes, only two weeks ago we had dinner in Zurich."

"Zurich? He's left Brussels?"

"About six months ago. He had a relapse of consumption and came to Switzerland for a rest cure. I've been studying in Zurich and visited him there in the sanitarium. He'll be discharged in a couple of weeks and then move to Berlin for an advanced banking course. I happen to be moving to Berlin for study in a few weeks, so we'll be meeting often there. You know none of this?"

"No, we've gone our separate ways. We were never close and now have pretty much lost touch."

"Yes, Eugen mentioned that—wistfully, I thought. I know your mother died when you were an infant—that was hard for both of you—and I recall your father also died young, of consumption?"

"Yes, he was only forty-four. That was when I was eleven. Tell me, Herr Pfister—"

"Friedrich, please. A brother of a friend is also a friend. So we are now Friedrich and Alfred?"

A nod from Alfred.

"And Alfred, a minute ago you were going to ask? . . ."

"I wonder if Eugen ever mentioned me?"

"Not at our last meeting. We hadn't met for about three years and had a lot of catching up to do. But he has spoken of you many times in the past."

Alfred hesitated and then blurted out, "Could you tell me all he said about me?"

"All? I'll try, but first permit me to make an observation: on the one hand you tell me, matter-of-factly, that you and your brother have never been close and you seem to have made no efforts to contact one another. Yet today you seem eager—I would even say hungry—for news. A bit of a paradox. That makes me wonder if you're on a type of search for yourself and your past?"

Alfred's head jerked back for a moment; he was startled by the perceptiveness of the question. "Yes, that's true. I'm amazed you saw that. These days are . . . well, I don't know how to say it . . . chaotic. I saw roiling crowds in Moscow reveling in anarchy. Now it's sweeping across eastern Europe, across all of Europe. Oceans of displaced people. And I'm unsettled along with them, perhaps more lost than others . . . cut off from everything."

"And so you seek an anchor in the past—you yearn for the unchanging past. I can understand that. Let me dredge my memory for Eugen's comments about you. Give me a minute, let me concentrate, and I'll jostle the images and let them surface."

Friedrich closed his eyes, then shortly opened them. "There's an obstacle—my own memories of you seem to get in the way. First let me convey them, and then I'll be able to retrieve Eugen's comments. All right?"

"Yes, that's fine," mumbled Alfred. But it wasn't entirely fine. On the contrary, this entire conversation was most odd: every word that came out of Friedrich's mouth was strange and unexpected. Even so, he trusted this man who had known him as a child. Friedrich had the aroma of "home."

Closing his eyes again, Friedrich commenced to speak in a faraway voice: "Pillow fight—I tried but you wouldn't play . . . I couldn't get you to play. Serious—so, so serious. Order, order . . . toys, books, toy soldiers, everything very orderly . . . you loved those toy soldiers . . . deadly serious little boy . . . I carried you piggyback sometimes . . . I think you liked it . . . but you always jumped off quickly . . . was fun not all right? . . . house felt cold . . . motherless . . . father removed, depressed . . . you and Eugen never spoke . . . where were your friends? . . . never saw friends at your house . . . you were fearful . . . running to your room, closing your door, always running to your books . . ."

Friedrich stopped, opened his eyes, took a hearty gulp of ale, and turned his eyes to Alfred. "That's all that comes out of my memory bank about you—perhaps other memories will surface later. Is this what you wanted, Alfred? I want to be sure. I want to give the brother of my closest friend what he wants and needs."

Alfred nodded and then quickly turned his head, self-conscious about his amazement: never had he heard such talk before. Though Friedrich's words were German, his language was an alien tongue.

"Then I'll continue and retrieve Eugen's comments about you." Friedrich once again closed his eyes and a minute later spoke again in the same strange, faraway tone, "Eugen, speak to me of Alfred." Friedrich then slipped into yet another voice, a voice perhaps meant to be Eugen's voice.

"Ah . . . my shy fearful brother, a wonderful artist—he got all the family talent—I loved his sketches of Reval—the port and all the ships at anchor, the Teutonic castle with its soaring tower—they were accomplished drawings even for an adult, and he was only ten. My little brother—always reading—poor Alfred—a loner . . . so fearful of other children . . . not popular—the boys mocked him and called him 'the philosopher'—not much love for him—our mother dead, our father dying, our aunts good-hearted but always busy with their own families—I should have done more for him, but he was hard to reach . . . and I was living on mere scraps myself."

Friedrich opened his eyes, blinked once or twice and then, resuming his natural voice, said, "That's what I remember. Oh, yes there was one other thing, Alfred, which I have mixed feelings about saying: Eugen blamed you for your mother's death."

"Blamed me? Me? I was only a couple of weeks old."

"When someone dies, we often look for something, someone, to blame."

"You can't be serious. Are you? I mean Eugen really said that? It makes no sense."

"We often believe things that make no sense. Of course you didn't kill her, but I imagine Eugen harbors the thought that if his mother had never gotten pregnant with you, then she'd be alive now. But, Alfred, I'm guessing. I can't recall his exact words, but I do know he had a resentment toward you that he himself labeled irrational."

Alfred, now ashen, remained silent for several minutes. Friedrich stared at him, sipped some ale, and said gently, "I fear I may have said too much. But when a friend asks, I try to give all I can."

"And that is a good thing. Thoroughness, honesty—good, noble German virtues. I commend you, Friedrich. And so much rings true. I have to admit that I have sometimes wondered why Eugen did not do more for me. And that taunt—'Little philosopher'—how often did I hear that from the other boys! I think it influenced me greatly, and I plotted my revenge on all of them by becoming a philosopher after all."

"At the Polytechnic? How is that possible?"

"Not exactly a certified philosopher—my degree is in engineering and architecture, but my true home was philosophy, and even at the Polytechnic I found some learned professors who guided my private readings. More than anything I have come to worship German clarity of thought. It is my only religion. Yet right now, at this very moment, I'm floundering in a muddled state of mind. In fact, I'm almost dizzy. Perhaps I just need time to assimilate all you've said."

"Alfred, I think I can explain what you feel. I've experienced it myself, and I've seen it in others. You're not responding to the memories I've shared. It's something else. I can best explain it by speaking in a philosophical mode. I, too, have had much philosophy training, and it is a pleasure to speak with one of similar inclination."

"It would be a pleasure for me as well. I have been surrounded by engineers for years and yearn for a philosophical conversation."

"Good, good. Let me start in this way: remember the shock and disbelief toward Kant's revelation that external reality is not as we ordinarily perceive it—that is, we constitute the nature of external reality by virtue of our internal mental constructs? You're well acquainted with Kant, I imagine?"

"Yes, very well acquainted. But his relevance to my current state of mind is? . . ."

"Well, what I mean is that suddenly your world, I refer now to your internal world, constituted so much by your past experiences, *is not as you thought it was*. Or, to put it another way, let me use a term from Husserl, and say your *noema* has exploded."

"Husserl? I avoid Jewish pseudo-philosophers. And what is a *noema*?"

"I advise you, Alfred, not to dismiss Edmund Husserl—he's one of the greats. His term *noema* refers to the thing as we experience it, the thing as structured by us. For example, think of the idea of a building. Then think of leaning against a building and finding that the building is not solid and that your body passes right through it. At that moment your *noema* of a building explodes—your *Lebenswelt* (life-world) suddenly is not as you thought."

"I respect your advice. But please clarify further—I understand the concept of a structure that we impose upon the world, but still I'm puzzled about the relevance for Eugen and me."

"Well, what I'm saying is that your view about the lifelong relationship you had with your brother is, in one big stroke, altered. You thought of him one way, and suddenly the past shifts, just a bit, and you find out now that he sometimes regarded you with resentment—*even though*, of course, the resentment was irrational and unfair."

"So you're saying that I'm dizzy because the solid ground of my past has been shifted?"

"Precisely. Well put, Alfred. Your mind is on overload because it is totally preoccupied with reconstituting the past, and it has not the capacity to do its normal jobs—like taking care of your equilibrium."

Alfred nodded, "Friedrich, this has been an astounding conversation. You're giving me a lot to ponder. But let me point out that some of this dizziness preceded our talk."

Friedrich waited calmly, expectantly. He seemed to know how to wait.

Alfred hesitated, "I don't usually share this much. In fact I hardly talk about myself to anyone, but there is something about you that is very—what shall I say—trusting, inviting."

"Well, in a way I'm family. And, of course, you know that you can't make old friends anew."

"Old friends anew . . ." Alfred thought for a moment, then smiled, "I understand. Very clever. Well, I started the day feeling estranged—I just arrived yesterday from Moscow. I'm alone now. I was married for a brief time—my wife has consumption, and her father placed her in a sanitarium in Switzerland a few weeks ago. But it's more than the consumption: her wealthy family strongly disapproves of me and my poverty, and I'm certain our very short marriage is over. We have spent little time together and even stopped writing much to one another."

Alfred hastily took a swallow of his ale and continued. "When I arrived here yesterday, my aunts and uncles and nieces and nephews seemed glad to see me and their welcome felt good. I felt I belonged. But not for long. By the time I woke this morning I once again felt estranged and homeless and walked around the city looking and looking in search of . . . what? I guess, for home, for friends, even for familiar faces. Yet I saw only strangers. Even in the Realschule, I met no one I knew except for my favorite teacher, the art teacher, and he only pretended to recognize me. And then, less than an hour ago, came the final blow. I decided to go where I truly belonged, to stop living in exile, to reconnect with my race and to return to the Fatherland. Intending to join the German army, I went to the German military headquarters across the street. There, the enlistment sergeant, a Jew named Goldberg, flicked me off like an insect. He waved me away with the words that the German army was for Germans, not for citizens of combatant countries."

Friedrich nodded sympathetically. "Maybe the final blow was a blessing. Maybe you were fortunate to get a reprieve, a pardon from a senseless, muddy death in the trenches."

"You said I was an oddly serious child. I guess I'm still that way. For example, I take my Kant seriously: I consider it a moral imperative to enlist. What would our world be like if everyone deserted the mortally wounded Fatherland? When he calls, his sons must answer."

"It is odd, isn't it," said Friedrich, "how we Baltic Germans are so much more German than the Germans. Perhaps all of us who are displaced Germans have that same powerful longing you describe—for home, a place where we really belong. We Baltic Germans are in the midst of a plague of rootlessness. I feel it especially keenly at this moment because my father died earlier this week. That's why I'm in Reval. Now I, too, don't know where I belong. My maternal grandparents are Swiss, and yet I don't really belong there, either."

"My condolences," Alfred said.

"Thank you. In many ways I've had it easier than you: my father was almost eighty, and I had his full healthy presence my entire life. And my mother is still alive. I've spent my time here helping her move into her sister's home. In fact, I just left her napping and must rejoin her shortly. But before I leave, I want to say that I believe the issue of home is deep and urgent for you. I can stay a bit longer if you'd like to explore that more."

"I don't know *how* to explore it. In fact your ability to talk about deeply personal things with such ease amazes me. I've never heard anyone express his inner thoughts as openly as you."

"Would you like me to help you do that?"

"What do you mean?"

"I mean help you identify and understand your feelings about home." Alfred looked wary but, after a long slow gulp of his Latvian ale, agreed.

"Try this. Do just what I did when I dredged up my memories of you as a child. Here's my suggestion: think of the phrase 'not at home,' and say it to yourself several times: 'not at home,' 'not at home,' 'not at home.'"

Alfred's lips silently mouthed the words for a minute or two, and then he shook his head. "Nothing comes. My mind is on strike."

"The mind never goes on strike; it is always working, but something often blocks our knowledge of it. Usually it's self-consciousness. In this case, I imagine it is self-consciousness about me. Try again. Let me suggest you close your eyes and forget about me, forget about what I will think of you, forget about how I might judge what you say. Remember I am trying to help, and remember that you have my word that this conversation will remain only with me. I'll not share it even with Eugen. Now close your eyes, let your thoughts pop into your mind about 'not at home,' and then give voice to them. Just say what comes to mind—it doesn't have to make sense."

Alfred again closed his eyes, but no words came.

"Can't quite hear you. Louder, a little louder, please."

Softly Alfred began to speak. "Not at home. Nowhere. Not with Aunt Cäcilie, or Aunt Lydia . . . no place for me, not in school, not with other boys, not in my wife's family, not in architecture, not in engineering, not in Estonia, not in Russia . . . Mother Russia, what a joke . . ."

"Good, good—keep going," urged Friedrich.

"Always outside, looking in, always want to show them . . ." Alfred grew silent, opened his eyes. "Nothing else comes . . ."

"You said you want to show them. Show who, Alfred?"

"All those who mocked me. In the neighborhood, at the Realschule, at the Polytechnic, everywhere."

"And how will you show them, Alfred? Stay in your loose frame of mind. You don't have to make sense."

"I don't know. Somehow I will make them notice me."

"If they notice you, will you be at home then?"

"Home doesn't exist. Is that what you're trying to tell me?"

"I have no preordained plan, but I do now have an idea. It's just a guess, but I wonder if you can ever be at home anywhere, because home is not a place—it's a state of mind. Really being at home is feeling at home in your own skin. And, Alfred, I don't think you feel at home in your skin. Perhaps you never have. Perhaps you have been searching for home in the wrong place all your life."

Alfred looked thunderstruck. His jaw sagged; his eyes riveted on Friedrich. "Your words speed right to my heart. How come you know such things, such miraculous things? You said you were a philosopher. Is that where this comes from? I must read this philosophy."

"I'm an amateur. Just like you, I would have loved spending my life in philosophy, but I have to earn a living. I went to medical school in Zurich and learned a lot about helping others talk about difficult things. And now," Friedrich rose from his seat, "I must leave you. My mother is waiting, and I must return to Zurich the day after tomorrow."

"Unfortunate. This has been enlightening, and I feel as though we were just starting. Is there no time for a continuation before you leave Reval?"

"I have only tomorrow. My mother always rests in the afternoon. Perhaps the same time? Shall we meet here?"

Alfred restrained his greediness and his wish to exclaim, "Yes, yes." Instead he bowed his head in just the proper manner: "I look forward to it."

CHAPTER ELEVEN

AMSTERDAM—1656

At the van den Enden academy the following evening, Clara Maria's assiduous Latin drill was interrupted by her father. He bowed formally to his daughter and said, "Forgive me for intruding, Mademoiselle van den Enden, but I must have a word with Mr. Spinoza." Turning toward Bento, he said, "Please come to the large alcove in an hour and join the Greek class, where we shall discuss some texts by Aristotle and Epicurus. Even though your Greek is still rudimentary, these two gentlemen have something important to say to you." To Dirk he said, "I know that you have little interest in Greek since it is, disgracefully, no longer a requirement for medical school, but you may find aspects of this discussion useful in your future work with patients."

Van den Enden bowed again formally to his daughter. "And now, Mademoiselle, I shall leave you to continue putting them through their Latin paces."

Clara Maria continued reading short passages from Cicero, which Bento and Dirk took turns translating into Dutch. Several times she tapped her ruler on the table to alert the distracted Bento, who, rather than attend to Cicero, was caught up entirely with the delightful movement of Clara Maria's lips when she pronounced her *m*'s and *p*'s in *multa, pater, puer,* and, most wonderfully of all, *praestantissimum.*

"Where is your concentration today, Bento de Spinoza?" said Clara Maria, trying hard to contort her most pleasing thirteen-year-old, pear-shaped face into a stern frown.

"Sorry, I was, for a moment, lost in thought, Miss van den Enden."

"No doubt thinking about my father's Greek symposium?"

"No doubt," dissembled Bento, who had been thinking far more about the daughter than the father. He also continued to be haunted by Jacob's angry words a few hours earlier, predicting his destiny as a lonely, isolated man. Jacob was opinionated, closed-minded, and wrong on so many issues, but in this he was right: Bento knew he could have no wife—no family, no community. Reason told him that freedom should be his goal and that his struggle to free himself from the constraints of the superstitious Jewish community would be farcical if he were simply to exchange them for the shackles of a wife and family. Freedom was his only quarry, the freedom to think, to analyze, to transcribe the thunderous thoughts echoing in his mind. But it was hard, oh so hard, to wrench his attention from the lovely lips of Clara Maria.

Van den Enden began his discussion with his Greek class by exclaiming, "*Eudaimonia*. Let's examine the two roots: *eu*?" He cupped his ear with his hand and waited. Students timidly called out "good," "normal," "pleasant." Van den Enden nodded and repeated the exercise with *daimon* and received a more invigorated chorus of "spirit," "imp," "minor deity."

"Yes, yes, and yes. All are correct but in consort with *eu* the meaning veers toward 'good fortune' and, thus, *eudaimonia* usually connotes 'well-being' or 'happiness' or 'flourishing.' Are these three terms synonyms? At first they appear to be, but in fact philosophers beyond count have discoursed on their shades of difference. Is *eudaimonia* a state of mind? A way of life?" Without waiting for an answer, van den Enden added, "Or is it sheer hedonistic pleasure? Or might it be connected to the concept of *arete*, which means?" Cupping his ears, he waited until two students simultaneously called out "virtue."

"Yes, exactly, and many ancient Greek philosophers incorporate virtue into the concept of *eudaimonia*, thus perhaps elevating it from the *subjective* state of feeling happy to a greater consideration of living a moral, virtuous, desirable life. Socrates had strong feelings about that. Recall your last week's reading of Plato's *Apologia*, in which he accosts a fellow Athenian and raises the question of *arete* with these words . . ." At this point van den Enden assumed a theatrical pose and recited Plato in Greek and then, slowly, translated the text into Latin for Dirk and Bento: "Are you not ashamed of your eagerness to possess as much wealth, reputation, and honors as possible, while you do not care for nor give thought to wisdom or truth or the best possible state of your soul?"

"Now, keep in mind that Plato's earlier works reflect the ideas of his teacher, Socrates, whereas in his later work, such as *The Republic*, we see the emergence of Plato's own ideas emphasizing absolute standards for justice and other virtues in the metaphysical realm. What is Plato's idea of our fundamental goal in life? It is to attain the highest form of knowledge, and that, in his view, was the idea of the 'good,' from which all else derives value. Only then, Plato says, are we able to reach *eudemonia*—in his view, a state of *harmony of the soul*. Let me repeat that phrase: 'harmony of the soul.' It's worth remembering; it may serve you well in your life.

"Now let's look at the next great philosopher, Aristotle, who studied with Plato for perhaps twenty years. *Twenty years*. Remember that, those of you who have whimpered about my curriculum being too hard and too long.

"In the parts of *The Nichomachean Ethics* you shall be reading this week, you will see that Aristotle also had some strong views on the good life. He was certain that it did *not* consist of sensual pleasure or fame or wealth. What *did* Aristotle hold to be our purpose in life? He thought it was to fulfill *our innermost unique function*. 'What is it,' he asks, 'that sets us off from other forms of life?' I pose that question to you."

No instant answers from the class. Finally one student said, "We can laugh, and other animals can't," eliciting some chuckles from his classmates.

Another: "We walk on two legs."

"Laugh and legs—is that the best you can do?" exclaimed van den Enden. "Such foolish answers trivialize this discussion. Think! What is the major attribute that sets us off from lower life forms?" Suddenly he turned to Bento: "I pose that question to you, Bento de Spinoza."

Without a moment's reflection, Bento said, "I believe it is our unique ability to reason."

"Precisely. And hence Aristotle claimed that the happiest person is the one who most fulfills that very function."

"So the highest and happiest of endeavors is to be a philosopher?" asked Alphonse, the cleverest student in the Greek class, who felt unnerved by Bento's rapid-fire answer. "Doesn't it seem self-serving for a philosopher to make that claim?"

"Yes, Alphonse, and you're not the first thinker to draw that conclusion. And that very observation provides us with a segue to Epicurus, another important Greek thinker who weighed in with radically different ideas about *eudemonia* and about the mission of the philosopher. When you read some of Epicurus in two weeks, you'll see that he, too, spoke of the good life but used another word entirely. He speaks much of *ataraxia*, which translates . . ." Again van den Enden cupped his ear.

Alphonse instantly called out "tranquility," and soon others added "calm" and "peace of mind."

"Yes, yes, and yes," said van den Enden, obviously growing more pleased with his class's performance. "For Epicurus, *ataraxia* was the only true happiness. And how do we achieve it? Not through Plato's harmony of the soul nor Aristotle's attainment of reason but simply *by the elimination of worry or anxiety*. If Epicurus were speaking to you at this moment, he would urge you to simplify life. Here's how he might put it if he were standing here today."

Van den Enden cleared his throat and spoke in a collegial manner: "Lads, your needs are few, they are easily attained, and any necessary suffering can be easily tolerated. Don't complicate your life with such trivial goals as riches and fame: they are the enemy of *ataraxia*. Fame, for example, consists of the opinions of others and requires that we must live our life as others wish. To achieve and maintain fame, we must like what others like and shun whatever it is that they shun. Hence, a life of fame or a life in politics? Flee from it. And wealth? Avoid it! It is a trap. The more we acquire the more we crave, and the deeper our sadness when our yearning is not satisfied. Lads, listen to me: if you crave happiness, do not waste your life struggling for that which you really do not need."

"Now," continued van den Enden, settling back into his own voice, "note the difference between Epicurus and his predecessors. Epicurus thinks the greatest good is to attain *ataraxia* through freedom from all anxiety. Now, comments and questions? Ah, yes, Mr. Spinoza. A question?"

"Does Epicurus propose only a negative approach? I mean, does he say that removal of distress is all that is needed and that man without extraneous worry is perfect, naturally good, happy? Are there no positive attributes for which we should strive?"

"Excellent question. And the readings I have selected shall illuminate his answer. Fortunately, Mr. Spinoza, you shall not have to wait to perfect your Greek, because you can read the ideas of Epicurus in Latin written by the Roman poet Lucretius, who lived about two hundred years later. I shall select the appropriate pages for you in due time. Today I sought only to touch on the central idea that distinguishes him from others: that the good life consists of the removal of anxiety. But even a light reading will indicate that Epicurus is far more complex. He encourages knowledge, friendship, and virtuous, temperate living. Yes, Dirk, you have a question? It appears as if my Latin students are more inquisitive about the Greeks than my Greek class."

"In Hamburg," Dirk said, "I know a tavern that is called 'The Epicurean Delight.' So good wine and ale are part of his good life?"

"I've been waiting for that question—it was certain to appear. Many mistakenly use his name to indicate good food or wine. Were he to know this, Epicurus would be astonished. I believe that this curious error stems from his strict materialism. He believed that there is no afterlife and that since this life is all there is, we should strive for earthly happiness. But do *not* make the error of concluding that Epicurus suggests we should spend our lives wallowing in sensual or lustful activities. Absolutely not—he lived and advocated an almost ascetic life. I repeat: he believed we could best maximize pleasure by minimizing pain. One of his major conclusions was that the fear of death was a major source of pain, and he spent much of his life seeking philosophical methods to lessen the fear of death. Further questions, please."

"Does he mention service to others and one's community or love?" asked Dirk.

"An apt inquiry from a future physician. You will be interested to know that he considered himself a medical philosopher, ministering to the ailments of the soul just as a physician ministers to the ailments of the body. He once said that a philosophy unable to heal the soul has as little value as medicine unable to heal the body. I've already mentioned some of the soul's ailments arising from a pursuit of fame, power, wealth, and sexual lust, but they were only secondary. The behemoth of anxieties underlying and feeding all the other worries is the fear of death and the afterlife. In fact one of the first principles in the 'catechism' that his students had to learn was that we are mortal, that there is no afterlife, and therefore we have nothing to fear from the gods after death. You'll read more about this in Lucretius very soon, Dirk. Now I've forgotten what the rest of your question was."

"First," said Dirk, "I have to say that I don't know the word 'behemoth.'"

"Good question. Who here knows that word?" Only Bento raised his hand.

"Mr. Spinoza, tell us."

"Monstrous beast," said Bento. "From the Hebrew *b'hëmāh* that appears in Genesis and also in Job."

"Job, eh. I didn't know that myself. Thank you. Now, back to your question, Dirk."

"I asked about love and service to one's community."

"As far as I know, Epicurus did not marry but believed in marriage and the family for some—those who are ready for the responsibility. But he staunchly disapproved of irrationally impassioned love that enslaves the lover and ultimately leads to more pain than pleasure. He says that once lustful infatuation is consummated, the lover experiences boredom or jealousy or both. But he gave great weight to a higher love, the love of friends, that awakens us to a state of blessedness. It is of interest to know that he was inclusive and treated all human souls equally: his was the only school in Athens that welcomed both women and slaves.

"But your question about service, Dirk, is important. His position was that we should live a quiet, secluded life, avoid public responsibilities, holding office, or any other type of responsibility that might threaten our *ataraxia.*"

"I hear nothing about religion," said a Catholic student, Edward, whose uncle had been the bishop of Antwerp. "I hear about the love of friends but nothing about the love of God or of God's purpose in his scheme of happiness."

"You've put your finger on an important point, Edward. Epicurus is shocking to today's readers because his formula for happiness pays so little attention to the Divine. He believed that happiness emanates only from our own mind and places no importance on our relationship with anything supernatural."

"Are you saying," asked Edward, "that he denied the existence of God?"

"You mean *gods*, in the plural? Remember the time period, Edward. This is the fourth century BC, and Greek culture, like every early culture aside from the Hebrews, was polytheistic," said van den Enden.

Edward nodded and rephrased his question: "Did Epicurus deny the Divine?"

"No, he was bold, but not foolhardy. He was born about sixty years after Socrates had been executed for heresy, and he knew that disbelief in the gods would have been bad for one's health. He took a safer position and stated that the gods existed, lived blissfully on Mount Olympus, but were entirely unconcerned with human life."

"But what kind of God is that? How can one imagine that God would not want us to live according to His plan?" asked Edward. "It is unimaginable that a God who sacrificed His own son for us did not intend for us to live in a particular holy manner."

"There are many conceptions of gods invented by many cultures," Bento interjected.

"But I know with the deepest certainty that Christ, our Lord, loves us and has a place for us in his heart and a design for us," said Edward, looking upward.

"The strength of a belief has no relationship to its veracity," shot back Bento. "Every god has his deep and fierce believers."

"Gentlemen, gentlemen," van den Enden intervened, "let us postpone this discussion until we have read and mastered the texts. But let me say to you, Edward, that Epicurus was not flippant about the gods: he incorporated them into his view of *ataraxia* and urged us to keep the gods close to our hearts by emulating them and using them as models for a life of blissful tranquility. What's more, in the service of avoiding disturbance"—at this point van den Enden cast a glance in Bento's direction—"he strongly advised his followers to participate serenely in all community activities, including religious ceremonies."

Edward was not mollified. "But to pray simply to avoid disturbance seems a sham observance."

"Many have voiced that opinion, Edward, and yet Epicurus also writes that we should honor the gods as perfect beings. Moreover we obtain aesthetic pleasure from contemplating their perfect existence. The time is late, gentlemen. These are all excellent questions, and we'll consider every one of them as we read his work."

The day ended with Bento and his teachers switching roles. He gave a half-hour Hebrew lesson to father and daughter, after which van den Enden asked him to stay a bit longer for a private discussion.

"You remember our talk the first time we met?"

"I remember very well, and you are indeed introducing me to like-minded companions."

"No doubt you've noted that some of Epicurus's comments are most apt to your current predicament in your community."

"I wondered if you had aimed some of his comments about participating serenely in the community's religious ceremonies in my direction."

"Exactly so. And did they reach their target?"

"Almost, but they were so weighted down with self-contradiction that they fell short."

"How so?"

"For me I cannot imagine tranquility sprouting from the soil of hypocrisy."

"You refer, I assume, to Epicurus's advice to do anything necessary to fit in with a community, including participating in public prayer."

"Yes, I call that hypocrisy. Even Edward responded to that. How can inner harmony be present if one is untrue to oneself?"

"I particularly wanted to speak to you about Edward. What do you think about how he feels about our discussion and about you?"

Surprised at this question, Bento paused. "I don't know the answer to that."

"I ask for a guess."

"Well, he's not happy with me. He's angry, I suppose. Perhaps threatened."

"Yes, good guess. Highly predictable, I would say. Now answer this question. Is that what you want?"

Bento shook his head.

"And would Epicurus think that you've acted in a way conducive to the good life?"

"I must agree that he would not. At the moment, however, I believed that I was acting wisely in refraining from other utterances."

"Such as?"

"That God did not make us in His image—we made Him in our image. We imagine He is a being like us, hears our murmured prayers and cares about what we wish—"

"Good Lord! If this is what you almost said, then I see your point. Let us say, then, you acted unwisely but not entirely foolishly. Edward is a devout Catholic. His uncle was a Catholic bishop. To expect him to lay down his beliefs on the basis of a few comments, even rational comments, is highly irrational and perhaps dangerous. Amsterdam has a reputation for being the most tolerant city in Europe at the moment. But remember the meaning of the word 'tolerant'—it connotes that we all be tolerant of others' beliefs, even though we deem them irrational."

"More and more," said Bento, "I believe that if one lives among men with greatly different beliefs, then one cannot accommodate them without greatly changing oneself."

"Now I begin to understand my spy's report of unrest about you in the Jewish community. Do you express all your ideas to other Jews?"

"About a year ago in my meditations I resolved to be truthful at all times—"

"Ah," van den Enden interjected, "now I see why business is so bad. A truth-telling businessman is an oxymoron."

Bento shook his head. "Oxymoron?"

"From the Greek: *oxys* means sharp; *moros* means foolish. Hence oxymoron alludes to an internal paradox. Imagine what a truth-telling merchant might say to his customer: 'Please buy these raisins—it would be a great favor to me. They are years old, wizened, and I must be rid of them before the shipment of succulent raisins arrives next week.'"

Perceiving no trace of a grin from Bento, van den Enden was reminded of something he had already discerned—Bento de Spinoza had no sense of humor. He retraced his steps. "But I do not mean to make light of the serious things you tell me."

"You asked about my discretion in my community. I have maintained silence about my views aside from my brother and those two strangers from Portugal who sought my advice. In fact, I saw them a few hours ago, and in an effort to be helpful to the one professing to be in a spiritual crisis, I did not hold back from expressing my opinions about superstitious beliefs. I have been engaged in a critical reading of the Hebrew Bible with those two visitors. Ever since I unburdened myself to them I've experienced what you called 'internal harmony.'"

"You sound as though you have long stifled yourself."

"Not fully enough for my family or for my rabbi, who is entirely displeased with me. I long for a community that is not in thrall to false beliefs."

"You will search the world over and not find a nonsuperstitious community. As long as there is ignorance, there will be adherence to superstition. Dispelling ignorance is the only solution. That is why I teach."

"I worry that it is a losing battle," replied Bento. "Ignorance and super-stitious beliefs spread like wildfire, and I believe that religious leaders feed that fire to secure their positions."

"Dangerous words, those. Words beyond your years. Again I say to you that discretion is required to remain a part of *any* community."

"I'm persuaded I must be free. If such a community is not to be found, then perhaps I must live without a community."

"Remember, what I said about *caute*. If you are not cautious, it is possible that your wishes, and perhaps your fears, will come to pass."

"It is now beyond the pale of 'possible.' I believe I have already started the process," replied Bento.

CHAPTER TWELVE

ESTONIA—1918

On the day after their first meeting, Alfred got to the beer hall early and sat staring at the entrance until he spotted Friedrich. He jumped to his feet to greet him. "Friedrich, good to see you. Thank you for making the time for me."

After collecting their beer at the counter, they sat again at the same quiet corner table. Alfred had resolved not to be the focus of the entire conversation once again and began, "How are you and your mother doing?"

"My mother's still in shock, still trying to grasp that my father is gone from existence. At times she seems to forget he's gone. Twice she thought she saw him in a crowd of people outside. And the denial in her dreams, Alfred—it's extraordinary! When she woke this morning, she said it was terrible to open her eyes: she was so happy walking and talking to my father in her dream that she hated waking to rejoin a reality in which he was still dead."

"As for me," Friedrich continued, "I'm struggling on two fronts, just like the German army. Not only do I have to grapple with the fact of his death, but in this short time I'm here, I have to help my mother. And that is tricky."

"What do you mean by 'tricky'?" asked Alfred."

"To help someone, I believe you have to enter into that person's world. But whenever I try to do that with my mother, my mind flits away, and in a moment or two I'm suddenly thinking of something entirely different. Just a little while ago my mother was weeping, and as I put my arm around her to console her, I noted how my thoughts were wandering to meeting with you today. For a moment I felt guilty. Then I reminded myself that

I'm only human and that humans have an inbuilt tendency toward protective distraction. I've been pondering why I cannot stay focused on my father's death. I believe the reason is that it confronts me with my own death and that prospect is simply too fearsome to behold. I can think of no other explanation. What do you think?" Friedrich stopped and turned to look squarely into Alfred's eyes.

"I don't know about these things, but your conclusion seems plausible. I, too, never allow myself to think deeply about death. I always hated it when my father insisted on taking me to my mother's grave."

Friedrich remained silent until he was certain Alfred intended to say no more and said, "So, Alfred, that's a very long answer to your polite inquiry about how I am doing, but as you see, I love observing and discussing all these machinations of my mind. Did I give a more involved answer than you expected or wished?"

"It was a longer answer to my inquiry than I expected, but it was real, it was deep, and it was heartfelt. I admire how you avoid superficiality—how willing you are to share your thoughts so honestly and unself-consciously."

"And you, Alfred, you too went deep within yourself at the end of yesterday's conversation. Any after-effects?"

"I confess I've been unsettled: I'm still trying to understand our talk."

"What part wasn't clear?"

"I'm not referring to clarity of ideas but to the strange feeling I had when talking with you. I mean we only spoke a brief time—what, perhaps three-quarters of an hour? And yet I revealed so much and felt so involved, so strangely . . . close. As though I've known you intimately all my life."

"That an uncomfortable feeling?"

"It's mixed. It was good because it takes the edge off my isolation, my sense of homelessness. But it was uncomfortable because of the extreme oddness of the conversation yesterday—as I keep saying to you, I've never had an intimate talk like that nor trusted a stranger so quickly."

"But I'm not a stranger because of Eugen. Or let's say I'm a familiar stranger who has had access to the inner chambers of your childhood home."

"You've been in my mind a great deal since yesterday, Friedrich. One matter has arisen, and I wonder if you would permit a personal question . . ."

"Of course, of course. No need to ask—I *like* personal questions."

"When I asked you how you acquired such skills in speaking and exploring the mind, you answered that it was your medical training. Yet I've been thinking of all the doctors I've known, and none, not a single one, has shown even a trace of your engaging manner. With them it's all business— a few cursory questions, never a personal inquiry, then a quick scribbling of some mysterious Latin prescription followed by 'Next patient, please.' Why are you so different, Friedrich?"

"I haven't been totally candid, Alfred," replied Friedrich, looking into Alfred's eyes with his usual straightforwardness. "It *is* true I am a physician, but I've withheld something from you—I've also completed training in psychiatry, and it was that experience that has shaped the way that I think and speak."

"That fact seems so . . . so innocuous. Why such pains to conceal it?"

"Nowadays more and more people become nervous, back away, and look for the exit when they learn I am a psychiatrist. They have silly notions that psychiatrists can read minds and know all their dark secrets."

Alfred nodded. "Well, perhaps not so silly. Yesterday it was as if you could read my mind."

"No, no, no. But I am learning to read my own mind, and by virtue of that experience I can serve as a guide for you to read your own mind. That's the major new direction of my field."

"I have to confess that you're the first psychiatrist I've ever met. I know nothing about your field."

"Well, for centuries, psychiatrists have primarily been diagnosticians and custodians for hospitalized psychotic, almost always incurable patients, but all that has changed in the last decade. The change began with Sigmund Freud in Vienna, who invented a talking treatment called psychoanalysis, which permits us to help patients overcome psychological problems. Today we can treat such ailments as extreme anxiety or intractable grief or something we call hysteria—an ailment in which a patient has psychologically caused physical symptoms like paralysis or even blindness. My teachers in Zurich, Carl Jung and Eugen Bleuler, have been pioneers in this field. I'm intrigued by this approach and will soon be starting advanced training in psychoanalysis in Berlin with Karl Abraham, a highly regarded teacher."

"I've heard some things about psychoanalysis. I've heard it referred to as another Jewish intrigue. Are your teachers all Jews?"

"Certainly not Jung or Bleuler."

"But, Friedrich, why involve yourself in a Jewish field?"

"It *will* be a Jewish field unless we Germans step in. Or put it another way: It's too good to be left to the Jews."

"But why contaminate yourself? Why become the student of Jews?"

"It's a field of science. Look, Alfred, consider the example of another scientist, the German Jew Albert Einstein. All of Europe is buzzing about him—his work will forever change the face of physics. You can't speak of modern physics as Jewish physics. Science is science. In medical school one of my instructors in anatomy was a Swiss Jew—he didn't teach me Jewish anatomy. And if the great William Harvey were Jewish, you'd still believe in the circulation of the blood, right? If Kepler were Jewish, you'd still believe in the earth revolving about the sun? Science is science regardless of the discoverer."

"It's different with the Jews," Alfred interjected. "They corrupt, they monopolize, they suck every field dry. Take politics. I saw firsthand the Jewish Bolsheviks undermine the entire Russian government. I saw the face of anarchy on the streets of Moscow. Take banking. You've seen the role of the Rothschilds in this war: they pull the strings, and all of Europe dances. Take the theater. Once they take over, they allow only Jews to work."

"Alfred, we all love to hate the Jews, but you do it with such . . . such intensity. It's come up so often in our brief conversations. Let's see . . . There was the attempted enlistment with the Jewish sergeant, and Husserl, Freud, the Bolsheviks. What do you say to our making a philosophical inquiry into this intensity?"

"What do you mean?"

"One of the things I love about psychiatry is that, unlike any other field of medicine, it veers close to philosophy. Like philosophers, we psychiatrists rely on logical investigation. We not only help patients identify and express feelings, but we also ask 'why'? What is their source? Why do certain complexes arise in the mind? Sometimes I think our field really began with Spinoza, who believed that everything, even emotion and thought, has a cause that can be discovered with proper investigation."

Noting the baffled expression on Alfred's face, Friedrich continued. "You seem puzzled. Let me try to clarify. Consider our very brief excursion into something that haunts you—the sense of not being at home. Yesterday, in only a few minutes of informal meandering, we came upon several sources of your feeling of being unrooted. Think of them—there was the absence of your mother and your ill and distant father. Then you talked of having chosen the wrong academic field, and now your lack of self-esteem, which results in your not being at home in your skin—right? You follow me?"

Alfred nodded.

"Now, just imagine how much richer our excavation would be if we had many, many hours over several weeks to explore these sources more fully. Do you see?"

"Yes, I understand."

"That is what my field is all about. And what I was suggesting earlier is that even your particularly powerful Jew-hatred must have psychological or philosophical roots."

Drawing back slightly, Alfred said, "There we differ. I prefer to say that I am fortunate to be enlightened enough to understand the dangers that the Jew poses for our race and the damage they have done to great civilizations in the past."

"Please understand, Alfred, you have no quarrels with me about your conclusions. We both have these feelings about the Jews. My point is only that you feel them so very keenly and with such extraordinary passion. And the love of philosophy that you and I share dictates that we can examine the logical base of all thoughts and beliefs. Not true?"

"Here I cannot go with you, Friedrich. I cannot follow you. It seems almost obscene to subject such obvious conclusions to philosophic inquiry. It's like analyzing why you feel the sky is blue or why you love beer or sugar."

"Ah yes, Alfred, perhaps you're right." He recalled Bleuler admonishing him on more than one occasion: "Young man, psychoanalysis is not a battering ram: we do not just hammer away until exhausted egos raise tattered white flags of surrender. Patience, patience. Win the patient's confidence. Analyze and understand resistance—sooner or later resistance will melt away and the road to the truth will open up." Friedrich knew he should drop the topic. But his internal impetuous demon who had to know could not be stilled.

"Let me make one last point, Alfred. Let's consider the example of your brother, Eugen. You'd agree he is deeply intelligent, brought up in the exact culture as you, same heredity, environment, same relatives surrounding him, and yet he does not invest the Jewish problem with much passion. He is not German-intoxicated and prefers to think of Belgium as his real home. Fascinating puzzle. Brothers with the same environment yet such different points of view."

"We had similar but not identical environments. For one thing, Eugen did not have my bad luck of encountering a Jew-loving headmaster in the Realschule."

"What? Headmaster Peterson? Impossible. I knew him well when I attended that school."

"No, not Peterson. He was on sabbatical my senior year, and his place was taken by Herr Epstein."

"Wait a minute, Alfred—I'm just beginning to recall Eugen telling me a story about you and Herr Epstein and some serious trouble you got into just before your graduation. What happened exactly?"

Alfred told Friedrich the entire story—about his anti-Semitic speech, about Epstein's fury, about his immersion in Chamberlain, about the forced assignment of reading Goethe's comments about Spinoza, and about his promise to read Spinoza.

"Quite a story, Alfred. I'd like to see those chapters in Goethe's autobiography. Promise that you'll point them out to me some day. And tell me this: Did you keep your promise to read Spinoza?"

"I tried again and again but could not get into it. It was such abstruse fluff. And the incomprehensible definitions and axioms in the beginning were an insurmountable roadblock."

"Ah, you started with the *Ethics*. A big mistake. It's a difficult work to read without a guide. You should have begun with his simpler *The Theological and Political Treatise*. Spinoza is a paragon of logic. I put him up there in my pantheon of Socrates, Aristotle, and Kant. Someday we must meet again in the Fatherland, and if you wish, I shall help you read the *Ethics*."

"As you can imagine, I have highly charged feelings about reading the work of this Jew. Yet the great Goethe revered him, and I did give my oath to the headmaster to read him. So you could help me understand Spinoza? Your offer is kind. Even enticing. I shall try to make our paths cross in Germany, and I look forward to learning about Spinoza from you."

"Alfred, I must return to my mother, and as you know, I leave tomorrow for Switzerland. But I wish to say one last thing before we part. I feel in a bit of a dilemma. On the one hand I care about you and wish only for your welfare, but on the other hand I am burdened with some information that may pain you but will, I think, ultimately lead you to some truths about yourself."

"How can I, as a philosopher, refuse to pursue the truth?"

"I expected no less a noble answer from you, Alfred. What I must tell you is that your brother over the years and even last month has spent hours with me discussing the fact that his mother's grandmother—your great-grandmother—was Jewish. He said he once visited her in Russia and that, even though she had converted to Christianity in childhood, she acknowledged her Jewish forebears."

Alfred silently glared into the distance.

"Alfred?"

"I deny this. This is a scurrilous rumor that has long hovered about, and I resent your propagating it. I deny it. My father denies it. My aunts, my mother's sisters, deny it. My brother is a confused fool!" Alfred's face was suffused with anger. Refusing to meet Friedrich's gaze, he added, "I cannot imagine why Eugen embraces this lie, why he tells others, and why you tell me."

"Please, Alfred." Friedrich lowered his voice to nearly a whisper. "First, let me assure you I do not propagate it. You are the only person I have mentioned this to, and it shall remain that way. You have my oath, my German oath. As for why I told you—let's reason it out. I did say to you I had a dilemma: telling you seemed painful, and yet *not* telling you seemed worse. How can I pretend to be your friend and not tell you? Your brother told me this, and it seemed relevant to our discussion. Good friends, not to mention fellow philosophers, can and should speak of everything. Your resentment to me is great?"

"I am stunned that you say this to me."

Friedrich thought of his supervision with Bleuler, who had admonished him many times: "You do not have to say everything you think, Doctor Pfister. Therapy is not a place for you to feel better by discharging troublesome thoughts. Learn to hold them. Learn to be a vehicle for unruly thoughts. Timing is everything." He turned to Alfred. "Then, perhaps I erred and should have kept it to myself. I must learn that there are some things that must be left unsaid. Forgive me, Alfred. I told you out of friendship, out of my belief that your unbridled passion may ultimately be self-destructive. Look how close you came to being thrown out of the Realschule. Your future education, your degree, your bright future ahead of you would have all been sacrificed. I wanted to help make sure such events did not happen in the future."

Alfred looked far from persuaded. "Let me ponder upon it. And now I know you must be on your way."

Taking a folded sheet of paper out of his shirt pocket and handing it to Alfred, Friedrich said, "Should you wish to see me again for any reason— a continuation of any part of our discussion, guidance for reading Spinoza, anything—here is my current address in Zurich and my contact information in Berlin, where I shall be after three months. Alfred, I do hope we meet again. *Auf wiedersehen.*"

Alfred sat glumly for fifteen minutes. He emptied his stein and stood to leave. He unfolded the sheet of paper Friedrich had left, stared at Friedrich's addresses, then ripped it into quarters and threw it on the floor, and headed out of the beer hall. Just as he reached the exit, however, Alfred stopped, reconsidered, walked back to his table, and bent down to retrieve the pieces of the torn page.

CHAPTER THIRTEEN

AMSTERDAM—1656

About 10 o'clock the following morning the Spinoza brothers were hard at work in their shop, Bento sweeping and Gabriel opening a newly arrived crate of dried figs. They were interrupted when Franco and Jacob appeared at the door and stood there hesitating until Franco said, "If your offer is still open, we would like to continue our discussion. Please, we are available any time that is convenient for you."

"I am glad to resume," Bento said, but turning to Jacob, he asked, "You wish this also, Jacob?"

"I wish only what is best for Franco."

Bento considered that response for a moment and replied, "Wait one minute, please," and then, after a whispered conference with his brother in the back of the shop, Bento announced, "I can be at your service now. Shall we walk to my house and continue our study of the scriptures?"

The massive Bible was on the table and the chairs in place as if Bento had been expecting them. "Where shall we begin? We touched on many questions last time."

"You were going to tell us about Moses not writing the Torah," said Jacob, speaking in a softer, more conciliatory manner than the day before.

"I've studied the matter for many years and believe that a careful and open-minded reading of the books of Moses provides much internal evidence that Moses could not possibly have been the author."

"Internal evidence? Explain to me," said Franco.

"There are inconsistencies in the story of Moses; some parts of the Torah contradict other parts, and many passages don't hold up to simple logic. I'll give examples and start with an obvious one that others before me have noted.

"The Torah not only describes the manner of Moses' death and burial, and the thirty days' mourning of the Hebrews, but further compares him with all the prophets who came after him and states that he surpassed them all. A man obviously cannot write about what happens to him after his death, nor can he compare himself with other prophets yet to be born. So it's certain that part of the Torah cannot have been written by him. Not true?"

Franco nodded. Jacob shrugged.

"Or look here." Bento opened the Bible to a page marked by a thread and pointed to a passage in Genesis 22. "You see here that Mount Moriah is called the mount of God. And historians inform us it acquired that name *after* the building of the Temple, a great many centuries *after* the death of Moses. Look at this passage, Jacob: Moses clearly says that God will at some future time choose a spot to which this name will be given. So earlier it says one thing and later an opposing thing. You see the internal contradiction, Franco?"

Both Franco and Jacob nodded.

"May I present another example?" Bento asked, still troubled by Jacob's outbursts of temper at their last meeting. Confrontations were always uncomfortable for him, but at the same time he was thrilled to finally share his thoughts with an audience. He steadied himself; he knew what to do—a temperate delivery and a presentation of undeniable evidence. "The Hebrews in the time of Moses indisputably knew what territories belonged to the tribe of Judah but absolutely did not know them under the name of Argob or the Land of the Giants, as cited in the Bible. In other words, the Torah uses names that did not come into existence until many centuries after Moses."

Seeing nods from both, Bento continued. "Similarly, in Genesis. Let's consider this passage." Bento turned to another page marked with a red thread and read the Hebrew passage for Jacob: "and the Canaanite was *then* in the land." Now that passage could not have been written by Moses because the Canaanite were driven out *after* the death of Moses. It has to have been written by someone else looking back upon that time, someone who knew that the Canaanite had been driven out."

After nods from his audience, Bento went on, "Here's another obvious problem. Moses is supposed to be the author, and yet the text not only speaks of Moses in the third person but also bears witness to many details concerning him; for instance, 'Moses talked with God'; 'Moses was the meekest of men'; and that passage I cited yesterday, 'The Lord spoke with Moses face to face.'"

"This is what I mean by internal inconsistencies. The Torah is so crammed with them that it is clearer than the sun at noontime that the books of Moses could *not* have been written by Moses, and it is irrational to continue claiming Moses himself was the author. Do you follow my argument?"

Again Franco and Jacob nodded.

"The same can be said for the book of Judges. No one can possibly believe that each judge wrote the book bearing his name. The way the several books are connected one with the other suggests that they all have the same author."

"If so, then who wrote it, and when?" asked Jacob.

"The dating is helped by such statements as this"—he turned to a page in Kings for Jacob to read—"'In those days there was no king.' You see the wording, Jacob? That means this passage had to be written after a kingship was established. My best guess is that a major writer-compiler of the book of Kings was Ezra."

"Who is he?" asked Jacob.

"A priestly scribe who lived in the fifth century BC. He was the one who led five thousand Hebrew exiles from Babylon back to their home city of Jerusalem."

"And when was the entire Bible compiled?" asked Franco.

"I think we can be certain that before the time of the Maccabees—that is, around 200 BC—there was no official collection of sacred books called the Bible. It seems to have been compiled from a multitude of documents by the Pharisees at the time of the restoration of the Temple. So please keep in mind that what is holy and what is *not* holy is merely the collected opinion of some very human rabbis and scribes, some of whom were serious-minded, blessed men while others may have been struggling for their own personal status, battling upstarts in their own congregation, getting hunger pangs, thinking about dinner, and worrying about their wives and children. *The Bible was put together by human hands.* There is no other possible explanation for the many inconsistencies. No rational person could imagine that a divine omniscient author deliberately wrote with the object of contradicting himself freely."

Jacob, looking confounded, attempted a parry. "Not necessarily. Are there not learned Kabbalists who suggest that the Torah contains deliberate errors that contain many hidden secrets and that God has preserved from corruption every word, indeed every letter, of the Bible?"

Bento nodded. "I have studied the Kabbalists and believe they wish to establish that they alone possess the secrets of God. I find in their writings nothing that has the air of a divine secret, but instead only childish lucubrations. I wish us to examine the words of the Torah itself, not the interpretation of triflers."

After a brief silence he asked, "Have I now made clear to you my thoughts about the authorship of the scriptures?"

"That you have," said Jacob. "Perhaps we should move on to other topics. For example, please address Franco's questions about miracles. He asked why the Bible is replete with them and yet there are none to be seen since then. Tell us your thoughts about miracles."

"Miracles exist only through man's ignorance. In ancient times any occurrence that could not be explained through natural causes was considered a miracle, and the greater the ignorance of the masses about the workings of Nature, the greater the number of miracles."

"But there are great miracles that were seen by multitudes: the Red Sea parting for Moses, the sun staying still for Joshua."

"'Seen by multitudes' is solely a manner of speaking, a way of trying to claim the veracity of unbelievable events. In the case of miracles I am of the opinion that the larger the multitude that claimed to have seen it, the less believable is the event."

"Then how can you explain these unusual events that happen at precisely the right moment, when the Jewish people were in peril?"

"I'll start by reminding you of the millions of precisely right moments when miracles do *not* occur, when the most pious and righteous of individuals are greatly imperiled, cry out for help, and are answered only with silence. Franco, you spoke of that at our very first meeting, when you asked where were the miracles when your father was burned to death. Right?"

"Yes," Franco agreed softly, glancing at Jacob. "I said that, and I say it again—where were the miracles when the Portuguese Jews were in peril? Why was God silent?"

"Such questions *should* be asked," encouraged Bento. "Let me offer a few further thoughts about miracles. We must keep in mind that there are always attendant natural circumstances that are omitted in miracle reporting. For example, Exodus tells us, 'Moses stretched forth his hand and the seas returned to their strength . . .' but *later* in the song of Moses, we read additional material: 'Thou didst blow with thy wind and the sea covered them.' In other words, some descriptions omit the natural causes, the winds. Thus, we see that the scriptures narrate them in the order that has the most power to move men, particularly uneducated men, to devotion."

"And the sun stood still for Joshua's great victory? That too was fiction?" asked Jacob, straining to remain calm.

"That miracle is most wobbly. First, remember that the ancients all believed the sun moved and the Earth stood still. We know now that it is the Earth that revolves around the sun. That error itself is evidence of the human hands behind the Bible's construction. What's more, the particular form of the miracle was shaped by political motivations. Was not the sun god worshipped by the enemies of Joshua? Hence, the miracle is a message trumpeting that the Hebrews' God was more powerful than the Gentiles' God."

"That is wonderfully explained," said Franco.

"Don't believe everything you hear from him, Franco," said Jacob. "So, Bento," he asked, "is that the whole explanation of the miracle in Joshua?"

"That's only part. The rest of the explanation lies in the idioms of the day. Many so-called miracles are only manners of expression. It's the way people talked and wrote in those times. What the writer of Joshua probably meant when he said the sun stood still was simply that the day of the battle seemed long. When the Bible states that God hardened Pharaoh's heart, it only means that Pharaoh was obstinate. When it says that God clave the rocks for the Hebrews and water gushed forth, it merely meant that the Hebrews found springs and quenched their thirst. In the scriptures almost anything unusual was attributed to an act of God. Even trees of unusual size are called trees of God."

"And," Jacob asked, "what about the miracle of the Jews surviving whereas the other nations have not?"

"I see nothing miraculous in it, nothing that cannot be explained by natural causes. The Jews have survived since the Diaspora because they have always refused to blend in with other cultures. They have remained separate by virtue of their complex rites, their dietary rules, and the sign of circumcision, which they scrupulously observe. Thus they survive, but at a cost: their stubborn adherence to separateness has drawn down upon them universal hatred."

Bento paused and, seeing the shocked faces of both Franco and Jacob, said, "Perhaps I give you indigestion by serving up too many difficult things for you to swallow today?"

"Do not worry about me, Bento de Spinoza," said Jacob. "Surely you know that listening is not the same as swallowing,"

"I may be mistaken, but I believe you nodded at least thrice to my words. Am I correct?"

"Most of what I hear is arrogance. You believe you know more than countless generations of rabbis, more than Rashi, Gersonides, more than Maimonides."

"Yet you nodded."

"When you show *evidence*, when you show two statements in Genesis that contradict one another, *that* I cannot deny. Yet, even so, I am certain there are explanations for that beyond your knowledge. I am certain it is *you*, not the Torah, that is mistaken."

"Is there no contradiction in your words? On the one hand you respect evidence and at the same time remain certain of something for which there is no evidence." Bento turned to Franco. "And you? You have been unusually silent. Indigestion?"

"No, no indigestion, Baruch—do you mind my calling you by your Hebrew rather than your Portuguese name? I prefer it. I don't know why. Perhaps it is because you are unlike any Portuguese man I ever saw. No indigestion—you give me the reverse. What would that be? Soothing, I think. Stomach soothing. Soul soothing too."

"I remember how frightened you were during our first talk. You risked so much by sharing your reaction to rituals in both the synagogue and the cathedral. You referred to them both as madness. You remember?"

"How could I forget? But to know that I am not alone, to know that others—especially you—share them. That is a gift that saves my sanity."

"Franco, your answer gives me the fortitude to go further and teach you more about ritual. I have reached the conclusion that rituals of our community have nothing to do with divine law, nothing to do with blessedness and virtue and love, and everything to do with civic tranquility and perpetuation of rabbinical authority—"

"Once again," Jacob interrupted, his voice rising, "you go too far. Is there no limit to your arrogance? A schoolchild knows that the scriptures teach that observation of ritual is the law of God."

"We disagree. Again, Jacob, I do not ask you to believe me. I appeal to your reason and simply ask you to look at the words of the Holy Book with your own eyes. There are many places in the Torah that tell us to follow your heart and not take ritual too seriously. Let us look at Isaiah, who teaches most plainly that the divine law signifies a true manner of life, not a life of ceremonial observances. Isaiah plainly tells us to forego sacrifices and feasts and sums up the whole of divine law in these simple words"—Bento opened the Bible to a bookmark in Isaiah and read—"Cease to do evil, learn to do well; seek judgment, relieve the oppressed."

"So you're saying that rabbinical law is not the Torah's law?" asked Franco.

"What I'm saying is that the Torah contains two kinds of law: there is moral law, and there are laws designed to keep Israel together as a theocracy separate from its neighbors. Unfortunately the Pharisees, in their ignorance, failed to understand the difference and thought that the observance of the state laws was the sum total of morality, whereas such laws were merely intended for the welfare of the community. They were not meant to instruct the Jews but instead to keep them under control. There is a fundamental difference in the purpose of each of the two kinds of laws: observation of ceremonial law leads only to civic tranquility, whereas observation of divine or moral law leads to blessedness."

"So," said Jacob, "do I hear correctly? Do you counsel Franco not to heed ceremonial law? Not to attend the synagogue, not to pray, not to observe Jewish dietary laws?"

"You misunderstand me," said Bento, drawing on his recently acquired knowledge of the views of Epicurus. "I do not negate the importance of civic tranquility, but I do differentiate it from true blessedness." Bento turned to Franco. "If you love your community, wish to be a part of it, wish to raise your family here, wish to live among your own, then you must participate agreeably in community activities, including religious observances."

Turning back to Jacob, he asked, "Can I be more clear?"

"I hear that you say we should follow ritual law only for the sake of appearances, and that it really doesn't count for much because the only thing that matters is this other divine law that you still have not defined," said Jacob.

"By divine law, I mean the highest good, the true knowledge of God and love."

"That's a vague answer. What is 'true knowledge'?"

"True knowledge means the perfection of our intellect that permits us to know God more fully. Jewish communities have penalties for failing to follow ritual law: public criticism by the congregation and the rabbi or, in extreme instances, banishment or *cherem*. Is there a penalty for failing to follow divine law? Yes, but it is not some particular punishment; it is the absence of the good. I love the words of Solomon, who says, 'When wisdom enters into your heart and knowledge is pleasant to thy soul, then shalt thou understand righteousness, and judgment, and equity, yea, every good path.'"

Jacob shook his head. "These high-sounding phrases do not conceal the fact that you are challenging basic Jewish law. Maimonides himself teaches that those who follow the commandments of the Torah are rewarded by God with bliss and happiness in the world to come. With my own ears, I have heard Rabbi Mortera himself emphatically declare anyone who denies the divinity of the Torah will be cut off from immortal life with God."

"And I say his phrases—'the world to come' and 'immortal life with God'—are human words, not divine words. Moreover, these words are not to be found in the Torah; they are the phrases of rabbis writing commentaries on commentaries."

"So," insisted Jacob, "do I hear you deny the existence of the world to come?"

"The world to come, immortal life, blissful afterlife—I repeat, all such phrases are the inventions of rabbis."

"You deny," Jacob persisted, "that the righteous will find everlasting joy and communion with God and that the evil will be vilified and doomed to eternal punishment?"

"It is against reason to think that we, as we are today, will persist after death. The body and the mind are two aspects of the same person. The mind cannot persist after the body dies."

"But," Jacob spoke loudly, now visibly agitated, "we know the body will be resurrected. All of our rabbis teach us that. Maimonides stated this clearly. It is one of the thirteen articles of Jewish faith. It is the ground of our faith."

"Jacob, I must be a poor guide. I thought I had fully explained the impossibility of such things, yet now you're once more wandering into the land of miracles. Again, I remind you these are *all* human opinions; they have *nothing* to do with the laws of Nature, and *nothing* can occur contrary to the fixed laws of Nature. Nature, which is infinite and eternal and encompasses all substance in the universe, acts according to orderly laws that cannot be superseded by supernatural means. A decayed body, returned to dust, cannot be reassembled. Genesis tells us this most clearly: 'You will eat your bread until you return to the earth, from which you were taken, because earth you are and to earth you shall return.'"

"Does that mean I will never be reunited with my martyred father?" asked Franco.

"I, like you, yearn to see my blessed father again. But the laws of Nature are what they are. Franco, I share your longing, and when I was a child, I too believed that all time would come to an end and someday after death we should be reunited—I with my father and my mother, even though I was so young when she died that I can hardly remember her. And of course they would be reunited with their parents and they with theirs, ad infinitum."

"But now," Bento continued in a soft, teacherly voice, "I have given up these childish hopes and have replaced them by the certain knowledge that I hold my father inside me—his face, his love, his wisdom—and in this manner I am already united with him. Blessed reunion must occur in this life because this life is all we have. There is no eternal blessedness in the world to come because there is no world to come. Our task, and I believe the Torah teaches us this, is to attain blessedness in this life *now* by living a life of love and of learning to know God. True piety consists in justice, charity, and love of one's neighbor."

Jacob stood and gruffly pushed his chair aside. "Enough! I've heard enough heresy for one day. Enough for one lifetime. We're leaving. Let's go, Franco."

As Jacob grabbed Franco's hand, Bento said, "No, not yet. Jacob, there's one remaining important question that, to my surprise, you have neglected to ask."

Jacob let go of Franco's arm and looked warily at Bento. "What question?"

"I have told you that Nature is eternal, infinite, and encompasses all substance."

"Yes?" Jacob's face was furrowed and quizzical. "What question?"

"And have I not told you that God is eternal, infinite, and encompasses all substance?"

Jacob nodded, entirely bewildered.

"You say you have been listening, you say you have heard enough, but yet you have not asked me the most fundamental question."

"What fundamental question?"

"If God and Nature have the identical properties, then what is the difference between God and Nature?"

"All right," said Jacob. "I ask you: what is the difference between God and Nature?"

"And I give you the answer you already know: there is no difference. God is Nature. Nature is God."

Both Jacob and Franco stared at Bento, and without another word Jacob yanked Franco to his feet and dragged him into the street.

When out of sight, Jacob put his arm around Franco and squeezed him. "Good, good, Franco, we got just exactly what we needed out of him. And you regarded him a wise man? What a fool he is!"

Franco yanked himself away from Jacob's embrace. "Things are not always what they seem to be. You may be the fool to think him a fool."

CHAPTER FOURTEEN

MUNICH—1918-1919

Character is destiny. The new wave of psychoanalytic thought embraced by Friedrich agreed with Spinoza that the future is determined by what has gone before, by our physical and psychological makeup—our passions, fears, goals; our temperament, our love of self, our stances toward others.

But consider Alfred Rosenberg, a pretentious, detached, unloving, unlovable philosopher-manqué who lacked curiosity about himself and, despite his gerrymandered sense of self, walked the earth with a smug sense of superiority. Could Friedrich, could any student of human nature, have predicted the meteoric rise of Alfred Rosenberg? No, character alone is insufficient for prophecy. There is another core and unpredictable ingredient. What shall we term it? Fortune? Chance? The sheer good luck of being in the right place at the right time?

The right time? November 1918. The war was ending, and Germany, weeping and staggered by defeat, was in chaos awaiting a savior. And the right place? Munich. Alfred Rosenberg would soon be on his way to that chosen spot, whose back alleys and popular beer halls were incubating a momentous drama and awaiting only the arrival of its preternaturally malignant cast.

Alfred stayed for several weeks longer in Reval, struggling to support himself by teaching art at German-speaking schools. On one occasion he was astonished by winning a small prize for two of his drawings—the first and only money his art would ever generate. The following evening, in a celebratory mood, he wandered into a town meeting and stood rapt in the back of the audience listening to a debate about the future of Estonia. Suddenly, as in a trance, he impulsively strode to the front of the hall and delivered a short impassioned speech about the dangers of Jewish Bolshevism looming in neighboring Russia. Was he perturbed when the Jewish owner of a large warehouse interrupted and led a large group of Jews to the exit in protest? Not at all. Alfred's lips curled into a knowing smile, fully persuaded it was a good thing to have cleansed his audience. He didn't wish those Jews evil. He hoped they would be warm and happy in their own kitchens. He just wanted them gone from Reval. Slowly the seeds of a grand idea germinated: gone not just from Reval, not just from Estonia, but gone from all of Europe. The Fatherland would only be safe, only be prosperous, when every Jew had left Europe.

Day by day his resolve grew to emigrate to Germany; he would dwell no more in an insignificant peripheral country. Estonia, now being emptied of Germans, headed for an unstable future as a weak independent country or, worse, immediate takeover by the Jewish-Russian Bolshevists. Yet how to leave? The roads out of Estonia were closed, and all trains had been commandeered by the military for the dejected army troops returning to Germany. Trapped and directionless, Alfred had his first visit from the angel of good fortune.

In the working-class café where Alfred often dined, he sipped his beer and ate sausages while reading *The Brothers Karamazov*. He read in Russian but had a German copy open on the table and stopped from time to time to evaluate the accuracy of the translation. Soon, annoyed by the noisy merriment at an adjoining table, he stood to search for a quieter spot. As he scanned the café, he chanced to overhear a conversation in German at the other table.

"Yes, yes, I'm leaving Reval," said a middle-aged baker in a white apron, dusty with flour, that strained to contain an enormous belly. He smiled broadly as he opened a bottle of celebratory schnapps for his three companions, poured a glass, raised it over his head, and toasted them. "I drink a farewell to you, my dear friends, and hope we meet in the Fatherland. For once in my life I did something smart—baker smart."

He pointed to his head and then to his belly. "I brought the military commander two loaves of my German bread and my best apple-raisin strudel, toasty warm, right out of the oven. His military aide tried to look fierce and take them from me, saying he would deliver them to the commander, but I stared him down and promised to return later with a strudel for him, which was now baking in my oven. What's more, I told him that the commander asked me to deliver it personally—*that* I made up on the spot. Then I walked into the commander's office, showed him my gift, and begged him to let me go to Berlin. 'It would go bad for me once the army left,' I told him. "The Estonians would treat me as a collaborator because I bake good German bread and pastry for the troops. Here, look at this bread, heavy and crisp. Smell it. Taste it.' I broke off a chunk and put it into his open mouth. He chewed, and his eyes lit up with delight. 'Now smell the strudel,' I said as I held it to his nose. Again and again he inhaled the aroma steaming from it. Soon he was intoxicated: his eyes went in circles, and he began to weave on his feet. 'Now, open your mouth for a taste of heaven.' He opened his mouth. Like a mother bird I fed him bits of strudel, choosing pieces packed with raisins, and he began to moan with delight as he chewed. 'Yes, yes, yes,' he said and without another word ordered me a hardship pass to Germany. So I board the train tomorrow morning, and you, my friends, are welcome to the dough that rises in my oven as we speak."

Alfred ruminated about what he had heard for three days and then woke up one morning determined to emulate the baker's boldness. Arriving at the military headquarters with three of his best sketches of Reval, he, like the baker, told the aide-de-camp that he wished to deliver his gift directly to the commander. The aide's resistance quickly evaporated when Alfred offered him a gift of one of the sketches. Ushered into the commander's presence, Alfred presented his sketches and commented, "Here is a small remembrance of your time in Reval. I have been teaching Germans how to draw, and now I want nothing more than to teach Berliners my craft." The commander inspected Alfred's work, his lower lip protruding in appreciation of the sketches. When Alfred described his town meeting speech and the exodus of the Jews from the audience, the commander warmed even more and volunteered on his own that Alfred might not be safe in Estonia after the German military evacuation and offered him the last seat on a train to Berlin leaving at midnight that very evening.

Home! Finally heading home to the Fatherland! A home that he had never known. That thought crowded out all bodily discomfort during the several-day, freezing train trip to Berlin. Once he arrived, his exuberance was dampened by the sight of the drooping military parade of the returning defeated German army down the Unter den Linden. Berlin, Alfred learned quickly, was not to his liking, and he felt more alone than ever. He spoke to no one at the immigrants' relief station where he boarded, but he listened hungrily to conversations. "Munich" was on everyone's lips. Avant-garde artists were there, anti-Semitic political groups as well, and Munich was the meeting place for radical White Russian anti-Bolshevistic agitators. The pull to Munich was irresistible and, convinced that his destiny lay there, Alfred within a week had hitched a ride on a cattle truck to Munich.

His funds running low, Alfred took his free lunch and supper at the Munich emigrants' center, which offered decent food but required the indignity of bringing one's own spoon. Munich was open, sunny, bustling, crammed with galleries and street artists. To his chagrin, he examined the watercolors of the street artists—their work was far better than his, and they weren't selling. At times, anxiety set in: how would he live? Where would he find work? But for the most part, he felt unconcerned; confident that he was in the right place, he knew that sooner or later his future would be revealed to him. While he waited, he spent his days in art galleries and in libraries reading all he could find on Jewish history and literature and began sketching an outline for a book, *The Trace of the Jew*.

Again and again, Spinoza's name appeared in his readings of Jewish history. Even though he had left Reval with all his belongings in only one suitcase, he still retained his copy of Spinoza's *Ethics* but, recalling Friedrich's advice, did not try to read it again. Instead he placed his name on the library waiting list for Spinoza's other book, *Theological-Political Treatise*.

As he strolled the streets of Munich trying unsuccessfully to peddle some sketches, good fortune struck once again when he looked up at a building that bore a placard: *Edith Schrenk: Dancing Instruction*. Edith Schrenk— he knew that name. Years ago his estranged wife, Hilda, and Edith had been dancing students in the same class in Moscow. Though he was shy by nature and had only spoken with Edith once or twice, he longed for a familiar face and tapped meekly on her door. Edith, dressed in a black leotard with a stylish aqua foulard around her neck, greeted him cordially, asked him to sit, offered him coffee, and inquired about Hilda, whom she had always liked. During the course of a long conversation Alfred described his uncertainty about his future, his interests in the Jewish question, and his experience during the Russian Revolution. When he mentioned he had been writing a personal account of the dangers of Jewish Bolshevism, Edith put her hand on his.

"Why, then, Alfred, you must pay a visit to my friend Dietrich Eckart, the editor of the weekly newspaper *Auf gut Deutsch*. He has similar views and might be interested in your observations about the Russian Revolution. Here's his address. Be sure to use my name when you see him."

Without delay Alfred rushed out and headed to a life-changing meeting. On the way to Eckart's office, he searched for *Auf gut Deutsch* at two news-stands but was told they had sold out. As he climbed the stairs to Eckart's third-floor office, he recalled how Friedrich had warned him that impulsive fanatical actions could be his undoing. But throwing that advice to the wind, Alfred opened the door, introduced himself to Dietrich Eckart, mentioned Edith's name, and impulsively blurted out, "Can you use a fighter against Jerusalem? I am dedicated, and I will fight until I drop."

CHAPTER FIFTEEN

AMSTERDAM—JULY 1656

T wo days later, as Bento and Gabriel were opening the store for business, a young boy wearing a skullcap ran up to them, stopped to catch his breath, and said, "Bento, the rabbi wants to talk to you. Right now. He is waiting at the synagogue."

Bento was not surprised: he had been expecting this summons. He took his time putting his broom away, drank the last sip of coffee in his cup, nodded farewell to Gabriel, and silently followed the young boy toward the synagogue. With a look of grave concern on his face, Gabriel stepped outside and watched the two recede into the distance.

In his study on the second floor of the synagogue, Rabbi Saul Levi Mortera, dressed in the style of a prosperous Dutch burgher with camel-hair trousers and jacket and silver-buckled leather shoes, irritably tapped his pen on his desk awaiting Baruch Spinoza. A tall, imposing sixty-year-old man with a razor sharp nose, frightening eyes, stern lips, and a well-trimmed gray goatee, Rabbi Mortera was many things—an honored scholar, a prolific author, a fierce intellectual warrior, a survivor of bitter battles with competing rabbis, a gallant defender of the sanctity of the Torah—but he was not a patient man. It had been almost thirty minutes since he had sent his messenger, a lad in bar mitzvah training, to fetch his wayward former student.

Saul Mortera had presided majestically over the Amsterdam Jewish community for thirty-seven years. In 1619 he had been appointed to his first post as the rabbi of Beth Jacob, one of the three small Sephardic synagogues in the city. When his congregation merged with Neve Shalom and Beth Israel in 1639, Saul Mortera was chosen over other candidates to take the post of head rabbi of the new Talmud Torah Synagogue. A mighty bulwark of traditional Jewish law, he had for decades protected his community from the skepticism and secularism of the wave of Portuguese immigrants, many of whom had been forced to convert to Christianity and few of whom had had early traditional Jewish instruction. He was weary—indoctrinating adults into the old ways is hard work. He appreciated all too well the lesson all religious teachers ultimately grasp: it is essential to capture students when they are very young.

A tireless educator, he developed a comprehensive curriculum, hired many teachers, personally offered daily Hebrew, Torah, and Talmud classes to the older students, and endlessly dueled with other rabbis in order to uphold his interpretations of the laws of the Torah. One of his bitterest struggles had taken place fourteen years earlier with his assistant and rival, Rabbi Isaac Aboab de Fonseca, over the question of whether unrepentant Jewish sinners, even Jews forced under pain of death from the Inquisition to convert to Christianity, would live eternally in the world to come. Rabbi Aboab, who, like many members of the congregation, had converso family members remaining in Portugal, held that a Jew always remained a Jew and that all Jews would ultimately enter the blessed world to come. Jewish blood persevered, he insisted, and could be erased by nothing, not even conversion to another religion. Paradoxically, he supported his claim by citing Queen Isabella of Spain, the great enemy of the Jews, who acknowledged the indelibility of Jewish blood when she instituted the *Estatutos de Limpieza de Sangre*, blood laws that prevented "New Christians"—that is, Jewish conversos—from holding important civic and military positions.

Rabbi Mortera's hard-line position was consonant with his physique—unyielding, uncompromising, oppositional—and he insisted that all unrepentant Jews who broke Jewish law would be forever barred from the blissful world to come and would instead face eternal punishment. The law was the law, and there were no exceptions, even for those Jews who yielded under threat of death from the Portuguese and Spanish Inquisition. All Jews who were uncircumcised or violated dietary laws or failed to observe the Sabbath, or any of the myriad religious laws, were doomed for all eternity.

Mortera's unforgiving declaration infuriated Amsterdam Jews, who had converso relatives still dwelling in Portugal and Spain, but he would not budge. So acrimonious and divisive was the ensuing debate that the elders of the synagogue petitioned the rabbinate of Venice to intervene and provide a definitive interpretation of the law. The Venetian rabbis reluctantly agreed and listened to the delegates' arguments, often offered in shrill voices, for each side of the knotty controversy. For two hours they pondered their response. Stomachs churned. Dinner was delayed, and finally they reached a unanimous decision not to decide: they wanted no part of this thorny controversy and ruled that the problem must be solved by the Amsterdam congregation itself.

But the Amsterdam community could not reach resolution and, to prevent a descent into irreparable schism, sent an emergency second delegation to Venice pleading even more strongly for outside intervention. Ultimately the Venetian rabbinate reached a decision and supported the view of Saul Mortera (who, by the by, had been educated in the yeshiva of Venice). The delegation bearing the rabbinical decision rushed back to Amsterdam, and four weeks later many members of the congregation somberly stood at the harbor and waved farewell to the downcast Rabbi Aboab and his family, as their goods were loaded onto a ship headed for Brazil, where he would assume rabbinical duties in the distant seaside city of Recife. From that point on, no rabbi in Amsterdam would ever again challenge Rabbi Mortera.

Today Saul Mortera faced a far more personally painful crisis. The synagogue parnassim had met the evening before, reached a decision on the Spinoza problem, and instructed their rabbi to inform Baruch of his excommunication—to take place at the Talmud Torah synagogue two days hence. For forty years Baruch's father, Michael Spinoza, had been one of Saul Mortera's closest friends and supporters. Michael's name had appeared on the deed of trust for the original purchase of Beth Jacob, and throughout the decades he had generously supported the synagogue fund (which paid the rabbi's salary) as well as other synagogue charities. During that time Michael rarely missed a meeting of the Crown of the Law, Rabbi Mortera's adult study group that met in the rabbi's home, and, more times than he could count, Michael, sometimes accompanied by his prodigy son, Baruch, had eaten dinner at his table, along with as many as forty others. Moreover Michael, and also Michael's older brother, Abraham, had often served as a *parnas*, a member of the governing board, the ultimate authority for synagogue governance.

But now the rabbi brooded. Today, any minute . . . Where was Baruch anyway? He would have to tell his dear friend's son of the calamity awaiting him. Saul Mortera had said prayers over Baruch at his circumcision, supervised his flawless bar mitzvah performance, and watched him develop through the years. What prodigious talents the boy possessed, talents like no other! He absorbed information like a sponge. Every course of instruction seemed so elementary for him that each teacher assigned him advanced texts while the rest of the class struggled with the class assignment. Sometimes Rabbi Mortera worried that other students' envy would result in enmity toward Baruch. That never happened: his abilities were so evident, so far out of range, that he was much esteemed and befriended by other students, who often consulted him, rather than the teachers, for instruction on some knotty problem of translation or interpretation. Rabbi Mortera remembered how he, too, held Baruch in awe, and on many occasions asked Michael to bring Baruch for dinner in order to delight a celebrated guest. But now, Saul Mortera sighed, Baruch's golden period, from years four to fourteen, had long passed. The lad had changed, taken a wrong turn; now the entire community faced the danger of the prodigy turning into a monster that would devour its own.

Footsteps sounded on the stairs. Baruch was approaching. Rabbi Mortera remained seated, and when Baruch appeared at his door, he did not turn to greet him but instead pointed to a low and uncomfortable seat by his desk and said sharply, "Sit there. I have catastrophic news to deliver, news that will alter your life forever." He spoke in a slightly halting but passable Portuguese. Though Rabbi Mortera's background was Ashkenazi, not Sephardic, and though he had been born and educated in Italy, he had married a Marrano and learned to speak Portuguese well enough to deliver hundreds of Sabbath sermons to a congregation that was primarily Portuguese in origin.

Baruch replied in an unruffled tone, "No doubt what has happened is that the parnassim has decided to excommunicate me and instructed you to deliver the *cherem* at a public synagogue ceremony almost immediately?"

"As insolent as ever, I see. I should be accustomed to it by now, but I continue to be astounded by the transformation of a wise child into a foolish adult. You are correct in your assumptions, Baruch—that is precisely their instruction to me. Tomorrow you shall indeed be placed under *cherem* and be excommunicated forever from this community. But I object to your sloppy use of the verb 'happened.' Do not fall sway to the sentiment that the *cherem* is merely something that has *happened* to you. Instead it is *you* that have brought the *cherem* upon yourself with your own actions."

Baruch opened his mouth to answer, but the rabbi hurried on. "However, all may not yet be lost. I am a loyal man, and my long friendship with your blessed father mandates that I do everything in my power to offer you protection and guidance. What I want now is for you, at this moment, to simply sit and listen. I've instructed you since you were five, and you're not too old for additional instruction. I want to give you a particular type of history lesson.

"Let's go back," Saul Mortera began in his most rabbinical voice, "to ancient Spain, the land of your ancestors. You know that Jews first came to Spain perhaps a thousand years ago, and they lived in peace with the Moors and Christians for centuries despite the fact that Jews met with hostility elsewhere?"

Baruch nodded wearily while rolling his eyes.

Rabbi Mortera noted the gesture but let it pass. "In the thirteenth and fourteenth centuries, we were driven out of country after country, first from England, the source of the accursed blood libel that accused us of making matzo with the blood of Gentile children; then France ejected us, then the cities of Germany, Italy, and Sicily—all of Western Europe, in fact—except for Spain, where *La Convivencia* persisted and the Jews, Christians, and Moors mingled amicably with one another. But the gradual Christian reconquest of Spain from the Moors signaled the tarnishing of this golden period. And you know about the end of *La Convivencia* in 1391?"

"Yes, I know about the expulsions and about the 1391 pogroms at Castile and Aragon. I know all of this. And you know I know it. Why are you telling me this today?"

"I know you *think* you know it. But there is knowing, and there is true knowing, knowing in your heart, and you have not yet reached that stage. All I ask now is that you listen. Nothing else. All will become clear in time."

"What was truly different about 1391," the rabbi continued, "was that, after the pogrom, Jews, *for the very first time in history*, began to convert to Christianity—and convert in droves, by the thousands, by the tens of thousands. The Spanish Jews gave up. They were weak. They decided our Torah—the direct word of God—and our three-thousand-year-old heritage were not worth the price of continued harassment.

"Such massive Jewish conversions were of world-shaking significance; never before in history had we Jews given up our faith. Compare this with the response of the Jews in 1096. You know that date? You know what I'm referring to, Baruch?"

"No doubt you mean the Jews who were slaughtered in the pogroms during the crusades—the 1096 pogrom in Mainz."

"Mainz and elsewhere throughout the Rhineland. Yes, slaughtered, and you know who led the slaughterers? The monks! Whenever Jews are slaughtered, the men of the cross are to be found at the head of the pack. Yes, those fine Jews of Mainz, those magnificent martyrs, chose death over conversion—many held out their necks to the murderers, and many others slaughtered their own families rather than let them be defiled by the Gentiles' swords. They preferred death to conversion."

Baruch looked at him incredulously. "And you applaud that? You consider it praiseworthy to end your own existence and, incidentally, to murder your children in order to—"

"Baruch, you have much still to learn if you consider no cause worthy of laying down your own insignificant life, but there is too little time to educate you about such matters now. Today you are not here to display your insolence. There will be time enough for that later. Whether you appreciate it or not, you are at the great crossroads of your life, and I am trying to help you choose your way. I want you to listen *attentively and silently* to my account of how our entire Jewish civilization is now imperiled."

Bento held his head high, breathed easily, and took note of how the rabbi's fierce voice once terrified him and how little dread it held for him today.

Rabbi Mortera took a deep breath and continued. "In the fifteenth century there continued to be tens of thousands of new conversions in Spain, including members of your own family. But the Catholic Church's appetite for blood was still not satisfied. They claimed that conversos were not Christian enough, that some still harbored Jewish sentiments, and decided to send the inquisitors to sniff out everything Jewish. They asked, 'What did you do on Friday, on Saturday?' 'Do you light candles?' 'What day do you change the sheets?' 'How do you make your soups?' And if inquisitors found any traces of Jewish traits or Jewish customs or Jewish cooking, the kindly priests burned them alive at the stake. Even then they were not convinced of the cleanliness of the conversos. Every trace of the Jew had to be scrubbed out. They did not want the eyes of the conversos to light upon a true practicing Jew for fear of awakening the old ways, and so in 1492 they expelled all the Jews, every single one, from Spain. Many, including your own ancestors, went to Portugal but enjoyed only a brief respite there. Five years later the king of Portugal insisted that every Jew choose between conversion or expulsion. And, once again, tens of thousands chose conversion and were lost to our faith. This was the low point of Judaism in history, such a low point that many, and I among them, believe that the coming of the Messiah is imminent. You remember that I lent you the great three-volume Messianic trilogy by Isaac Abrabanel positing that very thing?"

"I remember that Abrabanel makes no rational case for why the Jews have to be at their lowest point for that mythical event to occur. Nor any explanation for an omnipotent God being unable to protect his chosen people and allowing them to get to that point, nor why—"

"Quiet. Just listen today, Baruch," the rabbi barked. "For once, maybe for the last time, *do exactly what I tell you.* When I ask a question, just reply yes or no. I have only a few more things to say to you. I was talking about the lowest point in Jewish history. Where could the Jews of the late fifteenth and the sixteenth century seek shelter? Where in *all the world* was there a safe haven? Some went east to the Ottoman Empire or to Livorno, in Italy, which tolerated them because of their valuable international trade network. And then, after 1579, when the northern provinces of the Netherlands proclaimed their independence from Catholic Spain, some Jews found their way here to Amsterdam.

"How did the Dutch greet us? *Like no other people in the world.* They were entirely tolerant about religion. No one inquired about religious beliefs. They were Calvinists but granted everyone the right to worship in their own manner—except for the Catholics. Toward them there was not much tolerance. But that is not our affair. Not only were we not harassed here, but we were welcomed, because the Netherlands wanted to become an important commercial center and they knew that Marrano traders could help build that commerce. Soon more and more immigrants from Portugal arrived, enjoying a tolerance not seen elsewhere in centuries. And other Jews came too: waves of poor Ashkenazi Jews also poured in from Germany and Eastern Europe to escape the mad violence against Jews there. Of course these Ashkenazi Jews lacked the culture of the Sephardic Jews: they had no education nor skills, and most became peddlers, old clothes traders, and shopkeepers, but *still* we welcomed them and offered charity. Did you know that your father made regular and generous donations to the Ashkenazi charity box in our synagogue?"

Baruch, remaining silent, nodded.

"And then," Rabbi Mortera continued, "after a few years, the Amsterdam authorities, in consultation with the great jurist Grotius, officially recognized our right to live in Amsterdam. At first we were meek and followed our old ways of remaining inconspicuous. Thus we did not mark our four synagogues outwardly but instead held our prayer services in buildings that resembled private homes. Only the passage of many harassment-free years allowed us to truly realize that we could practice our faith openly and be assured that the state would protect our lives and property. We Jews in Amsterdam have had the extraordinary good fortune to be living in *the one spot in the entire world* where Jews could be free. Do you appreciate that—the one spot in the entire world?"

Baruch stirred uncomfortably on his wooden seat and gave a perfunctory nod.

"Patience, patience, Baruch. Listen only a little longer—I am now veering very close to matters of urgent relevance to you. Our remarkable freedom comes with certain obligations that the Amsterdam city council has stated explicitly. No doubt you know what these obligations are?"

"That we do not defame the Christian faith and do not try to convert or marry Christians," answered Baruch.

"There was more. Your memory is prodigious, but you do not remember the other obligations. Why? Perhaps because they are inconvenient for you. Let me remind you of them. Grotius also decreed that all Jews over fourteen years of age must state their faith in God, Moses, the Prophets, the afterlife, and that our religious and civil authorities must guarantee, at the risk of losing our freedom, that none of our congregation said or did anything that would challenge or undermine any aspect of the Christian religious dogma."

Rabbi Mortera paused, shook his forefinger while speaking slowly and emphatically. "Let me stress this last point to you, Baruch—it is a crucial point for you to grasp. *Atheism or flouting of religious law and authority—either Jewish or Christian—is expressly forbidden.* If we show the Dutch civil authorities that *we cannot govern ourselves, then we lose our precious freedom and once again submit to rule by Christian authorities.*"

Rabbi Mortera paused again. "I have finished my history lesson. My major hope is that you will understand that we are still a people apart, that though we have some limited freedom today, *we can never be fully autonomous.* Even today it is not easy to support ourselves as free men because so many professions are closed to us. Keep that in mind, Baruch, when you contemplate life without this community. It may be that you are choosing starvation."

Baruch started to respond, but the rabbi silenced him with a wag of his right forefinger. "There's another point I want to stress. Today, *the very foundation of our religious culture is under attack.* The waves of immigrants continuing to flow in from Portugal are Jews without any Jewish education. They have been forbidden to learn Hebrew; they have been forced to learn the Catholic dogma and practice as Catholics. They are between two worlds with shaky faith in both Catholic dogma and Jewish beliefs. It is my mission to reclaim them, to bring them back home, back to their Jewish roots. Our community is prospering and evolving: we are already producing scholars, poets, playwrights, Kabbalists, physicians, and printers. We are on the brink of a great renaissance, and there is a place for you here. Your learning, your nimble mind, and your gifts as a teacher would be of tremendous help. If you taught by my side, if you took over my work when I am no longer here, you would fulfill your father's dreams for you—and my dreams as well."

Astonished, Baruch looked into the rabbi's eyes. "What do you mean 'work with you'? Your words mystify me. Keep in mind I am a shopkeeper, and I am under *cherem.*"

"The *cherem* is pending. It is not reality until I have pronounced it publicly at the synagogue. Yes, the parnassim holds ultimate authority, but I have great influence with them. Two newly arrived Marranos, Franco Benitez and Jacob Mendoza, gave witness, highly damaging witness, yesterday to the parnassim. They reported that you believe God is nothing more than Nature and that there is no world to come. Yes, that was damaging, but between you and me, I distrust their testimony, and I know they distorted your words. They are the nephews of Duarte Rodriguez, who remains incensed at you for turning to the Dutch court to avoid your debt to him, and I am persuaded that he has ordered them to lie. And, trust me, I am not the only one who believes that."

"They did not lie, Rabbi."

"Baruch, come to your senses. I've known you since your birth, and I know that from time to time you, like anyone else, can harbor foolish thoughts. I beseech you: study with me; let me purify your mind. Now listen to me. I will make you an offer that I would make to no one else on earth. I am certain I can grant you *a lifelong pension that will permanently take you out of the import-export business and into a life as a scholar.* You hear that? I offer you the gift of a life of scholarship, a life of reading and thinking. You can even think forbidden thoughts while you seek the confirmatory or negating evidence from rabbinical scholarship. Think about that offer: a lifetime of total freedom. It comes with only one stipulation: *silence.* You must agree to keep to yourself all thoughts that are injurious to our people."

Baruch seemed frozen in thought. After a long silence, the rabbi said, "What do you say, Baruch? Now, when it is time for you to speak, you remain silent."

"More times than I can remember," Baruch responded in a calm voice, "my father spoke of his friendship with you and his high regard for you. He also told me of your high opinion of my mind—'limitless intelligence' were the words he attributed to you. Were these indeed your words? Did he cite you correctly?"

"Those were my words."

"I believe the world and everything in it operate according to natural law and that I can use my intelligence, provided I employ it in a rational mode, to discover the nature of God and reality and the path to a blessed life. I've said this to you before, have I not?"

Rabbi Mortera placed his head in his hands and nodded.

"And yet today you suggest that I spend my life confirming or negating my views by consulting rabbinical scholarship. That is not and will not be my way. Rabbinical authority is not based on purity of truth. It rests only on the expressed opinions of generations of superstitious scholars, scholars who believed the world was flat, circled by the sun, and that one man named Adam suddenly appeared and fathered the human race."

"You deny the divinity of Genesis?"

"Do you deny the evidence showing that there were civilizations long predating the Israelites? In China? In Egypt?"

"Such blasphemy. Do you not realize how you jeopardize your place in the world to come?"

"There is no rational evidence for the existence of a world to come."

Rabbi Mortera looked thunderstruck. "This is exactly what Duarte Rodriquez's nephews quoted you as saying. I had thought they were lying at the orders of their uncle."

"I believe you did not hear me, or did not want to hear me, when I said earlier, 'They did not lie, Rabbi.'"

"And the other charges they made? That you deny the divine source of the Torah, that Moses did not write the Torah, that God exists only philosophically, and that ceremonial law is not sacred?"

"The nephews did not lie, Rabbi."

Rabbi Mortera glared at Baruch, his anguish turning to anger. "Any single one of these charges is cause for *cherem*; together they deserve the harshest cherem ever issued."

"You have been my Hebrew teacher, and you have taught me well. Allow me to repay you by composing the *cherem* for you. You once showed me some of the most brutal *cherems* issued by the Venetian community, and I remember every word of them."

"I said earlier you would have time enough for insolence. Now, I see, it already begins." Rabbi Mortera paused to collect himself. "You want to kill me. You want to destroy my work utterly. You know that my life work has been the vital role of the afterlife in Jewish thought and culture. You know about my book, *The Survival of the Soul*, which I placed into your hands at your bar mitzvah. You know of my great debate with Rabbi Aboab about that matter and my victory?"

"Yes, of course."

"You shrug that off lightly. Do you have any idea of the stakes involved? If I had lost that debate, if it were decreed that *all* Jews have an equal status in the world to come and that virtue would be unrewarded and transgression would have no penalty, can you not foresee the repercussions upon the community? If they are insured a place in the world to come, then what is the incentive to convert back to Judaism? If there is no penalty for wrongdoing, can you imagine how the Dutch Calvinists would regard us? How long would our freedom last? Do you think I was playing a child's game? Think of the implications."

"Yes, that great debate—your words have just demonstrated that it was not a debate about spiritual truth. No doubt that is why the Venetian rabbinate was confounded. Both of you argued for different versions of the afterlife for reasons that have nothing to do with the reality of the afterlife. You attempt to control the populace through the power of fear and hope— the traditional cudgels of religious leaders throughout history. You, the rabbinical authorities everywhere, claim to hold the keys to the afterlife, and you use those keys for political control. Rabbi Aboab, on the other hand, took his stand to minister to the anguish of his congregation who wanted to offer help for their converso families. This was not a spiritual disagreement. It was a political debate masquerading as a religious debate. Neither of you offered any proof for the existence of the world to come, either a proof from reason or even proof from the words of the Torah. I assure you it is not to be found in the Torah, and you know that."

"You obviously did not assimilate what I've been telling you about my responsibility to God and to the persistence of our people," Rabbi Mortera said.

"Much of what religious leaders do has little to do with God," Baruch replied. "Last year you gave a *cherem* to a man who bought meat from a kosher Ashkenazi butcher rather than a Sephardic butcher. You think that was relevant to God?"

"It was a short *cherem* highly instructive about the importance of community cohesion."

"And I learned last month that you told a woman who came from a small village without a Jewish baker that she could buy bread from a Gentile baker provided she tossed a wood chip into his oven so as to participate in the baking."

"She came to me distressed and left my presence relieved and a happy woman."

"She left a woman with a mind more stunted than before, a woman even less able to think for herself and to develop her rational faculties. This is exactly my point: religious authorities of all hues seek to impede the development of our rational faculties."

"If you think our people can survive without control and authority, you are a fool."

"I think that religious leaders lose their own spiritual direction by meddling into the business of the political state. Your authority or consul should be confined to counsel about inward piety."

"The business of the political state? Have you not understood what happened in Spain and Portugal?"

"That is precisely my point: they were religious states. Religion and statehood must be separated. The best imaginable ruler would be a freely elected leader who is limited in his powers by an independently elected council and who would act in accord with public peace and safety and social well-being."

"Baruch, you have now succeeded in persuading me that you shall live a lonely life and that your future will include not only blasphemy but treason as well. Be gone."

As he listened to Baruch's footsteps clattering down the stairs, Rabbi Mortera looked upward and muttered, "Michael, my friend, I have done what I could for your son. I have too many other souls to protect."

CHAPTER SIXTEEN

MUNICH—1919

I magine the scene: a shabbily dressed, unemployed, unpublished immigrant youth, soup kitchen spoon in shirt pocket, barges into the office of a well-known journalist, poet, and politician and blurts out, "Can you use a fighter against Jerusalem?"

Surely an ill-fated beginning of a job interview! Any responsible, well-bred, sophisticated editor in chief would be quick to dismiss the intruder as puerile, bizarre, and possibly dangerous. But no—the time was 1919, the place was Munich, and Dietrich Eckart was intrigued by the youth's beautiful words.

"Well, well, young warrior, show me your weapons."

"My mind is my bow, and my words are—" Taking a pencil from his pocket and waving it aloft, Alfred exclaimed, "My words are my arrows!"

"Well said, young warrior. And tell me of your exploits, your assaults against Jerusalem."

Alfred trembled with excitement as he recounted his anti-Jerusalem exploits: his near-memorization of Houston Stewart Chamberlain's book, his anti-Semitic election speech at age sixteen, his confrontation with the suspected Jew Headmaster Epstein (he omitted the Spinoza part), his revulsion at the sight of the Jewish-Bolshevist revolution, his recent, rousing anti-Jew speech at the Reval town meeting, his plan to write an eyewitness account of the Jewish Bolshevists in revolt, his historical research into the menace of Jewish blood.

"An excellent beginning. But only a beginning. Next we must inspect the caliber of your weapons. In twenty-four hours, bring me a thousand words of your eyewitness account of the Bolshevist revolution, and we'll see if it merits publication."

Alfred made no move to leave. He glanced again at Dietrich Eckart, an imposing man with a shaved head, dark-rimmed glasses shielding blue eyes, short fleshy nose, and a broad, rather brutal chin.

"Twenty-four hours, young man. Time to begin."

Alfred looked about him, obviously reluctant to leave Eckart's office. Then, timidly: "Is there a desk, a corner, and some paper I might use? I have only the library, which is now crammed with illiterate refugees trying to stay warm."

Dietrich Eckart signaled to his secretary. "Show this applicant to the back office. And give him some paper and a key." To Alfred, he said, "It's poorly heated but quiet and has a separate entrance, so you may work though the night, if necessary. *Auf Wiedersehen*, until tomorrow at precisely this time."

Dietrich Eckart put his feet on his desk, tamped out his cigar in the ashtray, and leaned back in his chair for a catnap. Though only in his early fifties, he had been unkind to his body, and his flesh hung heavily upon him. Born into a wealthy family, the son of a royal notary and attorney, he had lost his mother in childhood, his father a few years later, and in his late teens had drifted into a drug-immersed Bohemian life, which soon dissipated the fortune left by his father. After a series of false starts in the arts and radical political movements, and a year of medical school, he slipped into serious morphine addiction, which necessitated psychiatric hospitalization for several months. He then became a playwright, but none of his work ever saw the stage. Fully convinced of his literary merit, he placed the blame for his failure on the Jews, who he believed controlled German theaters and were offended by his political views. His desire for revenge gave birth to a career as a professional anti-Semite: born again as a journalist, he launched *Auf gut Deutsch* as the latest of a series of publications intended to combat the power of the Jews. In 1919 the time was propitious, his journalistic style compelling, and soon his paper became required reading for those interested in nefarious Jewish machinations.

Though Dietrich's health was poor and his energy level low, his thirst for change was huge, and he avidly awaited the arrival of the German savior— a man of extraordinary force and charisma who would lead Germany to its rightful position of glory. He saw immediately that this young handsome Rosenberg was not that man: Rosenberg's pitiful craving for approval stuck out too obviously from behind his brash presentation. But perhaps there might be a role for him in preparing the way for the one yet to come.

————

The following day Alfred sat in Eckart's office, nervously crossing and uncrossing his legs, as he watched the publisher read his thousand words.

Eckart removed his glasses and looked up at Alfred. "For someone who has a degree in architecture and has never written such prose before, I would say this work is not without promise. It's true that these thousand words contain not a single grammatically correct sentence, but despite that inconvenient fact your work has some power. There is tension, there is intelligence and complexity, and there are even a few, not enough, graphic images. I hereby announce that your journalistic virginity is at an end. I will publish this article. But there is work ahead: Every sentence shrieks for help. Pull your chair over here, Alfred, and we'll go over it line by line."

Alfred eagerly moved his chair next to Eckart.

"Here's your first lesson in journalism," Eckart continued. "The writer's job is to communicate. Alas, many of your sentences are unaware of that simple dictum and instead attempt to obfuscate or to convey that the author knows far more than he chooses to say. To the guillotine with every one of those sentences. Look here and here and here." Dietrich Eckart's red pencil started its work in a blur, and Alfred Rosenberg's apprenticeship began.

Alfred's revised piece was published as part of a series, "Jewry Within Us and Without," and he soon wrote several other eyewitness accounts of Bolshevist mayhem, each one showing gradual stylistic improvement. Within weeks, he was on the regular payroll as Eckart's assistant, and within months Eckart was so satisfied that he asked Alfred to write the introduction to his book, *Russia's Gravedigger*, which described in lurid detail how Jews had undermined the Russian tsarist regime.

These were Alfred's halcyon days, and to the end of his life he would glow with pleasure when he recalled working side by side with Eckart and accompanying him by taxi when they distributed Eckart's fiery pamphlet, *To All Workingmen*, all over Munich. Alfred, finally, had a home, a father, a purpose.

With Eckart's encouragement, he completed his historical research on the Jews and within a year published his first book, *The Trace of the Jew Through Changing Times*. It contained the seeds of what would become the major motifs of Nazi anti-Semitism: the Jew as the source of destructive materialism, anarchy, and Communism, the dangers of Jewish Freemasonry, the malignant dreams of Jewish philosophers from Ezekiel and Ibn Ezra to Marx and Trotsky, and, most of all, the threat to higher civilization posed by contamination with Jewish blood.

Under Eckart's tutelage, Alfred grew more aware that the German working man, oppressed by Jewish financial pressures, was yoked and trussed even further by Christian ideology. Eckart grew to rely on Alfred for the historical context not only for anti-Semitism but, by tracing the development of Jesuitism from the Judaism of the Talmud, for powerful anti-Christian sentiments as well.

Eckart took his young protégé to radical political rallies, introduced him to influential political figures, and soon sponsored Alfred for membership in the Thule Society and accompanied him to his first meeting of this august secret society.

At the Thule meeting, Eckart, after introducing Alfred to several members, left him on his own as he conferred privately with several colleagues. Alfred looked about him. This was a new world—not a beer hall but rather a meeting room in the magnificent Munich Four Seasons Hotel. Never before had he been in such a room. He tested the thick pile of the red carpet under his scuffed shoes and looked upward to an ornate ceiling depicting fleecy clouds and fleshy cherubs. There was no beer in sight, so he walked to the central table and helped himself to a glass of sweet German wine. Looking about at the other members, perhaps one hundred fifty, all obviously affluent, well-dressed, and overfed men, Alfred grew self-conscious about his clothes, each item purchased at a secondhand shop.

Aware that he was obviously the poorest and shabbiest man in the room, he tried his best to blend in with the Thule fellows and even tried to claim some distinction, referring to himself, whenever possible, as a philosopher-writer. When standing alone he busied himself practicing a new facial expression that combined a tiny curl of his lips with a minuscule nod and closing of his eyelids, by which he hoped to convey, "Yes, I know exactly what you mean—I am not only in the know, but I know even more than you think." Later in the evening, he checked out the expression in the mirror in the men's room and was pleased. It soon would become his trademark smirk.

"Hello! You're Dietrich Eckart's guest?" asked an intense-looking man with a long face, mustache, and black-rimmed glasses. "I'm Anton Drexler, part of the welcoming committee."

"Yes, Rosenberg, Alfred Rosenberg. I'm a writer and philosopher for *Auf gut Deutsch*, and yes, I'm Dietrich Eckart's guest."

"He has told me good things about you. It's your first visit, and you must have questions. What can I tell you about our organization?"

"Many things. First, I'm interested in the name, 'Thule.'"

"To answer that I should start by telling you that our original name was 'Study Group for German Antiquity.' Thule, many believe, was a land mass, now vanished, thought to be in the vicinity of Iceland or Greenland and to be the original home of the Aryan race."

"Thule . . . I know my Aryan history well from Houston Stewart Chamberlain, and I remember nothing about Thule."

"Ah, Chamberlain is a historian and one of our finest, but this is pre-Chamberlain and prehistory. The realm of myth. Our organization wishes to pay reverence to our noble ancestors whom we know only through oral history."

"So, then, all these impressive men are meeting here tonight because of their interest in myth, in ancient history? I'm not questioning it—in fact I think it admirable to see such calmness and scholarly devotion in a time so volatile that Germany may blast apart at any minute."

"The meeting has not yet begun, Herr Rosenberg. You'll see soon enough why the Thule Society holds your writings in *Auf gut Deutsche* in high regard. Yes, yes, we are keenly interested in ancient history. But even more interested in our postwar history, a history in the making that our children and grandchildren will one day read about."

Alfred was exhilarated by the public addresses. Speaker after speaker warned about the grave danger facing Germany from Bolshevists and Jews. Each speaker emphasized the pressing need for action. Toward the end of the evening, Eckart, tipsy from an uninterrupted stream of German wine, put his arm on Alfred's shoulder and exclaimed, "An exciting time, eh, Rosenberg! And it's going to get more exciting. Writing the news, changing attitudes, steering public opinion—all noble endeavors. Who can deny it? Yet making the news, yes, *making* the news—therein lies the true glory! And you'll be with us, Alfred. You'll see, you'll see. Trust me, I know what's coming."

Something momentous was in the air. Alfred sensed it keenly, and, too agitated to sleep, he continued pacing the streets of Munich for an hour after parting from Eckart. Recalling his new friend Friedrich Pfister's advice for the relief of tension, he inhaled deeply and quickly through his nostrils, held his breath for a few seconds, and then exhaled slowly from his mouth. After only a few cycles he felt better and also surprised at the effectiveness of such a simple maneuver. No doubt about it—Friedrich was a bit of a wizard. He had not liked the turn their conversation had taken about a possible Jewish strain in his grandmother's family but nonetheless felt positive toward Friedrich. He wanted their paths to cross again. He would make it happen.

Upon returning home he found a note on the floor dropped in through the mail slot; it read, "The Munich Public Library will hold *Theological-Political Treatise* by Spinoza for you for one week at the checkout desk." Alfred read it again several times. How oddly comforting was this little frail library notice that had found its way through the roiling, dangerous streets of Munich to his tiny apartment.

CHAPTER SEVENTEEN

AMSTERDAM—1656

B ento wandered through the streets of Vlooyenburg, the section of Amsterdam where most of the Sephardic Jews lived, viewing everything with poignancy. He stared at each image for a long time, as if to imbue it with permanence, so it might be called back again in the future, even though the voice of reason murmured that all will evaporate and life must be lived in the present.

Upon Bento's return to the shop, Gabriel, eyes full of alarm, dropped his broom and rushed over to him. "Bento, where have you been? All this time you've been talking to the rabbi?"

"We had a long, unfriendly talk, and since then I've been walking all over the city trying to settle myself. I'll tell you everything that happened, but I want to tell both you and Rebekah together."

"She won't come, Bento. And now it's more than just her anger at you— now it's her husband's anger. Ever since Samuel finished his rabbinical studies last year, he has taken a stronger and stronger stance. Now he forbids Rebekah to see you at all."

"She'll come if you tell her how serious it is." Bento clasped Gabriel's shoulders with both hands and looked into his eyes. "I know she will. Invoke the memory of our blessed family. Remind her we're the only ones still alive. She'll come if you tell her this will be the last talk we will ever have."

Gabriel was visibly alarmed. "What's happened? You're frightening me, Bento."

"Please, Gabriel. I cannot describe this twice—it's too hard. Please, get Rebekah here. You can find a way to do it. It is my last request to you."

Gabriel ripped off his apron, flung it on the back counter, and raced out of the shop. He returned in twenty minutes with a sullen Rebekah in tow. Unable to refuse Gabriel's plea—after all, she had raised Bento during the three years between the death of their mother, Hana, and their father's remarriage to Esther—Rebekah dripped with anger as she entered the shop. She greeted Bento with a frosty nod and splayed palms. "Well?"

Bento, who had already tacked a note on the door in both Portuguese and Dutch stating that the shop would reopen shortly, replied, "Let's go home, where we can talk privately."

Once home, Bento closed the front door and motioned to Gabriel and Rebekah to sit while he stood and paced about. "Much as I want this to be a private matter, I know it is not. Gabriel has made it clear how my affairs affect the whole family. I'm afraid that what I'm going to say will shock you. It is hard, but I must tell you everything. I want no one, absolutely no one in the community, to know more than you about what is going to happen."

Bento stopped. He had the full attention of his brother and sister, sitting still as granite. Bento took a deep breath. "I'll come right to the point. This morning Rabbi Mortera told me that the parnassim has met and that a *cherem* is imminent. I will be excommunicated tomorrow."

"A *cherem*?" exclaimed Gabriel and Rebekah simultaneously. Both were ashen-faced.

"There's no way to stop it?" asked Rebekah. "Rabbi Mortera will not stand up for you? Our father was his best friend!"

"I just spoke to Rabbi Mortera for an hour, and he told me it was not in his hands—the parnassim is elected by the community and holds all the power. He has no choice but to do as they bid. But then he also said he agreed with their decision."

Bento hesitated. "I must hold nothing back." Looking into the eyes of his sister and brother, he acknowledged, "He *did* say there might be a chance. He said that if I were to reverse all my views, if I were to publicly recant and proclaim that I would from this point forth embrace Maimonides' thirteen articles of faith, then he would petition the parnassim with all his strength to reconsider the *cherem*. In fact—and I'm not certain he wishes this to be known because he whispered it to me—he offered me a lifetime pension from synagogue funds if I vowed to devote my life to the respectful, and silent, study of Torah and Talmud."

"And?" Rebekah looked straight into Bento's eyes.

"And . . ." Bento looked at the floor. "I declined. For me, freedom is beyond price."

"You fool! Think what you are doing." Rebekah's voice was shrill. "My God, Brother, what is wrong with you? Have you lost your senses?" She leaned forward as though she meant to bolt from the room.

"Rebekah—" Bento strained to keep his voice calm. "This is the last time, the very last time, we shall be with one another. The *cherem* means absolute exile. It will forbid you to speak to me or contact me in any way ever again. Ever again. Think of how you, how all three of us, will feel if our last meeting is bitter and devoid of love."

Gabriel, too agitated to remain seated, also stood and paced about. "Bento, why do you keep saying 'last'? Last time we will see you, last request, last meeting? How long is the *cherem*? When will it end? I've heard of one-day *cherems* or one-week *cherems*."

Bento swallowed and looked into the eyes of his brother and sister. "This will be a different type of *cherem*. I know about *cherems*, and if they do it properly, this *cherem* will have no end. It will be for a lifetime, and it will be irreversible."

"Go back to the rabbi," said Rebekah. "Take his offer, Bento, please. We all make mistakes when we are young. Rejoin us. Honor God. Be the Jew you are. Be your father's son. Rabbi Mortera will pay you for life. You can read, study, do anything you want, think anything you want. Just keep it to yourself. Take his offer, Bento. Don't you see that for the sake of our father he is paying you not to commit suicide?"

"Please," Gabriel clasped Bento's hand, "take his offer. Make a new start."

"He would be paying me to do something I cannot do. I intend to pursue truth and to devote my life to knowing God, whereas the rabbi's offer demands I live dishonestly and thus dishonor God. I shall never do that. I shall follow no power on earth other than my own conscience."

Rebekah began to sob. She put her hands behind her head and rocked as she said, "I don't understand you, don't understand, don't understand."

Bento went to her and put his hand on her shoulder. She shrugged it away, then raised her head and turned to Gabriel. "You were too young, but I remember, as if it were yesterday, our blessed father bragging that Rabbi Mortera called Bento the best student he'd ever seen."

She looked at Bento, tears cascading down her face. "The cleverest and the deepest, he said. How our father beamed when he heard you might be the next great scholar, perhaps the next Gersonides. That you would write the great seventeenth-century Torah commentary! The rabbi believed in you. He said that your mind retained everything and that none of the synagogue elders could stand up to you in debate. And yet now, *despite* this, *despite* your God-given gifts, look at what you've done. How could you throw everything away?" Rebekah took the handkerchief Gabriel held out.

Bending to look directly into her eyes, Bento said, "Rebekah, please try to understand. Maybe not now but perhaps sometime in the future you will understand these words: I took my own path *because* of my gifts, not *despite* them. Do you understand? *Because* of my gifts, not *despite* them."

"No, I do *not* understand it, and I shall *never* understand you, even though I have known you since birth, even though the three of us slept in the same bed for so many years after mother died."

"I remember," said Gabriel. "I remember us sleeping together and you reading us stories from the Bible, Bento. And secretly teaching both Rebekah and Miriam to read. I remember how you said it was so unfair that girls weren't taught to read."

"I told my husband that," said Rebekah. "I tell him everything: I told him how you taught us, and read to us, and questioned everything, all the miracles. And how you used to run to father and ask, 'Father, father, did that really happen?' I remember your reading to us about Noah and the flood and asking father whether God could really be so cruel. You asked, 'Why did he drown everyone? And how did the human race start again?' And 'Who could Noah's children marry?'—the same question you asked about Cain and Abel. Samuel believes those were the first signs of your malady. A curse from birth. Sometimes I think I'm to blame. I confessed to my husband that I used to giggle at everything you said, all your blasphemous remarks. Maybe I encouraged you to think that way."

Bento shook his head. "No, Rebekah, take no blame for my curiosity. It is my nature. Why do we seek to take blame for something happening for reasons outside of ourselves? Remember how father blamed himself for our brother's death? How many times did we hear him say that if he hadn't sent Isaac to make deliveries of coffee beans into other neighborhoods, he would never have caught the plague. It's Nature's course. We can't control it. Taking blame is just a way of deceiving ourselves into thinking we are powerful enough to control Nature. And, Rebekah, please know that I respect your husband. Samuel is a fine man. It's just that we disagree about the source of knowledge. I don't believe that questioning is a malady. Blind obedience without questioning is the malady."

Rebekah had no reply. The three lapsed into silence until Gabriel asked, "Bento, a forever *cherem*? Is there such a thing? I've never heard of it."

"I'm sure that's what they will do, Gabriel. Rabbi Mortera says they must do this to show the Dutch we can govern ourselves. Perhaps it's best for everyone. It will reunite you and Rebekah with your community. You will have to join with the others and obey the *cherem*. You must be a part of the shunning. You, like everyone else, must obey the law and avoid me."

"Best for everyone, Bento?" asked Gabriel. "How can you speak like that? How can it be best for you? How is it best to live among people who despise you?"

"I will not stay here; I'll live elsewhere."

"Where could you live?" asked Rebekah. "Are you planning to convert to Christianity?"

"No. Rest easy about that. I find much wisdom in the words of Jesus. They are similar to the central message in our Bible. But I shall never ascribe to any superstitious views about a God who, like any human, has a son and sends him on a mission to save us. Like all religions, including our own, the Christians imagine a God who has human attributes and human desires and needs."

"But where will you live, if you're going to remain a Jew?" asked Rebekah. "A Jew can live only with Jews."

"I'll find a way to live without a Jewish community."

"Bento, you may be gifted, but you're also a simple-minded child," Rebekah said. "Have you really thought it through? Have you forgotten Uriel da Costa?"

"Who?" asked Gabriel.

"Da Costa was a heretic who got a *cherem* from Rabbi Modena, Rabbi Mortera's teacher," said Rebekah. "You were still an infant, Gabriel. Da Costa challenged all our laws—the Torah, the skullcap, the tefillin, circumcision, even the mezuzahs on our doors—just like your brother. Worst of all he denied the immortality of our soul and the resurrection of the body. One by

one other Jewish communities in Germany and Italy also expelled him by
cherem. No one here wanted him, but he kept pleading to come back. Finally
we accepted him. Then he started his lunacy again. And once again he
begged for forgiveness, and the synagogue held a ceremony of penance. You
were far too young, Gabriel, but Bento and I saw that ceremony together.
Do you remember?"

Bento nodded, and Rebekah continued, "In the synagogue he had to
strip, and he received thirty-nine terrible lashes to his back and then after
the ceremony ended had to lie down in the doorway while everyone in the
entire congregation stepped on him as they left, and all the children chased
him and spit on him. We didn't join them—father wouldn't permit it. A
short time after that he took a gun and shot himself in the head."

"That's what happens," she said, turning to Bento. "There is no life outside of the community. He couldn't do it, and you won't either. How will
you live? You will have no money—you won't be permitted to run a business
in this community—and Gabriel and I will be forbidden to help you. Miriam
and I took an oath to our mother that we'd take care of you, and when
Miriam was dying, she asked me to look out for you and Gabriel. But now
I can do nothing more. How will you live?"

"I don't know, Rebekah. My needs are few. You know that. Look around."
He swept his arm around the room. "I can do with little."

"But answer me, how will you live? Without money. Without friends?"

"I am thinking of working with glass for a living. Grinding lenses. I
think I'll be good at that."

"Glass for what?"

"Spectacles. Magnifying glasses. Maybe even telescopes."

Rebekah looked at her brother in amazement. "A Jew grinding glass.
What has happened to you, Bento? Why are you so bizarre? You have no
interest in real life. Not in a woman, a wife, a family. You used to say all the
time when we were children that you wanted to marry me, but for years—
ever since your bar mitzvah—you've never mentioned marriage again, and
I've never heard you take any interest in any woman. It's unnatural. You
know what I think? I think you never recovered from our mother's death.
You watched her die, wheezing and struggling to breathe. It was awful. I remember how you held my hand on the funeral barge taking her body to
Beth Haim burial ground at Ouderkerk. You would not speak a word that

whole day—you just fixated on the horse pulling the barge along the canal. The neighbors and friends were wailing and keening so loud that the Dutch bailiffs boarded and hushed us. And then, all through the burial ceremony, you had your eyes closed as though you were sleeping standing up. You didn't see how they circled mother's body seven times. I pinched you when she was placed in the ground, and you opened your eyes and were terrified and tried to run away when everyone started throwing handfuls of dirt on her. Maybe it was too much—maybe you were scorched too badly by her death. You hardly talked for weeks after that. Maybe you never got over it, and you won't risk loving another woman, won't risk another loss, another death like that. Maybe that's why you won't let anyone matter to you."

Bento shook his head. "That's not right, Rebekah. *You* matter to me. And Gabriel matters to me. Never seeing you again will be painful. You speak as though I'm not human."

Rebekah continued as though she hadn't heard him, "I believe you haven't recovered from all the deaths. At our brother Isaac's death you showed so little feeling, as though you weren't even comprehending it. And then when Father told you that you had to stop your rabbinical studies to take over the shop, you simply nodded. In one instant your whole life was changed, and yet you just nodded. As though it were of little matter."

"That doesn't make sense," said Gabriel. "Losing our parents is not the explanation. I've lived in this same family, suffered the same deaths, and I don't think like Bento. I want to be a Jew. I want a wife and family."

"And," said Bento, "when did you hear me say a family was unimportant? I am full of happiness for you, Gabriel. I love the idea of you starting your family. It deeply pains me to think I shall never see your children."

"But you love ideas, not people," interjected Rebekah. "Maybe it comes from the way Father raised you. You remember the honey board?"

Bento nodded.

"What?" asked Gabriel.

"When Bento was very young, maybe three or four—I don't remember—Father taught him how to read with a strange method. Later he told me it was common teaching practice hundreds of years ago. He gave Bento a board on which was painted the entire *aleph, bet, gimmel* and covered it with honey. He told Bento to lick off all the honey. Father thought it would help Bento love the Hebrew letters and love language.

"Maybe it worked too well," Rebekah continued. "Maybe *that's* why you care more about books and ideas than you care for people."

Bento hesitated. Anything he might say would make matters worse. Neither his sister nor his brother could open their minds to his ideas, and perhaps that was best after all. If he succeeded in helping them see the problems of blind obedience to the authority of the rabbi, then their hopes of contentment in their marriages and their community would be jeopardized. He would have to leave them without their blessing.

"I know you're angry, Rebekah, and you, too, Gabriel. And when I see this from your viewpoint, I can understand why. But you cannot see it from mine, and it saddens me that we must part without understanding. Small comfort that it may be, my parting words are these: I promise you that I shall live a holy life and follow the words of the Torah by loving others, doing no harm, following the path of virtue, and directing my thoughts upon our infinite and eternal God."

But Rebekah was not listening. She had more to say. "Think of your father, Bento. He does not lie next to his wives, neither our mother nor Esther. He lies in hallowed ground next to the holiest of men. He lies in his eternal sleep, honored for his devotion to the synagogue and to our law. Our father knew about the imminent arrival of the Messiah, and he knew about the immortality of the soul. Think—think how he would feel about his son Baruch. Think how he *does* feel, because his spirit does not die. It hovers, it sees, it knows the heresy of his chosen son. He curses you at this moment!"

Bento could not restrain himself. "You are doing precisely what the rabbis and scholars do. And this is precisely where they and I part company. You all proclaim with such certainty that our father's spirit watches me and curses me. Whence cometh your certainty? Not from the Torah! I know it by heart, and it doesn't contain a word of this. There is no evidence whatsoever for your claims about Father's spirit. I know you hear such fairy tales from our rabbis, but don't you see how it serves their purposes? They control us by fear and hope: *fear* of what will happen after death and *hope* that if we live in some particular fashion—one that is good for the congregation and for the continued authority of the rabbis—we will enjoy a blissful life in the world to come."

Rebekah had put her hands over her ears, but Bento merely spoke louder, "I say to you that when the body dies, the soul dies. *There is no world to come.* I shall not permit the rabbis or anyone else to forbid me to reason, for it is only through reason that we can know God, and this quest is the only true source of blessedness in this life."

Rebekah stood and prepared to leave. She moved close to Bento and looked into his eyes. "I love you as you once were in our family," and she hugged him. "And now"—she slapped him hard in the face—"I hate you." She grabbed Gabriel's hand and tugged him out of the room.

CHAPTER EIGHTEEN

MUNICH—1919

The next morning, while Alfred waited for Spinoza's book in the library line, a dream from the night before drifted into his mind: *I'm walking and talking with Friedrich in the forest. Suddenly he vanishes, and I'm alone and pass other people who seem not to see me. I feel invisible. I am unseen. Then the forest darkens. I feel frightened.* That was all he could recall. There was more, he knew, but he could not retrieve it. Strange, he thought, how fleeting dreams could be. In fact he had not even remembered having a dream at all until this snippet simply popped into his mind. The recollection must have been prompted by a linkage between Spinoza and Friedrich. Here he was in line to get Spinoza's *Theological-Political Treatise*, the book that Friedrich had suggested he read before attempting to read the *Ethics*. How odd that Friedrich came to mind so often—after all, they had only met twice. No, that wasn't entirely true. Friedrich knew him as a child. Perhaps it was simply the singular, oddly personal nature of their conversation.

When Alfred arrived in the office, Eckart had not yet put in an appearance. That was not unusual, as Eckart drank heavily every evening and his morning working hours were irregular. Alfred began browsing through the preface of Spinoza's book, which described what he intended to prove. No problem reading *this* book—the prose was crystal clear. Friedrich was right, it was a mistake to have started with the *Ethics*. The very first page riveted Alfred's attention. "Fear breeds superstition," he read. And: "Weak and greedy people in adversity use prayers and womanish tears to implore help from God." How could a seventeenth-century Jew have written that? Those were the words of a twentieth-century German!

The next page described how the "pomp and ceremony invested in religion clogs the mind of men with dogmatism, crowds out sound reason leaving not enough room for even a modicum of doubt." Amazing! And it didn't stop there! Spinoza went on to speak of religion as "a tissue of ridiculous mysteries" that attracts men "who flatly despise reason." Alfred gasped. His eyes grew wider.

The Hebrews as God's "chosen people"? "Nonsense," said Spinoza. An informed and honest reading of Mosaic law, Spinoza insisted, revealed that God favored the Jews only by selecting for them a thin strip of territory where they could live in peace.

And scripture the "word of God"? Spinoza's powerful prose scattered that idea to the winds as he claimed that the Bible contains only spiritual truth—namely, the practice of justice and charity—not terrestrial truths. All those who find terrestrial laws and truths in the Bible are mistaken or self-interested, Spinoza insisted.

The preface ended with a warning, "I ask the multitude not to read my book," and went on to explain that the "superstitious, unlearned populace, who hold that reason is nothing but a handmaid to theology, will gain nothing from this work. Indeed their faith may be disturbingly unsettled."

Stunned by these words, Alfred could not help marveling at Spinoza's audacity. The short, biographical introduction stated that though the book was published anonymously in 1670 (when Spinoza was thirty-eight) the identity of the author was widely known. To state these words in 1670 took courage: 1670 was only two generations after Giordano Bruno was burned at the stake for heresy and only a single generation after Galileo's trial by the Vatican. The introduction noted that the book was quickly banned by the state, by the Catholic Church, by the Jews, and soon after, by the Calvinists. All that spoke well for it.

There could be no denying the extraordinary intelligence of the author. Now, finally, finally, he understood why the great Goethe and all the other Germans he loved so much—Schelling, Schiller, Hegel, Lessing, Nietzsche— revered this man. How could they not admire a mind like this? But, of course, they lived in another century and knew nothing about the new science of race, nothing of the dangers of poisoned blood—they simply admired this mutation, this extraordinary blossom emerging from slime. Alfred looked at the title page: "Benedictus de Spinoza"—hmm, Benedictus, a name with the greatest possible distance from a Semitic name. The biographical sketch noted that he was excommunicated by the Jews in his twenties and never again had contact with a Jew. So he was not truly a Jew. He was a mutation—the Jews recognized he was not a Jew, and, in taking this name, he must have realized it too.

Dietrich appeared by eleven and spent much of the day teaching Alfred how to be a more effective editor. Soon he was given the responsibility of editing most of the work submitted to the paper. Within weeks, Alfred's red pencil moved lightning fast as he skillfully elevated the style and intensity of others' work. Alfred felt blessed; not only did he have a superb teacher, but he was Dietrich's only "child." However, soon that was to change. A littermate for Alfred was on his way—a littermate who would take up all the room.

The change was set into motion several weeks later, in September 1919, when Anton Drexler, the man who had welcomed Alfred to the Thule Society, appeared at the office in an excited state. Dietrich was about to close his door for a private talk when Drexler, with Dietrich's approval, beckoned Alfred to enter.

"Alfred, let me orient you," Drexler said. "You know, I am sure, that not long after your first meeting at the Thule Society, several of us started a new political party—the German Workers Party? I recall you attended one of the first meetings, a small one. But now we're ready to expand. Dietrich and I want to invite you to attend our next meeting and write a lead article on the party. We're one among a legion of parties and need to make ourselves more prominent."

Alfred, after glancing at Eckart, whose sharp nod suggested that the invitation was more than an invitation, replied, "I shall make it a point of attending the very next meeting."

Drexler seemed satisfied. He closed the door and gestured to Alfred to take a seat. "So, Dietrich, I think we've found the one you've been waiting for. Let me tell you what's happened. You remember, of course, that when we decided to turn the party from a Thule members' debating society into an active political party with open meetings, we had to apply to the army for permission? And we were notified that military observers would periodically attend our meetings?"

"I remember and fully approve of that regulation. It's necessary to keep the Communists in line."

"Well," Drexler continued, "at a meeting last week with about twenty-five or thirty attendees, this rather coarse-looking, poorly dressed man arrived late and sat in the last row. Carl, our bodyguard and bouncer, whispered to me that he's an army observer in civilian clothes and has been seen at other political meetings, and at theaters and clubs, looking for dangerous agitators."

"So this observer—his name is Hitler, a corporal in the army, but to be discharged in a few months—remained entirely silent as he listened to the main speaker giving a dull talk on the elimination of capitalism. But then, in the ensuing discussion period, things got lively. Someone in the audience made a long statement favoring that stupid plan that's floating around for Bavaria to break away from Germany and merge with Austria into a South German state. Well, instantaneously, this Hitler got enraged, bolted to his feet, strode to the front of the room, and delivered a blistering attack on that idea or any proposal that deliberately weakened Germany. He continued for a few minutes excoriating enemies of Germany—those allied with the Versailles criminals who are trying to murder our country, fragment us, deprive of our glorious destiny—and so on.

"It was a wild tantrum, and he looked like a madman on the brink of losing all control. The audience was stirring uneasily, and I was about to ask Carl to remove him—I hesitated only because, well, he's from the army. But just then, as though he knew what I was thinking, he took hold of himself, regained restraint, and delivered a stunning fifteen-minute, far-ranging, impromptu speech. Nothing original in the content. His views—anti-Jews, pro-military, anti-Communist—parallel our own. But his delivery was astounding. After a few minutes, everyone, and I mean everyone, was transfixed, their attention riveted to his blazing blue eyes and to his every word. This man has a gift. I knew it instantaneously, and after the meeting I ran after him and gave him my pamphlet, *My Political Awakening*. I also handed him my card and invited him to contact me to learn more about the party."

"And?" Eckart asked.

"Well, he visited me last night. We talked at length about the aims and goals of the party, and he is now member number 555 and will address the party at the next meeting."

"Five hundred fifty-five?" interjected Alfred. "Amazing! You're grown that large already?"

"Between us, and only between us, Alfred, it's 55," Drexler whispered. "For publication we want you to add a digit and make it 555. We'll be taken more seriously if we're thought to be larger."

A few nights later, Eckart and Alfred went together to hear Corporal Hitler speak. Afterward, they were to dine at Eckart's home. Hitler strode confidently to the front of the audience of forty and with no introduction launched quickly into an impassioned warning of the danger posed to Germany by the Jews. "I have come," he spat out, "to warn you about the Jews and to urge a new kind of anti-Semitism. I urge an anti-Semitism based on fact, not emotions. Emotional anti-Semitism leads only to ineffective pogroms. That is not the solution. We need more, far more, than that. We need a rational anti-Semitism. Rationality leads us to only one absolutely unshakeable conclusion: the elimination of Jews from Germany altogether."

Then he issued another warning. "The revolution that swept the crowned head of Germany from power must not open the door for Judeo-Bolshevism."

Alfred was startled by Hitler's term "Judeo-Bolshevism." He had been using that exact phrase for some time, and here this corporal was thinking in the same way—using the same words. That was both bad and good. Bad because he felt proprietary about the term, but good because he realized he had a forceful ally.

"Let me tell you more about the Jewish danger," Hitler continued. "Let me tell you more about rational anti-Semitism. It's not because of the Jews' religion. Their religion is no worse than the others—they're all part of the same great religious swindle. And it's not because of their history or abominable parasitic culture—though their sins against Germany through the centuries are legion. No, these things are not the reason. The real issue is their race, their tainted blood that is every day, every hour, every minute, weakening and threatening Germany.

"The tainted blood can never become pure. Let me tell you about the Jews that choose baptism, the converted Christian Jews. They are the worst kind. They pose the greatest danger. They will insidiously infect and destroy our great country, just as they have destroyed every great civilization."

Alfred jerked his head at this statement. He's right, he's right, he thought. This Hitler reminded him of what he knew. The blood cannot be changed.

Once a Jew, always a Jew. Alfred needed to rethink his whole approach to the Spinoza problem.

"And now, today"—Hitler continued and began to pound on his chest with each point—"you must realize you cannot turn a blind eye to this problem. Nor can small steps solve this problem—this problem of whether our nation can ever recover its health. The Jewish germ must be eradicated. Don't be misled into thinking you can fight a disease without killing the carrier, without destroying the bacillus. Do not think you can fight racial tuberculosis without taking care to rid the nation of the carrier of that racial tuberculosis."

Hitler made each point with a voice that grew more and more shrill, each sentence at a higher pitch, until it seemed certain his voice would crack into slivers—but it never did. When he ended by screaming, *"This Jewish contamination will not subside, this poisoning of the nation will not end until the carrier himself, the Jew, has been banished from our midst,"* the entire audience leapt to its feet, applauding wildly.

Dinner that evening at Eckart's home was intimate—only four were present: Alfred, Drexler, Eckart, and Hitler. But this was a different Hitler—not the chest-pounding, angry Hitler but a polite, gracious Hitler.

Eckart's wife, Rosa, a refined woman, escorted them into the parlor but after a few minutes discreetly retired, leaving the four men to their private conversation. Eckart, with an affable flourish, brought up one of his best wines from his cellar, but his exuberance was dashed to find that Hitler was a teetotaler and Alfred a one-glass man. He was dashed even more to learn that Hitler was a vegetarian and would not partake of the steaming roasted goose that the housekeeper proudly carried into the dining room. After the housekeeper quickly prepared some scrambled eggs and potato for Hitler, the four ate and talked for over three hours.

"So, Herr Hitler, tell us about your current assignment and your future in the army," Eckart prompted.

"There is not much future for the army since the Versailles Treaty—may it be cursed forever—has set a limit of one hundred thousand soldiers and no limits at all for our enemies. This shrinkage means I'll be mustered out in about six months. Currently I have few duties aside from observing meetings of the most threatening of our fifty political parties now operating in Munich."

"And why is the German Workers Party considered threatening?" asked Eckart.

"Because of your word 'workers.' That arouses suspicions of Communist influence. But, Herr Eckart, I assure you that after my report, the army shall offer you nothing but support. It is a dangerous situation for us all. The Bolsheviks were responsible for the Russian surrender in the war, and now they are dedicated to infiltrating Germany and turning us into a Bolshevist state."

"You and I spoke yesterday," said Drexler, "about the recent wave of assassinations of leftist leaders. Would you mind repeating to Herr Eckart and Herr Rosenberg how you think the army and the police should respond?"

"I believe there are far too few assassinations, and if it were left to me, I'd supply more bullets to the assassins."

Eckart and Drexler both smiled broadly at that answer, and Eckart inquired, "And your view of our party thus far?"

"I like what I see. I agree entirely with the party platform, and after thinking the matter through, I have no misgivings whatsoever about casting my lot with your party."

"And our small size?" asked Drexler. "Alfred, our journalist here, was a trifle startled to learn that our first five hundred soldiers were of the mythic variety."

"Ah, as a journalist," Hitler turned to Alfred, "I hope you will come to agree that the truth is whatever the public believes. To speak frankly, Herr Drexler, our small size is, for me, an advantage, not a disadvantage. I have my military pay, few demands from my commanding officer, and for the next six months I plan to work unceasingly for the party and hope soon to put my imprint upon it."

"May I take the liberty of asking for more information about your army service, Herr Hitler?" Eckart asked. "What particularly interests me is your rank. You have so much obvious leadership potential. You should be of high rank, and yet you are a corporal?"

"You must pose that question to my superior officers. I suspect they would say I was potentially a great leader but that I too strongly resisted being a follower. But what is more pertinent are the facts." He turned to Alfred to make sure that he was taking notes. "I was awarded two Iron Crosses for bravery. Check that with the army, Herr Rosenberg. A good journalist needs to check the facts, even though there are times he may not choose to use them. And I was wounded twice in front-line action. The first time was shrapnel wounds to my leg. But rather than enjoy a long convalescence, I insisted on returning immediately to my regiment. The second was a gift from our British friends—mustard gas. Several of us were blinded temporarily and survived only because one was merely half-blinded. He led us, each holding on to the next in a chain of hands, from the front to medical care. I was treated at Pasewalk Hospital and discharged about a year ago, with some damage to my vocal chords."

Alfred, busily taking notes, looked up to say, "Your vocal cords sounded hale and hearty tonight."

"Yes, I thought so. It's strange, but those who knew me before the injury say that the chlorine gas seemed to have made my voice stronger. Trust me, I shall not fail to use it against the French and British criminals."

"You're an excellent speaker, Herr Hitler," said Eckart, "and I think you'll become invaluable to our party. Tell me: have you had any professional training in public speaking?"

"Only briefly, in the army. On the basis of a few impromptu speeches to other soldiers I was given a couple of hours' training and assigned to lecture returning German prisoners of war on the major dangers to Germany: Communism, the Jews, and pacifism. My army record contains a report from my commanding officer calling me a 'born orator.' I believe that. I have a gift, and I intend to use it in the service of our party."

Eckart continued asking questions about Hitler's education and reading. Alfred was surprised to hear he had been a painter and sympathized with his outrage at Jews controlling the Viennese Art Academy and denying him entry to the painting school. They agreed to sketch together sometime. At the end of the evening, as the guests were preparing to leave, Eckart asked Alfred to remain a bit longer to discuss some work issues. When they were alone, Eckart poured some brandy for the two of them, ignoring Alfred's refusal, and said, "Well, Alfred, he's arrived. I believe tonight we've seen the future of Germany. He's coarse and rough-hewn—many deficits, I know. But there is power, much power! And all the right sentiments. Do you not agree?"

Alfred was hesitant. "I see what you see. But when I think about elections, I envision large segments of Germany who might not agree. Can they embrace a man who has not spent a single day at university?"

"One vote per man. The great majority, like Hitler, have had their school-ing on the streets."

Alfred ventured yet further: "Yet I believe the greatness of Germany emanates from our great souls—Goethe, Kant, Hegel, Schiller, Leibniz. Don't you agree?"

"That is precisely why I've asked you to stay. He needs . . . what shall I say? Polishing. Completion. He's a reader but a highly selective one, and we need to fill in the gaps. That, Rosenberg, will be our job—yours and mine. But we must be deft and subtle. I sense great pride in him, and the herculean task lying before us is to educate him without his knowing it."

Alfred walked home with a heaviness to his step. The future had grown clearer. A new drama was opening upon the stage, and though he was now certain he would be a cast member, his assigned role was not the one he had dreamed of.

CHAPTER NINETEEN

AMSTERDAM—JULY 27, 1656

T he exterior of the Talmud Torah Synagogue, the major synagogue
of the Sephardic Jews, resembled the exterior of any other house
on the Houtgracht, a large and busy boulevard where many of Amsterdam's Sephardic Jews lived. But with its lavish Moorish furnishings,
the synagogue's interior belonged to another world. Against the side wall—
the wall closest to Jerusalem—stood an elaborately carved Holy Ark containing
the Sifrei Torah hidden behind a dark red velvet, embroidered curtain. In
front of the Ark a wooden bimah served as a platform on which the rabbi,
the cantor, the reader of the day, and other dignitaries stood. All windows
were covered with heavy drapes embroidered with birds and vines, pre-
venting any passerby from seeing the synagogue interior.

The synagogue served as a Jewish community center, Hebrew school,
and house of prayer for simple morning services, lengthier Sabbath ceremonies, and the festive celebrations of the High Holidays.

Not many people regularly attended the short, weekday prayer services;
often there were only ten men—the required minyan—and if ten were not
present, then an urgent street search was launched for additional men.
Women, of course, could not be part of the minyan. On the morning of
Thursday, July 27, 1656, however, there were not ten quiet pious worshippers
but nearly three hundred clamoring congregation members occupying every
seat and every inch of standing room. Present were not only regular, weekday
worshippers and Sabbath Jews but even the rarely seen "High Holiday Jews."

The reason for the hubbub and momentous turnout? The frenzy was
fueled by the same thrill, the same horror and dark fascination that, through

the ages, had inflamed crowds rushing to witness crucifixions, hangings, be-headings, and autos-da-fé. Throughout the Jewish community of Amsterdam word had spread swiftly that Baruch Spinoza was to be excommunicated.

Cherems were commonplace in Amsterdam's seventeenth-century Jewish community. A *cherem* was issued every several months, and every adult Jew had witnessed many. But the enormous crowd of July 27 anticipated no ordinary *cherem*. The Spinoza family was well-known to every Amsterdam Jew. Baruch's father and his uncle, Abraham, often had served on the *mahamad*, the governing board of the synagogue, and both men lay buried in the cemetery's most hallowed ground. Yet it is the fall from grace of the most highly placed that has always most excited crowds: the dark side of admiration is envy combined with disgruntlement at one's own ordinariness.

Of ancient lineage, *cherems* were first described in the second century BCE, in the Mishnah, the earliest written compilation of oral rabbinical traditions. A systematic compendium of offenses warranting *cherem* was compiled in the fifteenth century by Rabbi Joseph Caro in his influential book *The Prepared Table (Shulchan Arukh)*, which was widely printed and well-known to seventeenth-century Amsterdam Jews. Rabbi Caro listed a large number of offenses warranting *cherem*, including gambling, behaving lewdly, failing to pay one's taxes, publicly insulting fellow community members, marrying without parental consent, committing bigamy or adultery, disobeying a decision of the *mahamad*, disrespecting a rabbi, engaging in theological discussion with Gentiles, denying the validity of oral rabbinic law, and questioning the immortality of the soul or the divine nature of the Torah.

It was not only the *who* and the *why* of the impending *cherem* that incited curiosity among the crowd at Talmud Torah Synagogue: rumors presaged extreme severity. Most *cherems* were mild, public rebukes, resulting in a fine or being shunned for days or weeks. In more serious cases involving blasphemy, the sentence typically was longer—in one case, eleven years. Yet reinstatement always was possible if the individual was willing to repent and to accept some prescribed penalty—generally, a large fine or, as in the case of the infamous Uriel da Costa, public lashing. But in the days leading to July 27, 1656, rumors had circulated about a *cherem* of unprecedented severity.

According to custom for *cherem*, the synagogue interior was lit only by candles of black wax, seven resting on a large, hanging chandelier and twelve in surrounding wall niches. Rabbi Mortera and his assistant, Rabbi Aboab, who had returned from thirteen years in Brazil, stood side by side on the bimah in front of the Holy Ark, flanked by the six members of the parnassim. Waiting solemnly until the congregation grew quiet, Rabbi Mortera held aloft a Hebrew document and, without greeting or opening statement, read the Hebrew proclamation in his booming voice. Most of the congregation listened in silence. The few who understood spoken Hebrew whispered in Portuguese to their neighbors, who in turn passed the information along the rows. By the time Rabbi Mortera had finished reading, the congregation's mood had grown sober, almost grim.

Rabbi Mortera took two steps back as Rabbi Aboab stepped forward and began to translate the Hebrew *cherem*, word for word, into Portuguese.

The Lords of the Parnassim announce that, having long known of the evil opinions and acts of Baruch de Spinoza, they have endeavored by various means and promises to turn him from his evil ways. But having failed to make him mend his wicked ways, and, on the contrary, daily receiving more and more serious information about the abominable heresies that he practiced and taught and about his monstrous deeds, and having for this numerous trustworthy witnesses who have deposed and born witness to this effect in the presence of the said Spinoza, they became convinced of the truth of this matter; and after all of this has been investigated in the presence of the honorable rabbis, they have decided that the said Spinoza should be excommunicated and expelled from the people of Israel.

"Abominable heresies"? "Evil acts"? "Monstrous deeds"? Murmuring arose from the congregation. Astonished members searched one another's faces. Many had known Baruch Spinoza for his entire life. Most admired him, and none knew of any involvement with wickedness, monstrous deeds, or abominable heresies. Rabbi Aboab continued:

By decree of the angels and by the command of the holy men, we excommunicate, expel, curse, and damn Baruch Spinoza with the consent of God, Blessed be He, and with the consent of the entire holy congregation, and in front of these holy scrolls with the 613 precepts which are written therein; cursing him with the excommunication with which Joshua banned Jericho and with the curse which Elisha cursed the boys and with all the castigations which are written in the Book of the Law.

From the men's section of the congregation, Gabriel searched the women's area for Rebekah, trying to gauge her reaction to this violent cursing of their brother. Gabriel had witnessed *cherems* before but never one with such vehemence. And it immediately got worse. Rabbi Aboab continued:

Cursed be Baruch Spinoza by day, and cursed be he by night; cursed be he when he lies down, and cursed be he when he rises up. Cursed be he when he goes out, and cursed be he when he comes in. The Lord will not spare him, but then the anger of the Lord and his jealousy shall lie upon him, and the Lord shall blot out his name from under heaven. And the Lord shall separate him unto evil out of all the tribes of Israel, according to all the curses of the covenant that are written in this Book of the Law. But you that cleave unto the Lord your God are alive every one of you this day.

As Rabbi Aboab retreated, Rabbi Mortera stepped forward and glared at the congregation, as if to make eye contact with every member, then slowly, laying emphasis upon each syllable, he pronounced the shunning:

We order that no one should communicate with Baruch Spinoza, neither in writing nor accord him any favor nor stay with him under the same roof nor within four cubits in his vicinity, nor read any treatise composed or written by him.

Rabbi Mortera nodded to Rabbi Aboab. Without a word, the men locked arms and descended in unison from the bimah. Then, followed by the six members of the parnassim, they strode down the aisle and out of the synagogue. The congregation broke into raucous clamor. Not even the eldest of members could recall a *cherem* so harsh. There had been no mention of repentance or reinstatement. Everyone in the congregation appeared to understand the implications of the rabbi's words. This *cherem* was forever.

CHAPTER TWENTY

MUNICH—MARCH 1922

As the weeks passed Alfred changed his opinion about his assigned role. No longer onerous, it was now a glorious opportunity, the perfect role for him to exert vast influence upon the fate of the Fatherland. The party was still small, but Alfred knew it was the party of the future.

Hitler lived in a small apartment near the office and almost daily visited Eckart, who mentored his protégé by sharpening his anti-Semitism, extending his political vision, and introducing him to prominent right-wing Germans. Three years later Hitler would dedicate the second volume of *Mein Kampf* to Dietrich Eckart, "that man who devoted his life to awakening our people in his writings, his thoughts, his deeds." Alfred, too, often saw Hitler, always in the late afternoon or evening, because Hitler kept late hours and slept till noon. They talked and walked and visited galleries and museums.

There were two Hitlers. One was Hitler the ferocious orator, who electrified and mesmerized every crowd he addressed. Alfred had never seen anything like it, and Anton Drexler and Dietrich Eckart were ecstatic to have finally found the man to lead their party into the future. Alfred attended many of the talks, and they were legion. With limitless energy Hitler spoke wherever he could find an audience, on corners of busy boulevards, on crowded trams, and, mainly, in beer halls. His fame as a speaker quickly spread, and his audiences grew—at times to over a thousand. Moreover, to make the party more inclusive Hitler suggested changing the name from the German Workers Party to the National Socialist German Workers Party (Nationalsozialistische Deutsche Arbeiterpartei, or NSDAP).

Occasionally Alfred also gave speeches to party members that Hitler generally attended and always applauded. "The thoughts were *wunderbar,*" Hitler would say. "But more fire, more fire."

And then there was the other Hitler—the amiable Hitler, the relaxed, courteous Hitler who listened to Alfred's musings on history, on aesthetics, on German literature. "We think alike," Hitler often exclaimed, oblivious of the fact that it was Alfred who planted many of the seeds now sprouting in his mind.

One day Hitler visited him in his new office at the *Völkischer Beobachter* (the People's Observer) to hand him an article on alcoholism he wished to publish. Earlier that year, the Nazi Party had purchased the Thule Society newspaper, *Münchener Beobachter*, promptly rechristened it, and turned it over to Dietrich Eckart, who closed his old newspaper and moved his entire staff to the new one. Hitler waited as Alfred read over the article and was surprised when Alfred opened his desk drawer and pulled out a draft of an article he, by sheer chance, was writing on alcoholism.

Quickly reading Alfred's article, Hitler looked up and declared, "They are twins."

"Yes, they're so similar that I'll withdraw my article," Alfred replied.

"No, I insist not. Publish both. They'll have greater impact if they're both published in the same issue."

As Hitler assumed more executive power in the party, he decreed that all party speakers submit their speeches to him before delivery. He later excused Alfred from that step—it was unnecessary, he said, because their talks were so similar. But Alfred noticed some differences. For one thing, Hitler, despite his limited formal education and the huge gaps in his knowledge, had extraordinary self-confidence. Over and over again Hitler used words like "unshakeable," implying total certainty of his convictions and total commitment to never, under any circumstance, changing a single aspect of his convictions. Alfred marveled as he listened to Herr Hitler. Where did that certainty come from? Alfred would have sold his soul for such confidence and cringed with disgust as he observed himself forever looking about for wisps of agreement and approval.

There was another difference too. Whereas Alfred often spoke of the necessity of "removing" Jews from Europe, or "resettling" or "relocating" or "evicting" the Jews, Hitler used different language. He spoke of "exterminating" or "eradicating" Jews, even of hanging all Jews from lampposts. But surely that was a matter of rhetoric, of knowing how to galvanize audiences.

As the months passed, Alfred realized that he had underestimated Hitler. This was a man of significant intelligence, an autodidact who voraciously scanned books, retained information, and had a keen appreciation of art and Wagner's music. Even so, without a systematic university education, his knowledge base was uneven and contained yawning chasms of ignorance. Alfred did his best to address them, but the task was challenging. Hitler's pride was such that Alfred could never explicitly tell him what to read. Instead he learned to tutor indirectly, for he had noted that whenever he spoke of, say, Schiller, a few days later Hitler could discourse at length and with unshakable certainty about Schiller's dramatic works.

One spring morning that year, Dietrich Eckart approached the door of Alfred's office, peered for a few moments through the glass panel at his protégé busily editing a story, and then, shaking his head, tapped on the glass and beckoned Alfred to follow him into his office. Inside he pointed to a chair.

"I have something to tell you—for Christ's sake, Alfred, stop looking so worried. You're doing fine. I'm completely satisfied with your diligence. If anything I'd suggest a little *less* diligence, a few more beers, and a lot more schmoozing. Too much work is not always a virtue. But that's for another time. Listen, you're growing valuable to our party, and I want to accelerate your development. Would you agree that editors who publish what they know about are advantaged?"

"Of course." Alfred strained to keep a smile on his face but was uneasy about what was coming. Eckart was entirely unpredictable.

"Have you visited much of Europe?"

"Very little."

"How can you write about our enemies without seeing them with your own eyes? A good warrior must stop sometimes to sharpen his weapons. Not true?"

"Without question," Alfred agreed warily.

"Then go pack your bags. Your flight to Paris leaves in three hours."

"Paris? Flight? Three hours?"

"Yes. Dimitri Popoff, one of the party's major Russian donors, has an important business meeting there. He is flying today with two associates and has agreed to raise funds from the White Russian community there. He's flying in one of the new Junker F 13s, which has room for four passengers. I had planned to accompany him, but a few inconvenient chest pains yesterday have made that impossible. My doctor and my wife forbid me to go. I want you to go in my place."

"I'm sorry about your illness, Herr Eckart. But if the doctor is advising rest, I shouldn't leave you alone with the next two editions—"

"The doctor said nothing about rest. He is simply being cautious because he knows too little about the effects of flying on this kind of condition. The editions are mostly written. I'll take care of them. Go to Paris."

"What would you like me to do there?"

"I want you to accompany Herr Popoff as he meets with potential donors. If he wishes, you will make some presentations to donors yourself. It's time for you to learn how to talk to the rich. After that you are to travel home slowly by train. Take a whole week or ten days. Be a free man. Travel wherever you want and simply observe. See how our enemies feast off the Versailles Treaty. Take notes. Everything you observe will be useful to the paper. By the way, Herr Popoff has also agreed to supply you with ample French francs. You'll need them. The deutschmark is nearly worthless abroad, thanks to inflation. It's nearly worthless here!"

"A loaf of bread costs more every day," Alfred agreed.

"Exactly. And I'm writing a piece right now for the next issue about why we must once again increase the price of the paper."

On takeoff, Alfred gripped the arms of his seat and stared out the window as Munich grew smaller by the second. Tickled by Alfred's fright, Herr Popoff, his gold teeth gleaming, yelled over the roar of the engines, "First time flying?" Alfred nodded and looked out the window, grateful that the noise made further conversation with Herr Popoff and the other two passengers impossible. He thought of Eckart's comment about schmoozing . . . why *was* he so bad at easy conversation? Why so secretive? Why didn't he tell Eckart that he had once traveled to Switzerland with his aunt and that a few years ago, just before the outbreak of the war, he and his fiancée, Hilda, had visited Paris. Perhaps he simply wished to blot out his Baltic past and to be born again as a German citizen in the Fatherland. No, no, no—he knew it ran deeper.

Opening himself had always been threatening. That was precisely why his two beer-hall conversations with Friedrich had been so extraordinary and so liberating. He tried to delve deeper into himself but, as always, lost his way. *I have to change . . . I'll go to visit Friedrich again.*

The following day Herr Popoff relied on Alfred to discuss the party's platform and to explain why the party was the only one capable of stopping the Judeo-Bolshevists. A banker wearing a dazzling diamond ring on his little finger said to Alfred, "I understand your official party name is now the National Socialist German Workers party—the Nationalsozialistische Deutsche Arbeiterpartei?"

"Yes."

"Why such a lumpish and confusing name? 'National' implies 'right,' 'socialist' left, 'German' right, and 'worker' left! It's impossible. How can your party be everything at once?"

"That's exactly what Hitler wants, to be everything to all people—except Jews and Bolshevists of course. We have a long-range plan. Our first task is to enter Parliament in great numbers over the next few years."

"Parliament? You believe the ignorant masses can rule?"

"No. But first we must achieve power. Our parliamentary democracy is fatally weakened by incursions from the Bolshevists, and I promise you we will ultimately do away with this parliamentary system altogether. Hitler has used these very words with me many times. And he has made the party goals very clear with his new platform. I've brought copies of the new twenty-five-point program."

At the end of their visits, Herr Popoff presented Alfred with a bulging envelope of French francs. "Good work, Herr Rosenberg. These francs should see you through your European travels. Your presentations were excellent, just as Herr Eckart assured me they would be. And in such fine Russian. Beautiful Russian. Everyone was favorably impressed."

A free week ahead of him! What a pleasure simply to wander wherever he wished. Eckart was right—he *had* been working too hard. As he strolled through the streets of Paris, Alfred contrasted the gaiety and opulence everywhere with the bleakness of Berlin and the poverty and agitation of

Munich. Paris showed few scars of war, its citizens seemed well-fed, restaurants were jammed, and yet France, along with England and Belgium, continued to suck Germany's life blood with draconian reparations demands. Alfred decided to spend two days in Paris—the galleries and art dealers beckoned—and then take the train north to Belgium and finally to Holland—Spinoza country. From there he would take the long train ride home via Berlin, where he would drop in on Friedrich.

In Belgium, Alfred found Brussels not to his liking and detested the sight of the Belgian legislative building, where Germany's enemies never ceased formulating new methods of pillaging the Fatherland. The following day he visited the German military cemetery at Ypres, where the Germans had suffered such horrendous losses in the world war and where Hitler had served so courageously. And then north to Amsterdam.

Alfred had no idea what he sought. He only knew that the Spinoza problem buzzed away in the back of his mind. He remained intrigued by the Jew Spinoza. *No*, he said to himself, not intrigued; be honest—you admire him—just as Goethe did. Alfred had never returned his library copy of Spinoza's *Theological-Political Treatise* and often read a few paragraphs of it in bed at night. He was a poor sleeper; for some inexplicable reason he grew anxious as soon as he got into bed, and he seemed to fight sleep. That was something else to talk about with Friedrich.

On the train he opened the *Treatise* to the page he had fallen asleep on the night before. Once again he was impressed by how intrepid Spinoza was by daring to question religious authority in the seventeenth century. Look at how he pointed out inconsistencies in the scriptures and the absurdity of considering a document to be of divine origin when it was riddled with human errors. He was especially tickled by passages in which Spinoza thumbed his nose at priests and rabbis who felt they had a privileged vision into God's meaning.

> If it be blasphemy to assert that there are any errors in scripture, what name shall we apply to those who foist onto it their own fancies, who degrade the sacred writers till they seem to write confused nonsense?

And look how Spinoza, with a flick of his wrist, dispatched Jewish mystical zealots: "I have read and known kabbalistic triflers, whose insanity provokes in me unceasing astonishment."

What a paradox! A Jew both courageous and wise. How would Houston Stewart Chamberlain respond to the Spinoza problem? Why not visit him in Bayreuth and ask him about the Spinoza problem? Yes, I will do that—and I will ask Hitler to accompany me. After all, aren't the two of us his intellectual heirs? Most likely, Chamberlain will conclude that Spinoza was not Jewish. And he would be right—how could Spinoza be a Jew? All that around-the-clock religious indoctrination, and still he rejected the Jewish God and the Jewish people. Spinoza had soul wisdom—he must have non-Jewish blood in him.

But thus far in his genealogical research he had found only that Spinoza's father, Michael D'Espinoza, had possibly come from Spain and immigrated to Portugal and then to Amsterdam in the early seventeenth century. Still, his investigations had yielded unexpected, interesting results. Just a week ago he had discovered that Queen Isabella, in the fifteenth century, proclaimed bloodstain laws (*limpiezas de sangre*) that prevented converted Jews from holding influential positions in the government and the military. She was wise enough to understand that the Jewish malignancy did not emanate from religious ideation—*it was in the blood itself.* And she put it into law! Hats off to Queen Isabella! He now revised his opinion of her. Previously, he had always connected her only with the discovery of America—that cesspool of racial mixing.

Amsterdam seemed more congenial than Brussels, perhaps because of Dutch neutrality in the world war. Joining a half-day tourist group but keeping to himself, Alfred cruised Amsterdam's canals and stopped to visit sites of interest. The last stop was at Jodenbreestraat, to visit the Great Sephardic Synagogue, which was hideous and enormous, seating two thousand and exhibiting Jewish mongrelization at its worst—such an amalgamation of Grecian pillars, arched Christian windows, and Moorish wooden carvings. Alfred imagined Spinoza standing before the central platform as he was cursed and damned by ignorant rabbis and then probably walking out secretly jubilant at his liberation. But he had to erase this image only a few minutes later when he learned from his guidebook that Spinoza had never set foot in this synagogue. It was built in 1675, about twenty years after Spinoza's excommunication, which, Alfred knew, would have prevented him from entering any synagogue or, indeed, conversing with any Jew.

Across the street was a large Ashkenazi synagogue, darker, sturdier, and less pretentious. About a block from both synagogues was the site of Spinoza's birth. The house had been demolished long ago and replaced by the massive Moses and Aaron Catholic Church. Alfred could hardly wait to tell Hitler about this. It was an example of what both felt so keenly—that Judaism and Christianity were two sides of the same coin. Alfred smiled as he recalled Hitler's apt phrase—that amazing man had such a way with words: "Judaism, Catholicism, Protestantism—what difference does it make? *They are all part of the same religious swindle.*"

The following morning he boarded a steam tram to Rijnsburg, the site of the Spinoza Museum. Though it was only a two-hour journey, the long, hard wooden benches seating six made it seem far longer. The stop closest to the small village of Rijnsburg was three kilometers from his destination, which he reached by horse-drawn cart. The museum was a small brick house with the address "29" and two plaques on the outside wall.

THE HOUSE OF SPINOZA

DOCTOR'S HOUSE FROM 1660

THE PHILOSOPHER B. DE SPINOZA LIVED HERE FROM 1660 TO 1663.

The second plaque read:

ALAS, IF ALL HUMANS WERE WISE

AND HAD MORE GOOD WILL

THE WORLD WOULD BE A PARADISE

NOW IT IS MOSTLY A HELL

Drivel, thought Alfred. Spinoza was surrounded by idiots. Walking around the building Alfred discovered that half the house was the museum and half was inhabited by a village family who used a separate entrance on the side. An old plow in the driveway suggested that they were probably farmers. The museum door was so low that Alfred had to bow his head to enter. He then had to pay an entrance fee to a shabbily dressed Jewish guard who seemed to have just awakened from a nap. The guard was a sight to behold! He obviously hadn't shaved for days, and sagging bags hung under his bleary eyes.

Alfred was the sole visitor and looked about in disappointment. The entire museum consisted of two small, eight-foot-by-ten-foot rooms, both with a small-paned window that looked out on an apple orchard in the back. One room was of little interest, containing generic seventeenth-century lens-grinding equipment, but the other, the one that excited Alfred, held Spinoza's personal library in a six-foot-long bookcase extending along the side wall and covered by glass panels badly in need of washing. A thick red tasseled cord supported by four upright stands prevented close access to the bookcase. The shelves were crammed with heavy volumes, most upright but the larger ones lying horizontal, all bound with sturdy covers dating from the seventeenth century and earlier. Here was a treasure, indeed. Alfred strained to count the titles—well over a hundred volumes. The guard, sitting on a chair in the corner, peered over his newspaper and called out, "*Honderd een en vijftig.*"

"No Dutch. I speak only German and Russian," replied Alfred, where-upon the guard instantly switched to excellent German—"*Ein hundert ein und funfzig*"—and returned to his reading.

On the adjacent wall a small glass case displayed five first editions (1670) of the *Theological-Political Treatise*—the very book Alfred carried in his small bag. Each edition was opened to the title page, and as the legend ex-plained in Dutch, French, English, and German, the publishers adjudged this book so incendiary that neither the author nor the publishing company was identified. Moreover, each of the five editions claimed to be published in a different city.

The guard beckoned Alfred to come to the desk and sign the guest reg-ister. After signing, Alfred flipped through the pages scanning the names of other guests. The guard reached over, turned back a few pages, pointed to the signature of Albert Einstein (dated November 20, 1920), and, tapping the page, proudly said, "Nobel laureate for physics. A famous scientist. He spent almost a whole day reading in this library and writing a poem to Spin-oza. Look there," he pointed to a small framed page of paper hanging on the wall behind him. "It's his handwriting—he made us a copy. It's the first stanza of his poem."

Alfred stepped over and read:

> *How I love this noble man*
> *More than I can say with words.*

Still, I fear he remains alone
With his shining halo.

Alfred felt like throwing up. *More drivel. A Jewish pseudo-scientist giving a Jewish halo to a man who rejected all things Jewish.* "Who runs this museum?" Alfred asked. "The Dutch government?"

"No, it's a private museum."

"Sponsored by? Who pays for it."

"The Spinoza Association. Freemasons. Private Jewish donors. This man here paid for the house and most of the library"—the guard flipped the pages of the huge guest register all the way to the beginning and pointed to the first signature dated 1899: George Rosenthal.

"But Spinoza was not a Jew. He was excommunicated by the Jews."

"Once a Jew, always a Jew. Why so many questions?"

"I'm a writer and the editor of a newspaper in Germany."

The guard bent over to look closely at his signature. "Aha, Rosenberg? *Bist an undzericker?*"

"What are you speaking? I don't understand."

"Yiddish. I asked if you were Jewish."

Alfred drew himself up. "Take a good look. Do I look Jewish?"

The guard looked him up and down. "Not distinguished enough," he said, and sauntered back to his chair.

Cursing under his breath, Alfred turned back to the bookcase and leaned over the guardian cord as far as he could in order to read the titles of Spinoza's books. A bit too far. He lost his balance and fell heavily against the bookcase. The guard, sitting in his corner chair, threw down his newspaper and rushed over to assure himself no damage had been done to the books. He said, "What are you doing? Are you crazy? These books are priceless."

"Trying to see the names of the books."

"Why do you have to know?"

"I'm a philosopher. I want to see where he got his ideas."

"Aha, first you're a newspaper man, and now you're a philosopher?"

"Both. I'm both a philosopher and a newspaper editor. Get it?"

The guard glared at him.

Alfred glared back at his drooping lips, the fat misshapen nose, the hair sprouting from unclean fleshy ears. "That too hard to understand?"

"I understand a lot."

"Do you understand Spinoza is an important philosopher? Why keep his books so distant? Why is there no catalogue of the books displayed? Real museums are meant to display things, not conceal them."

"You're not here to learn more about Spinoza. You're here to destroy him. To prove he stole his ideas."

"If you knew anything at all about the world at large, you'd know that every philosopher is influenced and inspired by other preceding philosophers. Kant influenced Hegel; Schopenhauer influenced Nietzsche; Plato influenced everyone. It's common knowledge that—"

"Influenced, inspired. That's the point, the very point: you didn't say 'influenced.' And you didn't say 'inspired.' Your exact words were 'where he got his ideas from.' That's different."

"Aha, Talmudic disputation is it? That's what you people like to do. You know damned well what I meant—"

"I know exactly what you meant."

"Some museum. You let Einstein, one of yours, spend the whole day studying the library and keep others three feet away."

"I promise you Herr philosopher-editor Rosenberg—you win a Nobel Prize, and you can hug every book in this library. The museum is now closing. Get out."

Alfred had seen the face of hell: A Jewish guard with authority over an Aryan, Jews blocking access to non-Jews, Jews imprisoning a great philosopher who despised Jews. He would never forget this day.

CHAPTER TWENTY-ONE

AMSTERDAM—JULY 27, 1656

Two blocks from the Talmud Torah Synagogue, Bento, with help from Dirk, his fellow student at Van den Enden Academy, packed his library of fourteen volumes into a large, wooden case and then dismantled the Spinoza family four-poster bed. The pair then loaded bed and books onto a barge on the Nieuwe Herengracht Canal for shipping to the van den Enden house, where Bento would live temporarily. Dirk accompanied Bento's goods on the barge, while Bento stayed behind to pack his remaining possessions—two pairs of trousers, brass-buckled shoes, three shirts, two white collars, underclothes, a pipe, and tobacco—into a bag that he would carry to van den Enden's house. The bag weighed little, and Bento congratulated himself on having so few possessions. If not for his bed and books, he would be able to live entirely unfettered, like a nomad.

Taking a final look around the room, Bento collected his straight razor, soap, and towel, and then he spotted, on a high shelf, his tefillin. He had not touched his tefillin since the day his father died. He reached for the two small leather boxes with their straps, and he held them gently—perhaps, he thought, for the last time. What strange objects! And strange, too, he considered, how they both repelled and beckoned him. Holding up the leather boxes, he examined each of them. Affixed to the box marked "*rosh*"—for the head—were two leather straps. To the "*yad*" box—for the arm—was attached one long strap. The hollow boxes contained verses of holy scripture written upon parchment. And, of course, everything—the leather from which the boxes had been made, the sinews used as ties, the parchment, the straps—came from kosher animals.

A memory from fifteen years earlier drifted into his mind. Often, as a child, he had watched with insatiable curiosity as his father had put on his tallit and began laying tefillin before breakfast—something his father had done every workday morning of his life. (Tefillin were never used on the Sabbath.) One day, his father had turned to him and said, "You want to know what I'm doing, don't you?"

"Yes!" Bento had replied.

"In this as in all things," his father had replied, "I follow the Torah. The words of Deuteronomy instruct us, 'And you should bind them as a sign on your hand, and they should be as frontlets between your eyes.'"

A few days later, his father came home with a gift—the very set of tefillin Bento now held in his hand.

"This is for you, Baruch, but not for today. We'll keep it until you are twelve, and then, a few weeks before your bar mitzvah, you and I will start to lay tefillin together." So excited was Bento about the prospect of laying tefillin with his father, and so often did he ply his father with questions about the precise procedure, that, in only a few days, his father acquiesced. "Today, just this one time, we'll have a rehearsal, and then, after that, we'll put away the tefillin until your time comes. Agreed?" Bento nodded eagerly.

His father continued. "We'll practice together. You do exactly what I do. You place the *yad* box on the upper part of your left arm, facing your heart, and then you wrap the leather straps seven times around your arm, ending at your wrist. See—watch me. Remember, Baruch, exactly seven times—not six times, not eight—for so the rabbis have taught us."

Next, his father chanted the prescribed blessing:

*Baruch atah Adonai Eloheinu melech ha-olam asher kid'ishanu
b'mitzvotav v'tzivanu l'hani'ach tefillin.
(Blessed are you, God, our God, sovereign of the world who has made us
holy with his commandments and commanded us to lay tefillin.)*

His father opened his prayer book and handed it to Bento and said, "Here, *you* read the prayer." But Bento did not take the book. Instead, he raised his head so that his father could see that his eyes were closed; then he repeated the prayers precisely as his father had spoken it. Once Bento heard a prayer—or any other text—he never forgot it. Beaming, his father kissed him tenderly on each cheek. "Ah what a mitzvah, what a mind. In my heart, I know that you shall be one of the greatest of all Jews."

Bento broke the reverie to taste the words "the greatest of all Jews." Tears flowed down his cheeks as he returned to his memory.

"Now, let's continue with the *tefillin shel rosh* box," his father said. "Put it on your forehead just like I'm doing—high, just above your hairline, and exactly between your eyes. Then you place the tight knot right at the nape of the neck, like I'm doing. Now, say the next prayer."

> *Baruch atah Adonai Eloheinu melech ha-olam asher kid'ishanu*
> *b'mitzvotav v'tzivanu al mitzvat yefillin.*
> *(Blessed are you, God, our God, sovereign of the world, who has made us*
> *holy with his commandments and commanded us regarding the tefillin.)*

Once more, to his father's delight, Bento repeated the prayer word for word.

"Next, you put the two hanging *rosh* straps in front of your shoulders and make sure the blackened side faces outward and the left strap must reach right here"—his father put his finger on Bento's belly button and tickled him. "And you be sure to make the right strap end a few inches lower—right by your little watering spout."

"Now we go back to the *tefillin shel yad* strap and tie it around your middle finger, three times. See how I'm doing? Then wrap it around your hand. Do you see how it forms the shape of the letter *shin* around my middle finger? I know it's hard to see. What does *shin* stand for?"

Bento shook his head.

"*Shin* is the first letter of *Shaddai* (Almighty)."

Bento recalled an unusual state of calmness brought about by winding the leather straps around his head and arms. The sense of confinement, the binding, pleased him greatly, and he felt almost merged with his father, who was bound by the leather straps in the same manner.

His father ended the lesson: "Bento, I know you won't forget any step of this, but you must resist laying tefillin until formal rehearsals just before your bar mitzvah. And after your bar mitzvah, then you'll lay tefillin every morning for the rest of your life except for? . . ."

"For the holidays and the Sabbath."

"Yes." His father kissed his cheeks. "Just like me, just like every Jew."

Bento allowed his father's image to dissolve, returned to the present, stared at the bizarre little boxes, and, for a moment, felt an ache that he would never lay tefillin again, never again feel that pleasant sense of confinement and merger. Was he acting dishonorably by failing to obey his father's wish? He shook his head. His father, blessed be his name, had come from an age hobbled by superstition. Looking again at the inscrutably tangled *rosh* and *yad* straps, Bento knew that he had made the decision that was right for him. But what to do with his father's gift, his tefillin? He couldn't simply abandon them for Gabriel to find. That would greatly wound his brother. He would have to take them with him and dispose of them later. For now, he placed the little boxes into his bag beside the razor and soap and then sat down to write a long and loving letter to Gabriel.

Halfway through, Bento realized his folly. By now, along with the entire congregation, Gabriel would have been forbidden by the *cherem* to read anything that he had written. Not wanting to cause more pain for his brother, Bento tore up his letter and quickly composed a note containing a few lines of essential information that he placed on the kitchen table:

> Gabriel—final words, alas. I have taken the bed that father left me in his will, along with my clothes, soap, and books. All else I leave to you, including our entire business—poor thing that it is.

With all of its stops along the way, Bento knew the barge carrying his bed and books would take two hours to reach van den Enden's house. On foot he could cover the distance in a half hour, so he had time to take a final walk through the streets of the Jewish neighborhood where he had spent all his life. Leaving his bag, he set off with reasonable equanimity at a brisk pace, but soon felt oppressed by the eerily quiet streets reminding him that almost every person he knew was at this moment in the synagogue listening to Rabbi Mortera curse the name of Baruch Spinoza and ordering them to shun him forever. Bento imagined the scene if he were to take this walk tomorrow: all eyes would avoid his, and crowds would divide around him, as if making way for a leper. Though he had prepared himself for this moment for months, he was unexpectedly shocked by the ache coursing through him—the ache of homelessness, of being lost, of knowing he would never again walk these memory-laden streets of his youth, the streets of Gabriel and Rebekah and all his childhood friends and neighbors, the streets once walked on by those dear ones who no longer walked on any streets on earth—his father and mother, Michael and Hanna, his stepmother, Esther, and his dead brother and sister, Isaac and Miriam. Bento continued on past a little row of shops. These streets were his last tangible connection to the dead. They and he had both trod on these same streets, and their eyes had fallen on the same sights: Mendoza's kosher butcher shop, Manuel's bakery, Simon's herring stalls. But now the connection would be ruptured; never again would he set eyes upon anything his dead father, mother, and stepmother had also seen. Solitude—he knew it now as never before.

Almost instantly, Bento observed an opposing sentiment emerging in his mind. "Freedom," he whispered to himself. "How interesting!" He had not willed this thought—it emerged to offset the pain of solitude. It was as though his mind automatically strove for equilibrium. How could that be? Was there deep within him a force independent of conscious willing, that created thoughts, offered protection, and permitted him to flourish?

"Yes, freedom," he said—Bento had long been in the habit of holding lengthy conversations with himself—"freedom is the antidote. You are finally free from the yoke of tradition. Remember how you yearned and strained for freedom—from prayer and ritual and superstition. Remember how much of your life had been in bondage to ritual. The countless hours devoted to tefillin. Chanting the appointed prayers three times a day in the synagogue and again whenever drinking water or eating an apple or any morsel of food. Whenever engaging in any event of life. Remember the endless hours reciting the alphabetical list of sins and striking your entirely innocent breast and praying for forgiveness."

Bento stopped on a bridge over the Verwers Canal and leaned on the cold stone railing to gaze at the inky water below as he recalled his study of religious commentaries. Whatever time was left from observance of ritual was devoted to reading commentary. Day after day, night after night, for hours beyond count, he had pored over the words—some banal, some brilliant—of vast armies of scholars who had spent entire lifetimes writing on the meaning and the implications of God's words in the scriptures as well as the justification and implications of the prescribed 613 mitzvoth (commandments), which controlled every aspect of Jewish life. And then, when he began the study of the Kabbalah with Rabbi Aboab, his lessons became arcane beyond belief, as he confronted the secret meanings of each letter and the ramifications of numbers assigned to each letter.

And yet none of his rabbi teachers nor ancient scholars had ever questioned the validity of their basic text or whether the books of Moses were indeed the actual words of God. When in his Jewish history class, over a dozen years ago, he had dared to question how God could have written a document with so many inconsistencies, Rabbi Mortera slowly raised his head, glared at him unbelievingly, and responded, "How can you, a mere child, a single soul, question God's authorship and presume to know of God's infinite knowledge and God's intentions? Do you not know that the presentation of the Covenant to Moses was witnessed by the tens, by the hundreds of thousands, by the entire nation of Israel? It was seen by more people than any other event in all of history."

The rabbi's tone conveyed to the class the expectation that no student should ever again raise such a foolish question. And no one ever had. Nor, it seemed to Bento, had anyone but he himself observed that the people of Israel collectively in their reverential posture toward the Torah had committed the very sin that God, through Moses, had most warned them against: idolatry. The Jews everywhere worshipped not golden idols but idols of paper and ink.

As he watched a small boat disappear into a side canal, Bento heard the sound of someone running toward him. Looking up, he saw Manny, the baker's son, his pudgy and slightly slow-witted but faithful classmate and lifelong friend. By reflex, Bento smiled and stopped to greet his friend. But without breaking stride and with no sign of recognition, Manny rushed past, over the bridge, and down the street in the direction of his father's bakery.

Bento shivered. So the *cherem* had really happened! Of course he had known that it was real—Rabbi Mortera's glare had told him, as did the empty streets and Rebekah's slap, which still stung his cheek. But it was Manny's turning away from him that brought reality crashing down. He swallowed and thought, *It is all for the better—they force me to do nothing that I would not have done of my own accord. I dreaded scandal, but since they want it that way, I enter gladly on the path that is opened to me.*

"I am no longer a Jew," Bento murmured and listened to the sound of the words. He repeated it again and again. *I am no longer a Jew. I am no longer a Jew. I am no longer a Jew.* He shivered. Life felt cold and heartless.

But life had felt cold ever since his father and his stepmother had died. As of today, he was no longer a Jew. Perhaps now, as an excommunicated Jew, he could think and write as he wished, and he would be able to hold exchanges of opinions with Gentiles.

Several months earlier, Bento had silently vowed to live blessedly in honesty and love. Now as a non-Jew he could live more peacefully. The Jews had always held that true opinions and a true plan of life arrived at by reason, rather than through prophetic Mosaic documents, had no place in the path of blessedness. Railing against reason made no sense to Bento, so now that he was a non-Jew, should he not be able to live a life of reason?

As he descended from the bridge, Bento suddenly thought, *What am I? If not a Jew, then what am I?* He reached into his pocket for the notebook he always carried—the same notebook in which van den Enden had seen him writing at their first meeting. Turning right onto a small street, he sat down by the canal's edge and looked for an answer among his written observations of the last two years, stopping to reread the comments that particularly enhanced his resolve.

> If I am among men who do not agree at all with my nature, I will hardly be able to accommodate myself to them without greatly changing myself
>
> A free man who lives among the ignorant strives as far as he can to avoid their favors
>
> A free man acts honestly, not deceptively
>
> Only free men are genuinely useful to one another and can form true friendships
>
> And it is absolutely permissible, by the highest right of Nature, for everyone to employ clear reason to determine how to live in a way that will allow him to flourish.

Bento closed his notebook, stood up, and turned back through the deserted streets toward his house to collect his belongings. Suddenly, an anguished voice behind him called, "Baruch Spinoza. Baruch Spinoza."

CHAPTER TWENTY-TWO

BERLIN—1922

B erlin on the first day of spring was much as Alfred remembered it from his brief stay in the winter of 1919. Under a granite sky, with biting cold winds and continual light rain that never seemed to reach the ground, dour shopkeepers swaddled in several layers of clothes sat in unheated shops. The Unter den Linden was empty but guarded at every street corner by soldiers. Berlin was dangerous: violent political demonstrations and assassinations of both Communists and Social Democrats were every-day happenings.

At the end of their last meeting, four years earlier, Friedrich had written "Charité Hospital, Berlin" on the note that Alfred had torn up and thrown away, only to return to the spot a few minutes later to collect the scattered pieces. Approaching a guard, Alfred asked for directions to the hospital. He inspected Alfred from shoes to crown and growled, "Your vote?"

Alfred, puzzled, asked, "What?"

"Who did you vote for?"

"Oh." Alfred drew himself up. "I'll tell you who I will vote for in future elections: Adolf Hitler and the entire anti–Jewish-Bolshevist platform of the NSADP."

"Don't know any Hitler," replied the soldier, "and never heard of the NSDAP. But I like the platform. The Charité, huh—you can't miss it—it's the largest hospital in Berlin." He pointed to a street on his left. "Down that street, straight ahead."

"Thank you much. And, sir, keep the name Hitler in mind. You're going to be voting for Adolf Hitler soon enough."

The clerk in the receiving building recognized Friedrich Pfister's name instantly. "Ah, yes, Herr Doctor Pfister is a consultant in the out-patient department for nervous and mental disorders. Down the hall to your right, out the door, and straight ahead to the next building over."

So jammed was the reception area of the next building with young to middle-aged men still wearing their grey military overcoats that Alfred needed fifteen minutes to push his way to the front desk, where he finally caught the attention of the harried receptionist by smiling politely and announcing, "Please, please, I'm a close friend of Doctor Pfister. I assure you he will want to see me."

She looked straight into his eyes. Alfred was a handsome young man. "Your name?"

"Alfred Rosenberg."

"As soon as he finishes his session I'll tell him you're out here." Twenty minutes later, she gave Alfred a warm smile and beckoned him to follow her to a large office. Wearing a band with a mirror on his head, a white coat with pockets crammed with a flashlight, pen, ophthalmoscope, and wooden tongue depressors, and a stethoscope, Friedrich awaited him.

"Alfred, what a surprise! A good surprise. I never thought to see you again. How are you? What's happened to you since we met in Estonia? What brings you to Berlin? Or do you live here? You can see I'm a bit harried by my foolishly thrusting questions at you when I have no time to hear answers. The clinic is packed, as always, but I'm finished by half past seven—will you be free then?"

"Totally free. I'm, uh, just passing through Berlin. I thought I'd take a chance on seeing you," said Alfred, silently admonishing himself, *Why don't you tell him the real reason you're here?*

"Good, good. Let's have supper and a talk. I'd enjoy that."

"I would as well.

"I'll meet you at the receptionist's desk at 7:30."

Alfred spent the afternoon trudging through the city and comparing the tawdry Berlin streets with the resplendent boulevards in Paris. When the chill was too great, he tarried in the warmest rooms of the unheated museums. At 7 he returned to the hospital waiting room, now almost empty. Friedrich arrived at exactly 7:30 and escorted Alfred to the doctor's dining room, a large, windowless, sauerkraut-scented room with many waiters scurrying about serving white-coated patrons. "You see, Alfred, it's like all of Germany: many tables, plenty of help, but little to eat."

Supper at the hospital, invariably a cold meal, consisted of thin slices of *bierwurst*, *leberwurst*, country Limburger cheese, cold boiled potatoes, and sauerkraut and pickles. Friedrich apologized. "I'm sorry it's the best I can offer. I hope you had a hot meal today?"

Alfred nodded, "Wursts on the train. They weren't bad."

"We can look forward to dessert. I've asked the cook for something special—his son is one of my patients, and he often bakes treats for me. Now," Friedrich sat back and exhaled, obviously exhausted, "finally we can relax and talk. First, let me tell you about your brother. Eugen just wrote asking if I had heard from you. We saw a good bit of one another in Berlin, but about six months ago he moved to Brussels to take a good position at a Belgian bank. He continues to be in remission from his consumption."

"Oh, no," Alfred moaned.

"What is it? Remission is *good* news."

"Yes, of course. I was responding to 'Brussels.' If only I had known. I just spent a day there."

"But how could you have known? All Germany is dislocated. Eugen wrote that he had no idea where you were living. Or how. All I could tell him from our meeting in Reval is that you were hoping to get to Germany. If you wish, I'll serve as the intermediary and give both of you the other's address."

"Yes, I want to write him."

"I'll get his address after dinner—it's in my room. But what were you doing in Brussels?"

"The long or short version?"

"The long version. I've plenty of time."

"But you must be tired. Haven't you been listening to people all day? When did you start this morning?"

"Working since seven. But talking with patients is not the same as talking with you. You and Eugen are all I have left from my life in Estonia—I was an only child, and as you may remember, my father died just before we last met. My mother died two years ago. I treasure the past—perhaps to an irrational degree. And I deeply regret our parting last time on bad terms—all because of my thoughtlessness. So the long version, please."

Alfred spoke willingly of his life during the past three years. No, it was more than willingness: a warmth seeped through his bones as he spoke, a warmth emanating from sharing his life with someone who truly wanted to hear of it. He spoke of his escape out of Reval on the last train to Berlin, the cattle truck to Munich, the chance meeting with Dietrich Eckart, his job as a newspaper editor, his joining the NSDAP, his impassioned relationship with Hitler. He spoke of major achievements—writing *The Trace of the Jew* and, the previous year, publishing *The Protocols of the Elders of Zion*.

The Protocols of the Elders of Zion caught Friedrich's attention. Only a few weeks before, Friedrich had heard about the document during a presentation by an eminent historian at the Berlin Psychoanalytic Society on the topic of man's eternal need for a scapegoat. He had learned that *The Protocols of the Elders of Zion* was reputed to be a summary of speeches given at the 1897 First Zionist Congress in Basel that reveal an international Jewish conspiracy to undermine Christian institutions, bring about the Russian Revolution, and pave the way for Jewish world domination. The speaker at the psychoanalytic conference said that the *Protocols* had recently been republished in its entirety by an unscrupulous Munich newspaper, despite the fact that several major scholarly institutions had demonstrated convincingly that the *Protocols of Zion* was a hoax. *Had Alfred known that it was a hoax?* Friedrich wondered. *Would he have published it nevertheless?* But of this he spoke not a word. In his intensive personal psychoanalysis for the past three years, Friedrich had learned how to listen and learned, also, to think before he spoke.

"Eckart's health is failing," Alfred continued, turning to his ambitions. "I am saddened because he has been a wonderful mentor, but at the same time I know his impending retirement will open the path to my becoming editor in chief of the Nationalsozialistische Party newspaper, *Völkischer Beobachter*. Hitler told me himself that I am obviously the best candidate. The paper is growing robustly and is soon to become a daily. But even more I hope my editorial position, coupled with my closeness to Hitler, will eventually lead to my playing a major role in the party."

Alfred ended his account by sharing a big secret: "I am now planning a truly important book that I will entitle *The Myth of the Twentieth Century*. I hope it will bring home to every thinking person the magnitude of the Jewish threat to Western civilization. It will take many years to write, but eventually I expect it to be the successor to Houston Stewart Chamberlain's great work, *The Foundations of the Nineteenth Century*. So that's my story, up to 1923."

"Alfred, I'm impressed with what you've accomplished in such a short time. But you haven't finished. Bring me up to the present. What about Brussels?"

"Ah, yes. I told you everything except what you inquired about!" Alfred then described in detail his trip to Paris, Belgium, and Holland. For some reason he couldn't fathom, he omitted any mention of the visit to the Spinoza Museum in Rijnsburg.

"What a rich three years, Alfred! You must be proud of what you've accomplished. I am honored that you've trusted me so. I have a hunch that you may not have shared this, especially your aspirations, with anyone before. Right?"

"Right. You're very right. I haven't spoken so personally since we last talked. There's something about you, Friedrich, that encourages me to open up." Alfred felt himself edging toward telling Friedrich that he wanted to change some basic things about his personality, when the cook appeared with generous helpings of warm Linzer Torte.

"Freshly baked for you and your guest, Dr. Pfister."

"How kind of you, Herr Steiner. And your son, Hans? How is he this week?"

"His days are better, but the nightmares continue to be awful. Almost every night I hear him screaming. His nightmares have become my nightmares."

"The nightmares are normal for his condition. Have patience—they will fade, Herr Steiner. They always do."

"What's wrong with his son?" asked Alfred after the cook departed.

"I can't speak to you of any particular patient, Alfred—doctor's code of confidentiality. But I can tell you this: remember that crowd of men you saw in the waiting room? They are all, every single one, afflicted with the same thing—shell shock. And it is so in every waiting room for nervous disorders in every hospital in Germany. They all are suffering greatly: they're irritable, unable to concentrate, subject to terrible bouts of anxiety and depression. They never stop reliving their trauma. During the day horrifying images intrude into their mind. During the night in nightmares they see their comrades blown apart and their own deaths approaching.

Though they feely lucky to have escaped death, they all suffer from survivor guilt—guilt that they have survived while so many others perished. They ruminate about what they could have done to save their fallen comrades, how they might have died in their stead. Rather than feel proud, many feel like cowards. This is a gigantic problem, Alfred. I'm speaking of a whole generation of German men afflicted. And of course, in addition to this there is the grief of the families. We lost three million in the war, and almost every family in Germany lost a son or a father."

"And, all," Alfred added immediately, "probably made so much worse by the tragedy of the satanic Versailles Treaty, which made all their suffering pointless."

Friedrich noted how adroitly Alfred swung the discussion toward his knowledge base of politics but ignored that. "An interesting speculation, Alfred. To address it we'd need to know what is going on in the waiting rooms of Paris and London military hospitals. You may be in a great position to explore that question for your paper, and, frankly, I wish you would write about it. All the publicity we can get will help. Germany needs to take this more seriously. We need more resources."

"You have my word. I'll write a story about it as soon as I return."

As they both slowly enjoyed their linzer torte, Alfred turned to Friedrich. "So you've finished your training now?"

"Yes, most of my formal training. But psychiatry is a strange field because, unlike any other field of medicine, you never really finish. Your greatest instrument is you, yourself, and the work of self-understanding is endless. I'm still learning. If you see anything about me that might help me know more about myself, please do not hesitate to point it out."

"I can't possibly imagine that. What could I see? What could I tell you?"

"Anything you notice. Perhaps you might catch me looking at you in an odd way, or interrupting you, or using an inapt word. Maybe I'll misunderstand you or ask clumsy or irritating questions . . . anything. I mean it, Alfred. I want to hear it."

Alfred was speechless, almost destabilized. It had happened again. He had once more entered Friedrich's strange world, with radically different rules of discourse—a world he encountered nowhere else.

"So," Friedrich continued, "you said you were in Amsterdam and had to return to Munich. But Berlin is not exactly on the way."

Reaching into his overcoat pocket, Alfred pulled out Spinoza's *Theological-Political Treatise*. "A long train ride was the perfect venue for reading this." He held the book up to Friedrich. "I finished this on the train. You were so right to suggest it to me."

"I'm impressed, Alfred. You *are* a dedicated scholar. Not many like you around. Aside from professional philosophers, very few people read Spinoza after their university days. I would have thought that by now, with your new profession and all the shattering events in Europe, you'd have forgotten all about old Benedictus. Tell me what you thought of the book?"

"Lucid, courageous, intelligent. It's a devastating critique of Judaism and Christianity—or, as my friend Hitler puts it, the 'whole religious swindle.' However, I do question Spinoza's political views. There is no doubt he is naïve in his support for democracy and individual freedom. Only look at where those ideas have led us to in Germany today. He seems almost to be advocating an American system, and we all know where America is heading—to a half-caste mulatto disaster of a country."

Alfred paused, and both men took their last bites of the linzer torte, a true luxury in such lean times.

"But tell me more about the *Ethics*," he continued. "*That* was the book that offered Goethe so much tranquility and vision, the book that he carried in his pocket for a year. Do you remember offering to be my guide, to help me learn how to read it?"

"I remember, and the offer stands. I just hope I'm up to it, because I've been cramming my mind with the small and big thoughts of my profession. I haven't thought of Spinoza since I was with you. Where to begin?" Friedrich closed his eyes. "I'm transporting myself back to university days and listening to my philosophy professor's lectures. I remember him saying that Spinoza was a towering figure in intellectual history. That he was one lonely man who was excommunicated by the Jews, whose books were banned by Christians, and who changed the world. He claimed that Spinoza introduced the modern era, that the enlightenment and the rise of natural science all began with him. Some consider Spinoza as the first Westerner to live openly without any religious affiliation. I remember how your father publicly scorned the church. Eugen told me he refused to set foot in church, even at Easter or Christmas. True?"

He looked Alfred in the eyes, and Alfred nodded, "True."

"So in some real way your father was beholden to Spinoza. Before Spinoza, such an open opposition toward religion would have been unthinkable. And you were perceptive in spotting his role in the rise of democracy in America. The American Declaration of Independence was inspired by the British philosopher John Locke, who was in turn inspired by Spinoza. Let's see. What else? Ah, I remember my philosophy professor particularly emphasizing Spinoza's adherence to immanence. You know what I mean by this?"

Alfred looked uncertain as he rotated his hands quizzically.

"It contrasts with 'transcendence.' It refers to the idea that this worldly existence is all there is, that the laws of nature govern everything and that God is entirely equivalent to Nature. Spinoza's denial of any future life was monumentally important for the philosophy that followed, for it meant that all ethics, all codes of life meaning and behavior must start with *this* world and *this* existence." Friedrich paused. "That's about all that comes to mind . . . Oh yes, one last thing. My professor claimed that Spinoza was the most intelligent man who ever walked the earth."

"I understand that claim. Whether you agree with him or not, he is clearly brilliant. I'm certain that Goethe and Hegel and all our great thinkers recognized this."

And yet how could such thoughts have come from a Jew? Alfred started to add, but refrained. Perhaps both men took care to avoid the topic that had led to such acrimony in their last meeting.

"So, Alfred, do you still have your copy of the *Ethics*?"

The cook stopped by the table and served tea.

"Are we keeping you?" Friedrich asked after looking around and discovering that he and Alfred were the only diners left in the room.

"No, no, Dr. Pfister. A lot to do. I'll be here for hours yet."

After the cook left, Alfred said, "I still have my *Ethics* but haven't opened it for years."

Blowing on his tea and taking a sip, Friedrich turned back to Alfred. "I think now is the time to start reading it. It is a difficult read. I took a yearlong course in it, and often in class we spent an entire hour discussing one page. My advice is to go slow. It's inexpressibly rich and addresses almost every important aspect of philosophy—virtue, freedom, and determinism, the nature of God, good and evil, personal identity, mind-body relationship. Perhaps only Plato's *Republic* had such a wide scope."

Friedrich looked around again at the empty restaurant. "Regardless of Herr Steiner's polite demurrals, I fear we're keeping him here late. Let's go to my room, and I can jog my memory by a quick scan of my Spinoza notes and also get Eugen's address for you."

Friedrich's room in the doctors' dormitory was Spartan, containing only bookcase, desk, chair, and a tidily made-up bed. Offering Alfred the chair, Friedrich handed him his copy of the *Ethics* to peruse while he sat on the bed leafing through an old folder of notes. After ten minutes, he began: "So, a few general comments. First—and this is important—do not be discouraged by the geometric style. I don't believe any reader has ever found this congenial. It resembles Euclid, with precise definitions, axioms, propositions, proofs, and corollaries. It's devilishly hard to read, and no one is certain why he chose to write in this manner. I remembering your saying that you gave up trying because it seemed impenetrable, but I urge you to stay with it. My professor doubts that Spinoza actually thought in this manner but rather regarded this as a superior pedagogical device. Perhaps it seemed the natural way of presenting his fundamental idea that nothing is contingent, that everything in Nature is orderly, understandable, and necessitated by other causes to be exactly that which it is. Or perhaps he wanted logic to reign, to make himself entirely invisible and let his conclusions be defended by logic, not by recourse to rhetoric or authority, nor prejudged on the basis of his Jewish background. He wanted the work to be judged as a mathematical text is judged—by the sheer logic of his method."

Friedrich took his book back from Alfred and flipped through the pages. "It's divided into five parts," he pointed out. "'On God,' 'On the Nature and Origin of the Mind,' 'On the Origin and Nature of the Emotions,' 'On Human Bondage,' 'Of Human Freedom.' It's the fourth section, 'On Human Bondage,' that interests me the most because it has the most relevance to my field. Earlier I said that I've not thought of him since we last met, but as we talk, I realize now that's not true. Quite frequently, as I read or listen to psychiatry lectures or talk with patients, I ruminate about Spinoza's vastly unappreciated influence on my field of psychiatry. And the fifth part, 'On the Power of the Understanding, or Of Human Freedom,' also has relevance to my work and should have interest for you. This is the part that I imagine was the most beneficial for Goethe."

"A couple of thoughts about the first two parts—" Friedrich glanced at his watch. "They are for me the most difficult and most abstruse sections, and I've never been able to understand every concept. The major point is that everything in the universe is a single eternal substance, Nature or God. And never forget he uses the two terms interchangeably."

"Mentions of 'God' litter every page?" asked Alfred. "I didn't think he was a believer."

"Lot of controversy about that. Many refer to him as a pantheist. My professor preferred to call him a devious atheist, repeatedly using the term 'God' to encourage seventeenth-century readers to keep reading. And to prevent both his books and his person from being consigned to flames. For sure he is not using 'God' in the conventional sense. He rails against the naïveté of humans' claim they are made in God's image. Somewhere, I think in his correspondence, he says that if triangles could think they would create a triangular god. All anthropomorphic versions of God are just superstitious inventions. To Spinoza, Nature and God are synonyms; you might say he naturalizes God."

"So far I don't hear anything about ethics."

"You have to wait until parts four and five. First he establishes that we live in a deterministic world loaded with obstacles to our well-being. Whatever occurs is a result of the unchanging laws of nature, and we are part of nature, subject to these deterministic laws. Furthermore, nature is infinitely complex. As he puts it, nature has an infinite number of modes or attributes, and we humans can only apprehend two of them, thought and material essence."

Alfred asked a few more questions about the *Ethics*, but Friedrich noted that he seemed to be straining to keep the conversation going. Choosing his time carefully, Friedrich ventured an observation. "Alfred, it is wonderful for me to remember and discuss Spinoza with you. But I want to be sure I haven't missed anything. As a therapist I've learned to pay attention to hunches that pass through my mind, and I have a hunch about you."

Alfred's eyebrows raised. He waited expectantly.

"I have a hunch that you came to speak not only about Spinoza but also for some other reason."

Tell him the truth, Alfred said to himself. *Tell him about your tightness. About your inability to sleep. About being unloved. About always being an outsider apart from, rather than a part of.* But instead he said, "No, it's been great to see you, to catch up, to learn more about Spinoza—after all, how often does one stumble upon a Spinoza tutor? What's more, I have a good story for the paper. If you can supply me with some medical reading on shell shock, I will write the story on the train ride to Munich and put it in next week's edition. I'll send it to you."

Friedrich walked over to his desk and rifled through several journals. "Here's a good review in the *Journal of Nervous Diseases*. Take the issue with you, and mail it back when you're finished with it. And here also is Eugen's address."

As Alfred slowly, somewhat reluctantly, started to rise, Friedrich decided to try one last thing—another device he had learned from his own analyst and that he had often used with patients. It rarely failed.

"Stay a moment, Alfred. I've one last question. Let me ask you to imagine something. Close your eyes and imagine leaving me now. Imagine walking away from our talk, and then imagine sitting on the long train ride to Munich. Let me know when your imagination is there."

Alfred closed his eyes and soon nodded readiness.

"Now, here's what I'd like you to do. Think back upon our talk tonight, and ask yourself these questions: Do I have any regrets about my talk with Friedrich? Were there important issues I did not raise?"

Alfred kept his eyes closed and, after a long silence, slowly nodded. "Well, there is *one* thing . . ."

CHAPTER TWENTY-THREE

AMSTERDAM—JULY 27, 1656

Bento wheeled when he heard his name called and saw a disheveled, tearful Franco, who immediately sank to his knees and bowed his head until his brow touched the pavement.

"Franco? What are you doing here? And what are you doing on the ground?"

"I have to see you, to warn you, to beg forgiveness. Please forgive me. Please allow me to explain."

"Franco, stand up. It's not safe for you to be seen talking to me. I'm heading to my house. Follow at a distance, and then just come right in without knocking. But first be certain you're not seen by anyone."

A few minutes later, in Bento's study, Franco continued in a tremulous voice, "I just came from the synagogue. The rabbis cursed you. Vicious— they were vicious. I could understand everything because they translated into Portuguese—I never imagined they would be so vicious. They ordered no one to speak to you or look at you or—"

"That's why I told you it was unsafe to be seen with me."

"You already knew? How could you? I just came from the synagogue. I ran out immediately after the service."

"I knew it was coming. It was fated."

"But you're a good man. You offered to help me. You did help me. And look what they've done to you. Everything is my fault." Franco fell to his knees again and took Bento's hand and pressed it to his forehead. "It's a crucifixion, and I'm the Judas. I betrayed you."

Bento extricated his hand and placed it on Franco's head for a moment. "Please stand. I have things to tell you. Above all, you must know *it is not your fault*. They were looking for an excuse."

"No, there are things you do not know. It is time: I must confess. We betrayed you, Jacob and I. We went to the parnassim, and Jacob told them everything you said to us. And I did nothing to stop him. I just stood there as he talked and nodded my head. And each nod pounded a nail into your crucifixion. But I had to. I had no choice . . . Believe me, I had no choice."

"There is always choice, Franco."

"That sounds good, but it is not true. Real life is more complex than that."

Startled, Bento took a long look at Franco. This was a somewhat different Franco. "Why is it not true?"

"What if you're faced with only two choices, and both are deadly?"

"Deadly?"

Franco avoided Bento's eyes. "Does the name Duarte Rodriguez mean anything to you?"

Bento nodded. "The man who tried to rob my family. The man who needed no rabbi's proclamation to hate me."

"He is my uncle."

"Yes, I know that, Franco. Rabbi Mortera told me yesterday."

"Did he tell you that my uncle offered me two choices? If I agreed to betray you, he would rescue me from Portugal, and then, after I had fulfilled my bargain, he would immediately send a ship to Portugal to rescue my mother, my sister, and my aunt, Jacob's mother. They are all in hiding and in great danger from the Inquisition. If I refused, he would strand them in Portugal."

"I understand. You made the correct choice. You saved your family."

"Even so, that does not erase my shame. I am planning to go back to the parnassim the moment my family is safe and confess that we provoked you into saying the things you said."

"No, do not do that, Franco. The best thing you can give me now is silence."

"Silence?"

"It is best for me, for all of us."

"*Why* is it best? We *did* trick you into saying what you said."

"But that is not true. I said what I said freely."

"No, you're being merciful to me, to assuage my pain. My guilt remains. It was all an act, all planned. I sinned. I deceived you. I caused you great harm."

"Franco, you did not deceive me. I *knew* you would bear witness against me. I deliberately spoke rashly. I *wanted* you to testify. I'm the one who is guilty of deception."

"*You?*"

"Yes, I took advantage of you. Worst of all, I did so even though I had an inkling that you and I might be like-minded."

"You understood right. But our like-mindedness compounds my guilt. When Jacob described your views to the parnassim, I kept silent, whereas I should have shouted at the top of my lungs, 'I agree with Baruch Spinoza. His views are my views too.'"

"If you had done that, you would have had the worst of all worlds. Your uncle would retaliate, your family would be imperiled, I would still have been excommunicated, and the parnassim would have excommunicated you along with me."

"Baruch Spinoza—"

"Please—Bento now. There is no longer a Baruch Spinoza."

"All right, *Bento*. Bento de Spinoza, you are an enigma. Nothing about today makes sense. Answer one simple question: if you wanted to quit this community, why did you not just leave of your own choice? Why bring such disgrace and catastrophe upon yourself? Why not just move away? Go elsewhere?"

"Where? Do I look Dutch? A Jew cannot just disappear. And think of my brother and sister. Think of how hard it would be to leave them and then keep deciding over and over again to stay away from them. Better this way. And better, too, for my family. Now they no longer have to choose again and again not to talk to their brother. The rabbi's *cherem* decides for me and for them once and for all time."

"So you say it is better to hand your own fate to others. Better not to choose, but to force others to make the choice for you? Did you not just say there was always a choice?"

Jolted, Bento looked again at this different Franco, a thoughtful, forthright Franco with no trace of the shy, buffoonish Franco of their previous meetings. "There is much truth in what you say. How came you to think in such ways?"

"My father, he who was burned by the Inquisition, was a wise man. Before he was forced to convert, he was the main rabbi and advisor of our community. Even after we all became Christians, the villagers continued to visit him to discuss serious life problems. I often sat by his side, and I learned many things about guilt and shame and choice and grief."

"You, the son of a wise rabbi? So in our meetings with Jacob, you concealed your knowledge and your true thoughts. When I talked of the words of the Torah, you feigned ignorance."

Franco lowered his head and nodded. "I acknowledge that I played a deceptive role. But, in truth, I *am* ignorant of Jewish things. My father, in his wisdom and his love for me, desired that I not be educated in our tradition. If we were to stay alive, we had to be Christians. He deliberately taught me nothing of the Jewish language or customs because the cunning Inquisitors were so good at spotting all traces of Jewish ideas."

"And your outburst about the madness of religions? That, too, was pretense?"

"Not in any way! Yes, Jacob's scheme was for me to voice great religious doubt in order to encourage you to loosen your tongue. But that role was easy—no actor has ever been assigned an easier part. In fact, Bento, it was a great relief to utter those words. I have always concealed my feelings before. The more Christian dogma and stories of miracles I was forced to learn, the more I realized how both the Christian and the Jewish faiths were based on childish, supernatural fantasies. But I could never express this to my father. I could not wound him so. Then he was murdered for hiding Torah pages that he believed contained the very words of God. And again I could say nothing. Hearing your thoughts was so liberating that my sense of deception diminished, even though my honest sharing with you was itself in the service of deception. A complex paradox."

"I understand exactly. During our talk I, too, felt exhilarated at finally telling the truth about my beliefs. Knowing that I was shocking Jacob did not deter me in the least. Quite the contrary—I confess I rather enjoyed shocking him even though I was aware that dark consequences would follow."

They fell into silence. Bento's anguished sense of absolute isolation after Manny, the baker's son, had shunned him began to fade. This meeting, this moment of honesty with Franco, touched and warmed him. As was his wont, he did not linger long with feelings but shifted into the observer role and examined his mind, noting especially the mellowness spreading through him. Even full awareness of its fleeting nature did not deter its pleasantness. Ah, friendship! So *this* is the glue that holds people together—this warmth, this loneliness-dispelling state of mind. Doubting so much, fearing so much, revealing so little, he had sampled friendship far too rarely in his life.

Franco glanced at Bento's packed bag and broke the silence. "You're leaving today?"

Bento nodded.

"Going where? What will you do? How will you support yourself?"

"Hopefully I head toward an unencumbered life of contemplation. For the past year I've been trained by a local lens maker to make lenses for spectacles and, of much greater interest to me, optical instruments, both telescopes and microscopes. My needs are few, and I should be able to support myself easily."

"You'll stay here in Amsterdam?"

"For the time being. At the home of Franciscus van den Enden, who operates a teaching academy near the Singel. Eventually I may move to a smaller community, where I can pursue my own study in a quieter setting."

"You'll be all alone? I imagine the stigma of excommunication will keep others at a distance?"

"On the contrary, it will be easier to live among Gentiles as an excommunicated Jew. Perhaps especially as a permanently excommunicated Jew, rather than a renegade Jew who just wants Gentile company."

"So that's another reason why you welcomed a *cherem*?"

"Yes, I admit that and something more: I plan eventually to write, and it may be that there is a better chance the world at large will read the work of an excommunicated Jew than a member of the Jewish community."

"You know for sure?"

"Sheer speculation, but I've already developed relationships with several like-minded colleagues who urge me to write down my thoughts."

"These are Christians?"

"Yes, but a different kind of Christian from the fanatic Iberian Catholics you have met. They don't believe in the miracle of resurrection or drink the blood of Jesus during Mass or burn alive those who think otherwise. These are liberal-minded Christians who call themselves Collegiants and think for themselves without preachers or churches."

"Then you're planning to convert to be one of them?"

"Never. I plan to live a religious life without the interference of any religion. I believe that all religions—Catholicism, Protestantism, Islam, as well as Judaism—simply block our view of the core religious truths. I hope for a world someday without religions, a world with a universal religion in which all individuals use their reason to experience and to venerate God."

"Does that mean you wish for the end of Judaism?"

"For the end of *all* traditions that interfere with one's right to think for oneself."

Franco fell silent for a few moments. "Bento, you're so extreme it's frightening. It takes my breath away to imagine that, after surviving thousands of years, our tradition should perish."

"We should cherish things because they are true, not because they are old. Old religions trap us by insisting that if we forsake the tradition, we dishonor all past worshippers. And should one of our ancestors have been martyred, then we are trapped even more because we feel honor-bound to perpetuate the martyrs' beliefs, even though we know them to be fraught with error and superstition. Did you not intimate that you felt something of that as a result of your father's martyrdom?"

"Yes—that I'd render his life meaningless if I negated the very thing he died for."

"But would it not also be meaningless to dedicate your one and only life to a false and superstitious system—a system that chooses only one people and excludes all other beings?"

"Bento de Spinoza, you stretch my mind too far. Any farther and it will shatter. I have never dared to think upon such things. I cannot imagine living without belonging to my community, my own group. How is it so easy for you?"

"Easy? It is not easy, but it is easier if one's dear ones are dead. My permanent excommunication gives me the task now of refashioning my entire identity and learning to live without being Jewish or Christian, or any other religion. Perhaps I shall be the first man of such a sort."

"Be careful! It's possible that your permanent excommunication will not be so permanent. In the eyes of others you may not have the luxury of being a non-Jew. Baruch, what do you know about the *limpiezas de sangre*?"

"The Iberian blood laws? Not very much, except that Spain implemented them to prevent converted Jews from gaining too much power."

"They began, my father told me, with Torquemada, the grand Inquisitor, who persuaded Queen Isabella two hundred years ago that the Jewish stain remained in the blood despite conversion to Christianity. Since Torquemada, himself, had Jewish ancestry four generations before, he drew the line of the Blood Laws three generations back. Thus recent conversos, or even those two or three generations old, remain under deep suspicion and are blocked from many careers—in the church, military, many guilds, and civil service."

"Patently false beliefs such as 'three but not four generations' obviously are invented to convenience the inventor. Like the poor of the earth, false beliefs will always be with us, and their persistence is out of my control. I strive now to care only about those things over which I do have control."

"Such as?"

"I think I have true control only over one thing: the progress of my understanding."

"Bento, I have the strongest desire to say something to you that I know is impossible."

"But not impossible to say?"

"I know it is impossible, but I want to come with you! You think great thoughts, and I know you will think greater ones. I want to follow you, be your student, your servant, share in what you shall do, be a copier of your manuscripts, make your life easier."

Bento paused for a moment. He smiled, then shook his head.

"I find what you say pleasing, even enticing. Let me answer you from both the inside and from the outside."

"First the inside. Though I desire and insist upon a solitary life to pursue my meditations, I can sense another part of me longing for intimacy. Sometimes I can slip into an inexpressibly intense longing for the old feelings of being cradled and held by a loving family and that part of me—that craving part—welcomes your wish and makes me want to embrace you and answer, 'Yes, yes, yes!' Simultaneously another part of me, my stronger and higher part, clamors for freedom. I ache that the past is gone and will never return.

I ache to think that all those who once cradled me are dead, and I also hate this ache that shackles me and holds me back. I cannot affect past events, but I have resolved to avoid future intense attachments. I shall never again wrap myself in my childish desire to be cradled. You understand?"

"Yes, far too well."

"That's the inside. Now let me answer from the outside. I assume your word 'impossible' referred to the impossibility of abandoning your family. If I were in your situation, I, too, would find it impossible. It is difficult enough for me to abandon my younger brother. My sister has her own family, and I worry less about her. But, Franco, it's not just your family that prevents you joining me. There are other obstacles. Only a few minutes ago, you told me you cannot imagine life without a community. Yet my way is one of solitude and craves no community other than absolute absorption into God. I will never marry. Even should I desire marriage, it would not be possible. As a solitary oddity I may be able to live without a religious affiliation, but it is doubtful that even Holland, the most tolerant country in the world, would allow a couple to live in that fashion and raise children without religious membership. And my solitary life means no aunts or uncles or cousins, no family holiday celebrations, no Passover meals, no Rosh Hashanah. Only solitude."

"I understand, Bento. I understand I am more gregarious and perhaps more needy. I marvel at your extraordinary self-sufficiency. You don't seem to want or need anyone."

"I've been told that so many times that I begin to believe it myself. It's not that I don't enjoy the company of others—at this moment, Franco, I cherish our conversation. But you're right, a social life is not essential for me. Or at least not as essential as it seems for others. I remember how undone my sister and brother would be when they weren't invited to some event with their friends. That kind of thing has never affected me in the least."

"Yes," Franco nodded, "it is true: I could not live in your fashion. It is indeed alien to me. But, Bento, consider my other choice. Here I am a man who shares so many of your doubts and your wishes to live without super-stition, and yet I am fated to sit in synagogue praying to a God who does not hear me, following foolish ritual, living as a hypocrite, embracing a meaningless life. Is that what is left to me? Is that what life is all about? Won't I be forced into a solitary life even in the midst of a crowd?"

"No, Franco, it is not so bleak. I've been observing this community for a long time, and there will be a way for you to live here. Conversos from Portugal and Spain pour into Amsterdam every day, and many, it is true, fervently long to return to their ancestral Jewish roots. Since none have had a Jewish education, they must start learning Hebrew and Jewish law as though they were children, and Rabbi Mortera works day and night to bring them back home to Judaism. Many will emulate him and become more religious than the rabbi, but, trust me, there will be others like you who, because of their forced Christian conversion, are disenthralled with all religion and will join the Jewish community with no religious fervor. You will find them if you look, Franco."

"But still the pretense, the hypocrisy—"

"Let me tell you something of the ideas of Epicurus, a wise, ancient Greek thinker. He believed, as any rational person must, that there is no world to come and that we should spend our only life as peacefully and joyfully as possible. What is the purpose of life? His answer was that we should seek *ataraxia*, which might be translated as 'tranquility,' or as 'freedom from emotional distress.' He suggested that a wise man's needs are few and easily satisfied, whereas people with implacable cravings for power or wealth, perhaps like your uncle, never attain *ataraxia* because cravings breed. The more you have, the more they have you. When you think of fashioning a life here, think of attaining *ataraxia*. Embed yourself in the part of the community that creates the least stress for you. Marry someone with sentiments similar to yours—you'll find many conversos who, like you, will cling to Judaism only for the comfort of belonging to a community. And if the rest of the community, a few times a year, goes through the ritual of prayer, then pray with them knowing that you do so *only* for the sake of *ataraxia*, for the sake of avoiding the turmoil and distress of nonparticipation."

"Do you speak down to me, Bento? Is it that *I* should settle for *ataraxia* while *you* reach for something higher? Or will you seek *ataraxia* as well?"

"A difficult question. I think—" Suddenly the church bells pealed. Bento stopped for a moment to listen and to glance at his packed bag and then continued. "Alas, the time for reflection is short. I must leave very soon, before the streets become too crowded. But quickly—I haven't pointedly chosen *ataraxia* as my goal but instead point myself toward the goal of perfecting my reason. Perhaps, however, the goal is the same, though the method is different. Reason is leading me to the extraordinary conclusion that everything in the world is one substance, which is Nature or, if you wish, God, and that everything, with no exception, can be understood through the illumination of natural law. As I gain more clarity about the nature of reality, I, on occasion, knowing I am but a ripple on the surface of God, experience a state of joyousness or blessedness. Maybe that is my variant of *ataraxia*. Perhaps Epicurus is right to advise us to aim for tranquility. But each person, according to his external circumstances and his natural bent of mind and inner mental characteristics, must pursue it in his own particular manner."

The bells pealed again.

"Before we part, Franco. I have a last request of you."

"Tell me. I am greatly in your debt."

"My request is simply for silence. I have said things to you today that are but half-born thoughts. I have much thinking ahead of me. Promise me that all we have said today is our secret. Secret from the parnassim, from Jacob, from anyone, forever."

"You have my promise to carry your secrets to the grave. My father, blessed be he, taught me much about the sanctity of silence."

"Now we must say good-bye to one another, Franco."

"Wait one more moment, Bento de Spinoza, for I too have a final request. You have just said that we may have similar aims in life and similar doubts but each of us must take a different path. Thus, in a fashion, we will live alternate lives heading toward the same goal. Perhaps, had fate and time just slightly rotated and altered our external circumstances and temperament, you could have lived my life, and I could have lived yours. Here's my request: I want to know about your life from time to time, even if it is only every year or two or three. And I want you to know my life as it unfolds. Thus we may each see *what could have been*—the other life we could have led. Will you promise to remain in contact with me? I don't yet know the mechanism whereby this may happen. But will you let me know of your life?"

"I want this no less than you, Franco. My mind is clear about the necessity of leaving my home, but my heart wavers more than I expected, and I welcome your intriguing offer to view my alternative life. I know two people who will always know my whereabouts, Franciscus van den Enden and a friend, Simon de Vries, who lives on the Singel. I will find a way to communicate with you through them by letter or through personal meetings. Now you must go. Be careful not to be seen."

Franco opened the door, peered about him, and strode off. Bento took a last glance around his home, moved his note to Gabriel to a chair near the entrance so that it would be more easily visible, and, bag in hand, opened the door and stepped out into a new life.

CHAPTER TWENTY-FOUR

BERLIN—1922

W ell . . . ," Alfred hesitated. "There *is one thing* that I would regret not discussing with you, but . . . hmm . . . I'm having trouble bringing it up. I've been unable to speak of it all evening."

Friedrich waited patiently. Words from his supervisor, Karl Abraham, flashed into his mind: "In an impasse, forget the content and focus instead on the resistance. You'll find that you'll learn even more about your patient." With that in mind, Friedrich began. "I think I can help, Alfred. Here's my suggestion. For the time being, just forget about *what* you were going to tell me, and, instead, let's explore all the *obstacles* to speaking it."

"Obstacles?"

"Anything that gets in your way of talking to me. For example, what would be the repercussions of your saying what you want to say?"

"Repercussions? Not sure what you mean."

Friedrich was patient. He knew that resistance had to be approached tactfully and from all sides. "Let me put it this way. You have something you desire to say but cannot. What negative things might happen if you were to speak? Keep in mind that I'm a central part of this. You're not trying to say something in an empty room—you're trying to say it to *me*. Right?"

A reluctant nod from Alfred. Friedrich continued, "So now try to imagine that you've just revealed to me what's on your mind. What's your guess about how I would regard you?"

"I don't know how you'd react. I guess I'd just be embarrassed."

"But embarrassment always requires another person, and today that person is *me*, someone who's known you since you were a small child."

Friedrich was very proud of his gentle voice. Dr. Abraham's admonitions to stop charging at resistance like a raging bull had had their effect.

"Well"—Alfred took a breath and jumped in—"for one, you might feel I'm exploiting you for help. I'm embarrassed by asking for your professional services for free. And also, it makes me feel like the weak one and you the strong one."

"That's a great start, Alfred. Exactly what I meant. And now I can see your predicament. This must seem so uneven to you. I wouldn't like being so beholden to another, either. Then again, you've already reciprocated by agreeing to run a newspaper story for me."

"It's not the same. You receive nothing personally."

"I understand that. But tell me, do you believe I resent offering something to you?"

"I don't know—you might. After all, your time is valuable. You do this for pay all day long."

"And my response that you're like family to me isn't relevant either?"

"Right. I hear that as placating."

"Tell me, how is it when we're talking about Spinoza, about philosophy? I get the feeling you're more relaxed then."

"Yes, that's different. Even though you're teaching me, I get the impression that philosophy talk is enjoyable to you."

"Yes, you're correct about that. Whereas listening to you discussing yourself would *not* be enjoyable to me?"

"I can't imagine why on earth it would be."

"Here's a thought—just a sheer guess. Perhaps you have negative feelings about yourself and think that if you opened up, I would also feel negatively about you?"

Alfred looked puzzled. "It's possible I guess, but if so, it's not the major factor. I just can't imagine myself taking that kind of interest in anyone else."

"That sounds important, and I imagine it's a risk to say that to me. Tell me, Alfred: is that close to the very thing you would regret not bringing up today?"

Alfred smiled broadly. "My God! You are *really* good at this, Friedrich! Yes, more than close. It is exactly the thing."

"Say more." Friedrich relaxed. He coasted in familiar waters now.

"Well, just before I left, my boss, Dietrich Eckart, called me into his office. He simply wanted to talk about my trip to Paris, but I didn't know that, and the first thing he did when I got to his office was chide me for looking so worried. Then, after assuring me I was doing a good job, he said it would be much better for me to be less diligent and do a bit more drinking and a lot more schmoozing."

"And that statement hit home."

"Yes, because it's true—it has been said to me in one way or another many times. I say it to myself. But I just cannot sit around with empty-headed people talking about nothing."

A scene entered Friedrich's mind: the time, twenty-five years earlier, when he had attempted unsuccessfully to give Alfred a piggyback ride. At their last meeting he had described that to Alfred and added, "You didn't like to play." The lifelong persistence of such traits fascinated Friedrich. What a rare opportunity to study the genesis of personality formation! This might be a major professional breakthrough. What other analyst had ever had the chance to analyze someone he knew as a child? And what's more, he had personally known the patient's significant adults: Alfred's father, brother, and surrogate mother, his Aunt Cäcilie, even Alfred's doctor. And he was familiar with the same physical surroundings—Alfred's home, playground—and they had gone to the same school and had the same teachers. What a pity Alfred didn't live in Berlin so that he could take him on for a full psychoanalysis.

"And it was right then, right after Dietrich Eckart's comment," Alfred continued, "I decided to see you. I knew he was right. Only a few days before I had overheard a conversation about me between a couple of employees. They referred to me as the sphinx."

"How did that make you feel?"

"Mixed. They weren't important, just cleaning and delivery people, and I usually pay no attention to any opinions from their type. But in this instance they caught my attention because they were so right. I am closed and tight, and I know I've got to change this part of myself if I'm to be successful in the Nationalsozialist Party."

"You said 'mixed.' What's *positive* about being a sphinx?"

"Hmm, not sure, perhaps it is—"

"Wait, let's stop for a minute, Alfred. I've gotten ahead of myself. This is unfair to you. I'm pelting you with personal questions, and we really haven't agreed upon what we're doing here. Or, in the technical language of my profession, we haven't defined the *frame* of our relationship, have we?"

Alfred seemed puzzled. "Frame?"

"Let's just back up and establish an agreement about what we're up to. I'm making the assumption that you want to make changes in yourself by working in therapy. Is that right?"

"I'm not sure what work in therapy means."

"It's what you've been doing so well the last ten minutes: speaking honestly and openly about your concerns."

"I definitely want to make changes in myself. So, yes, I want therapy. And also I want to work with you."

"But, Alfred, change requires many, many meetings. Tonight we're just having an introductory chat, and I'm leaving tomorrow for a three-day psychoanalytic conference. I'm thinking of the future. Berlin is a long way from Munich. Wouldn't it make more sense to see a psychoanalyst in Munich whom you could see more often? I can give you a good referral—"

Alfred vigorously shook his head. "No. No one else. I can't possibly trust anyone else, certainly no one in Munich. I have a belief, a very strong belief, that one day I'll have a powerful position in this country. I'll have my enemies, and I could be ruined by anyone who knew my secrets. I know I'm safe with you."

"Yes, you are safe with me. Well, let's think about our schedule—when might you visit Berlin next?"

"I can't be sure, but I know that the *Völkischer Beobachter* will become a daily shortly, and we'll be covering more national and international news. In the future I may be able to visit Berlin frequently, and I hope I can see you for one or two sessions whenever I come."

"I'll always try to make time for you if you give me some advance notice. I want you to know I will keep everything you say in complete and absolute confidence."

"I'm sure you will. That's of the utmost importance to me, and I was very reassured when you declined to tell me anything personal about your patient, the cook's son."

"And rest assured I will never share your secrets, not even the fact that you are in therapy with me, with anyone in the world, your brother included. Confidentiality is crucial in my field, and you have my oath."

Alfred patted himself over his heart and mouthed the words, "Thank you. Thank you much."

"You know," Friedrich said, "maybe you are right. I think our arrangement would work better if it weren't unequal. I think I should, starting next time, charge you the analytic standard fee. I'll be sure it is affordable for you. What do you think?"

"Perfect."

"So, now, back to work. Let's continue. A few minutes ago when we were talking about your being called the sphinx, you said you had 'mixed' feelings. Now, I want you to free associate to 'sphinx.' By that I mean you should try to let your thoughts about 'sphinx' freely enter into your mind and think out loud. It doesn't have to make sense."

"Now?"

"Yes, just for a couple of minutes."

"Sphinx . . . desert, huge, mysterious, powerful, enigmatic, keeps its own counsel . . . dangerous—the sphinx strangled those who did not answer his riddle." Alfred paused.

"Keep going."

"Did you know that the Greek root meant 'strangler,' or one who squeezes? 'Sphincter' is related to Sphinx—all the sphincters of the body squeezing . . . tight . . . tight-assed."

"So," Friedrich asked, "by 'mixed' you meant that you disliked being considered so silent and aloof and tight-assed but that you liked being thought of as enigmatic, mysterious, powerful, threatening?"

"Yes, that's right. Precisely right."

"Then, perhaps the positive aspects—your pride in being powerful and mysterious, even dangerous—will get in the way of schmoozing and being open. It means you have a choice—schmooze and be an insider, or remain mysterious, dangerous, and an outsider."

"I see what you're getting at. It's complex."

"Alfred, weren't you, as I recall, also an outsider in your youth?"

"Always a loner. Didn't belong to any group."

"But you also mentioned that you are very close to the party leader, Herr Hitler. That must feel good. Tell me about that friendship."

"I spend a great deal of time with him. We have coffee; we talk about politics and literature and philosophy. We visit galleries, and one day last autumn we went to Marienplatz—you know it?"

"Yes, Munich's main square."

"Right. Amazing light there. We set up our easels and sketched together for hours. That day stands out as one of my finest days. Our sketches were good; we complimented one another and discovered similarities in our work. Both of us are strong on architectural details and weak on human figures. I had always wondered if my inability to draw figures was symbolic and was relieved to see he had the same limitations. It's certainly not symbolic for Hitler—no one has better skills in relating to people."

"Sounds enjoyable. Have you sketched with him again?"

"He's never suggested it."

"Tell me about other good times you've had with him."

"The very best day in my life happened about three weeks ago. Hitler took me out shopping for a desk for my new office. He had a purse stuffed with Swiss francs—I don't know how he got them, and I never pry. I prefer to let him tell me details at his own pace. He came into the *Beobachter* one morning and said, 'We're going shopping. You can buy any desk you wish—and buy all the things you want to put on the desk.' And for the next two hours we went on a spree through the most expensive furniture stores in Munich."

"The best day of your life—that's saying a lot. Tell me more."

"Part of it was simply the thrill of the gift. Imagine someone taking you out and saying, 'Buy any desk you want. At any price.' And then to have Hitler give me so much time and attention was really bliss."

"Why is he so important for you?"

"From a practical standpoint, he's the party head now, and my newspaper is the party newspaper. So he's my real boss. But I don't think you meant that."

"No, I meant 'important' in a deeper personal sense."

"Hard to put into words. Hitler just has that effect on you, on everybody."

"Taking you out for a wonderful shopping spree. Sounds like something you'd have liked your father to do."

"You knew my father! Can you imagine him taking me out and offering me anything, even a piece of candy? Yes, he lost his wife, and his health was terrible, and he had big money problems, but still I got nothing, absolutely nothing from him."

"Lots of feeling in those words."

"A lifetime of feeling."

"I knew him. And I know you got precious little fathering—and, of course, you never even knew your mother."

"Aunt Cäcilie did the best she could. I never blame her—she had her own children. Too many shoulders to hug."

"So perhaps some of your exhilaration about Hitler comes from getting, finally, some real fathering. What's his age?"

"Oh, he's a few years older. He's like no one I've ever met. He has come from nowhere, like me, from an undistinguished, uneducated family. He was just a corporal in the war, though much decorated. He has no financial means, no culture, no university education. But, even so, he mesmerizes everyone. It's not just me. People gather round him. Everyone seeks his company and his counsel. Everyone senses he is a man of destiny, the pole star of Germany's future."

"So you feel privileged to be with him. Is your relationship progressing into a close friendship?"

"That's just the point—it's not progressing. Aside from the 'desk day,' Hitler doesn't seek me out. I think he likes me, but he doesn't love me. He never asks to have meals with me. He is far closer to others. I saw him last week in intimate discussions with Hermann Göring. Their heads were so close together they were touching. They had just met, yet they laughed and joked and walked arm in arm, and poked each other in the stomach as though they had known one another all their lives. Why doesn't that ever happen to me?"

"Your phrase, 'He doesn't love me'—think about that. Let your mind meander about that. Think out loud."

Alfred closed his eyes.

"I can't quite hear you," said Friedrich.

Alfred smiled. "Love. Someone to say, 'I love you.' I heard those words only once, with Hilda in Paris before we married."

"You're married! Yes, I had almost forgotten. You rarely mention your wife."

"I should say I *was* married. Guess I still am officially. Very short marriage in 1915. Hilda Leesmann. We were together a couple of weeks in Paris, where she was studying to be a ballerina, and at the most three to four months in Russia. Then she developed severe consumption."

"How awful. Like your brother and mother and father. What happened then?"

"We've been out of touch for a long time. The last I heard, her family put her in a sanatorium in the Black Forest. I'm not sure if she's still alive. When you said, 'how awful,' I winced inside because I *don't* feel much about this. I never think of her. And I doubt she thinks of me. We became strangers. I remember that one of the last things she said to me was that I had never inquired about her life, never asked her how she spent her day."

"So," Friedrich said, looking at his watch, "we return full circle to the reason you contacted me. We began with no schmoozing, no interest in others. Next we looked at the part of you that desires to be sphinx-like. Then we returned to your yearning for love and attention from Hitler and how painful it is to watch him favor others while you're left on the outside watching. And then we spoke of your distance from your wife. Let's take a moment to look at closeness and distance right here with me. You said you feel safe here?"

Alfred nodded.

"And what about your feelings toward me?

"Very safe. And very understood."

"And you find yourself feeling close? Liking me?"

"Yes, both."

"Therein lies our great discovery today. I think you *do* like me, and a major reason for that is that I'm interested in you. I'm recalling your earlier comment that you don't think you're interested in others. And yet people like people who are interested in them. That is the most important message I have for you today. I'll say it again: *People like people who are interested in them.*

"We did good, hard work today. It's our first session, and you're plunging right in. I'm sorry it has to end, but it *has* been a long day, and my energy ebbs. I do hope you'll come to see me again often. I feel I can help you."

CHAPTER TWENTY-FIVE

AMSTERDAM—1658

Over the next year Spinoza—no longer Baruch but now and forever after known as Bento (or in his written work, Benedictus)—maintained an odd nocturnal relationship with Franco. Almost every night, as Bento lay in his four-poster bed in a small garret in van den Enden's house, anxiously awaiting sleep, Franco's image entered his thoughts. So seamless and stealthy was his entrance that, uncharacteristically, Bento never tried to understand why he so often brought Franco to mind.

But at no other time did Bento think of Franco. His waking hours were crammed with intellectual endeavors that offered more joy than anything he had ever before experienced. Whenever he imagined himself as a wizened old man reflecting upon his life, he knew that he would select these very days as the best of days, these days of fellowship with van den Enden and the other students, mastering Latin and Greek and savoring the great themes of the classical world—Democritus's atomistic universe, Plato's Form of the Good, Aristotle's Unmoved Mover, and the Stoic's freedom from the passions.

His life was beautiful in its simplicity. Bento entirely agreed with Epicurus's insistence that man's needs were few and easily satisfied. Needing only room and board, a few books, paper, and ink, he could earn the necessary guilders by grinding lenses for spectacles only two days a week and by teaching Hebrew to Collegiants who desired to read the scriptures in their original tongue.

The academy offered not only a vocation and a home but a social life—more, at times, than Bento wished. He was meant to take dinner with the van den Enden family and the students boarding at the academy but instead often chose to take a plate of bread and hard Dutch cheese and a candle to his room to read. His absences at dinner disappointed Madame van den Enden, who found him an enlivening conversationalist and tried, without success, to increase his sociability, even offering to cook his favorite dishes and to avoid nonkosher foods. Bento assured her he was in no way observant but was simply indifferent to food and quite content with the simplest fare—his bread, cheese, and daily glass of ale followed by a smoke on his long-stemmed clay pipe.

Outside his classes he avoided socializing with fellow students aside from Dirk, soon to be off to medical school and, of course, the precocious and adorable Clara Maria. Yet generally, after a short period, he slipped away even from them, preferring the company of the two hundred weighty, musty volumes in van den Enden's library.

Aside from his interest in the fine paintings displayed in the shops of art dealers in the small streets branching off of the town hall, Bento had little affinity for the arts and resisted van den Enden's attempts to increase his aesthetic sensibility in music, poetry, and narrative. But there was no resisting the schoolmaster's passionate devotion to the theater. Classical drama can be appreciated, van den Enden insisted, only if read aloud, and Bento dutifully participated with the other students in dramatized class readings, even though he was too self-conscious to speak his lines with sufficient emotion. Generally twice a year van den Enden's close friend, the director of the Amsterdam Municipal Theater, permitted the academy to use its stage for major productions before a small audience of parents and friends.

The production in the winter of 1658, over two years after the excommunication, was *Eunuchus*, by Terence, with Bento assigned the role of Parmenu, a precocious slave. When he first looked over his lines, he grinned as he came to this passage:

> If you think that uncertain things can be made certain by reason, you'll accomplish nothing more than if you strived to go insane by sanity.

Bento knew that van den Enden's wry sense of humor was undoubtedly at play when he assigned him this role. He had been persistently chiding Bento for his hypertrophied rationalism that left no space for aesthetic sensibility.

The public performance was splendid, the students played their roles with zest, the audience laughed often and applauded long (though they understood little of the Latin dialogue), and in high spirits Bento left the theater walking arm in arm with his two friends, Clara Maria (who had played Thaïs, the courtesan) and Dirk (who had played Phaedria). Suddenly out of the shadows stepped a frenzied, wild-eyed man brandishing a long butcher knife. Screaming in Portuguese, "*Herege, herege!*" ("Heretic, heretic!"), he lunged at Bento and slashed him twice in the abdomen. Dirk grappled with the attacker, knocking him to the ground, while Clara Maria rushed to Bento's aid, cradling his head in her arms. Of slight build, Dirk was no match for the attacker, who flung him off and quickly fled into the darkness, knife in hand. Van den Enden, a former physician, rushed to examine Bento. Noting the two gashes in the heavy black coat, he quickly unbuttoned it and saw that his shirt, also slashed, was splotched with blood, but the wounds themselves were only skin deep.

In a state of shock, Bento, with the support of van den Enden and Dirk, was able to walk the three blocks home and slowly make his way up the stairs to his room. With much gagging he swallowed a valerian draught prepared by the schoolmaster physician. He stretched out and, with Clara Maria sitting by his bed and holding his hand, soon lapsed into a deep twelve-hour sleep.

The following day disorder reigned in the household. Early in the morning municipal authorities appeared at the door seeking information about the attacker, and later two servants arrived bearing notes from outraged parents criticizing van den Enden not only for staging a scandalous play about sexuality and transvestism but also for permitting a young woman (his daughter) to play a role—and of a courtesan at that. The schoolmaster, however, remained remarkably placid—no, more than placid—he was amused by the letters and chuckled at how tickled Terence would have been by these outraged Calvinist parents. Soon his jocularity calmed the family, and the schoolmaster returned to teaching his Greek and classics courses.

Upstairs in the garret, Bento remained racked with anxiety and could barely tolerate the gripping pressure in his chest. Again and again he was assaulted by visions of the assault, the cries of "Heretic!," the gleaming knife, the pressure of the knife cutting through his coat, his fall to the ground under the weight of the assailant. To calm himself, he called upon his customary weapon, the sword of reason, but on this day it was no match for his terror.

Bento persisted. He tried to slow his breathing with long deliberate breaths and deliberately conjured up the fearful image of his attacker's face—heavily bearded, wide-eyed, and frothing like a mad dog—and stared directly at him until the image dissolved. "Calm yourself," he murmured. "Think only of this moment. Waste no energy on what you cannot control. You cannot control the past. You are frightened because you imagine this past event occurring now in the present. Your mind creates the image. Your mind creates your feelings about the image. Focus only on controlling your mind."

But all these well-honed formulae that he had been compiling in his notebook did nothing to slow his pounding heart. He continued attempting to soothe himself with reason: "Remember that everything in Nature has a cause. You, Bento de Spinoza, are an insignificant part of this vast causal nexus. Think of the assassin's long trajectory, the long chain of events that led inevitably to his attack." What events? Bento asked himself. Perhaps inflammatory speeches by the rabbi? Perhaps some misery in the assailant's past or present personal life? Upon all these thoughts Bento mused as he paced back and forth in his room.

Then a soft knock sounded. Within a step of the door, he reached and opened it instantly, to find Clara Maria and Dirk standing in the doorway, their hands touching, their fingers intertwined. They instantly drew their hands apart and entered his room.

"Bento," said a flustered Clara Maria. "Oh, you're up and walking? Only an hour ago we knocked, and when you didn't open, we looked in, and you were so deep asleep."

"Uh, yes, it's good to see you up," said Dirk. "They haven't caught the maniac yet, but I had a good look at him, and I'll recognize him when they catch him. I hope they put him away for a long time."

Bento said nothing.

Dirk pointed at Bento's abdomen, "Let's take a look at the wound. Van den Enden asked me to check on it." Dirk approached closer and signaled to Clara Maria to leave them.

But Bento instantly stepped back and shook his head. "No, no. I'm all right. Not just now. I'd rather be alone for a while longer."

"All right, we'll be back in an hour." Dirk and Clara Maria glanced quizzically at one another as they left the room.

Now Bento felt even worse: those hands touching and pulling apart lest he see them—that intimate glance between them. Only a few minutes ago these were his two closest friends. Only last night Dirk had saved his life; only last night he had adored Clara Maria's performance, enchanted by her every movement, every flirtatious gesture of her lips and flutter of her eyelids. And suddenly now he felt hatred toward both of them. He had been unable to thank Dirk or even utter his name or thank Clara Maria for sitting with him last night.

"Slow down," Bento murmured to himself. "Back away and look at yourself from a great distance. Look at how your feelings whirl about in a frenzy—first love, now hate, now anger. How fickle, how capricious are passions. Look at how you are tossed, first here, then there by the actions of others. If you want to flourish, you must overcome your passions by anchoring your feelings to something unchangeable, something eternally enduring."

Another knock on the door. The same soft knock. Could it be her? Then her melodious voice, "Bento, Bento, can I come in?"

Hope and passion stirred. Bento felt instantly buoyant and forgot all about the eternal and the unchanging. Perhaps Clara Maria would be alone, changed, remorseful. Perhaps she would take his hand again.

"Come in."

Clara Maria entered alone holding a note in her hand. "Bento, a man gave me this for you. A strange, agitated, rather short man with a heavy Portuguese accent who kept looking up and down the street. I think he's a Jew, and he's waiting for an answer in front by the canal."

Bento snatched the note from her extended hand, opened it, and read it quickly. Clara Maria watched with much curiosity: never before had she seen Bento devour anything so ravenously. He read it aloud to her, translating the Portuguese words into Dutch.

Bento, I've heard about last night. The whole congregation knows of it. I want to see you today. It's important. I'm standing close to your place in front of the red houseboat on the Singel. Can you come? Franco

"Clara Maria," Bento said, "he is a friend. My one remaining friend from my old life. I must go to see him. I can make it down the stairs."

"No, Papa said you must not climb stairs today. I'll tell your friend to return in a day or two."

"But he stresses 'today.' It must be related to last night. My wounds are merely scratches. I can do it."

"No, Papa placed you in my care. I forbid it. I'll bring him up here. I'm sure Papa would approve."

Bento nodded. "Thank you, but take care that the streets are clear—no one must see him enter. My excommunication forbade any Jew to speak to me. He must not be seen visiting."

Ten minutes later Clara Maria returned with Franco. "Bento, when shall I return to escort him out?" Receiving no answer from the two men entirely absorbed in staring into one another's eyes, she discreetly departed. "I'll be in the next room."

At the sound of the door closing, Franco approached and clasped Bento firmly by the shoulders. "Are you all right, Bento? She tells me you're not wounded badly."

"No, Franco, a couple of scratches here"—pointing to his belly—"but a very deep gash *here*," pointing to his head.

"It's such a relief to see you."

"For me, too. Here, let's sit down." He gestured toward the bed, where they sat while Franco continued.

"At first news went through the congregation that you were dead, struck down by God. I went to the synagogue, and the mood there was exultant—people were saying that God had heard their cries and delivered his justice. I was beside myself with anguish, and it was only when I spoke to police officials searching the neighborhood for the assassin that I learned you were wounded and, of course, not by God but by a crazy Jew."

"Who is he?"

"No one knows. Or at least, no one says they know. I've heard he is a Jew who has just arrived in Amsterdam."

"Yes, he's Portuguese. He screamed '*Herege*' when he attacked me."

"I heard that his family was killed by the Inquisition. And perhaps he had a special grievance against ex-Jews. Some ex-Jews in Spain and Portugal have become the Jews' greatest enemies: priests who gain rapid promotion by helping Inquisitors see through subterfuge."

"So, now the causal network becomes clearer."

"Causal network?"

"Franco, it is good to be with you again. I always like the way you stop me and ask for clarification. I mean simply that everything has a cause."

"Even this attack?"

"Yes, everything! All is subject to the laws of Nature, and it is possible, through our reason, to grasp this chain of causality. I believe this is true not only for physical objects but for everything human, and I am now embarking on the project of treating human actions, thoughts, and appetites just as if they were a matter of lines, planes, and bodies."

"Are you saying that we can know the cause of every thought, appetite, whim, dream?"

Bento nodded.

"Does that mean we can't simply decide to have certain thoughts? I can't decide to turn my head one way and then another way? That we have no simple free choice?"

"I do mean exactly that. Man is a part of Nature and therefore subject to Nature's causative network. Nothing, including us, in Nature can simply choose capriciously to initiate some action. There can be no separate dominion within a dominion."

"No separate dominion in a dominion? I'm lost again."

"Franco, it's over a year since we last spoke, and here I am immediately talking philosophy instead of finding out everything about your life."

"No. Nothing is more important to me than to speak like this with you. I am like a man dying of thirst coming upon an oasis. The rest can wait. Tell me about a dominion within a dominion."

"I mean that since man in every way is a part of Nature, it is incorrect to think that man disturbs, rather than follows, the order of Nature. It is incorrect to assume that he, or any entity in Nature, has free will. Everything we do is determined by either outside or inside causes. Remember how I demonstrated to you earlier that God, or Nature, did not choose the Jews?"

Franco nodded.

"So, too, is it true that God did not choose mankind to be special, to be outside of Nature's laws. That idea, I believe, has nothing to do with natural order but instead comes from our deep need to be special, to be imperishable."

"I think I'm grasping your meaning—it is a gigantic thought. No freedom of will? I'm skeptical. I want to dispute it. You see, I think I'm free to decide to say, 'I want to dispute it.' Yet I have no arguments to offer. By the next time we meet I'll have thought of some. But you were talking about the assassin and the causal network when I interrupted you. Please continue, Bento."

"I think it is a law of Nature to respond to entire classes of things in the same way. This assassin, probably maddened by grief for his family, heard that I was an ex-Jew and classified me with other ex-Jews who harmed his family."

"Your line of reasoning makes sense, but it must also include the influence of others who may have encouraged him to do this."

"Those 'others' are also subject to the causal network," Bento said.

Franco paused, nodding his head. "You know what I think, Bento?"

Bento looked at him with raised eyebrows.

"I think this is a lifetime project."

"In that we are in full agreement. And I am agreeable, most agreeable, to devote my life to this project. But what were you going to say about the influence of others upon the assassin?"

"I believe the rabbis instigated this and shaped your assailant's thoughts and actions. Rumors are that he is now being hidden in the cellar of the synagogue. I believe the rabbis wanted your death to serve as a warning to the congregation of the dangers of questioning rabbinical authority. I'm planning to inform the police of where he might be hidden."

"No, Franco. Do *not* do that. Think of the consequences. The cycle of grief, anger, revenge, punishment, retribution will be endless and ultimately will engulf you and your family. Choose a religious path."

Franco looked startled. "Religious? How can you use the term 'religious'?"

"I mean a moral path, a virtuous path. If you desire to change this cycle of anguish, you must meet this assassin," Bento said. "Comfort him, soothe his grief, try to enlighten him."

Franco nodded slowly, sat silently as he digested Bento's words, and then said, "Bento, let's go back to what you said earlier about your deep wound in your head. How serious is that wound?"

"To be honest, Franco, I am paralyzed by fear. My tight chest feels as if it were going to burst. I can't calm myself even though I've been working on it all morning."

"Working how?"

"Just what I've been describing—reminding myself that everything has a cause and that what happened *necessarily* happened."

"What does 'necessarily' mean?"

"Given all the factors that have previously occurred, this incident *had* to occur. There was no avoiding it. And one of the most important things

I've learned is that it is unreasonable to try to control things over which we have no control. This, I am convinced, is a true thought, yet the vision of this attack returns to haunt me again and again." Bento paused for a moment as his eyes lighted upon his slashed coat. "Just now it's occurred to me that the sight of that coat over there on the chair may be aggravating the problem. A big mistake keeping it there. I must dispose of it entirely. For an instant, I thought of offering it to you, but of course you cannot be seen with that coat. It was my father's coat and will be easily recognized."

"I disagree. Getting it out of sight is a bad idea. Let me say to you what I heard my father say to others in very similar situations. 'Don't dispose of it. Don't close off part of your mind, but, rather, do exactly the opposite.' So, Bento, I suggest that you hang it always in plain view, somewhere you see it at all times to remind you of the danger you face."

"I can understand the wisdom of that advice. It requires much courage to follow it."

"Bento, it is essential to keep that coat in view. I think you underestimate the danger of your situation in the world now. Yesterday, you almost died. Surely you must fear death?"

Bento nodded his head. "Yes. Though I am working to overcome that fear."

"How? Every man fears death."

"Men fear it to different degrees. Some ancient philosophers I am reading have sought for ways to soften death's terror. Remember Epicurus? We once talked about him."

Franco nodded. "Yes, the man who said the purpose of life was to live in a state of tranquility. What was that term he used?"

"*Ataraxia*. Epicurus believed that the major disturber of *ataraxia* was our fear of death, and he taught his students several powerful arguments to diminish it."

"Such as?"

"His starting point is that there is no afterlife and that we have nothing to fear from the gods after death. Then he said that death and life can never coexist. In other words: where life is, death is not, and where death is, life is not."

"That sounds logical, but I doubt it would offer calmness in the middle of the night when one awakes from a nightmare about dying."

"Epicurus has yet another argument, the symmetry argument, that may be stronger yet. It posits that the state of nonbeing after death is identical to the state of nonbeing before birth. And though we fear death, we have no dread when we think of that earlier, identical state. Therefore we have no reason to fear death either."

Franco inhaled deeply. "That catches my attention, Bento. You speak the truth. *That* argument has calming power."

"For an argument to have 'calming power' supports the idea that no things, in and of themselves, are really good or bad, pleasant or fearsome. It is only your mind that makes them so. Think of that, Franco—*it is only your mind that makes them so.* That idea has true power, and I am convinced it offers the key to healing my wound. What I must do is to alter my mind's reaction to last night's event. But I have not yet discovered how to do it."

"I'm struck how you continue to philosophize even in the midst of your panic."

"I have to see it as an opportunity for understanding. What can be more important than to learn firsthand how to temper the fear of death? Just the other day I read a passage by a Roman philosopher named Seneca, who said, 'No dread dares to enter the heart that has purged itself of the fear of death.' In other words, once you conquer the fear of death, you also conquer all other fears."

"I'm beginning to understand more about your fascination with your panic."

"The problem grows clearer, but the solution is still concealed. I wonder if I fear death particularly keenly now because I feel so full."

"What?"

"I mean full in my mind. I have many undeveloped thoughts swirling in my mind, and I am inexpressibly pained to think that those thoughts may die stillborn."

"Then take care, Bento. Protect these thoughts. And protect yourself. Though you are on the path of being a great teacher, you are, in some ways, very naïve. I think you possess so little rancor that you underestimate its existence in others. Listen to me: *you are in danger and must leave Amsterdam.* You must get out of the sight of the Jews, go into hiding, and do your thinking and writing secretly."

"I think you have a fine teacher gestating inside of you. You give me good advice, Franco, and soon, very soon, I shall follow it. But now it is your turn to tell me of your life."

"Not quite yet. I have a thought that may help with your terror. I have a question: do you think you'd be so wounded up here," Franco pointed to his head, "if the assassin were just a plain crazy man, not a Jew with a particular grievance toward you?"

Bento nodded his head. "A most excellent question." He leaned back against the bed poster, closed his eyes, and pondered it for several minutes. "I think I understand your point, and it is a most insightful one. No, I'm sure if he were *not* a Jew, the wound in my mind would *not* be so grievous."

"Ah," said Franco, "and so that means—"

"It has to mean that my panic is not *only* about death. It has an additional component, linked to my forced exile from the Jewish world."

"I think so too. How painful is that exile right now? When last we talked, you expressed only relief at leaving the world of superstition and much joy at the prospect of freedom."

"Indeed. And that relief and joy are with me still, but only in my waking life. Now I live two lives. During the day I am a new man who has shed his old skin, reads Latin and Greek, and thinks exciting, free thoughts. But at night I am Baruch, a Jewish wanderer being comforted by my mother and sister, being quizzed on the Talmud by the elders, and stumbling about in charred ruins of a synagogue. The further I get from full waking consciousness, the more I circle back to my beginnings and clutch at those phantoms of my childhood. And this may surprise you, Franco: Almost every night as I lie in this bed awaiting sleep, you pay me a visit."

"I hope I am a good guest."

"Far better than you could ever imagine. I invite you in because you bring comfort to me. And you are a good guest today. Even as we speak, I feel *ataraxia* seeping back into me. And something more than *ataraxia*— you help me think. Your question about the assassin—how I would react if he were not a Jew—helps me truly grasp the complexity of determinants. I know now I must look deeper at antecedents and consider thoughts not fully conscious, nighttime as well as daytime thoughts. Thank you for that."

Franco smiled broadly and clasped Bento's shoulder.

"And now, Franco, you *must* tell me about your life."

"Much has happened, even though my life is less adventuresome than yours. My mother and sister arrived a month after you left, and we found, with the help of the synagogue fund, a small flat not far from your import store. I pass the store often and see Gabriel, who will nod but not speak to me. I think it is because he knows, as does everyone, of my role in your *cherem*. He is married now and lives with his wife's family. I work in my uncle's shipping business and help inventory his arriving ships. I study hard and take Hebrew lessons several times a week with other immigrants. Learning Hebrew is tedious but also exciting. It comforts me and offers a lifeline, a sense of continuity with my father and his father and *his* father back for hundreds of years. That sense of continuity is immensely stabilizing.

"Your brother-in-law, Samuel, is now a rabbi and teaches us four times a week. Other rabbis, even Rabbi Mortera, take turns teaching the other days. I get the impression from comments of Samuel that your sister, Rebekah, is well. What else?"

"And what of your cousin Jacob?"

"He has moved back to Rotterdam, and I rarely see him."

"And the important question: *are you content*, Franco?"

"Yes, but a melancholy sort of contentment. Knowing you has shown me another facet of life, a life of the mind that I do not fully experience. I am greatly comforted to know that you will be there and continue to share your explorations with me. My world is smaller, and I can already see its future contours. My mother and sister have selected my wife, a girl of sixteen from our village in Portugal, and we shall marry in a few weeks. I approve of the selection—she is comely, pleasant, and brings a smile to my face. She will make a good wife."

"Will you be able to talk to her of all your interests?"

"I believe so. She, too, is starved for knowledge. Like most girls from our village, she doesn't even know how to read. I have begun her education."

"Not too much education, I hope. There may be danger in that. But, tell me, is there talk of me in the community?"

"Until this incident, I have heard none. It's as though the community were ordered not only to avoid you but also not to speak your name. I don't hear it uttered, though of course I know nothing about what is said behind closed doors. Perhaps it is only my imagination, but I do believe your spirit floats about the community and influences much. For example, our Hebrew training sessions are extraordinarily intense and permit no questioning whatsoever. It's as though the rabbis were making certain that another Spinoza will never be born."

Bento bowed his head.

"Perhaps I should not have said that, Bento. I was unkind."

"You can be unkind only by shielding me from the truth."

A gentle knock at the door and then Clara Maria's voice: "Bento."

Bento opened the door.

"Bento, I must go out soon. How much longer will your friend stay?"

Bento glanced questioningly at Franco, who whispered that he had to leave shortly, for he had no good reason to be absent from work. Bento replied, "Clara Maria, give us just a few more minutes, please."

"I'll be waiting in the music room." Clara Maria closed the door softly.

"Who is she, Bento?"

"The schoolmaster's daughter and my teacher. She's teaches me Latin and Greek also."

"Your *teacher*? Impossible. How old is she?

"About sixteen. She started teaching me at thirteen. She is a prodigy. Quite unlike any other girl."

"She seems to regard you with love and tenderness."

"Yes, that is so, and I reciprocate those sentiments but . . ." Bento hesitated; he was not accustomed to share his innermost feelings. "But today she has much aggravated my distress by showing even more tenderness toward my friend and classmate."

"Ah, jealousy. That can indeed be painful. I am so sorry, Bento. But last time did you not speak to me of embracing a life of solitude and forsaking the idea of a mate? You seemed so committed or perhaps *resigned* to a life alone."

"Committed *and* resigned. I am absolutely committed to a life of the mind and know I can never take on the responsibility of a family. And I also know that it is impossible legally to marry either Christian or Jew. And Clara Maria is Catholic. A superstitious Catholic at that."

"So you have difficulty giving up that which you really don't want and cannot have?"

"Right! I like the way you drill directly to the heart of my absurdity."

"And you say you love her? And your good friend whom she favors?"

"I had love for him as well, until today. He helped me move after the *cherem*; he saved my life last night. He is a good man. And planning to be a physician."

"But you want her to desire you rather than him, even though you know that would make all three of you unhappy. "

"Yes, that is true."

"And the greater the desire she has for you, the greater will be her despair at not having you."

"Yes, that is undeniable."

"But you love her, and you desire her happiness. And if she is in pain, you too will suffer?"

"Yes, yes, and yes. Everything you say is correct."

"And one last question. You say she is a superstitious Catholic? And Catholics adore ritual and miracles. How then does she relate to your ideas of God as Nature, to your rejection of ritual and superstition?"

"I would never speak of those views with her."

"Because she will reject them and perhaps reject you as well?"

Bento nodded. "Every word you say is true, Franco. I have strived so hard, given up so much to be free, and now I've given up my freedom and become enthralled by Clara Maria. When I think of her, I am quite incapable of thinking of other loftier thoughts. In this matter it is obvious that I am not my own master but am enslaved by passion. Though reason shows me what is better, I am forced to follow what is worse."

"It's a very old story, Bento. We have always been enslaved by love. How shall you liberate yourself?"

"I can be free only if I absolutely sever my connections to sensual pleasure, wealth, and fame. If I do not heed reason, I will remain a slave to passion."

"Yet, Bento," said Franco, standing and preparing to depart, "we know that reason is no match for passion."

"Yes. Only a stronger emotion can conquer an emotion. My task is clear: I must learn to turn reason into a passion."

"*To turn reason into a passion*," whispered Franco as they walked toward the music room, where Clara Maria waited. "A stupendous task. When next we meet I hope to hear of your progress."

CHAPTER TWENTY-SIX

BERLIN—MARCH 26, 1923

I find it difficult to get on with our Baltic families: they seem to possess some negative sort of quality, and at the same time to assume an air of superiority, of being masters of everything, that I have encountered nowhere else.

Adolf Hitler on Alfred Rosenberg

Dear Friedrich,

With regret, I must cancel my upcoming visit. Though this is the third time I've done so, please don't give up on me. I am entirely serious in my desire for consultation with you, but demands on my time have sharply increased. Last week Hitler asked me to replace Dietrich Eckart as editor in chief of the Völkischer Beobachter. *Hitler and I are closer now—he is much pleased about my publication of* The Protocols of the Elders of Zion. *A month ago, with the help of a generous donor, the VB became a daily and now has a circulation of 33,000 (and, by the way, you can now find copies available on Berlin newsstands).*

Every day there is a new crisis to report. Every day the future of Germany seems to hang in the balance. For example, at the moment we must decide how to cope with the French, who have invaded the Ruhr in order to extract their criminal reparation payments. And every day spiraling inflation brings our entire country to the edge of the precipice. Can you believe that a U.S.

dollar, that only a year ago was worth 400 marks, is worth 20,000 marks this morning? Can you believe employers in Munich are beginning to pay workers three times a day? Is it also true in Berlin? The wife accompanies her husband to work, and they are paid once in the morning, and then she runs to buy breakfast before prices rise. She appears at noon to collect the pay (higher now) and must again rush to buy lunch—100,000 marks that bought four wursts the day before now buys only three—and a third time, again at a higher rate, at the end of the day, when the money is safe once the markets close until the morning stock exchange opens. It's a scandal, a tragedy.

And it will get worse. I believe this will be the greatest hyperinflation in history: all Germans will be pauperized except, of course, the Jews, who, naturally, profit from this nightmare. Their company safes bulge with gold and foreign currency.

My life as a publisher is so hectic I find it impossible to leave the office for lunch, much less board the train for the ten-hour, 20-million-mark journey to Berlin. Please let me know if ever anything brings you to Munich so we could meet here. I would be most grateful. Have you ever considered practicing in Munich? I could help: think of all the free ads I could run for you.

Dr. Karl Abraham read the letter and handed it back to Friedrich. "And how do you plan to respond?"

"I don't know. I'd like to use my supervisory hour today to discuss it. You remember him? I described my talk with him some months ago."

"The publisher of *The Protocols of Zion*? How could I forget him?"

"I haven't seen Herr Rosenberg since then. Just some letters. But here's yesterday's copy of his paper, the *Völkischer Beobachter*. Just look at this headline:

CHILD ABUSE IN VIENNA BORDELLO: MANY JEWS INVOLVED

Glancing at the headline, Dr. Abraham shook his head in disgust and asked, "And *The Protocols*—have you read it?"

"Only extracts and a few discussions that label it a fraud."

"An obvious fraud, but a dangerous one. And I have no doubt that your patient, Rosenberg, knew that. Reliable Jewish scholars in my community tell me that the Protocols were concocted by a disreputable Russian writer, Serge Nilus, who wished to persuade the tsar that the Jews were trying to dominate Russia. After reading *The Protocols*, the tsar ordered a series of bloody pogroms."

"So," Friedrich said, "my question is how can I do therapy with a patient who commits such vile acts? I know he is dangerous. How do I handle my countertransference?"

"I prefer to think of countertransference as the therapist's neurotic response to the patient. In this case, your feelings have a rational basis. The proper question becomes, 'How do you work with someone who is, by any objective standard, a repulsive, malignant person capable of much destruction?'"

Friedrich considered his supervisor's words. "Repulsive, malignant. Strong words."

"You're right, Dr. Pfister—those were my terms, not yours, and I believe you're alluding, quite correctly, to another issue—the countertransference of the *supervisor*—which may interfere with my ability to teach you. Being a Jew makes it impossible for me personally to treat this lethal, anti-Semitic individual, but let's see if perhaps I can still be of use as a supervisor. Tell me more about your feelings toward him."

"Though I'm not Jewish, I'm personally offended by his anti-Semitism. After all, the people I am closest to here are almost all Jews—my analyst, you, and most of the faculty of the institute." Friedrich picked up Alfred's letter. "Look. He writes proudly of his career advancements, expecting me to be pleased. Instead I feel increasingly offended and frightened for you, for all civilized Germans. I think he's evil. And his idol, this Hitler, may be the devil incarnate."

"That's one part. Yet there is another part of you that wants to continue seeing him. Why?"

"It's what we discussed before—my intellectual interest in analyzing someone whose past I shared. I've known his brother all my life; I knew Alfred as a young child."

"But Dr. Pfister, it's obvious that you'll never be able to analyze him. The distance alone makes that impossible. At best you'll see him only for a few scattered sessions and never be able to do deep archaeological work on his past."

"Right. I have to let that idea go. There must be other reasons."

"I remember your telling me about your sense of an annihilated past. There is only your good friend, the brother. I've forgotten his name—"

"Eugen."

"Yes, there remains only Eugen Rosenberg and to a much lesser extent, in that you were never close to him, Eugen's younger brother, Alfred. Your parents are dead, no siblings, you have no other contacts with your early life—neither persons nor places. It seems to me that you're trying to deny aging or transience by searching for something imperishable. You're dealing with that, I hope, in your personal analysis?"

"Not yet. But your comments are helpful. I cannot stop time by clinging to Eugen or Alfred. Yes, Dr. Abraham, you're making it clear that seeing Alfred does nothing for my inner conflicts."

"That is so important, Dr. Pfister, I will repeat it. *Seeing Alfred Rosenberg can do nothing for your inner conflicts.* The place for that is in your own analysis. Right?"

Friedrich nodded, resigned.

"So I ask again—why do you want to see him?"

"I'm unsure. I agree that he is a dangerous man, a man who spreads hatred. Yet I still think of him as the little boy next door rather than a man who is evil. I consider him misguided, not demonic. He truly believes that racial nonsense, and his thoughts and actions follow in a perfectly consistent manner from Houston Stewart Chamberlain's premises. I don't believe he is a psychopath, a sadist, or a violent person. He's rather timid in fact, almost cowardly and insecure. He relates poorly to others, and is entirely given over to the hope of love from his leader, Hitler. But still, he seems aware of his limitations and surprisingly ready to do some therapeutic work."

"So, then, your goals in therapy are . . ."

"Perhaps I'm being naïve, but isn't it true that if I can change him into a more moral person, then he'll do less mischief in the world? That has got to be better than doing nothing. Perhaps I can even help him address the power and the irrationality of his anti-Semitism."

"Ah, if you could successfully analyze anti-Semitism, you'd get the Nobel prize that has, so far, eluded Freud's grasp. You have ideas about how to approach that?"

"Not yet—it's off in the distance, and certainly it's *my* goal, not the patient's goal."

"And his goal? What does he want?"

"His explicit goal is to relate more effectively to Hitler and other party members. I would have to smuggle in anything loftier than that."

"Are you a good smuggler?"

"Just a novice, but I have an idea. I've mentioned to you that I've tutored him on Spinoza. Well, in Part 4 of the *Ethics*—the section on overcoming the bondage of passion—there is a phrase that caught my attention. Spinoza says that reason is no match for passion and what we must do is to turn reason into a passion."

"Hmm, interesting. How do you propose to do that?"

"I don't have a precise method in mind. But I know that I must fertilize his curiosity about himself. Doesn't everyone have an intense interest in himself? Doesn't everyone want to know everything about himself? I know I do. I shall strive to inflame Alfred's self-curiosity."

"Interesting way of framing therapy, Dr. Pfister. An original way. Let's hope he'll cooperate, and I'll do what I can to be helpful in supervision. But I wonder if there's not a flaw in your argument."

"Which is?"

"Overgeneralization. Therapists are different. We're odd ducks. Most other people don't share our passionate curiosity about the mind. So far, I hear that his goal is vastly different from yours: what he wants is to make himself more lovable to his fellow Nazis. So keep in mind the danger that therapy just might make things worse for all of us! Let me be more concrete. If you succeed in helping Rosenberg change in a way that would make Hitler love him more, then you'll have only made him more efficiently evil."

"I understand. My task is to help him embrace another, quite opposite goal—to understand and diminish his desperate and irrational need for Hitler's love."

Dr. Abraham smiled at his young student. "Precisely. I love your enthusiasm, Friedrich. Who knows? Maybe you can do this. Let's search for some professional meetings in Munich you might attend and have additional sessions with him there."

————

Bayreuth—October 1923

Despite his work pressures, Alfred followed through on his plan to pay a visit to Houston Stewart Chamberlain and easily persuaded Hitler to join him. Hitler, too, had been set afire by Chamberlain's *Foundations of the Nineteenth Century* and would claim, to the end of his life, that Chamberlain (along with Dietrich Eckart and Richard Wagner) were his primary intellectual mentors.

Chamberlain lived in Bayreuth, in Wahnfried, Wagner's massive old home, with his wife, Eva (Wagner's daughter), and Cosima, Wagner's eighty-six-year-old widow. The hundred-and-fifty-mile drive to Bayreuth was most pleasant for Alfred. It was his first trip in Hitler's gleaming new Mercedes and an opportunity to enjoy Hitler's sole attention for several hours.

A servant greeted them and led them upstairs, where Chamberlain sat in a wheelchair, his legs neatly covered by a blue and green tartan blanket, and stared out of the large window overlooking the Wagner inner courtyard. Ailing from some mysterious nervous disorder that left him partially paralyzed and unable to speak clearly, Chamberlain looked far older than his seventy years: his skin was blotchy, his eyes vacant, half of his face distorted by spasm. Fixing his eyes on Hitler's face, Chamberlain nodded from time to time and appeared to comprehend Hitler's words. He never glanced at Rosenberg. Hitler leaned forward, his mouth close to Chamberlain's ear, and said, "I treasure your words in your great book, *Foundations of the Nineteenth Century*: 'The Germanic race is engaged in a mortal struggle with the Jews that is to be fought not only with cannon but with every weapon of human life and society.'" Chamberlain nodded, and Hitler continued, "Herr Chamberlain, I promise that I am the man who will wage that war for you," and went on at great length to describe his twenty-five-point program and his absolute unshakeable determination to have a Jew-free Europe. Chamberlain nodded vigorously and from time to time croaked, "Yes, yes."

Later, when Hitler left the room for a private audience with Cosima Wagner, Rosenberg was left alone with Chamberlain and told him that at the age of sixteen he, like Hitler, had been enthralled by *Foundations of the Nineteenth Century* and that he, too, owed an enduring debt to Chamberlain. Then, leaning closer to Chamberlain's ear, as Hitler had done, he confided, "I'm starting to write a book that I hope will continue your work for the next century." Perhaps Chamberlain smiled—his face was so distorted that it was hard to tell. Alfred continued, "Your ideas and your words shall be everywhere in my pages. I am just beginning. It will be a five-year project— there is so much to be done. I have, however, just written a passage for the ending: 'The sacred hours of the Germans will reappear when the symbol of awakening—the flag with the swastika sign of resurgent life—has become the sole prevailing creed of the Reich.'" Chamberlain grunted. Perhaps he said, "Yes, yes."

Alfred sat back in his chair and looked about. Hitler was still nowhere to be seen. Alfred again bent over to Chamberlain's ear, "Dear teacher, I need your help with something. It's the Spinoza problem. Tell me how this Jew from Amsterdam could have written works so greatly revered by the greatest of German thinkers, including the immortal Goethe. How could this be possible?" Chamberlain moved his head in agitated fashion and uttered some garbled sounds of which Rosenberg could only distinguish, "*Ja, Ja.*" Shortly afterward he slumped into a deep sleep.

On their drive home, the two men spoke little of Chamberlain, for Alfred had another agenda: to persuade Hitler that the time had come for the party to act. Alfred reminded Hitler of the basic facts. "Chaos envelops Germany," Alfred said. "Inflation is veering out of control. Four months ago, a dollar was worth 75,000 deutschmarks, while yesterday a dollar was worth 150 million marks. Yesterday my corner grocer was charging 90 million deutschmarks for a pound of potatoes. And I know for a fact that, shortly, the treasury printing presses will be rolling out 1-trillion-mark notes."

Hitler nodded wearily. He had heard all this from Alfred several times.

"And look at all the coups cropping up all over," Alfred continued. "The Communist putsch in Saxony, the Reichswehr reserve putsch in East Prussia, the Kapp coup in Berlin, the Rhenish separatists' coup. But it's Munich and all of Bavaria that's the real powder keg ready to explode. Munich is crammed with a host of right-wing parties opposing the government in Berlin, but, of these, we are by far the strongest, the most powerful, and the best organized. It is our time! I've stirred up the populace with article after article in our newspaper, readying them for a major action by the party."

Hitler still appeared uncertain. Alfred pressed him, "Your time has come. You must act now, or you will lose your moment."

When the car arrived at the office building of the *Völkischer Beobachter*, Hitler merely said, "Much to think about, Rosenberg."

A few days later Hitler visited Alfred at his office and with a big smile waved a letter he had just received from Houston Stewart Chamberlain and read parts of it aloud:

> *Oct. 7, 1923*
>
> *Most respected and dear Herr Hitler:*
>
> *You have every right to be surprised at this intrusion, having seen with your own eyes how difficult it is for me to speak. But I cannot resist the urge to address a few words to you.*
>
> *I have been wondering why it was you of all people, you who are so extraordinary in awakening people from sleep and humdrum routines, who recently gave me a longer and more refreshing sleep than I have experienced since that fateful day in August 1914, when I was first struck down by this insidious sickness. Now I believe I understand that it is precisely this that characterizes and defines your being: the true awakener is at the same time the bestower of peace. . .*
>
> *That you brought me peace is related very much to your eyes and hand gestures. Your eye works almost as a hand: it grips and holds a person; and you have the singular quality of being able to focus your words on one particular listener at any given moment. As for your hands, they are so expressive in their movement that they rival your eyes. Such a man brings rest to a poor suffering spirit! Especially when he is dedicated to the service of the Fatherland.*
>
> *My faith in Germandom has never wavered for a moment, though my hopes had, I confess, reached a low ebb. At one blow you have transformed the state of my soul. That Germany in its hour of greatest need has given birth to a Hitler is proof of vitality; your actions offer further evidence, for a man's personality and actions belong together.*
>
> *I was able to sleep without a care. Nothing caused me to awaken again. May God protect you!*
>
> *Houston Stewart Chamberlain*

"He must have recovered his speech and dictated it—a magnificent letter," said Alfred as he strained to conceal his envy. Then he quickly added, "And well deserved, Herr Hitler."

"Now, let me give you some real news," Hitler said. "Erich Ludendorff has joined forces with us!"

"Well done! Well done!" replied Alfred. Ludendorff was, to put it mildly, eccentric, but he was still universally respected as the world war field marshal.

"He agrees with my idea of a putsch," Hitler continued. "He agrees that we should combine forces with other right-wing groups, even the monarchist groups and the Bavarian separatists, and storm into the evening meeting on November 8, kidnap several Bavarian government officials, and force them at gunpoint to accept me as their leader. The following day we will all march through the center of the city to the war ministry and, with the help of the hostages and the reputation of Field Marshal Ludendorff, win over the German army. And then we will emulate Mussolini's march to Rome by marching on to Red Berlin and bring down the German democratic government."

"Excellent! We're on our way." Alfred was so joyful that he barely minded Hitler overlooking that Alfred had suggested this very plan to him. He was used to having Hitler appropriate his ideas without crediting him.

But everything went wrong. The putsch was a complete fiasco. On the evening of November 8, Hitler and Alfred went together to the meeting of the coalition of right-wing parties. These parties had never before conferred together, and the meeting grew so unruly that at one point Hitler had to jump on a table and fire his pistol at the ceiling to establish order. The Nazis then kidnapped the delegates of the Bavarian government to hold as hostages. However, thinking they had come over to the Nazi view, the kidnappers failed to guard them properly, and the hostages escaped into the night. Nonetheless, Hitler acceded to Ludendorff's insistence that they proceed with their mass march in the morning, with the hope of creating an uprising among the citizens. Ludendorff was certain that neither the army nor the police would dare to fire upon him. Rosenberg rushed back to the office and prepared the VB's headlines calling for general revolt. Early in the morning of November 9, 1923, a column of two thousand men, many of them armed, including Hitler and Rosenberg, began their march to the center of Munich. In the front row were Hitler; Field Marshal Ludendorff, resplendent in his full military uniform with his world war pickle helmet; Hermann Göring, the popular world war ace wearing all his many war dec- orations; and Scheubner-Richter, who walked arm in arm with his close friend Hitler. Rosenberg was in the second row directly behind Hitler. Rudolf Hess marched behind Rosenberg, as did Putzi Hanfstaengl (the donor who had enabled the VB to become a daily paper). A few rows back, Heinrich Himmler marched, carrying the Nazi Party flag.

As they reached an open square, a barricade of troops awaited them. Hitler yelled to the troops to surrender. Instead they opened fire, and a three-minute firefight ensued during which the marchers immediately dis- banded. Sixteen Nazis and three troops were killed. Field Marshal Luden- dorff marched straight ahead unflinchingly to the barricade, pushed the rifles aside, and was greeted politely by an officer who apologized for the necessity of taking him into protective custody. Göring was wounded twice in the groin but crawled to safety and was taken to a kindly Jewish physician who gave him excellent treatment, after which he was quickly driven out of the country. Scheubner-Richter, who had locked arms with Hitler, was instantly killed and dragged Hitler to the ground, dislocating his shoulder. A bodyguard, Ulrich Graf, fell on Hitler and took several bul- lets, saving Hitler's life.

Though the man standing next to Alfred was killed, Alfred was un- harmed and crawled to the sidewalk away from the carnage and scampered into the crowd. He did not dare go home or to the office—the government immediately closed the VB indefinitely and posted guards before the news- paper offices. Ultimately Alfred persuaded an elderly woman to allow him to hide in her house during the next few days, while at night he wandered through Munich trying to learn the fate of his comrades. Hitler, in great pain, had crawled a few feet, was pulled into a waiting car, and, accompanied by a party physician, was driven to the home of Putzi Hanfstaengl, where his shoulder was treated and he was hidden in the attic. Just before he was ar- rested, he scribbled a note addressed to Alfred and asked Frau Hanfstaengl to deliver it. She found Alfred the following day and handed him the note, which he immediately ripped open and to his great surprise read:

DEAR ROSENBERG, LEAD THE MOVEMENT FROM NOW ON.
ADOLF HITLER

CHAPTER TWENTY-SEVEN

RIJNSBURG—1662

Within a few days, Bento's fear had subsided. Gone were the racing pulse, the tight chest, and the intrusive visions of the assassin's attack. And what a blessed relief to breathe easily and feel safe in his skin! With some dispassion, he could even visualize the assassin's face and, following Franco's suggestion, look at the slashed black overcoat hanging in plain sight on the wall of his room.

For weeks after the assassination attempt and Franco's visit, he pondered the mechanisms of overcoming terror. How had he recovered his equanimity? Was it not his improved understanding of the causes motivating the assassin? Bento leaned toward that explanation—it felt robust; it felt reasonable. Yet he was suspicious of his strong attachment to the power of understanding. After all, it hadn't helped him at first; it was only after Franco appeared that the idea gained purchase. The more he thought about it, the clearer it was that Franco offered something essential to his recovery. Bento knew he had been at his worst when Franco arrived and then, very quickly, began to improve. But what precisely had Franco offered? Perhaps his major contribution was to have dissected the ingredients of the terror and to have demonstrated that Bento was particularly unsettled by the fact that his assassin was a Jew. In other words, the terror was augmented by his buried pain of separation from his people. That might explain Franco's healing power: not only had he helped the process of reason, but, possibly even more importantly, he offered his sheer presence—his Jewish presence.

And Franco had also jolted Bento out of his tormented jealousy by confronting him with the irrationality of yearning for something that he neither truly desired nor could possibly have. Bento steadily regained his tranquility and before long reestablished his camaraderie with Clara Maria and Dirk. Still, dark clouds gathered in his mind once again the day Clara Maria appeared wearing a pearl necklace given to her by Dirk. The clouds became a major squall a few days afterward, when they announced their engagement. But this time reason prevailed; Bento maintained his equilibrium and refused to allow passions to rupture his relationships with his two good friends.

Even so, Bento clung to the tactile memory of Clara Maria holding his hand throughout that night after the attack. And he recalled, too, the way Franco had clasped his shoulder and also how he and his brother Gabriel had often held hands. But there would be no more touching for him, however much his body yearned for it. Sometimes fantasies of touching and embracing Clara Maria or her aunt Martha, whom he also found attractive, stole into his mind, but they were easily swept away. Nighttime yearnings were another matter: he could lock no doors barring entry into his dreams, nor could he stem the nocturnal flow of his seed often staining his bedclothes. All this, of course, he held in the deepest vaults of silence, but were he to share it with Franco, he could predict the response: "It has always been thus—sexual pressure is part of our creatureliness; it is the force that allows our kind to persevere."

Though Bento saw the wisdom of Franco's advice to leave Amsterdam, he nonetheless lingered there for several more months. His linguistic skills as well as his powers of logic resulted in many Collegiants seeking his help with translation of Hebrew and Latin documents. Soon the Collegiants had formed a philosophy club headed by his friend Simon de Vries that met regularly and often discussed ideas formulated by Bento.

But this growing appreciative circle of acquaintances, so salutary for his self-esteem, also intruded heavily into his time, making it difficult for him to attend fully to the thoughts burgeoning within him. He spoke to Simon de Vries of his desire for a quieter life, and soon Simon, with the help of other philosophy club members, identified a house in Rijnsburg where he could live. Rijnsburg, a small community on the river Vliet forty kilometers from Amsterdam, was not only the center of the Collegiant movement but conveniently close to the University of Leiden, where Bento, now proficient in Latin, would be able to attend philosophy classes and enjoy the company of other scholars.

Bento found Rijnsburg much to his liking. The house was made of sturdy stone, with several small-paned windows looking out to a well-tended apple orchard. On the entry wall was painted a brief verse echoing the discontent of many Collegiants about the state of the world:

> *Alas! If all humans were wise,*
> *And had more good will*
> *The world would be a Paradise*
> *Now it is mostly a Hell!*

Bento's quarters consisted of two ground-floor rooms, one for his study, burgeoning library, and four-poster bed; the other a smaller work room holding his lens-grinding equipment. Dr. Hooman, a surgeon, lived with his wife in the other half of the house—a combined large kitchen and living room and an upstairs bedroom, reached by a steep stairway.

Bento paid a small additional fee for supper, which he usually took with Dr. Hooman and his most congenial wife. Sometimes, after his long days of solitary writing and lens grinding, he looked forward to their company, but when he was particularly engrossed in an idea, he reverted to old habits and for several days supped in his room, staring at the fecund apple trees in the rear orchard, while he thought and wrote.

A year passed most agreeably. One September morning Bento awoke feeling out of sorts, listless, and achy. Yet he decided to proceed with his plans to travel to Amsterdam to deliver some fine telescope lenses to a client. Moreover, his friend Simon de Vries, the secretary of the Collegiant Philosophy Club, had arranged for him to be present at a meeting for a discussion of the first part of Bento's new work. Bento pulled Simon's most recent letter from his bag and reread it.

> *Most Honorable Friend—I await your arrival with impatience. I sometimes complain of my lot, in that we are separated from each other by so long a distance. Happy, yes, most happy is Doctor Hooman, abiding under the same roof with you, who can talk with you on the best of subjects, at dinner, at supper, and during your walks. However, though I am far apart from you in body, you have been very frequently present to my mind, especially in your writings, while I read and turn them over. But as they are not all clear*

*to the members of our club, for which reason we have begun a fresh series
of meetings, and we look forward to your explanation of difficult passages,
so that we may be better able under your guidance to defend the truth against
those who are superstitiously religious and to withstand the attack of the
whole world.*

> *Your most devoted,*
> S. J. DE VRIES

As he folded up the letter, Bento experienced both joy and uneasiness—
joy at Simon's good words but suspiciousness of his own yearning for an
admiring audience. Without doubt moving to Rijnsburg was a wise decision.
Wiser yet, he imagined, might be an even farther move from Amsterdam.

He walked the short distance to Oegstgeest, where, for 21 stuivers, he
boarded the morning *trekschuit*, a horse-drawn barge that took passengers
down the small *trekvaart*, the canal recently dug that ran straight to Amsterdam. For a few stuivers more he could have sat in the cabin, but it was
a fine sunny day, and he sat on the deck and reread the beginning of his
paper, "Treatise on the Emendation of the Intellect," to be discussed the following day by Simon's philosophy club. He had begun by describing his
personal search for happiness.

> After experience had taught me that all the usual surroundings of so-
> cial life are vain and futile; seeing that none of the objects of my fears
> contained in themselves anything either good or bad, except in so far
> as the mind is affected by them, I finally resolved to inquire whether
> there might be some real good having power to communicate itself,
> which would affect the mind singly, to the exclusion of all else:
> whether, in fact, there might be anything of which the discovery and
> attainment would enable me to enjoy continuous, supreme, and un-
> ending happiness.

Next he described his inability to achieve his goal while still clutching his
cultural beliefs that the highest good consisted of riches, fame, and the sensual
pleasures. These goods, he insisted, were not good for one's health. He carefully
read his comments about the limitations of these three worldly goods.

By *sensual pleasure* the mind is enthralled to the extent of quiescence, as if the supreme good were actually attained, so that it is quite incapable of thinking of any other object; when such pleasure has been gratified it is followed by extreme melancholy, whereby the mind, though not enthralled, is disturbed and dulled.

In the case of *fame* the mind is still more absorbed, for fame is conceived as always good for its own sake, and as the ultimate end to which all actions are directed. Further, the attainment of *riches* and *fame* is not followed as in the case of sensual pleasures by repentance, but, the more we acquire, the greater is our delight, and, consequently, the more are we incited to increase both the one and the other; on the other hand, if our hopes happen to be frustrated, we are plunged into the deepest sadness.

Fame has the further drawback that it compels its votaries to order their lives according to the opinions of their fellow-men, shunning what they usually shun, and seeking what they usually seek.

Bento nodded, particularly satisfied with his description of the problem of fame. Now to the remedy: he had expressed his difficulties letting go of a sure and accustomed good for something uncertain. Then he had immediately tempered that idea by saying that, since he sought for a fixed good, something unchangeable, it was clearly not uncertain in its nature but only in its attainment. Though he was pleased with the progression of his arguments, he grew uncomfortable as he continued to read. Perhaps he had said and revealed too much of himself in several passages:

I thus perceived that I was in a state of great peril, and I compelled myself to seek with all my strength for a remedy, however uncertain it might be; as a sick man struggling with a deadly disease, when he sees that death will surely be upon him unless a remedy be found, is compelled to seek a remedy with all his strength, inasmuch as his whole hope lies therein.

He felt flushed as he read and began to murmur to himself. "This is not philosophy. This is far too personal. What have I done? This is simply passionate argument intended to evoke emotions. I resolve . . . no, more than resolve, I *vow* . . . that in the future, Bento de Spinoza and his search, his fears, his hopes, will be invisible. I write falsely if I cannot persuade readers entirely by the reason of my arguments."

He nodded as he continued reading passages describing how men have sacrificed all, even their lives, in pursuit of riches, reputation, and indulgence in sensual pleasures. Now to introduce the remedy in short strong passages.

(1) All these evils seem to have arisen from the fact that happiness or unhappiness is made wholly dependent on the quality of the object which we love.

(2) When a thing is not loved, no quarrels will arise concerning it— no sadness be felt, no hatred, in short no disturbances of the mind.

(3) All these arise from the love of what is perishable, such as the objects already mentioned.

(4) But love towards a thing eternal and infinite feeds the mind wholly with joy, and is itself unmingled with any sadness, wherefore it is greatly to be desired and sought for with all our strength.

He could read no more. His head began to throb—he definitely did not feel himself today—and he closed his eyes and dozed for what seemed a quarter of an hour. The first thing he saw when he awakened was a tightly clustered group of twenty to thirty strolling next to the canal. Who were they? Where were they going? He could not take his eyes off of them as the *trekschuit* neared and then passed the group. At the next stop, still at least an hour's walk to Simon de Vries's home in Amsterdam, where he would spend the night, he surprised himself by grabbing his bag, jumping off the barge, and heading backward, toward the strolling group.

Soon he drew close enough to notice that the men, who were dressed in working-class Dutch garb, all wore yarmulkes. Yes, without doubt, they were Jews, but Ashkenazi Jews, who would not recognize him. He drew closer. The group had stopped at a clearing by the banks of the canal and gathered about their leader, undoubtedly their rabbi, who began chanting at the very edge of the water. Bento edged closer to the group to hear his words. One elderly woman, short and stocky, her shoulders covered with heavy black cloth, eyed Bento for several minutes and then slowly approached him. Bento looked at her wrinkled face, so kind, so maternal that he thought of his own mother. But no, his mother had died at a younger age than he was now. This old woman would be *her* mother's age. She moved closer to him and said, "*Bist an undzeriker?*" ("Are you one of us?").

Though Bento had picked up only small bits of Yiddish from his commercial dealings with Ashkenazi Jews, he understood her question perfectly yet was unable to answer. Finally, shaking his head, he whispered, "Sephardic."

"*Ah, ir zayt an undzeriker. Ot iz a matone fun Rifke.*" ("Then you are one of us. Here, here is a gift from Rifke.") She reached into her apron pocket, handed him a sizeable chunk of fresh bread, and pointed to the canal.

He nodded thanks, and as she walked away, Bento slapped his forehead and murmured to himself, "Tashlich. Astounding . . . it's Rosh Hashanah—how could I have forgotten?" He knew the ceremony of Tashlich well. For centuries congregations of Jews had held a Rosh Hashanah service near the banks of running water that ended by their throwing bread into the water. The words of the scriptures came back to him: "The Lord will take us back in love; He will cover up our iniquities. You will cast all their sins into the depths of the sea" (Micah 7:19).

He edged closer to listen to the rabbi, who urged his congregation, the men clustered about him and the women in an outer circle, to think of all their regrets of the past year, all their acts of unkindness and their ignoble thoughts, their envy and pride and guilt, and told them to shed them, to toss unworthy thoughts away just as they now threw away their bread. The rabbi tossed his bread into the water, and immediately the others followed suit. Bento momentarily reached into his pocket where he had put his bread but pulled his hand back. He disliked participating in any ritual, and, besides, he was a bystander and was too far from the canal. The rabbi chanted the prayers in Hebrew, and Bento reflexively murmured the words with him. It was, all in all, a pleasing and most sensible ceremony, and as the crowd turned back to walk to their synagogue, many nodded to him and said, "*Gut Yontef*" ("Good holiday"). He reciprocated with a smile, "*Gut Yontef dir*" ("Good holiday to you"). He liked their faces; they seemed like good people. Even though their appearance differed from his own Sephardic community, still they resembled the people he had known as a child. Simple but thoughtful. Serene and comfortable with one another. He missed them. Oh, he missed them.

As he walked to Simon's house, nibbling Rifke's bread, Bento pondered his experience. Obviously he had underestimated the power of the past. Its stamp is indelible; it cannot be erased; it colors the present and vastly influences feelings and actions. More clearly than ever before, he understood how nonconscious thoughts and feelings are a part of the causative network. So many things became clear: the healing power with which he imbued Franco, the strong sweet tug of the Tashlich ceremony, even the extraordinary taste of Rifke's bread that he chewed slowly as if to extract every particle of flavor. What's more, he knew for certain that his mind undoubtedly contained an unseen calendar: though he had forgotten Rosh Hashanah, some part of his mind had remembered that today marked the beginning of a new year. Perhaps it was this hidden knowledge that lay behind the malaise that had plagued him the entire day. With this thought, his aches and his heaviness vanished. His stride quickened as he headed toward Amsterdam and Simon de Vries.

CHAPTER TWENTY-EIGHT

FRIEDRICH'S OFFICE, OLIVAER PLATZ 3, BERLIN—1925

For it is not you, gentlemen, who pass judgment on us. That judgment is spoken by the eternal court of history . . . Pronounce us guilty a thousand times over: the goddess of the eternal court of history will smile and tear to pieces the State Prosecutor's submissions and the court's verdict; for she acquits us.

—Adolf Hitler, final lines of his 1924 Munich trial speech

On April 1, 1925, the VB had reappeared as a daily again. And who was reinstalled as editor, in spite of all my pleadings and arguments?—Rosenberg, the insufferable, narrow-minded, mock mythologist, the anti-Semitic half-Jew, who, I maintain to this day, did more harm to the movement than any man except Goebbels.

—Ernst (Putzi) Hanfstaengl

Hitler's note utterly astounded me. Here, Friedrich, I want you to see it with your own eyes. I carry it in my wallet at all times. I now keep it in an envelope—it's starting to fall apart."

Friedrich took the packet gingerly, unfolded the envelope, and extracted the note.

DEAR ROSENBERG, LEAD THE MOVEMENT FROM NOW ON.

ADOLF HITLER

"So this was given to you just after the failed putsch—two years ago?"

"The day after. He wrote it on November 10, 1923."

"Tell me more about your reaction."

"As I say, stunned. I hadn't a single clue he would select me to succeed him."

"Keep going."

Alfred shook his head. "I . . ." He choked up for a moment and then regained his composure and blurted out: "I was jolted. Bewildered. How could it be? Hitler never spoke of my leading the party before this note—and never spoke of it again after he wrote it!"

Hitler never spoke of it before or after. Friedrich tried to digest that odd thought but continued focusing on Alfred's emotions. His analytic training had made him more patient. He knew all would unfold in time. "A lot of emotion in your voice, Alfred. It's important to follow feelings. What comes up for you?"

"Everything fell apart with the putsch. The party was dispersed. The leaders were either in jail, like Hitler, or out of the country, like Göring, or in hiding, like me. The government outlawed the party and permanently closed the *Völkischer Beobachter.* It reopened only a few months ago, and I'm back at my old job."

"I want to hear about all of this, but for the moment go back to your feelings about the note. Do what we've done before: imagine the scene when you opened the note for the first time, and then say whatever floats into your mind."

Alfred closed his eyes and concentrated. "Pride. Great pride—he chose *me, me above all the rest*—he passed his mantle to me. It meant everything. That's why I carry it with me. I had *no* idea he trusted me and valued me so much. What else? Great joy. It was perhaps the proudest moment of my life. No, not perhaps, it *was* my proudest moment. I loved him so much for that. And then . . . and then . . ."

"And then what, Alfred? Don't stop."

"And then it all turned to shit! That note. Everything! My greatest joy turned into the greatest . . . the greatest *pestilence* of my life."

"From joy to pestilence. Fill me in on the transformation." Friedrich knew his comments were unnecessary. Alfred was bursting to talk.

"It would take all my time today to answer in detail, so much has happened." Alfred looked at his watch.

"I know you can't tell me everything about the last three years, but I'll need at least some brief overview if I'm to really understand your distress."

Alfred looked at the high ceiling of Friedrich's spacious office and gathered his thoughts. "How to put it? In essence that note gave me an impossible task. I was asked to lead a sorry cadre of venomous men all scheming for power, all with personal agendas, each one set on defeating me. Each one shallow and stupid, each one threatened by my superior intelligence and entirely unable to comprehend my words. Each profoundly ignorant of the principles the party stood for."

"And Hitler? He asked you to lead the party. No support from him?"

"Hitler? He has been entirely bewildering and has made my life more difficult. You've not followed the drama of our party?"

"Sorry, but I'm not keeping up with political events. I continue to be consumed by new developments in my field and by all the patients calling upon me—mostly ex-soldiers. Besides, it's best I hear everything from your perspective."

"I'll summarize. As you probably know, in 1923 we tried to persuade the leaders of the Bavarian government to join us in a march on Berlin patterned on Mussolini's march on Rome. But our putsch was an utter fiasco. In everyone's view it could not have been worse. It was poorly planned and poorly executed and disintegrated at the first sign of resistance. When Hitler wrote that note to me, he was hiding in Putzi Hanfstaengl's attic, facing imminent arrest and possible deportation. When Frau Hanfstaengl delivered the note, she described what had happened. Three cars of policemen came to the house, and Hitler grew frenzied and waved his pistol, saying he would shoot himself before he let those swine take him. Fortunately, her husband had taught her jujitsu, and Hitler, with his injured shoulder, was no match for her. Frau Hanfstaengl wrestled the gun from his hands and threw it into a huge two-hundred-kilo barrel of flour. After quickly scribbling a note to me, Hitler went meekly to jail. Everyone thought his career was over. Hitler was finished—he was a national laughing stock.

"Or so it seemed. But it was at this lowest point that his true genius emerged. He turned the fiasco into pure gold. I'll be honest: he has treated me like shit. I'm devastated by what he did to me, and yet at this moment I am more convinced than ever that he is a man of destiny."

"Explain that to me, Alfred."

"His moment of redemption came at the trial. There, all the other putsch participants meekly pleaded not guilty to the charges of treason. Some were given light sentences—for example, Hess got seven months. Some, like the untouchable Field Marshal Ludendorff, were found not guilty and freed immediately. But Hitler alone insisted on pleading guilty to treason and at his trial entranced the judges, the spectators, the reporters from every major newspaper in Germany with a four-hour miraculous speech. It was his greatest moment—a moment that made him a hero to all Germans. Surely you know of this?"

"Yes. All the papers reported on the trial, but I've never actually read the speech."

"Unlike all the other weaklings pleading not guilty, he proclaimed his guilt again and again. 'If,' he said, 'overthrowing this government of November criminals, who stabbed the valiant German army in the back, is high treason, *then I am guilty*. If wanting to restore the glorious majesty of our German nation is treason, *then I am guilty*.' If wanting to restore the honor of the German army is treason, *then I am guilty*. The judges were so moved, they congratulated him, shook his hand, and wanted to acquit him, but they could not: he insisted on pleading guilty to treason. In the end, they sentenced him to five years in the minimum security prison at Landsberg but assured him of an early pardon. And, thus, in one extraordinary afternoon, he suddenly went from being a small-time politician and laughing stock to a universally admired national figure."

"Yes, I've noticed his name is now known to all. Thanks for filling me in. There's something sticking in my mind I'd like to return to—your strong term 'pestilence.' What happened between you and Adolf Hitler?"

"What *didn't* happen? The most recent thing—the real reason I'm here—is that he publicly humiliated me. He had one of his major tantrums, and in a rage he viciously accused me of incompetence, disloyalty, and all the crimes in the calendar. Don't ask me for more details. I have blotted it out and remember only fragments, the way one remembers a flitting nightmare. It has been two weeks, and I still haven't recovered."

"I see how shaken you are. What prompted this rage?"

"Party politics. I decided to run some candidates in the 1924 parliamentary elections. Clearly our future is in that direction. The disastrous putsch proved that we had no choice but to enter the parliamentary system. Our party was in tatters and would have dissolved entirely otherwise. Since the NSDAP was outlawed, I proposed that our members join forces with a different party, led by Field Marshal Ludendorff. I discussed this at length with Hitler in one of my many visits to the Landsberg prison. For weeks he refused to make a decision but finally granted me the authority to decide. That's like him—he'll rarely make a decision on policy, leaving it instead to his subordinates to battle it out. I made the choice, and we did well in the election. Later, however, when Ludendorff attempted to marginalize him, Hitler publicly denounced my decision and proclaimed that no one could speak for him—thus withdrawing all authority from me."

"It sounds as though his rage at you is displaced anger—that is, it was misdirected and flowed from other sources, especially the prospect of losing his power."

"Yes, yes, Friedrich. Exactly. Hitler is preoccupied now with one thing and one thing only—his position as leader. Nothing else, certainly not our basic principles, matters as much. Ever since he was pardoned after thirteen months in Landsberg, he has changed. He has developed a faraway look, as though he sees what others cannot, as though he is above and beyond terrestrial matters. And he now absolutely insists on everyone calling him 'Führer'—nothing else. He's grown inexpressibly distant with me."

"I remember your talking during our last meeting about how you felt he stayed distant from you, how chagrined you were when you witnessed him being more intimate with others—was it Göring you talked about?"

"Yes, exactly. But it's far more extensive now. In public he holds himself back from everyone. And this lout, Göring, is a big part of the problem. Not only is he unctuous, divisive, and abusive to me, but his open drug addiction is a disgrace. I'm told that in public meetings he takes out his bottle of pills every hour and gulps a handful. I tried to throw him out of the party but could not obtain Hitler's agreement. In fact, Göring is the other major reason I'm here today. Though he is still out of the country, I've heard from good sources that Göring is spreading the vicious rumor that Hitler *deliberately* chose me to lead the party in his absence *because he knew I was the most unsuitable candidate imaginable*. In other words, I'd be so inept that Hitler's own position and power would be unthreatened. I don't know what to do. I'm ready to jump out of my skin." Alfred sank back into his chair, hands over his eyes. "I need your help. I keep imagining talking to you."

"What do you imagine my saying or doing?"

"There I draw a blank. I never get that far."

"Try to imagine my speaking to you in a manner that would relieve your pain. Tell me, what would be the perfect thing for me to say?" This was one of Friedrich's favorite ploys, as it always led to deeper investigation of the therapist-patient relationship. Not today.

"I can't, I can't do it. I need to hear from you."

Seeing that Alfred was too agitated to do much reflection, Friedrich offered support as best he could. "Alfred, here's what I've been thinking as you spoke. First, I feel the weight of your burden. This is a horror story. It's as though you're in a viper's nest and you're dealt with unfairly and viciously by everyone. And though I'm listening hard, I haven't heard any affirmation from any source."

Alfred exhaled loudly. "You already understand. I knew you would. No one else validates anything I do. I made the correct decision about the election, and the Führer now pursues exactly the same path I proposed. But never, never do I ever hear praise."

"From no one in your life?"

"There's praise from my wife, Hedwig—I remarried recently—but her praise isn't important. Only Hitler's words count."

"Let me ask you something, Alfred. This abuse you're getting, the vicious rumors, Hitler's demeaning tirade, the total lack of appreciation—why do you put up with it? What keeps you locked in, asking for more? Why aren't you taking better care of yourself?"

Alfred shook his head as though he had been expecting this query. "I dislike sounding banal but I have to live. I need the money. What else can I do? I'm well-known as a radical journalist, and there are no other work opportunities. My professional training as an architect won't find me work. Did I ever tell you my dissertation project was designing a crematorium?"

When Friedrich shook his head, Alfred continued, "Well, I'm afraid that in Catholic Bavaria no one is clamoring to build more crematoriums. No, I have no other work options."

"But to yoke yourself to Hitler and to put up with such abuse and allow your whole self-esteem to soar or plunge depending upon his mood is not a good recipe for stability or well-being. Why does his love for you mean so very much?"

"That's not the way I look at it. It's not just his love I seek; it's his facilitation. My raison d'être is race purification. I know in my heart this is my life work. If I want Germany to rise again, if I want a Jew-free Germany and a Jew-free Europe, then I *must* remain with Hitler. Only through him can I bring these things to pass."

Friedrich glanced at the clock. There was still ample time, for they had scheduled a double session and another double session tomorrow. "Alfred, I have a thought about Hitler's change in behavior toward you. I think it's linked to his change in demeanor, his assumption of a visionary posture. It seems he is trying to re-create himself, to become larger than life. And I think he wishes to distance himself from all those who knew him when he was simply an ordinary human being. Perhaps that lies behind his detaching himself from you."

Alfred pondered that thought. "I hadn't quite put it that way. But I think there is much truth to what you're saying. He has a new in-group, and all of us in the out-group have to work hard to catch his ear. With the single exception of Göring, he's excluded the entire old guard. There's one particularly malignant newcomer, Joseph Goebbels, who I believe is going to be the Mephisto of our once upright movement. I can't stand him, and the feeling is fully reciprocated. Right now, Goebbels is the editor of a Nazi daily in Berlin, and soon he'll be managing all Nazi elections. And there is another insider: Rudolf Hess. He's been around for a while and commanded an SA division in the putsch. But still he came into Hitler's life much later than I. He was in a nearby cell in Landsberg and visited Hitler daily. Since he had been planning to go into his father's business, Hess had training as a stenographer and began taking dictation of Hitler's *Mein Kampf*. I admit I envied Hess. I'd gladly have gone to jail if I could have met with Hitler daily. They finished the first volume in prison, and I believe Hess did a lot of the editing—much of it very badly. Here I am, the party's leading intellectual and best writer by far—you'd think he would have asked *me* to edit it. I could have improved it so much. For sure I would have cut several passages that he now openly regrets having written—the crackpot section on syphilis for sure. But not once did he ask."

"Why didn't he ask?"

"I've got some good hunches that I can't share with anyone else but you. For one thing, I think he knew I would not have been an impartial editor because of all the ideas he'd purloined from me. You see, before he went to jail, I was the official party philosopher. In fact, some of the leftist papers regularly published such statements as "Hitler is Rosenberg's mouthpiece" or "Hitler commands what Rosenberg wills." This vexed him no end, and now he wants to make it crystal clear that he is the sole author of party ideology and that I had no role in this work. In *Mein Kampf* he is quite explicit about this. I've memorized this line: 'Within long spans of human progress it may occasionally happen that the practical politician and political philosopher are one.' He wants to be regarded as this rare kind of leader."

Alfred leaned back in his chair and closed his eyes for a moment.

"You look more relaxed, Alfred."

"It helps to talk to you."

"Shall we explore that. How do I help?"

"You give me new ways to look at what's happened to me. It's a relief to talk to an intelligent fellow being. I am surrounded by such mediocrity."

"It's as though this place, this manner of talking offers some respite from your isolation. Right?"

Alfred nodded.

"Yes," Friedrich continued, "and I'm glad to offer that. But it's not enough. I wonder if there is some way I can offer you something more substantial than relief. Something deeper and more enduring."

"I'm all for that. But how?"

"Let me try. I'll start with a question. There is a lot of negative feeling coming toward you from Hitler and from many others. My question is: what role do *you* play in this?"

"I've already addressed that. Over and over again, I am resented because of my superior intelligence. I have a complex mind, and most people cannot follow the intricacies of my thought. It's not *my* fault, but people feel intimidated by me. As a result of not being able to fully comprehend my ideas, many feel stupid and then lash out at me as though it were *my* fault."

"No, that's not quite what I'm after. I'm really trying to get at the question of 'What do you want to change about yourself?' Because that is what I try to do—help my patients change. Your answer that your problem stems from your superior mind leads us to a dead end because naturally you don't want to want to sacrifice any of your superior mind. No one would want that."

"I'm lost, Friedrich."

"What I mean is that therapy consists of change, and I'm trying to help you sort out what you want to change in yourself. If you say that your problems are due entirely to others, then I don't have any therapeutic leverage other than simply soothing you and helping you learn to tolerate abuse or suggesting you find other associates." Friedrich tried another tact that almost always was fruitful. "Here, let me put it this way—what percentage of the problems you're facing are caused by others? Is it 20 or 50 or 70 or 90 percent?"

"There is no way to measure that."

"Of course, but I don't expect accuracy; I simply want your wildest estimate. Humor me on this, Alfred."

"All right, let's say 90 percent."

"Good. And that means that 10 percent of these aggravating events that upset you so are *your* responsibility. That can give us some direction. You and I need to explore that 10 percent and see if we can understand and then change it. Are you with me, Alfred?"

"I'm getting that strange light-headed feeling I've gotten each time I've spoken to you."

"That's not necessarily a bad thing. The process of change often feels destabilizing. So back to work. Let's examine that 10 percent. I want to know about what role you play in others treating you so abusively."

"I've already covered that. I told you it was the envy of the common man for the one with soaring imagination and intellect."

"People mistreating you because of your superiority belongs to the 90 percent category. Let's stay focused on the 10 percent—*your* part of it. You say you are excluded, disliked, the victim of rumors. What do you do to bring that about?"

"I've done my best to persuade Hitler to get rid of the chaff, the small minds—the Görings, the Streichers, the Himmlers, the Röhms—but to no avail."

"But Alfred, you speak of the superiority of the Aryan bloodline, and yet these very men will, if Hitler prevails, become the Aryan rulers. How can that be if they are part of the Aryan bloodline? Surely they must have *some* strengths, *some* virtues?"

"They need education and enlightenment. The book I'm working on will provide the education that our future Aryan leaders will require. If Hitler will only back me, I can elevate and purify their thinking."

Friedrich felt dazed. How could he have so greatly underestimated the strength of Alfred's resistance? He tried again. "The last time we met, Alfred, you spoke of how others in your office referred to you as the 'sphinx' and also how Dietrich Eckart's criticism had persuaded you to make some significant changes in yourself. Remember?"

"Past history. That saga and the influence of Dietrich Eckart are over. He died several months ago."

"I'm sorry to hear that. A big loss for you?"

"It's mixed. I owe much to him, but our relationship deteriorated when Hitler decided Eckart was too ill and too weak to continue as editor in chief of the VB, and appointed me in his stead. It was not my fault, but Eckart blamed me for it. Though I tried my best, I could not persuade him that I didn't scheme against him. Only as he approached death did his rancor toward me lessen. At my last visit he beckoned me to come close to his bed and whispered in my ear, 'Follow Hitler. He will dance. But remember it is I who called the tune.' After his death Hitler called him the 'pole star' of the Nazi movement. But, as with me, Hitler never credited him with teaching him anything specific."

Friedrich's energy ebbed, but he kept trying. "Let's go back to the point I was trying to make. When you worked for Eckart, you told me you wanted to make changes in yourself, to be less of a sphinx, to schmooze—"

"That was then. Now I have no intention of weakening myself to curry the favor of inferior minds. In fact, I now find that thought repugnant. That very idea is a microcosm of the great issue we as a nation must face: *the weak are not equal to the strong.* If the strong lessen their will and power, if they forsake their destiny as rulers, or pollute their bloodline through intermarriage, then they undermine the true greatness of the *Volk.*"

"Alfred, you see the world only in terms of strong or weak. Surely there are other ways to view—"

"All of history," Alfred interrupted, his voice stronger, "is a saga of the strong and the weak. Let me speak frankly. The task of strong men like Hitler, like me, and like you, Friedrich, is to enhance the flourishing of the superior Aryan race. You suggest seeing history in 'other ways.' You are referring, no doubt, to the ways of the church that attempt to free us from blood ties and create the sovereign individual who is nothing but an abstraction lacking polarity or potency? All notions of equality are fantasies and contrary to nature."

Friedrich was seeing a different Alfred today—Alfred Rosenberg the Nazi ideologue, the propagandist, the speaker at mass Nazi rallies. He didn't like what he saw but, as though by reflex, persevered in his role. "I recall that the very first time we spoke as adults, you said that you took great pleasure in a philosophic conversation. You told me that you had had no opportunities for that in years."

"That is certainly true. Still is."

"So, can I proffer some philosophic questions about your comments?"

"I welcome it."

"All that you've been arguing this morning rests on a basic assumption: that the Aryan race is superior and that great and drastic efforts should be made to increase the purity of that race. Correct?"

"Go on."

"My question is, simply, What is your evidence? I have no doubt that every other race, if asked, would proclaim its own superiority."

"Evidence? Look around at the great Germans. Use your eyes, your ears. Listen to Beethoven, Bach, Brahms, Wagner. Read Goethe, Schiller, Schopenhauer, Nietzsche. Look at our cities, our architecture, and look at the great civilizations our Aryan forebears launched that ultimately crumbled after pollution by inferior Semitic blood."

"I believe you're citing Houston Stewart Chamberlain. I've now read some of his work and frankly am unimpressed with his evidence, which consists of little more than claiming to see occasional blue-eyed, blond-haired Aryans in paintings of Egyptian or Indian or Roman court figures. This is not evidence. The historians I've consulted say Chamberlain simply invented the history that would support his original claims. Please, Alfred, give me some substantial evidence for your premises. Give me evidence that Kant or Hegel or Schopenhauer would respect."

"Evidence, you say? My blood feelings are my evidence. We true Aryans trust our passions, and we know how to harness them to regain our rightful place as rulers."

"I hear passion, but I still hear no evidence. In my field we search for causes of strong passions. Let me tell you of a theory in psychiatry that seems most relevant to our discussion. Alfred Adler, a Viennese physician, has written much about the universal feelings of inferiority that accrue simply as a result of growing up as a human and experiencing a prolonged period in which we feel helpless, weak, and dependent. There are many who find this sense of inferiority intolerable and compensate by developing a superiority complex, which is simply the other side of the same coin. Alfred, I believe that dynamic may be at play in you. We talked about your unhappiness as a child, at not being at home anywhere, of being unpopular and striving to attain success partly in order to 'show them'—do you remember?"

No response from Alfred, who sat staring at him. Friedrich continued, "I believe you're making the same error as the Jews, who for two millennia have thought of themselves as a superior people, as God's chosen people. You and I agreed that Spinoza demolished that argument, and I have no doubt that, if he were alive, the power of his logic would demolish your Aryan argument as well."

"I warned you about entering this Jewish field. What does psychoanalysis know about race and blood and soul? I warned you, and now I fear that you've already been corrupted."

"And I told *you* that this knowledge and this method are too good and too powerful to be the sole property of Jews. I and my colleagues have used the principles of this field to offer enormous help to legions of wounded Aryans. And you're wounded too, Alfred, but, despite your own wishes, you will not allow me to help you."

"And I thought I was dealing with an *Übermensch*. How much was I mistaken!" Alfred stood, extracted an envelope of deutschmarks from his pocket, placed it with great precision on the corner of Friedrich's desk, and strode toward the door.

"I'll see you tomorrow at the same time," Friedrich called after him.

"Not tomorrow," Alfred called from the vestibule, "and not ever! And I'll make sure these Jew thoughts will leave Europe along with the Jews."

CHAPTER TWENTY-NINE

RIJNSBURG AND AMSTERDAM—1662

As Bento trudged toward Amsterdam, he actively turned his thoughts away from the past, away from nostalgic images of the Rosh Hashanahs shared with his family that had been evoked by the Ashkenazi Jews observing Tashlich, and turned toward what lay ahead. In about an hour he would see Simon again, dear generous Simon, his most ardent supporter. It was good that Simon lived near enough for occasional visits, but it was also good that Simon did not live even closer, since on several occasions, he had shown signs of wishing to be too close. A scene from Simon's last visit to Rijnsburg drifted into his mind.

"Bento," Simon says, "even though we are close, I still find you elusive. Humor me, my friend, and tell my exactly how you spend your day. Yesterday, for example."

"Yesterday was as every day. I started my day by collecting and writing thoughts that my mind had accrued during the night, and then I turned to my lens grinding for the next four hours."

"What exactly do you do? Tell me about the process step by step."

"Better than tell you, I'll show you. But it will take time."

"I want nothing more than to share your life."

"Come into the other room with me."

In the laboratory Bento points to a large slab of glass. "This is where I start. I picked this up yesterday from the glass factory just a kilometer from here." He picks up a hacksaw. "This is sharp but not sharp enough. I'm wiping it now with oil and diamond grit." Bento then cuts a circular three-centimeter blank. "The next step is to grind this blank to the proper curve and angle. First

I'll fix it in place to the stamper—like this." Bento applies black pitch with great care to fix the blank in place. "And now to use the lathe for the rough grinding with feldspar and quartz." After ten minutes of grinding, Bento places the glass into a mold on a fast-rotating wooden disc. "And finally we finish by delicate fine grinding. I use a corundum and tin oxide mixture. I'll just do the beginning, lest I bore you with the long and tedious grinding process."

He turns to Simon. "So now you know how I spend my mornings and also you know where spectacles come from."

Simon responds, "As I watch you, Bento, I am of two minds. On the one hand, please know that I admire greatly your skills and fine technique, yet the other, the grander part of my mind, clamors loudly, 'Leave this to the artisans. Every community in Europe has its artisans. There are untold hosts of artisans, but where in the world is there another Bento de Spinoza?' Do what only you can do, Bento. Finish the philosophical project that all the world awaits. All this din, this dust, this bad air, these odors, all this precious time consumed. Please, once again I plead, let me free you from the burden of this craft. Let me provide a lifetime annual stipend—any amount you wish—so you may use all your hours to philosophize. It is well within my means, and it would give me unimaginable joy to extend this aid to you."

"Simon, you are a generous man. And know that I love you for your generosity. But my needs are few and easily attained, and excessive money will distract rather then aid my concentration. What's more—and Simon, you may not find this credible, but believe me—lens grinding is good for thinking. Yes, I concentrate hard on the lathe, the angle and the radius of the glass, the delicate polishing, but while I do this, my thinking germinates in the background at such a rapid pace that I often finish a lens and discover that, mirabile dictu, *there are new solutions to thorny philosophical arguments ready at hand. I, or at least the attentive I, do not seem to be needed. It's not unlike the phenomenon of problems being solved in dreams, which many ancients have reported. Independent of this, the science of optics fascinates me. At present, I'm developing an entirely different method of grinding fine telescope lenses that I believe will be a major advance."*

The conversation had ended with Simon grasping Bento's hand with both his hands and holding it overly long while saying, "You shall not escape me. I shall not give up my attempts to facilitate your work. Please know that my offer shall remain open however long I live."

That was the moment Bento thought it was good that Simon did not
live too near.

In Amsterdam on a bench by the Singel, Simon Joosten de Vries awaited
his friend's visit. The son of wealthy merchants, Simon lived a few blocks
from van den Enden in a substantial four-story house twice the width of
the adjoining houses fronting the canal. Not only did Simon adore Bento,
but he resembled him in appearance—frail, small-boned, with beautiful,
delicate facial features and a carriage of great dignity.

As the sun set and the glowing orange sky turned charcoal gray, Simon
paced impatiently in front of his home and grew increasingly anxious about
the whereabouts of his friend. The *Trekschuit* should have arrived an hour
ago. Suddenly spotting Bento strolling on the Singel two blocks away, Simon
waved his arms, rushed to meet him, and insisted on carrying the heavy shoulder bag containing notebooks and the newly ground lenses. Once inside the
house Simon led his guest to the table set with rye bread and cheese and a
freshly baked spicy *oudewijvenkoek* (old ladies' cake), a northern Dutch
aniseed delicacy.

As Simon prepared coffee, he went over plans for the morrow. "The
Philosophy Club will meet here about 1900 hours. I expect twelve members,
all of whom will have read the ten pages you mailed me. I had two copies
made and asked them to read it in a day and pass it along to the others.
And in the afternoon I have a gift for you from the Philosophy Club, which
I am sure you will not turn down. I've found some interesting volumes at
two booksellers—the establishments of Abraham de Wees and Lubbert
Meyndertsz—and will escort you there to select one of your choice from a
tasty menu of Virgil, Hobbes, Euclid, and Cicero."

Bento did not decline this offer; instead his eyes lit up. "Simon, I thank
you. You are too generous."

Yes, Bento had one weak spot, and Simon had discovered it. Bento was
in love with books—not only the reading of books but the possession of
them. Though he politely and consistently declined all other gifts, he could
never refuse a worthy book, and Simon and many of the other Collegiants
were gradually building him a fine library that had almost filled the large

bookcase standing on the side wall of his living room in Rijnsburg. Sometimes late at night, when unable to sleep, Bento would go to his bookcases and smile as he gazed at the volumes. Sometimes he would rearrange them, sometimes for size or for subject or simply alphabetically, and sometimes he would inhale the aroma of the books or caress them, luxuriating in the heft or the feel of the variegated bindings upon his palms.

"But before the book shopping," Simon continued, "there will be a surprise. A visitor! I hope it will be a welcome one. Here, read this letter that arrived last week."

Bento opened a letter that had been tightly rolled and bound by twine. The first line was written in Portuguese, and Bento immediately recognized Franco's handwriting. "My dear friend, it has been far too long." At this point, much to Bento's surprise, the letter switched to excellent Hebrew. "I have many things to discuss with you. First among them is that I am now a serious student and a father. I am wary of writing too much and only hope your friend can arrange a way for us to meet."

"When did this arrive, Simon?"

"About a week ago. The deliverer was a caricature of furtiveness as he zipped through my door as soon as I opened it. He immediately handed me the letter and then, after opening the door slightly and peering carefully up and down the street to make sure he was not seen, quickly slipped out. He would not leave his name but said you had told him to use me as a contact. I assumed he is the man who was so helpful after the assassination attempt?"

"Yes, Franco is his name, but even that should be kept secret. He runs a great risk—remember that the excommunication expressly forbids any Jew from speaking to me. He is my one link to the past, and you are my one link to him. I want very much to meet with him."

"Good. I took the liberty of telling him you'd be in Amsterdam today, and his eyes brightened so much that I suggested that he stop here to see you tomorrow morning."

"His response?"

"He said that obstacles existed, but he would do all that is humanly possible to get here at some point before noon."

"Thank you, Simon."

The next morning, a loud rap at the door echoed throughout the house. When Simon opened the door, Franco, wearing a robe with a hood covering his head and much of his face, slipped inside. Simon led him to Bento, waiting in the front salon facing the canal, and then discreetly left them alone. Franco beamed as he grabbed Bento's shoulders with both hands. "Ah, Bento, what a blessing to see you."

"And a blessing for me to see you. Take off your cloak and let me look at you, Franco." Bento strolled around him. "Well, well, well. You've changed: you've gained weight; your face is more full, hearty. But that beard and your black clothes—you look like a Talmudic student. And how dangerous is it for you to be here? And how is it being married? And being a father? And are you content?"

"So many questions!" Franco laughed. "Which one to answer first? The last one I think. Wouldn't your friend Epicurus have considered that the main question? Yes, I am very content. My life has changed much for the better. And you, Bento? Are you content?"

"I, too, am more content than ever. As Simon may have told you, I live in Rijnsburg, a small, quiet village, and I live exactly as I wish—alone with few distractions. I think, I write, and no one tries to stab me. What could be better? But my other questions?"

"My wife and my son are true blessings. She is the soul mate I hoped for—and now evolving into an educated soul mate. I've been teaching her to read Portuguese and Hebrew, and we learn Dutch together. What else did you ask? Oh, my clothes and my shrubbery?" Franco stroked his beard. "This may come as a shock, but I am a student at your old school, the Pereira Yeshibah. Rabbi Mortera has granted me such a generous stipend from the synagogue that I no longer need to work for my uncle or anyone else."

"That is rare."

"I've heard the rumor that you were once offered such a stipend. Perhaps by some quirk of fate it has been redirected to me. Perhaps I am being rewarded for betraying you."

"What reason did Rabbi Mortera give?"

"When I asked him 'How am I worthy?' he surprised me. He said the stipend is his way, the Jewish community's way, of honoring my father, whose reputation, and the reputation of his long line of rabbinical ancestors, is far greater than I had ever imagined. But he also added that I was a promising student who might one day follow in my father's steps."

"And—" Bento took a deep breath. "Your response to the rabbi?"

"Gratitude. Bento de Spinoza, you've made me thirsty for knowledge and, to the rabbi's pleasure, I have plunged into a joyous study of Talmud and Torah."

"I see. Uh . . . well . . . you've accomplished much. The Hebrew in your note is most excellent."

"Yes, I am pleased with myself, and my joy in learning increases day by day."

A short silence ensued. They both opened their mouths to speak at the same time and then stopped. After another brief silence Franco asked, "Bento, you were in much anguish when I last saw you after the attack. You recovered quickly?"

Bento nodded. "Yes, and in no small part thanks to you. You should know that even now in Rijnsburg I keep my old slashed overcoat hanging in plain sight. It was excellent counsel."

"Tell me more of your life."

"Ah, what to say? I grind glass half my day and think, read, and write the rest of the time. I have little to tell on the outside. I live entirely in my mind."

"And that young woman who brought me up to your room? The one who gave you so much pain?"

"She and my friend Dirk are planning to marry."

A short silence. Franco asked, "And? Tell me more."

"We remain friends, but she is a devout Catholic and he is converting to Catholicism. I imagine our friendship will suffer once I publish my views on religion."

"And your concern about the power of your passions?"

"Ah . . ." Bento hesitated. "Well, since I last saw you, I've enjoyed tranquility."

Again, a silence ensued, finally broken by Franco.

"You notice something different between us today."

Bento, puzzled, shrugged. "What do you mean?"

"I mean the silences. We never had silences before. There was always far too much to say—we chattered without stop. There was never an instant of silence."

Bento nodded.

"My father, blessed be his name," Franco continued, "always said that when something big is not talked about, nothing else of importance can be said. Do you agree, Bento?"

"Your father was a wise man. Something big? What do you think?"

"Without a doubt it is related to my appearance and my enthusiasm for my Jewish education. I'm assuming that this has unsettled you and you don't know what to say."

"Yes, there is truth in your words. But . . . uh . . . I'm uncertain what to—"

"Bento, I am unaccustomed to hear you fumble with words. If I may speak for you, I think the 'something big' is your disapproval of my course of studies, and yet, at the same time, your heart cares for me, and you wish to respect my decision and say nothing that will cause me discomfort."

"Well put, Franco. I couldn't find the right words. You know you are uncommonly good at this."

"This?"

"I mean at understanding the nuances of what is said and what is unsaid between people. You startle me with your acuity."

Franco bowed his head. "Thank you, Bento. It is a gift from my blessed father. I learned at his knee."

Again a silence.

"Please, Bento, try to share your thoughts about our meeting today so far."

"I'll try. I agree, something *is* different today. We've changed, and I am uncommonly awkward in coping with that. You have to help me sort it out."

"Best just to talk about how we've changed. From your perspective, I mean."

"Before, it was *I* who was the teacher and *you* the student who agreed with my views and wanted to spend his life in exile with me. Now it's all changed."

"Because I have entered into a study of Torah and Talmud?"

Bento shook his head. "It is more than study: your words were 'joyous study.' And you were correct in your diagnosis of my heart. I did fear offending you or lessening your joy."

"You think our ways are parting?"

"Are they not? Surely, now, even if unencumbered by family, would you still choose to go my way with me?"

Franco hesitated and thought long before answering. "My answer, Bento, is yes and no. I think I would *not* go your way in life. Yet, even so, our ways have *not* parted."

"How can that be? Explain."

"I still fully embrace all the critiques of religious superstition you offered in those talks with Jacob and me. In that I am one with you."

"Yet now you obtain great joy in your studies of superstitious texts?"

"No, that is not correct. I have joy in the *process* of studying, not always the *content* of what I study. You know, teacher, there is a difference between the two."

"Please, teacher, explain." Bento, now much relieved, smiled broadly and reached out to tousle Franco's hair.

Franco smiled in return, paused for a moment to enjoy Bento's touch, and continued. "By 'process' I mean that I love to be engaged in intellectual study. I relish the study of Hebrew and take delight in the whole ancient world opening up to me. My Talmud studies class is far more interesting than I had imagined. Just the other day we discussed the story of Rabbi Yohanon—"

"Which story about him?"

"The story of his curing another rabbi by giving his hand to him, and then when he himself fell ill, he was visited by another rabbi, who asked, 'Are these sufferings acceptable to you?' And Rabbi Yohanon responded, 'No, neither they nor their reward.' The other rabbi then cured Rabbi Yohanon by giving him his hand."

"Yes, I know that story. And in which way did you find this interesting?"

"In our discussion we raised many questions. For example, why didn't Rabbi Yohanon simply cure himself?"

"And of course the class discussed the point that the prisoner cannot free himself and that the reward of suffering lies in the world to come."

"Yes, I know that is very familiar, perhaps tiresome to you, but for someone like me, such discussions are exhilarating. Where else would I have the opportunity for such soul-searching conversations? Some of my class said one thing, others disagreed, others wondered why certain words were used when another word might have had greater clarity. Our teacher encourages us to examine every little scrap of information in the text.

"And to take another example," Franco continued, "last week we discussed a story about a famous rabbi who lingered near death, suffering great agony, but was kept alive by the prayers of his students and fellow rabbis. His handmaiden took pity on him and threw a jar from the rooftop that shattered with such a great din that they were startled and stopped praying. At that very moment, the rabbi died."

"Ah, yes—Rabbi Yehudah haNasi. And I am certain you discussed such things as whether the handmaid did the correct thing or whether she was guilty of homicide and also whether the other rabbis lacked mercy in keeping him alive and delaying his arrival in the joyous world to come."

"I can imagine your response to this, Bento. I remember all too well your attitude toward belief in an afterlife."

"Exactly. The fundamental premise of a world to come is flawed. Yet your class was not open to questioning that premise."

"Yes, I agree, these are limitations. But even so, it is a privilege, a joy, to sit with others for hours and discuss such weighty matters. And our teacher instructs us how to argue. If a point seems overly obvious, we are taught to question why the writer even said it—perhaps there was a deeper point lurking beneath the words. When we are fully satisfied in our understanding, then we are taught to ferret out the underlying general principle. If some point is irrelevant, then we learn to question why the author included it. In short, Bento, Talmudic study is teaching me how to think, and I believe that may have been true for you as well. Maybe it was your Talmud study that honed your mind so keenly."

Bento nodded. "I cannot deny there is merit in that, Franco. In retrospect I would have preferred a less circuitous, more rational route. Euclid, for example, gets right to the point and doesn't muddy the waters with enigmatic and often self-contradictory stories."

"Euclid? The inventor of geometry?"

Bento nodded.

"Euclid is for my next, my worldly education. But, for now, the Talmud is doing the job. For one thing, I *like* stories. They add life and depth to the lessons. Everyone loves stories."

"No, Franco, not everyone! Consider your evidence for that statement. It is an unwarranted conclusion that I personally know to be false."

"Ah, you don't like stories. Not even as a child?"

Bento closed his eyes and recited, "'When I was a child, I talked like a child, I thought like a child, I reasoned like a child—'"

Franco interrupted and continued in the same tone. "'When I became a man, I put childish ways behind me.' Paul, Corinthians 1."

"Astonishing! You are now so quick, Franco, so self-confident. So different from that disheveled, uneducated young man just off the boat from Portugal."

"Uneducated in Jewish matters. But don't forget we conversos had a forced but full Catholic education. I read every word of the New Testament."

"I *had* forgotten that. That means you've already started some of your second education. That's good. There is much wisdom in both the Old and the New Testament. Especially in Paul. Just a couple of lines earlier he expresses my exact view toward stories: 'when the perfect comes, the partial will be done away.'"

Franco paused, repeating to himself, "'Partial'? 'Perfect'?"

"The 'perfect,'" Bento said, "is the moral truth. The 'partial' is the wrapping—in this case the story that is no longer necessary once the truth is delivered."

"I'm not sure I accept Paul as a model for living. His life, as it is taught, seems out of balance. So severe, so fanatic, so joyless, so damning of all worldly pleasures. Bento, you are so hard on yourself. Why forsake the pleasure of a good story, a pleasure that seems so benign, so universal? What culture doesn't have stories?"

"I remember a young man who railed against stories of miracles and prophecies. I remember an agitated and volatile and rebellious young man who pushed back so hard against Jacob's orthodoxy. I remember his reactions to the synagogue service. Though he had no Hebrew, he followed the Portuguese translation of the Torah and was outraged at the stories in the Torah and referred to the madness and the nonsense of both the Jewish and the Catholic service. I remember him asking, 'Why is the season of miracles over? Why didn't God perform a miracle and save my father?' And the same young man agonized that his father gave up his life for a Torah riddled with superstitious beliefs in miracles and prophecies."

"Yes, all that is so. I remember."

"And so where are those feelings now, Franco? You speak now only of joy in your studies of Torah and Talmud. And yet you say you still fully embrace my critique of superstition. How can that be?"

"Bento, it's the same answer—it's the *process* of study that gives me joy. I don't take the content very seriously. I like the stories, but I don't take them for historical truth. I attend to the morality, to the messages in the scriptures about love and charity and kindness and ethical behavior. And I put the rest out of mind. Plus, there are stories, and there are stories. Some stories of miracles are, as you say, the enemy of reason. But other stories elicit the student's attention, and that I find useful in my studies and in the teaching I am starting to undertake. One thing I know for sure—students will always be interested in stories, whereas there will never be a long line of students eager to learn about Euclid and geometry. And, oh, my mentioning my teaching causes me to remember something I've been eager to tell you! I'm starting to teach the elements of Hebrew, and guess who one of my students is. Be prepared for a shock—your would-be assassin!"

"Oh! My assassin! A shock indeed! You, my assassin's teacher! What can you tell me?"

"His name is Isaac Ramirez, and your guess about his circumstances was entirely correct. His family was terrorized by the Inquisition, his parents were killed, and he was maddened with grief. It was the very fact that his story is so similar to mine that prompted me to volunteer to teach him, and so far it is working out well. You gave me some strong advice about how I should regard him that I've never forgotten. Do you remember?"

"I remember telling you not to tell the police where he was."

"Yes, but then you said something else. You said, 'Take a religious path.' Remember? That puzzled me."

"Perhaps I haven't been clear. I love religion, but I hate superstition."

Franco nodded. "Yes, that was how I understood you—that I should show understanding and compassion and forgiveness. Right?"

Bento nodded.

"So that, too, a moral code of behavior, not only stories of miracles, is in the Torah."

"Without question that is so, Franco. My favorite Talmud story is the one about a heathen approaching Rabbi Hillel and offering to convert to Judaism if the rabbi could teach him the entire Torah while he stood on one foot. Hillel replied, 'What is hateful to you, do not do to your neighbor. That is the whole Torah—all the rest is commentary. Go and study it.'"

"You see you *do* like stories—"

Bento started to respond, but Franco quickly corrected himself: "—or at least *one* story. Stories can act as a memory device. For many, more effectively than bare geometry."

"I see your point, Franco, and I do not doubt that your studies *are* sharpening your mind. You're turning into a formidable debate opponent. It is obvious why Rabbi Mortera selected you. Tonight I discuss some of my writing with Collegiant members of a philosophy club, and how I wish the world were such that you could be there. I would attend more to your critique than to that of anyone else."

"I would be honored to read anything of yours. In what language do you write? My Dutch is improving."

"In Latin, alas. Let us hope that will be part of your second education, for I doubt it will ever see a Dutch translation."

"I learned the rudiments of Latin in my Catholic training."

"Aim toward a full Latin education. Rabbi Menasseh and Rabbi Mortera are well trained in Latin and may permit it, perhaps encourage you."

"Rabbi Menasseh died last year, and I'm afraid Rabbi Mortera is failing quickly."

"Ah, sad news. But even so you will find others to encourage you. Perhaps there is a way you could spend a year in the Venetian Yeshibah. It is important: Latin opens up a whole new—"

Franco stood up suddenly and rushed to the window for a closer look at the retreating figures of three men who had passed. He turned back. "Sorry, Bento—I thought I saw someone from the congregation. I am more than a bit nervous at being seen here."

"Yes, we never got to my question about the risk. Tell me, how great is your risk, Franco?"

Franco bowed his head. "It is very great—so great it is the one thing I cannot share with my wife. I cannot tell her that I put at risk everything we have struggled to build in this new world. It is a risk I take only for you, not for anyone else walking this earth. And I shall have to leave soon. I have no reason to give my wife or my rabbis for my absence. I've been scheming that, if I were seen, I could lie and say that Simon approached me for Hebrew lessons."

"Yes, I thought of that, too. But don't use Simon's name. My connection with him is known, at least in the Gentile world. Better to give a name of someone else that you could have met here, perhaps Peter Dyke, a member of the Philosophy Club."

Franco sighed. "Sad to be entering the land of lies. It is a terrain I have not trod since my betrayal of you, Bento. But before I leave, please share something of your philosophical progress. Once I learn Latin, perhaps Simon may make your work available to me. But for now, today, all I will have is your spoken word. Your thoughts intrigue me. I still puzzle about things you said to Jacob and me."

Bento raised his chin quizzically.

"The very first time we met you said that God was full, perfect, without insufficiencies, and needed no glorification from us."

"Yes, that is my view, and those were my words."

"And then I remember your next comment to Jacob—and it was a state- ment that made me love you. You said, 'Please allow me to love God in my own fashion.'"

"Yes, and your puzzlement?"

"I know, thanks to you, that God is not a being like us. Nor like any other being. You said emphatically—and that was the final blow for Jacob—that God was Nature. But tell me, teach me. How can you be in love with Nature? How can you love something not a being?"

"First, Franco, I use the term 'Nature' in a special way. I don't mean the trees or forests or grass or ocean or anything that is not manmade. I mean everything that exists: the absolute necessary, perfect unity. By 'Na- ture' I refer to that which is infinite, unified, perfect, rational, and logical. It is the immanent cause of all things. And everything that exists, without exception, works according to the laws of Nature. So when I talk about love of Nature, I don't mean the love you have for your wife or child. I'm talking about a different kind of love, an intellectual love. In Latin I refer to it as *Amor dei intellectualis.*"

"An intellectual love of God?"

"Yes, the love of the fullest possible understanding of Nature, or God. The apprehension of the place of each finite thing in its relationship to finite causes. It is the understanding, in so far as it is possible, of the universal laws of Nature."

"So when you speak of loving God, what you mean is the understanding of the laws of Nature."

"Yes, the laws of Nature are only another, more rational name for the eternal decrees of God."

"So it differs from ordinary human love in that it involves only one person?"

"Exactly. And the loving of something that is unchanging and eternal means that you are not subject to the loved one's vagaries of spirit or fickleness or finiteness. It means, too, that we do not try to complete ourselves in another person."

"Bento, if I comprehend you aright, it must also mean that we must expect no love in return."

"Exactly right again. We can expect nothing back. We derive a joyous awe from a glimpse, a privileged understanding of the vast, infinitely complex scheme of Nature."

"Another lifetime project?"

"Yes, God or Nature has an infinite number of attributes that will forever elude my full understanding. But my limited comprehension already yields great awe and joy, at times even ecstatic joy."

"A strange religion, if religion it may be called." Franco stood. "I must leave you still perplexed. But one last question: I wonder, do you deify Nature or naturalize God?"

"Well-phrased, Franco. I need time, much time to compose my response to that question."

CHAPTER THIRTY

BERLIN—1936

The Myth of the Twentieth Century—that thing that no one can understand written by a narrow minded Balt who thinks in a fearfully complicated way.

—Adolf Hitler

Few of the older members of the party are to be found among the readers of Rosenberg's book. I have myself merely glanced cursorily at it. It is in any case written in much too abstruse a style, in my opinion.

—Adolf Hitler

"Sigmund Freud Receives the Goethe Prize"

The Goethe Prize, the greatest scientific (scholarly) and literary prize in Germany, was given to Freud on August 28, 1930, Goethe's birthday, in Frankfurt, in the context of great festivities. The *Isrealitische Gemeindezeitung* rejoiced with cymbals and trumpets. The monetary award was 10,000 marks. . . It is known that notable scholars have rejected the psychoanalysis of the Jew Sigmund Freud in its entirety. The great anti-Semite Goethe would turn over in his grave if he discovered that a Jew had received a prize that carries his name.

—Alfred Rosenberg in *Völkischer Beobachter*

"*Mein* Führer, please look at this letter about Reichsleiter Rosenberg from Dr. Gebhardt, the chief physician at the Hohenlychen Clinic."

Hitler took the letter from Rudolf Hess's hand and scanned it, paying particular attention to the sections Hess had underlined.

I have found it remarkably difficult to make contact with Reichsleiter Rosen-berg . . . As a doctor, I have, above all, the impression that his delayed recovery . . . is in large measure attributable to his psychic isolation. . . In spite of my, if I may say so, tactful efforts to construct a bridge, these miscarried . . . due to the way in which the Reichsleiter is spiritually con-stituted and to his special position in political life. . . He can only be freed from restraint if he can open his mind to those who are at least entitled to speak to him on equal terms and out of similar intellectual capacity, so that he can find again the calm and determination necessary for action and, in-deed, for everyday life.

Last week, I inquired whether he had ever fully shared his innermost thoughts with anyone. Quite unexpectedly, he replied, offering the name of a Friedrich Pfister, a childhood friend in Estonia. I have since learned that this Friedrich Pfister is now Herr Oberleutnant Pfister, a well-regarded Wehrmacht physician stationed in Berlin. May I request that he be imme-diately ordered to assume duties as Reichsleiter Rosenberg's physician?

Hitler handed the letter back to Hess. "There is nothing in this letter that surprises us, but take care no else sees it. And issue the order to transfer Herr Oberleutnant Pfister immediately. Rosenberg is insufferable. Always has been. We all know that. But he's loyal, and the party still has use for his talent."

The Hohenlychen Clinic, one hundred kilometers north of Berlin, had been established by Himmler for the care of ailing Nazi leaders and high-ranking SS officers. Alfred had already spent three months there for an ag-itated depression in 1935. Now, in 1936, he was experiencing the same disabling symptoms: fatigue, agitation, and depression. Unable to concentrate on his editorial work at the *Beobachter*, he had totally withdrawn into himself for several weeks, rarely speaking to his wife and daughter.

Once hospitalized, he submitted to Dr. Gebhardt's physical examinations but persistently refused to answer questions about his mental state or his personal life. Karl Gebhardt was Himmler's personal physician and good friend and also treated the other Nazi leaders (aside from Hitler, who always kept his personal physician, Theodor Morell, close at hand). Alfred had no doubts that any words he uttered to Gebhardt would soon enough be broadcast to the whole brood of his Nazi enemies. For the same reason, Alfred would not speak to a psychiatrist. Stymied and fed up with sitting in silence facing Alfred's contemptuous stare, Dr. Gebhardt longed to transfer his irritating patient to another physician and took great pains in composing his carefully worded letter to Hitler, who, for reasons no one understood, valued Rosenberg and from time to time inquired about his condition.

Dr. Gebhardt had little psychological training, nor was he psychologically minded, but he easily recognized signs of great discord among the leaders—the incessant rivalry, the mutual contempt, the relentless scheming, the competition for power and Hitler's approval. They disagreed about everything, but Gebhardt discovered one thing they held in common: they all hated Alfred Rosenberg. After spending a few weeks visiting Alfred daily, he now saw why.

Though Alfred may have sensed this, he kept his silence and spent week after week at Hohenlychen Clinic reading the German and Russian classics and refusing to engage in conversation with the staff or any of the other Nazi patients. One morning, during his fifth week at the clinic, he felt extremely agitated and decided to take a short walk in the clinic grounds. When he found he was too fatigued to tie his own shoes, he cursed and slapped himself hard on each cheek to wake himself up. He had to do something to stop his slide into irreversible despair.

In his desperation he summoned Friedrich's face into his mind. Friedrich would have known what to do. What would he have suggested? No doubt he would have attempted to understand the cause of this cursed depression. Alfred imagined Friedrich's words: "When did it all start? Let your mind run free, and go back to the beginning of your decline. Simply observe all the ideas, all the images streaming into your mind. Take note of them. Jot them down if you can."

Alfred tried. He closed his eyes and observed the passing parade in his mind. He drifted back through time and watched a scene materialize.

It is several years ago, and he is in his VB office, sitting at the desk that Hitler bought for him. He makes the final edit on the final page of his masterpiece, Der Mythus des 20. Jahrhunderts (The Myth of the Twentieth Century), lays down his red pencil, grins triumphantly, arranges the seven-hundred-page manuscript into a tidy stack held in place with two thick rubber bands, and clasps it lovingly to his chest.

Yes, the recall of his finest moment brings, even now, a tear, perhaps two, streaming down his face. Alfred felt sympathy for that younger self, the young man who knew that the *Mythus* would astound the world. Its gestation had been long and laborious—ten years of Sundays plus every other hour in the week he could free—but worth the price. Yes, yes—he knew he had neglected his wife and his daughter, but how could that matter, compared to creating a book that would set the world on fire, a book that would offer a new philosophy of history based on blood and race and soul, a new appreciation of the *Volk*, of *völkisch* art, architecture, literature, and music and, most important of all, a new groundwork of values for the future Reich.

Alfred reached over to the bed table for his personal copy of the *Mythus* and flipped randomly through the pages. Certain passages instantly brought to mind the physical site of his inspiration. It was when he visited the cathedral of Cologne and was viewing stained-glass crucifixions of Christ and the hosts of emaciated, weakened martyrs that an inspired idea came to him—the Roman Catholic Church did not oppose Judaism. Though the church professed to be anti-Jewish, it was in fact the main channel through which Jewish ideas infected the healthy body of German thought. He read his own words with great pleasure:

> The great Germans lived in conformity with nature and esteemed their fine physiques and manly beauty. But that has been undermined by Christian antagonism to the flesh and by sentimental ideas about preserving the lives of defective children and by allowing criminals and those with hereditary diseases to propagate their defects into the next generation. Thus the contamination of race purity produces fragmentation of character, loss of the sense of direction and thought, and inner uncertainty. The German people are not born in sin but born in nobility. . . The Old Testament as a book of religious instruction must be ended once and for all. With it will end the unsuccessful attempt of the last one and a half millennia to make us all spiritual Jews. . . The spirit of fire—the heroic must take the place of the crucifixion.

Yes, he thought, such passages resulted in the *Mythus* being placed on the Catholic index of banned books in 1934. But that was no misfortune— that was a godsend that increased sales. Over three hundred thousand copies sold, and now my *Mythus* is second only to *Mein Kampf,* and yet here I am—emotionally bankrupt.

Alfred put the book away, rested his head on his pillow, and drifted into meditations. *My* Mythus *has brought me such joy but also such torment! The shithead literary reviewers—every single one of them used the term* unbegreiflich *(incomprehensible). Why didn't I respond to them? Why didn't I ask them in public print whether it had ever occurred to them that my writing might be too subtle and complex for insect brains? Why did I not remind them of the consequences of collisions between average minds and great works: invariably the inferior attack the superior thinkers. What does the public want? They clamor for the stupid vulgarity of Julius Streicher. Even Hitler prefers Streicher's prose. He twists the dagger every time he reminds me that Streicher's rag,* Der Stürmer, *regularly outsells my* Beobachter.

And to think that not a single one of the Nazi leaders has read my Mythus! *Only Hess had been forthright and apologetically told me that he had tried hard but could not negotiate the difficult prose. The others never even mentioned the book to me. Imagine—a huge best seller, and the envious bastards ignore me. But why should that trouble me? What could I expect from that lot? The problem is Hitler, always Hitler. The more I think about it, the more certain I am that my decline began the day I heard that Goebbels had been telling everyone Hitler had thrown down the* Mythus *after reading just a few pages and exclaimed, "Who can understand this stuff?" Yes, that was the moment of the deadly wound. In the end it's only Hitler's judgment that matters. But if he didn't love it, then why did he have it placed in every library and have it listed as essential reading on the official Nazi Party card? He is even ordering the Hitlerjugend (Hitler youth) to read it. Why do this and at the same time absolutely refuse to associate himself with my book?*

I can understand his public stance. I know that Catholic support is still vital to his position as Führer, and, of course, he can't publicly support a work so blatantly anti-Christian. When we were young, in the '20s, Hitler agreed wholeheartedly with my antireligious stance. I know he still does. In private he goes farther than I—how many times have I heard him say he'd hang the priests alongside the rabbis? I understand his public stance. But why not say something affirmative, anything, to me privately? Why not once invite me for lunch and a private talk? Hess told me that when the Archbishop of Cologne complained to Hitler about the Mythus, Hitler replied, "I have no use for the book. Rosenberg knows it. I told him. I do not want to know about heathen things like the Cult of Wotan and so on." When the archbishop persisted, Hitler proclaimed, "Rosenberg is our party dogmatist," and then chided the archbishop for boosting the sales of the Mythus by attacking the book so vehemently. And when I offered to resign from the party if my Mythus caused him embarrassment, he simply brushed the idea aside—again without offering to meet privately. And yet Hitler meets privately with Himmler all the time, and Himmler is more blatantly and aggressively anti-Catholic than I am.

I know he must have some respect for me. He offered me one important post after another: diplomatic assignments in London, then in Oslo, then head of the ideological education of the NSDAP and the German labor front, and all related organizations. Important positions. But why do I only find out about my appointments by mail? Why not call me into his office, shake my hand, sit down and talk? Am I so repulsive?

Yes, there's no doubt: Hitler is the problem. More than anything in the world I want his attention. More than anything, I dread his vexation. I run the most influential newspaper in Germany; I am in charge of the spiritual and philosophical education of all Nazis. But am I writing the necessary articles? Giving the necessary lectures? Planning curricula? Overseeing the education of all young Germans? No, Reichsleiter Rosenberg is too busy brooding about why he hasn't received a loving smile or nod or, God forbid, a lunch invitation from Adolf Hitler!

I disgust myself. This has got to stop!

Alfred arose and walked to the desk in his room. Reaching into his briefcase, he extracted his "No" folder. (He had two folders, a "Yes" folder containing positive reviews, fan letters, and newspaper articles and a 'No' folder, holding all contrary opinions.) The "Yes" folder was well-worn. Several times a week Alfred perused complimentary reviews and fan letters that served as a daily tonic—like taking his morning vitamins. But now the tonic was losing potency. Now all "Yes" comments barely penetrated, a millimeter at most, and rapidly evaporated. The "No" folder, on the other hand, was unknown territory—a cavern rarely visited. Today! Today would be the turning point! He would confront his demons. As Alfred reached into the unvisited folder, he imagined the surprised letters and articles scurrying for cover. A smile appeared on his lips, the first in many weeks, as he appreciated his droll sense of humor. He extracted an item randomly—it was time to overcome this foolishness. A brave man forces himself to read hurtful things every day until they no longer hurt. He looked at it—a letter from Hitler dated August 24, 1931:

> *My dear Herr Rosenberg: I am just reading in the* Völkischer Beobachter, *edition 235/236, page 1, an article entitled "Does Wirth Intend to Come Over?" The tendency of the article is to prevent a crumbling away from the present form of government. I myself am traveling all over Germany to achieve exactly the opposite. May I therefore ask that my own paper not stab me in the back with tactically unwise articles?*
>
> *With German Greetings,*
> *Adolf Hitler*

A wave of despair enveloped him. The letter was five years old but still potent, still hurtful. Paper cuts inflicted by Hitler never healed. Alfred shook his head vigorously to clear his head. Think about this man named Hitler, he told himself. He is, after all, only a man. Closing his eyes, he let his thoughts flow.

> *I introduced Hitler to the breadth and depth of German culture. I showed him the immensity of the Jewish scourge. I polished his ideas of race and blood. He and I walked the same streets, sat in the same cafés, talked incessantly, worked together on* Beobachter *articles, once even sketched together. But no longer. Now I can only watch him in astonishment, like a hen gazing up at a hawk. I was witness to his gathering together the scattered party members when he left prison, to his entering parliamentary elections, to his building a propaganda machine the likes of which the world had never before seen—a machine that invented direct mail and campaigned continuously, even when there were no elections. I saw him shrug off poor returns of less than 5 percent the first few years and keep improving until 1930, when his party became the second largest in Germany with 18 percent of the vote. And in 1932 I ran huge headlines announcing that the Nazis had become*

the largest party, with 38 percent of the vote. Some say it was Goebbels who was the mastermind, but I know it was Hitler. Hitler was behind everything. I covered every step of the way for the Beobachter. I saw him fly from city to city making appearances all over the county on the same day and persuading the populace that he was an Übermensch, capable of being everywhere at once. I admired his fearlessness as he deliberately scheduled meetings in the midst of dangerous Communist-controlled neighborhoods and commanded his storm troopers to battle the Bolshevists on the streets. I saw him reject my advice and run against Hindenburg in 1932. He gathered only 37 percent of the votes, but he showed me he was right to run: he knew no one could have defeated Hindenberg, but the election made him a household name. A few months later he agreed to a coalition Hitler/Papen government and then soon became chancellor. I followed every single political step, and I still don't know how he did it.

And the Reichstag fire. I remember how he showed up wild-eyed at my office at 5 am, yelling "Where is everyone?" and demanded huge coverage of the Communists burning down the Reichstag. I still don't think the Communists had anything to do with the fire, but no matter—in a stroke of genius he used the fire to ban the Communist Party and assume absolute one-man power. He never won a majority vote, never more than 38 percent, and there he was—an absolute ruler! How did he do it? I still don't know!

Alfred's reverie was interrupted by a knock on the door and the entry of Dr. Gebhardt, followed by Friedrich Pfister. "I have a surprise for you, Reichsleiter Rosenberg. I bring an old friend who may prove useful in treating your condition. I'll leave the two of you to discuss this alone."

Alfred glared at Friedrich for a long while before saying, "You betrayed me. You broke your vow to me about secrecy. How else could he have known that you and I—"

Friedrich wheeled about instantly and, without a word or glance at Alfred, strode out of the room.

Panicky, Alfred flopped back on the bed, closed his eyes, and tried to slow his rapid breathing.

A few minutes later Friedrich returned with Dr. Gebhardt, who said, "Dr. Pfister has asked me to tell you how I selected him. Do you not remember, Reichsleiter Rosenberg, our conversation three or four weeks ago, in

which I asked you whether you had ever bared yourself completely to anyone? Your exact words were, 'a friend from Estonia, now living here, Dr.
Friedrich Pfister.'"

Alfred shook his head slowly. "I vaguely remember our discussion but
do not recall using his name."

"You did indeed. How else could I have known it? Or known he was in
Germany? Last week, when your depression deepened and you would not
speak to me, I decided to try to locate your friend, thinking that a visit from
him might be salubrious. When I learned he was in the Wehrmacht, I asked
the Führer to order his transfer to the Hohenlychen Clinic."

"Would you mind," asked Friedrich, "telling Reichsleiter Rosenberg
about my response?"

"Only that you once knew him growing up in Estonia."

"And . . ." prodded Friedrich.

"There was nothing more . . . except that you regretted leaving the many
patients who depended on you but that nothing took precedence over following the Führer's orders."

"May I have a brief private conversation with Reichsleiter Rosenberg
before you leave the ward this morning?"

"Of course. I'll wait for you at the nurses' station."

When the door closed, Friedrich said, "Other questions, Reichsleiter
Rosenberg?"

"Alfred, please, Friedrich. I am Alfred. Call me Alfred."

"All right. Other questions, Alfred? He's waiting."

"You're to be my doctor? I assure you that under the old conditions I
would welcome it. But, now, how can I possibly speak to you? You're in the
Wehrmacht and under orders to report to him."

"Yes, I understand your dilemma. I would feel the same way if I were in
your position." Friedrich sat down on the chair next to the bed and thought
for a few moments; then he rose and left the room, saying, "I'll be back in a
minute," and soon returned with Dr. Gebhardt.

"Sir," he addressed Dr. Gebhardt, "my orders are to attend to Reichsleiter
Rosenberg, and, of course, I shall follow those orders to the best of my ability. But there is an impediment. He and I are old acquaintances, and we've
long shared intimate concerns with one another. If I'm to be helpful to him,
then it is essential he and I have complete privacy. I must be able to promise

him absolute confidentiality. I know that daily notes in the medical chart are mandatory, and I ask that I be permitted to enter notes describing only his medical condition."

"I'm not a psychiatrist, Dr. Pfister, but I can understand the necessity for privacy in this instance. It is not standard procedure, but nothing takes precedence over Reichsleiter Rosenberg's recovery and return to his important work. I agree to your request." He saluted both men and departed.

"Does this reassure you, Alfred?"

Alfred nodded. "I am reassured."

"And are there no other questions?"

"I am satisfied. Despite the fractious end of our last encounter I continue to have a strange trust in you. I say 'strange' because in truth I trust practically no one. And I need your help. Last year I was hospitalized here for three months in a similar state—a deep black hole. I could not climb out. I felt finished. I could not sleep. I was exhausted yet couldn't sit still, couldn't rest."

"Your condition—we call it 'agitated depression'—almost always resolves in about three to six months. I can help you shorten that."

"I will be eternally grateful. Everything—my whole life—is in jeopardy."

"Let's go to work. You know my approach and probably won't be surprised to hear me say that our first chore is to clear away all obstacles to our working together. I, like you, have concerns. Let me gather my thoughts."

Friedrich closed his eyes for a few moments and began. "It's best if I clear the air and just say what comes to mind. I have troubling doubts about our working together. We're too different. My propensity is to understand, to uncover the hidden roots of difficulties—that's the basic belief of the psychoanalytic method. Full knowledge removes conflicts and promotes healing. Yet, with you, I worry that I cannot take that path. Last time, when I attempted to explore the sources of your difficulties, you grew angry and defensive and charged out of my office. So I worry if I, or at least that approach, can be useful to you."

Alfred stood up and paced about his room.

"Am I unsettling you by my frankness?"

"No, it's just my nerves. I can't sit for too long. I appreciate your candor. No one else speaks so forthrightly to me. You're my one friend, Friedrich."

Friedrich tried to digest those words. He was moved despite himself. And he was furious at having been transferred with no advance notice to the Hohenlychen Clinic. His sudden transfer meant abandoning a large number of patients in the midst of their treatment without being able to provide a definite date of return. Nor did he relish seeing Alfred Rosenberg again. Six years ago, he watched Alfred Rosenberg's back as he stormed out of his office muttering sinister threats about the Jewish roots of his profession, and was relieved to have seen the last of him. Moreover, he had tried to read *The Myth of the Twentieth Century*. But like everyone else he found it incomprehensible. It was one of those best sellers everyone bought but no one read. What little he read alarmed him. *Alfred may be suffering, he plaintively says I'm his only friend, but he is a dangerous man—dangerous for Germany, for everyone.*

The thoughts in the *Mythus* and *Mein Kampf* were parallel—he remembered Alfred saying Hitler had stolen his ideas. Both books sickened him—so vile, so base. And so menacing that he had begun to consider emigration and had already written to Carl Jung and Eugen Bleuler to enquire about a post at the Zurich hospital where he had trained. But then came the accursed conscription letter congratulating him on his appointment as an Oberleutnant in the Wehrmacht. He should have acted earlier. He had been warned by his analyst, Hans Meyer, who several years ago read *Mein Kampf* over a weekend, foresaw the cataclysm to come, and began advising every single one of his Jewish patients to leave the country immediately. He himself had emigrated to London within a month.

So what to do? Friedrich had put aside the naïve thought that he could help Alfred become a better person—that seemed a piece of youthful foolishness. For the sake of his own career (and the welfare of his wife and his two young sons), there was only one viable option: follow orders, and do his best to get Alfred out of the hospital as quickly as possible and get himself back to his family and patients at his Berlin posting. He had to bury his contempt for his patient and act professionally. His first step was to construct a clear frame for therapy.

"I'm touched by your comment about our friendship," he said. "But your statement that I am your only friend concerns me. Everyone needs friends and confidants. We should try to address your isolation: there is no doubt it plays a major role in your illness. As for our work together, let me share some other concerns. These are more difficult to express, but it's essential that I do so. I, too, have privacy issues. As you know, it's now a

criminal offense to question any party positions. One's very speech is mon-
itored, and no doubt the monitoring will be even more intensive as time
goes by. It's always been so in authoritarian regimes. I, like the majority of
Germans, don't agree with all the tenets of the NSDAP. You, of course, know
well that Hitler never received a majority vote. Last time we met—it has
been many years—six, I think—you stormed out of my office in, if you'll
permit me to say, an angry, out-of-control state. In that state I could not
feel confident in your respecting my privacy. And that will result in my feeling constricted and less effective in my work with you. I'm being wordy
here, but I think you get my point: confidentiality must go both ways. You
have my personal and professional oath that what you say here remains
here. I need the same assurance."

Both men sat in silence for some time until Alfred said, "Yes, I understand.
I give you my word that all of your comments will be held in confidence. And
I can understand how you can't feel safe if I get in an out-of-control state."

"Right. So we must work more safely and strive to make us both
feel safe?"

Friedrich took a closer look at his patient. Alfred was unshaved. Dark
bags under his eyes gave testimony to sleepless nights, and his mournful
countenance stirred Friedrich's doctorly instincts; he tuned out his antipathy
and got to work. "Tell me, Alfred, what's our goal? I want to help. What
would you like to get from me?"

Alfred hesitated for several moments and then said, "Try this idea. These
last weeks I've been reading a great deal." He pointed to the stack of books
littering the room. "I'm going back to the classics, especially Goethe. Do
you remember my telling you about my problems with Acting Headmaster
Epstein just before high school graduation?

"Refresh my memory."

"Because of an anti-Semitic speech I had made as class president, I was
required to memorize some passages in Goethe's autobiography."

"Oh yes, yes—it's all coming back to me. Some passages about Spinoza.
They assigned them to you because Goethe so admired Spinoza."

"I was so frightened by the prospect of not graduating that I memorized
them well. I could recite them even now, but for the sake of brevity let me
summarize the major points: Goethe wrote that he was in a restless state,

and reading Spinoza gave him a remarkable sedative for his passions. Spinoza's mathematical approach provided a wonderful balance for his disturbing thoughts and led to calmness and a more disciplined way of thinking that allowed him to trust his own conclusions and to feel free from the influence of others."

"Well put, Alfred. And in reference to you and me? . . ."

"Well, that's what I want from you. I want what Goethe got from Spinoza. I need all these things. I want a sedative for my passions. I want—"

"This is good. Very good. Stop for a moment. Let me jot this down." Friedrich opened his fountain pen, a gift from his supervisor, and wrote "sedative for passions." Alfred continued while Friedrich took notes: "Freedom from the influence of others. Balance. Calm, disciplined way of thinking."

"Good, Alfred. It would be good for both of us to get back to Spinoza. And, what's more, trying to implement his ideas may be well suited for a philosophically inclined mind like yours. Perhaps, too, it will keep us out of contentious areas. Let's meet tomorrow at the same time, and in the meanwhile I'll get to work and do some reading. May I borrow your Goethe autobiography? And do you still have your copy of the *Ethics*?"

"The same copy I bought when I was twenty. They say Goethe carried the *Ethics* in his pocket for a whole year. I haven't kept it in my pocket. In fact, I haven't picked it up for years. Yet I can't bring myself to throw it away."

Though only a few minutes before, Friedrich had been eager to leave, he now sat back down. "I see my task. I'll try to locate passages and ideas that helped Goethe and may help you as well. But I think I need to know more about what precipitated this current bout of despair."

Alfred described the self-analysis he had been conducting earlier that day. He told Friedrich of his lack of pleasure in his successes and how the *Mythus*, his greatest achievement, had caused so much torment. He poured out everything, especially how everything inexorably led back to Hitler. Alfred ended: "More than ever, I see now how my entire sense of self depends on Hitler's opinion of me. I must get over this. I am a slave to the desire for his approval."

"I remember your struggling with this issue when we last met. You told me how Hitler always preferred the company of others and never included you in the inner circle."

"Now take the feeling I had then and multiply by ten, by a hundred. It's a curse; it has seeped into every corner of my mind. I need to exorcise it."

"I'll do my best. Let's see what Benedictus de Spinoza has to offer us."

The following afternoon, Friedrich entered Alfred's room and was greeted by a better shaved and better dressed patient who stood up briskly and said, "Ah, Friedrich, I'm eager to begin. The last twenty-four hours I've thought of little else but our meeting today."

"You look brighter."

"I feel that way. I feel better than I've felt in weeks. How is this possible? Even though twice our meetings ended badly, still I profited from seeing you. How do you do it, Friedrich?"

"Perhaps I bring hope?"

"That's part of it. But there's something else."

"I believe it has much to do with your very human need for caring and connection. Let's keep that on the agenda—it's important. But for now let's stay focused on our plan of action. I've picked out a few Spinoza passages that seem relevant. Let's start with these two phrases."

He opened his copy of the *Ethics* and read:

> Different men can be affected differently by the same object.
> The same man can be affected differently at different times by the same object.

Noting Alfred's puzzled look, Friedrich explained. "I cite this only as a starting place for our work. Spinoza is simply saying that each of us can be differently affected by the identical external object. Your reaction to Hitler may be quite different from the reaction of other men. Others may love and honor him as you do, yet their entire well-being and self-regard may not be so entirely dependent on their experience of him. Not so?"

"Maybe. But I have no way of knowing others' inner experiences."

"I spend much of my life exploring that territory and see much evidence supporting Spinoza's postulate. For example, my patients have varying responses to me even in their very first visits. Some distrust me, whereas others may have immediate confidence in me, while still others feel I'm out to do them injury. And in each instance I believe I am relating to them in the same way. How can that be explained? Only by assuming there are different inner worlds perceiving the single event."

Alfred nodded. "But what is the relevance to my situation?"

"Good. Don't let me wander. I'm only making the point that your relationship to Hitler is *to some degree* a function of your own mind. My point is simple. We must start with the goal of altering yourself, rather than attempting to alter Hitler's behavior."

"I accept that, but I'm glad you added 'to some degree' because Hitler looms large to everyone. Even Göring, in a moment of uncharacteristic candor, said to me that 'Everyone around Hitler is a yes-man because all the no-men are six feet under.'"

Friedrich nodded.

"But you have persuaded me that he looms excessively large for me," Alfred continued, "and I want you to help me to change that. Does Spinoza have a proposal for procedure?"

"Let's take a look at what he says about freeing oneself from the influence of others," said Friedrich, scanning his notes. "That is one of the things Goethe learned from Spinoza. Here's a relevant passage in Part 4, a section called 'Of Human Bondage': 'When a man is prey to his emotions, he is not his own master, but lies at the mercy of fortune.' That describes what's happening to you, Alfred. You're prey to your emotions, buffeted by waves of anxiety, fear, and self-contempt. Does that sound right?"

Alfred nodded.

"Spinoza continues by saying that if your self-esteem is based on love from the multitude, then you will always be anxious because such love is fickle. He refers to this as 'empty self-esteem.'"

"As contrasted with what? What is *full* self-esteem?"

"Goethe and Spinoza both insisted that we should never tie our fate to something corruptible or fickle. On the contrary Spinoza urges that we love something incorruptible and eternal."

"That being?"

"That being God or Spinoza's version of God, which is entirely equivalent to Nature. Recall Spinoza's phrase that influenced Goethe so much: 'Whosoever truly loves God must not desire God to love him in return.' He's saying that we live in folly if we love God in the expectation of receiving

God's love in return. Spinoza's God is not a sentient being. If we love God, we cannot receive love in return, but we do receive some other good."

"Which other good?"

"Something that Spinoza refers to as the highest state of blessedness—*Amor Dei Intellectualis*. Here, listen to these lines from the *Ethics*:

> Thus in life it is important before all things to perfect the understand-
> ing, or reason. . . In this man's highest happiness consists; indeed
> blessedness is nothing else but contentment of spirit which arises from
> the intuitive knowledge of God.

"You see," Friedrich continued, "Spinoza's religious feeling seems to be a state of awe that is experienced when one appreciates the grand scheme of the laws of Nature. Goethe fully embraces that idea."

"I'm trying to follow you, Friedrich, but I need something tangible, something I can use."

"I don't think I'm being a good guide. Let's go back to your original re-quest: 'I want what Goethe got from Spinoza.'"

Friedrich glanced at his notes. "Here's what you said you wanted: 'peace of mind, balance, independence from influence of others, and a calm, dis-ciplined way of thinking leading to clarity of vision of the world.' Your mem-ory is excellent, by the way. Last night I reread Goethe's comments about Spinoza in the autobiography, and you've cited him very accurately. Though he considers Spinoza as a noble, remarkable soul who lived an exemplary life, and credits Spinoza with altering his life, unfortunately, for our purposes he offers no specific details of the manner in which Spinoza helped him."

"So where does that leave us?"

"Here's what I suggest. Let me offer some informed guesses about how Spinoza influenced him. First, keep in mind that Goethe had already formed certain Spinoza-like ideas before he encountered Spinoza—the connected-ness of everything in Nature, the idea that Nature is self-regulatory, with nothing beyond or above it. Thus Goethe felt much affirmation when reading Spinoza. Both men were brought to a state of extreme joy by grasping the connectedness of everything in Nature. And remember that, for Spinoza, God was equivalent to Nature. He does not refer to the Christian or Jewish

God, but a universal religion of reason in which there would no longer be any Christian, Jew, Muslim, or Hindu."

"Hmm, I hadn't appreciated Spinoza wanted to eliminate all religions. Interesting."

"He was a universalist. He expected conventional religions to fade away as greater and greater numbers of men devoted themselves to seeking the fullest understanding of the cosmos. We talked about some of this years ago. Spinoza was the supreme rationalist. He saw an endless stream of causality in the world. For him there is no such entity as will or will power. Nothing happens capriciously. Everything is caused by something prior, and the more we devote ourselves to the understanding of this causative network, the more free we become. It was this view of an orderly universe with predictable, mathematically derived laws, a world with an infinite explanatory power, that offered Goethe a sense of calmness."

"Enough, Friedrich, my head is spinning. I feel only dread in this natural orderliness. This is so abstruse."

"I'm merely following your inquiry about how Goethe got help from Spinoza and your desire to reap those same benefits. There is no single technique in Spinoza's work. He doesn't offer a single exercise like confession or catharsis or psychoanalysis. One has to follow him step by step to arrive at his all-encompassing view of the world, behavior, and morality."

"I am tormented about Hitler. How would he suggest I alleviate it?"

"Spinoza took the position that we can overcome torment and all human passions by arriving at the understanding of the world as woven out of logic. His belief in this is so strong that he says"—Friedrich flipped through the pages—"'I shall consider human actions and feelings just as if it were a question of lines, planes, and bodies.'"

"And me and Hitler?"

"I'm sure he would have said that you are subject to passions that are driven by inadequate ideas rather than by the ideas that flow from a true quest for understanding the nature of reality."

"And how does one rid oneself of these inadequate ideas?"

"He states explicitly that a passion ceases to be a passion as soon as we form a more clear and distinct idea of it—that is, the causative nexus underlying the passion."

Alfred fell silent and slouched in his chair with a pinched face that looked as though he had tasted curdled milk. "There is something disturbing about this. Highly disturbing. I think I'm beginning to see the Jew in Spinoza—something flaccid, pale, weak, and anti-German. He denies the will and labels passions as inferior, whereas we modern Germans take the opposite viewpoint. Passion and will are *not* things to be eliminated. Passion is the heart and soul of the *Volk*, whose trinity is bravery, loyalty, and physical force. Yes, there is no doubt: there is something anti-German about Spinoza."

"Alfred, you're jumping to conclusions too quickly. Remember how you threw the *Ethics* down because the first few pages were crammed with abstruse axioms and definitions? To understand Spinoza, as Goethe did, we have to familiarize ourselves with his language and step by step, theorem by theorem, follow the construction of his worldview. You're a scholar. I am certain you spent years of historical research in writing your *Mythus*. And yet you refuse to give Spinoza, one of the greatest minds in history, more than a passing glance at his chapter headings. The great German intellectuals delved deep into his work. Give him the time he deserves."

"You always defend the Jews."

"He doesn't represent the Jews. He espouses pure reason. The Jews cast him out."

"I warned you about studying with Jews long ago. I warned you of entering this Jewish field. I warned you of your great danger."

"You may rest at ease. The danger is past. All the Jews in the psychoanalytic institute have left the country. As has Albert Einstein. As have the other great Jewish German scientists. And the great German non-Jewish writers—like Thomas Mann and two hundred fifty of our finest writers. Do you really believe this strengthens our country?"

"Germany grows stronger and more pure every time a Jew or a lover of Jews leaves the country."

"Do you believe such hatred—"

"It's not a matter of hatred. It's a matter of preserving the race. For Germany, the Jewish question is only solved when the last Jew has left the Greater German space. I wish them no harm. I just want them to live elsewhere."

Friedrich had hoped to force Alfred to look at the consequences of his goals. He sensed the pointlessness of going down this trail but could not control himself: "Do you see no harm in uprooting millions of people and doing—*what* with them?"

"They must go elsewhere—Russia, Madagascar, anywhere."

"Use your reason! You think of yourself as a philosopher—"

"There are higher things than reason—honor, blood, courage."

"Look at the implications of what you're proposing, Alfred. I urge you to muster the courage to look, to *really* look, at the human implications of your proposals. But maybe you do know at some level. Maybe your great agitation stems from the part of your mind that knows the horror—"

A knock on the door. Alfred stood, strode to the door, opened it, and was startled to see Rudolf Hess.

"Good day, Reichsleiter Rosenberg. The Führer is here to visit you. He has news for you and awaits your presence in the conference room. I'll wait outside and escort you."

Alfred froze for a moment. Then he stood more erect; strode to his closet, from which he removed his Nazi uniform; turned toward Friedrich— and seemed almost surprised to see him still there. "Herr Oberleutnant Pfister, go to your room. Await me there."

Quickly donning his uniform and putting on his boots, he joined Hess. They walked in silence to the room where Hitler awaited.

Hitler rose to greet Alfred, returned his salute, pointed for him to be seated, and indicated to Hess that he wait outside.

"You're looking well, Rosenberg. Not at all like a hospitalized patient. I am relieved."

Alfred, flustered by Hitler's affability, mumbled his thanks.

"I've just reread your *Völkischer Beobachter* article last year on the award of the Nobel peace prize to Carl von Ossietzky. An excellent piece of journalism, Rosenberg. Far superior to the pallid stuff published in our paper during your absence. Just the right tone of dignity and outrage at the Nobel committee awarding the peace price to a citizen who is in prison in his own country for treason. I entirely agree with your position. It is indeed an insult and a frontal attack upon the sovereign Reich. Please prepare Ossietzky's obituary. He is not tolerating the concentration camp very well, and we may have the good fortune to report his death shortly.

"But I am visiting today not only to inquire after your health and to give you my greetings but also to give you news. I very much liked your suggestion in the article that Germany should no longer tolerate the arrogance of Stockholm and should instead initiate our own German equivalent of the now-odorous Nobel prize. I have taken action and have created a selection committee to consider candidates for the German National Prize for Art and Science, and commissioned Müller-Erfurt to design an elaborate diamond-studded pendant. There will be a prize of 100,000 reichsmarks. I want you to be the first to know that I have nominated you for the first Deutscher National-alpreis. Here is a copy of the public statement that I shall release shortly."

Alfred took the sheet and read greedily:

> The National Socialist movement, and beyond that, the entire German people, will be deeply gratified that the Führer has distinguished Alfred Rosenberg as one of his oldest and most faithful fighting comrades by awarding him the German National Prize.

"Thank you. Thank you, *mein* Führer. Thank you for the proudest moment of my life."

"And when will you be going back to work? The *Völkischer Beobachter* needs you."

"Tomorrow. I am now entirely fit."

"The new doctor, that friend of yours, must be a miracle worker. We should commend and promote him."

"No, no—I recovered before he arrived. He deserves no credit. As a matter of fact, he was trained in that Jew-run Freud institute in Berlin and weeps tears that the Jewish psychiatrists have all left the country. I've tried, but I don't think I can get the Jew out of him. We should watch him. He may need some rehabilitation. And now I go to work. *Heil, mein* Führer!"

Alfred marched briskly to his room and quickly began to pack. A few minutes later Friedrich knocked on his door.

"Alfred, you're leaving?"

"Yes, I'm leaving."

"What's happened?

"What's happened is that I have no further use for your services, Herr Oberleutnant Pfister. Return immediately to your post in Berlin."

CHAPTER THIRTY-ONE

VOORBURG—DECEMBER 1666

My dear Bento,

Simon promises to deliver this letter within a week, and unless you tell him otherwise I shall visit you in Voorburg in the late morning of December 20. I have much to share with you and much to learn of your life. How I have missed you! I have been under such excruciating surveillance that I have not dared even to visit Simon to post a letter. Please know that even though we have not been together, you have been close to my heart all these years. Not a day passes without my seeing your radiant face and hearing your voice in my mind.

You most likely know that Rabbi Mortera died not too long after our last visit and that your brother-in-law, Rabbi Samuel Casseres, who gave the funeral oration, died a few weeks later. Your sister, Rebekah, lives with her son, Daniel, now sixteen and destined for the rabbinate. Your brother, Gabriel, now known as Abraham, has become a successful merchant and travels often to Barbados for trade.

I am now a rabbi! Yes, a rabbi! And until recently I was the assistant of Rabbi Aboab, who is now chief rabbi. Amsterdam is now under a madness, and no one speaks of anything else except the arrival of the Messiah, Sabbatai Zevi. Oddly, and I shall explain later, it is this madness about him that makes it possible for me to visit. Even though Rabbi Aboab continues to scrutinize my every move, it now no longer matters. I embrace you, and soon you shall know all.

Franco (also known as Rabbi Benitez)

Bento read Franco's letter a second and then a third time. He grimaced at the portentous phrase "it no longer matters"? What did that mean? And he grimaced again at the mention of the new Messiah. Sabbatai Zevi was in the air. Only the day before, he had received a letter about the coming of the Messiah from one of his regular correspondents, Henry Oldenburg, corresponding secretary of the British Royal Society of Science. Bento fetched Oldenburg's letter and reread the pertinent passage:

> *Here there is a widespread rumor that the Israelites, who have been dispersed for more than two thousand years, are to return to their homeland. Few hereabouts believe it, but many wish it. . . I am anxious to hear what the Jews in Amsterdam have heard about it and how they are affected by so momentous an announcement.*

Bento paced as he thought. His tile-floored room was more spacious than his Rijnsburg room. His two bookcases, now filled with over sixty large volumes, occupied one of his four walls; his slashed greatcoat hung next to the two small windows of a second wall; and the two remaining walls were adorned with borders of Delft tiles of windmills and a dozen fine Dutch landscapes by Dutch painters collected by Daniel Tydeman, his landlord, a Collegiant and an admirer of his philosophy. It was at Daniel's insistence that Bento had left Rijnsburg three years earlier to rent a room in his house in Voorburg, a charming village, only two miles from the seat of government in The Hague. Moreover, Voorburg was also the home of a valued acquaintance, Christiaan Huygens, the eminent astronomer, who often praised Bento's lenses.

Bento slapped his forehead as he muttered, "Sabbatai Zevi! The coming of the Messiah! What madness! Will there ever be an end to such foolish gullibility?" Few things irritated Bento more than irrational numerological beliefs, and 1666 was awash in fantastical predictions. Many superstitious Christians had long held that the great flood occurred 1656 years after the Creation and that a second coming or some other world-changing event was to occur in 1656. When that year passed uneventfully, they merely transferred expectations to 1666, a year given significance by a statement in the book of Revelation naming the number of the beast as 666 ("six hundred three score and six"—Revelation 13:18). Hence many had predicted the coming of the Antichrist in 666. When that prediction failed, latter-day prophets had set the ominous date one millennium ahead, to 1666—a belief given more credibility by the great fire of London only three months earlier.

The Jews were no less gullible. The messianists, especially among the Marranos, were fully anticipating the imminent coming of the Messiah, who would gather all the dispersed Jews and return them to the Holy Land. For many the arrival of Sabbatai Zevi was the answer to their prayers.

On Friday, the appointed date of Franco's arrival, Bento was unusually distracted by the sounds of the bustling Voorburg marketplace, only thirty meters from his room. This was odd for him—ordinarily he concentrated on his scholarly work despite all noises and outside events—but Franco's face kept dancing through his mind. After a half hour of rereading the same page of Epictetus, he gave up, closed the book, and returned it to the bookcase. This morning he allowed himself to daydream.

He tidied up the room, straightened the pillows, and smoothed the down blankets on the four-poster bed. He stepped back to admire his work and thought, *Someday I shall die upon that bed.* He eagerly anticipated Franco's arrival and wondered if the room were warm enough. Though he himself was indifferent to temperature, he imagined Franco would be chilled after his journey. Hence he gathered two armfuls of wood from the woodpile behind the house but tripped as he entered the house, scattering the logs on the floor. He collected them, carried them into his room, and bent to light a fire in the fireplace. Daniel Tydeman, who had heard the clatter of the falling logs, gently knocked on his door. "Good morning. A fire? Are you not feeling well?"

"The fire's not for me, Daniel. I'm expecting a visitor from Amsterdam."

"Amsterdam? He'll be hungry. I'll tell the *huishoudster* to prepare some coffee and some extra dinner."

Bento spent much of the morning looking out of his window. At midday, spotting Franco, he joyously rushed out to embrace him and lead him into his room. Once inside, he stepped back to admire Franco, who was now dressed as any proper Dutch citizen, with a tall, broad-brimmed hat, a long greatcoat, a jacket buttoned to the neck with a square white collar, and knee britches and hose. His hair was brushed and his short beard neatly trimmed. They sat together silently on Bento's bed and beamed at one another.

"Silence today," Bento said in familiar Portuguese of years past, "but this time I know why. There is simply too much to be said."

"And also great joy often overwhelms words," added Franco.

Their sweet silence was fractured by Bento's short coughing fit. The phlegm that he spat into his handkerchief was speckled brown and yellow.

"That cough again, Bento. You are ailing?"

He waved his hand to dismiss his friend's concern. "My cough and congestion have taken up lodging in my chest, and they never wander too far from home. But in all other ways, my life is good. Exile suits me, and, today excepted of course, I am grateful for my solitude. And you, Franco, or should I say *Rabbi* Franco Benitez, you look so different, so groomed . . . so . . . so Dutch."

"Yes, Rabbi Aboab, kabbalistic and otherworldly though he be, nonetheless wishes me to dress as the everyday Dutchman and even insists I trim my beard. I think he prefers to be the only full-bearded Jew in the community."

"And how have you possibly managed to arrive here so early from Amsterdam?"

"I came yesterday on the *trekschuit* from Amsterdam to The Hague and spent the night there with a Jewish family."

"Are you thirsty? Coffee?"

"Perhaps later, but now I am famished for only one thing—conversation with you. I want to know of your new writing and thinking."

"I'll converse more easily if I first ease my mind. A line in your letter gave me great concern." Bento walked over to his desk, fetched Franco's letter, and looked at it. "Here it is: 'Even though Rabbi Aboab continues to examine my every move, it now no longer matters.' What has happened, Franco?"

"What happened was that which *necessarily* happened—and I believe I use your term 'necessarily' correctly, in that things could not have happened otherwise."

"But what?"

"Don't be alarmed, Bento. For once we're not rushed. We have until two this afternoon, when I must take the *trekschuit* to Leiden, where I shall visit some Jewish families. We have ample time to go over the story of my life and of your life. All will be told, and all will be well, but stories are best told from the beginning rather than from the end backward. You see I still love stories and persist in my campaign to increase your respect for them."

"Yes, I remember your strange notion that I secretly enjoy stories. Well, you won't find many there"—Bento waved his hand toward his bookcase.

Franco walked over to peruse Bento's library and glanced over the titles of the four shelves of books. "Oh, they're beautiful, Bento. I wish I could spend months here reading your books and talking about them. But look here!" Franco pointed to one shelf. "What's this before my eyes? Do I not see the greatest storytellers of all? Ovid, Homer, Virgil? In fact I hear them whispering to me." Franco bent his ear to them. "They're pleading, 'Please, please read us—we have wisdom, but our unamused master ignores us so.'"

Bento burst out laughing, stood, and embraced his friend. "Ah, Franco, I miss you. Only you talk to me like this. Everyone else is so deferential to the Sage of Voorburg."

"Ah, yes. And, Bento, you and I both know that the Sage plays no role whatsoever in the deferential manner in which he is treated."

Another big guffaw from Bento. "How dare you keep the Sage waiting? Get to your story."

Franco took his seat next to Bento and began. "When last we met at Simon's home, I was just embarking on my study of Talmud and Torah and excited by the process of education."

"'Joyous study' was your term."

Franco smiled. "Precisely the phrase I used—but I expected no less from you. Three or four years ago, I asked the old caretaker of the synagogue, Abrihim, who was ailing and near death, about his memories of you, and he replied, 'Baruch de Espinoza forgets nothing. Total retention.' Yes, I was indeed joyous to learn, and my appetite and aptitude were so evident that Rabbi Aboab soon regarded me as his best student and extended my stipend so that I could continue on to rabbinical studies. I wrote you about that. You received my letter?"

Bento nodded. "I received it but was puzzled. In fact, astounded. Not by your love of learning—that I understand, that we share. But given your strong feelings about the dangers, the restrictions, the irrationality of religion, why choose to become a rabbi? Why join the enemies of reason?"

"I joined them for the same reason you left them."

Bento raised his eyebrows and then smiled slightly in comprehension.

"I think you understand, Bento. You and I both want to change Judaism—you from the outside and I from the inside!"

"No, no, I must disagree. My goal is not to change Judaism. My goal of radical universalism would eradicate all religions and institute a universal religion in which all men seek to attain blessedness through the full understanding of Nature. But let's return to this later. Exploring too many tributaries will impede your explanation of why Rabbi Aboab's surveillance no longer matters."

"So after my studies," Franco continued, "Rabbi Aboab ordained and blessed me and appointed me his assistant. For the first three years things went well. I participated by his side in all the daily services and eased his burden by taking over many of the bar mitzvahs and the marriage ceremonies. Soon his faith in me was so great that he sent me more and more of the individual congregation members who wished guidance and counseling. But the golden period, the time when we walked into the synagogue arm in arm, like father and son, was foreshortened. Dark clouds appeared on the horizon."

"Because of the coming of Sabbatai Zevi? I remember Rabbi Aboab as a fervent messianist."

"Even before that. Things went awry when Rabbi Aboab began to instruct me in the kabbalah."

"Ah yes. Of course. And I imagine that is when you ceased being a joyous student."

"Exactly. I tried my best, but my credulity was stretched to the breaking point. I attempted to convince myself that this text was an important historical document that I should study carefully. Shouldn't a scholar know the mythology of his own culture as well as others? But, Bento, your crystal-clear voice and your incisive method of Torah critique rang in my ears, and I was exquisitely attuned to the inconsistencies and to the insubstantially grounded premises on which the kabbalah rested. And of course Rabbi Aboab insisted he was not teaching me mythology—he was teaching me history, facts, the living truth, the word of God. No matter how hard I tried to dissimulate, my lack of enthusiasm shone through. Slowly, day by day, his loving smile faded; he no longer grasped my arm as we walked; he grew more distant, more disappointed. Then, when one of my students reported to him that I had used the term 'metaphor' to refer to Luria's description of kabbalistic cosmic creation, he publicly rebuked me and restricted my duties. I believe that he then placed informants in all my classes and enlisted observers who reported on all my activities."

"And now I understand why you could not contact Simon to correspond with me."

"Yes, although recently my wife picked up Simon's twelve-page Dutch translation of some of your thoughts about overcoming the passions."

"Your wife? I thought you could not share with—"

"Place a bookmark at this point. Patience. We'll return to it shortly, but, to continue with my personal chronology, my problems with the kabbalah were troublesome enough. But the real crisis with Rabbi Aboab concerned the supposed Messiah, Sabbatai Zevi."

"What can you tell me about him?"

"I imagine it has been a long time since you read the Zohar, but no doubt you recall the predictions about the coming of the Messiah."

"Yes, I recall my final talk with Rabbi Mortera, who believed that the sacred texts predicted the arrival of the Messiah when the Jews were at their lowest point. We had an unpleasant interchange about that when I asked, 'If we are indeed the chosen, why is it necessary for us to be at the point of greatest despair before the Messiah arrives?' When I suggested that it seemed likely that the idea of a Messiah was designed by humans to combat their hopelessness, he was outraged by my daring to question divine word."

"Bento, can you believe that I actually long for the good days of Rabbi Mortera? Rabbi Aboab is so extreme in his Messianic beliefs that Rabbi Mortera seems enlightened in comparison. Moreover, some coincidences have increased Rabbi Aboab's fervor. Do you recall the Zohar's prediction of the birth date of the Messiah?"

"I remember nine five—the ninth day of the fifth month."

"And, lo and behold, it is reported that Sabbatai Zevi was born on the ninth of *Av* in Smyrna in Turkey in 1626, and last year he was proclaimed to be the Messiah by Nathan, a cabbalist of Gaza, who has become his patron. Rumors of miracles abound. Zevi is said to be charismatic, tall as a cedar, beautiful, pious, and ascetic. He is said to fast for long periods while singing psalms in a melodious voice the whole night through. Everywhere he travels he seems to go out of his way to offend and threaten the entrenched rabbinical authorities. He was expelled by the rabbis of Smyrna because he dared to speak the name of God from the synagogue bimah and expelled by the rabbis of Salonica for holding a marriage ceremony with himself as the groom and the Torah as the bride. But he seemed little troubled by the rabbis' displeasure, and he continued to wander through the Holy Land gathering ever greater numbers of followers. Soon the news of the Messiah's arrival swept like a hurricane throughout the Jewish world. With my own eyes I saw Amsterdam Jews dance in the street when the news arrived, and many have sold or given away all their worldly goods and set sail to join him in the Holy Land. And not just the uneducated but many of our eminent citizens are under his spell—even the ever cautious Isaac Pereira has disposed of his entire fortune and gone to join him. And rather than restoring sanity, Rabbi Aboab celebrates and raises the enthusiasm about this man to a fever pitch. This despite the fact that many rabbis in the Holy Land threaten Sabbatai Zevi with *cherem*."

Bento, his eyes closed, held both hands to his head and moaned, "The fools, the fools."

"Wait. The worst is yet to come. About three weeks ago a traveler from the east arrived and reported that the Ottoman sultan was so displeased with the hordes of Jews pouring into the east to join the Messiah that he summoned Sabbatai Zevi to his palace and offered him the choice of martyrdom or conversion to Islam. Sabbatai Zevi's decision? The Messiah promptly chose to become a Muslim!"

"He converted to Islam! So that's it?" Bento's face registered surprise, "Just like that. The Messiah insanity is over?"

"One would think so! One would think that all the Messiah's followers would understand they'd been duped. But not in the least—instead, Nathan and others have convinced his followers that his conversion is part of the divine plan, and hundreds, perhaps thousands, of Jews have followed him into conversion to Islam."

"And what then happened with you and Rabbi Aboab?"

"I could no longer contain myself and publicly urged my congregation to come to their senses, to stop selling their homes and possessions, and to wait, at least wait a year, before emigrating to the Holy Land. Rabbi Aboab was irate and now has suspended me and threatens me with *cherem*."

"*Cherem*? *Cherem*? Franco, I must make a 'Franco' observation—something I learned from you."

"And that is?" Franco looked at Bento with great interest.

"Your words and your melody do not match."

"My words and my melody?"

"You describe such portentous events—Rabbi Aboab rebuking you publicly, withdrawing his love, sending observers, restricting your freedom, and now *cherem*. And yet, even though you were horrified by witnessing my *cherem*, I see no despair in your face, no fear in your words. In fact you seem—what? Almost buoyant. Whence comes your lightheartedness?"

"You observe accurately, Bento, though, if we had spoken even a month ago, I would not have been so buoyant. But just recently a solution occurred to me. I've decided to emigrate! At least twenty-five Jewish families who believe in my way of being a Jew will, in three weeks' time, set sail with me for the New World, to the Dutch island of Curaçao, where we will establish our own synagogue and our own way of religious life. Yesterday I visited two families in The Hague who had left Rabbi Aboab's congregation two years ago, and they too will most likely join us. This evening I hope to enlist two other families."

"Curaçao? Half the world away?"

"Believe me, Bento, though I am full of hope about our future in the New World, I am also greatly saddened to think that you and I may never again meet. Yesterday on the *trekschuit* ride I daydreamed, and not for the first time, that you came to visit us in the New World and then chose to remain with us as our sage and scholar. But I know it is a dream. Your cough and your congestion tell me you cannot make the journey, and your contentment with your life tells me you will not make it."

Bento stood and paced about the room. "I am too aggrieved even to sit still. Even though our meetings are perforce infrequent, your presence in my life is vital to me. The thought of a permanent farewell is such a shock, such a loss, I can find no words to speak of it. And at the same time my love for you raises other thoughts. The dangers! How will you live? Are there not already Jews and a synagogue in Curaçao? How will they accept you?"

"Danger is always present for Jews. We have always been oppressed—if not by Christians or Muslims, then by our own elders. Amsterdam is the one spot in the old world that offers us some degree of freedom, but many foresee the end of that freedom. Multiple enemies gain strength: the war with the English is over but most likely only briefly, Louis the XIV threatens us, and our own liberal government may not long withstand the Dutch Orangists, who want to create a monarchy. Don't you share these concerns, Bento?"

"Yes! So much so that that I have put aside my work on the *Ethics* and am now writing a book about my theological and political views. Religious authorities have influence over the governing bodies and are now meddling so much in politics that they must be stopped. We must keep religion and politics separate."

"Tell me more about your new project, Bento."

"Much of it is an old project. You remember the biblical critique I offered you and Jacob?"

"Every word."

"I am putting these on paper and shall include all those arguments and so much more that any reasonable person will come to doubt the divine sources of the scriptures and ultimately come to accept that everything happens according to the universal laws of Nature."

"So you're going to publish the very ideas that brought about your *cherem?*"

"Let's discuss that later. For now, Franco, let's return to your plans. There is more urgency there."

"More and more, our group has come to believe our only hope is in the New World. One of our merchant members has already visited and selected some land that we have purchased from the Dutch West Indies Company. And yes, you're right: there is already an established Jewish community in Curaçao. But we will be on the opposite side of the island on our own land, teach ourselves to farm, and create a different type of Jewish community."

"And your family? How do they react to this move?"

"My wife, Sarah, agrees to go but only under certain conditions."

"Certain conditions? Can a Jewish wife set conditions? What conditions?"

"Sarah is strong-willed. She agrees to go only if I agree to take seriously her views about changing the way Judaism regards and treats women."

"I cannot believe what I hear. How we regard women? I've never heard such nonsense."

"She asked me to discuss this very topic with you."

"You talked with her about me? I thought you had to keep your contact with me secret even from her."

"She has changed. We have changed. We have no secrets from one another. May I deliver her words to you?"

Bento nods warily.

Franco cleared his throat and spoke in a higher key. "Mister Spinoza, do you agree it is just for women to be treated as inferior creatures in every manner? In the synagogue we must sit separately from the men and in poorer seating and—"

"Sarah," Bento interrupted, immediately entering into the role play, "of course you women and your lustful glances are seated separately. Is it right that men be distracted from God?"

"I know her answer exactly," said Franco and, mimicking her, continued: "You mean that men are like beasts in continual heat and are driven from their rational minds by the mere presence of a woman—the very woman they sleep with side by side each night. And the mere sight of our faces will dispel their love of God. Can you imagine how that feels to us?"

"Oh foolish woman—of course you must be out of our sight! The presence of your tempting eyes and your fluttering fans and shallow comments are inimical to religious contemplation."

"So because men are weak and cannot stay focused, it is the woman's fault, not theirs? My husband tells me you have said that nothing is good or bad but it is the mind that makes it so. Not right?"

Bento reluctantly nods.

"So perhaps it is the mind of the man that needs to be edified. Perhaps men should wear mule-blinders instead of demanding that women wear veils! Do I make my point, or shall I continue?"

Bento started to reply in detail but stopped and, shaking his head, said, "Go on."

"We women are kept prisoners in the house and are never taught Dutch and thus are limited in shopping or conversing with others. We carry the burden of an unequal amount of work in the family, while men sit for much of the day and debate issues in the Talmud. Rabbis openly oppose educating us because they say we are of inferior intelligence and if they were to teach us the Torah, they would be teaching us nonsense because we women could never grasp its complexity."

"On this one instance I agree with the rabbi. You actually believe that women and men have equal intelligence?"

"Ask my husband. He's standing right next to you. Ask him if I don't learn as fast and understand as deeply as he does."

Bento raised his chin gesturing to Franco, who smiled and said, "She speaks the truth, Bento. She learns and comprehends as quickly, perhaps more quickly, than I. And you knew a woman like her. Remember that young woman who taught you Latin, whom you yourself labeled a prodigy? Sarah even believes women should be counted as one of the minyan and be called upon to read from the bimah and even become rabbis."

"Read from the bimah? Become a rabbi? This is beyond belief! If women were capable of sharing power, then we could consult history and find many such instances. But there are none to be found, no instances of women ruling equally with men, and no instances of women ruling men. We can only conclude that women have an inherent weakness."

Franco shook his head. "Sarah would say—and here I would agree with her—that your evidence is no evidence at all. The reason there is no power sharing is—"

A knock on the door interrupted their discussion, and the housekeeper entered, carrying a tray heavy with food. "Mr. Spinoza, may I serve you?'"

Bento nodded, and she began placing dishes steaming with food on Bento's table. He turned to Franco. "She's asking if we're ready for some lunch. We can eat in here."

Franco, startled, looked at Bento and replied in Portuguese, "Bento, how can you think I could eat this food with you? Have you forgotten? I'm a rabbi!"

CHAPTER THIRTY-TWO

BERLIN, THE NETHERLANDS—1939–1945

He is "almost Alfred." Rosenberg almost managed to become a scholar, a journalist, a politician—but only almost.

—Joseph Goebbels

Why does the world shed crocodile's tears over the richly
merited fate of a small Jewish minority? . . . I ask Roosevelt, I ask the American people: Are you prepared to
receive in your midst these well-poisoners of the German
people and the universal spirit of Christianity? We would
willingly give every one of them a free steamer ticket and
a thousand-mark note for traveling expenses, if we could
get rid of them.

—Adolf Hitler

Though Alfred did not suffer another debilitating depression, he
never grew comfortable in his skin, and for the rest of his life his
self-worth gyrated wildly: he was either puffed or deflated, depending on his perceived closeness to Adolf Hitler.

Hitler never loved him; yet, convinced that Alfred's skills were useful
to the party, he continued to heap responsibilities on him. These duties were
always in addition to Alfred's primary task as editor-in-chief of the party

newspaper. The *Völkischer Beobachter*, "the fighting newspaper of the Nazi Party," flourished under Alfred's direction: by the 1940s it had a daily circulation of well over a million. Personally, Hitler preferred the vulgar, anti-Semitic caricatures in Streicher's *Der Stürmer*, but the *Beobachter* was the official party newspaper, and Hitler or his deputy, Rudolf Hess, never failed to read it daily.

Alfred had a cordial relationship with Hess and, through him, gained access to Hitler. But that ended precipitously on May 10, 1941, when, after a long leisurely breakfast with Rosenberg, Hess drove to the airport and, for reasons still perplexing historians, flew a Messerschmitt BF110 to Scotland and parachuted out, only to be immediately captured and imprisoned by the British for the rest of his life. Martin Bormann assumed Hess's deputy post and, as Alfred put it, became "dictator of the antechamber." Except for rare occasions, Bormann granted access to the Führer only to the inner circle—and that never included Alfred Rosenberg.

Yet no one could deny Alfred the amazing success of his book *The Myth of the Twentieth Century*. By 1940 it had sold over a million copies and was second in Germany only to *Mein Kampf*. Other duties abounded: Alfred's role as director of the ideological education of the entire Nazi Party required frequent meetings and public addresses. His speeches never strayed far from the catechism outlined in his book: Aryan race superiority, the Jewish menace, purity of blood, dangers of impure breeding, necessity for Lebensraum, and the dangers posed by religion. He relentlessly hammered away at the threats posed to the Reich by Jews and never failed to insist that the Jewish question must be solved by the removal of every Jew from Europe. When, by 1939, it became clear that no country would accept the German, Polish, and Czech Jews, he argued for the relocation of the European Jews to a reservation (pointedly not a state) outside of Europe—for example, Madagascar or Guyana. For a time he considered Alaska but then decided that its harsh climate would be too severe for the Jews.

In 1939 Hitler summoned Rosenberg for a meeting.

"Rosenberg, in my hand I have my official announcement of your German National award. I'm certain you remember our conversation about my nominating you—you called it the proudest day of your life. I myself approved these lines. 'Rosenberg's indefatigable struggle to keep National

Socialist philosophy clean was especially meritorious. Only future times will be able to fully estimate the depth of the influence of this man on the philosophical foundation of the National Socialist Reich.'"

Alfred's pupils widened: he was stunned by Hitler's largesse.

"And today I plan to assign you to a position you were meant for. I've decided to formally establish the Hohe Schule, the party's elite university of Nazism. You are to be its leader."

"I am deeply honored, *mein* Führer. But I've heard nothing of the plans for the Hohe Schule."

"It shall be an advanced center of ideological and educational research to be located in northern Bavaria. I envision a three-thousand-seat auditorium, a library of five hundred thousand volumes, and different branches in various cities of the Reich."

Alfred took out his notepad. "Shall I write about this in the *Beobachter*?"

"Yes. My secretary will give you the background material on it. A brief *Beobachter* announcement of its establishment and your appointment to head it would be timely. Your first task—and this is not for publication"— Hitler lowered his voice—"is to build the university library. And build it quickly. Immediately. The books are available right now. I want you to take the lead in seizing the contents of all Jewish and Freemason libraries in occupied territories."

Alfred was euphoric: this task *was* meant for him. He began immediately. Soon Rosenberg's emissaries were ransacking Jewish libraries throughout Eastern Europe and sending thousands of rare books to Frankfurt, where librarians would select the best books for the Hohe Schule library. Hitler was also planning a museum for extinct peoples, and other valuable books would be selected for ultimate display there. Before long, Alfred's mandate was broadened to include artwork as well as books. Like an eager puppy craving attention, he wrote Hitler on the Führer's fiftieth birthday:

> *Heil, mein Führer:*
> *In my desire to give you, my Führer, some joy for your birthday, I take
> the liberty to present to you photos of some of the most valuable paintings
> that my special purpose staff, in compliance with your order, secured from
> ownerless Jewish art collections in the occupied territories. These photos rep-*

resent an addition to the collection of fifty-three of the most valuable objects
of art delivered some time ago to your collection.

I beg of you, my Führer, to give me a chance during my next audience
to report to you orally on the whole extent and scope of this art seizure action.
I beg you to accept a short written intermediate report of the progress and
extent of the art seizure action, which will be used as a basis for this later
oral report, and also accept three copies of the temporary picture catalogues,
which, too, show only part of the collection you own. I shall take the liberty
during the requested audience to give you, my Führer, another twenty folders
of pictures, with the hope that this short involvement with the beautiful
things of art that are nearest to your heart will send a ray of beauty and joy
into your revered life.

In 1940 Hitler formally notified the entire Nazi Party of the formation
of the ERR—Einsatzstab (task force) of Reichsleiter Rosenberg—whose mission was to confiscate all Jewish-owned European art and books for use by
the Reich. Rosenberg found himself at the head of an enormous organization
that moved together with the military into occupied territory to safeguard
and remove "ownerless" Jewish property deemed valuable to Germany.

Alfred was thrilled. This was his most rewarding assignment. As he
pranced down the streets of Prague and Warsaw with his ERR team, he mused:
Power! Finally, power! To have life-and-death decisions over the Jewish libraries
and galleries of Europe. And also to have bargaining chips with Göring, who is
suddenly so nice to me. His greedy hands grasp for art plunder everywhere. But
now I'm first in line. I get first pick of the art for the Führer before Göring can
snatch it away for his own collection. Such greed! Göring should have been elim-
inated a long time ago. Why does the Führer tolerate such betrayal of Aryan
tradition and ideology.

The seizure of the Jewish libraries of Poland and Czechoslovakia whetted
Alfred's appetite for the grandest treasure of all—the library at the Rijnsburg
Museum. With Spinoza's library clearly in his sights, Alfred avidly wrote
headline after triumphant headline about the Nazi progress on the Western
Front. "Nothing can stop our blitzkrieg," the *Beobachter* blared. Country
after country bowed to Hitler's force, and before long it was the Netherlands'
turn. Though that small country had remained neutral in World War I and

hoped to do the same in the new war, Hitler had different ideas. On May 10, 1940, Nazi troops invaded the Netherlands in full force. Four days later, the Luftwaffe carpet-bombed the industrial city of Rotterdam, destroying a full square mile of the city center, and on the following day the Dutch forces capitulated. Alfred was jubilant as he prepared the front-page headlines and story on the five-day Netherlands war for the *Völkischer Beobachter* and wrote an editorial about the invincibility of the Nazi blitzkrieg. *Beobachter* staff members were astonished by Alfred's behavior—never before had they seen him grin so broadly. Could this be Alfred Rosenberg opening bottles of champagne in the office, pouring drinks for everyone, and loudly offering toasts, first to the Führer and then to the memory of Dietrich Eckart?

A few weeks before, Alfred had come across a quote by Albert Einstein: "The secret to creativity is knowing how to hide your sources." At first he snorted—"Brazen dishonesty, typical Jewish hypocrisy"—and dismissed it. But for days Einstein's statement unaccountably returned to his mind. Was it a clue to solving the Spinoza problem? Perhaps the "original" ideas of Bento de Spinoza were not so original. Perhaps the real origins of his thoughts were hidden in the pages of the 159 books in his personal library.

The ERR, Alfred's plundering task force, was ready for action in the Netherlands in February 1941. Alfred flew into Amsterdam and attended a staff meeting organized by Werner Schwier, the German officer responsible for the liquidation of Freemasonry and related organizations in the Netherlands. The Nazis hated Freemasonry, Jewish and non-Jewish members alike. Hitler claimed in *Mein Kampf* that Freemasonry had "succumbed" to the Jews and had been a major force in Germany's loss of World War I. Present at the staff meeting were Schwier's staff of a dozen "provincial liquidators," each assigned to his own territory. Before the meeting Schwier had asked for Alfred's approval of the instructions he planned to distribute to the liquidators. All goods with Masonic emblems were to be destroyed: glasses, busts, paintings, badges, jewels, swords, circles, plumbs, trowels, gavels, seven-armed candelabras, and sextants. All wooden goods with irremovable emblems had to be smashed or burned. All Masonic leather aprons were to be cut into quarters and confiscated. Alfred smiled as he read and made only one correction—leather aprons should be cut into sixteen parts before confiscation. All else he approved, and he commended Schwier for his thoroughness.

Then, glancing at his list of sites to be confiscated, he asked, "Herr Schwier, I see you have the Rijnsburg Spinozahuis on this list. Why?"

"The entire Spinoza Association is crawling with Freemasons."

"Do they hold Freemason meetings in the Spinozahuis?"

"Not to my knowledge. We haven't discovered the Rijnsburg meeting places yet."

"I authorize you to arrest all suspected Freemasons but leave the Spinozahuis to the ERR. I'll personally pay a visit to the Spinozahuis to confiscate the library, and if I find any Freemason material, I'll turn it over to you."

"You *personally*, Reichsleiter? Of course. Do you need assistance? I'd be glad to assign some of my men."

"Thank you, no. My ERR men are in place, and we're fully prepared."

"Is it permissible, Reichsleiter, for me to inquire why this site is important enough to require your personal attention?"

"Spinoza's library and his works in general may have importance for the Hohe Schule. His library will require my personal attention. It may eventually be displayed in the Museum of Extinct Peoples that the Führer is planning."

Two days later, at 11 AM, Rosenberg and his chief assistant, Oberbereichsleiter Schimmer, arrived at Rijnsburg in a luxury Mercedes limousine followed by another limousine and a small truck carrying ERR personnel and empty crates. Alfred ordered two troops to guard the caretaker's house that adjoined the museum and two troops to apprehend the president of the Spinoza Society, who lived a block away. The museum door was locked, but it took little time to fetch the caretaker, Gerard van Egmond, who unlocked and opened the door. Alfred strode through the vestibule to the bookcase. It was not as he remembered it—far less packed. He silently counted the books. Sixty-eight.

"Where are the other books?" demanded Alfred.

Looking startled and frightened, the caretaker shrugged his shoulders.

"The other eighty-three books," said Alfred, drawing his pistol.

"I'm just the caretaker. I know nothing about this."

"Who does know?"

Just then his men entered with Johannes Diderik Bierens de Haan, the elderly president of the Spinoza Society, a dignified, well-dressed, elderly man with a white goatee and steel-rimmed spectacles. Alfred turned to him, waving his pistol at the half empty bookcase. "We're here for the library. To put it in a safe place. Where are the other eighty-three books? Do you think we are fools?"

Bierens de Haan appeared shaken but said nothing.

Alfred walked around the room. "And, Herr President, where is Einstein's poem that used to be hanging right there?" Alfred tapped his pistol against a spot on the wall.

At this point Bierens de Haan seemed entirely bewildered. He shook his head as he mumbled, "I know nothing about any of this. I never in my life saw a poem hanging there."

"How long have you been in charge?"

"Fifteen years."

"That guard, that fat disheveled disgrace, who worked here in the early twenties. Acted as if he owned the place. Where is he?"

"You probably mean Abraham. He's long dead."

"Lucky man. What a pity. I so wanted to meet him again. You have a family, Herr Spinozahuis President?"

A nod from Bierens de Haan.

"You have two choices: either lead us to the books, and you will return immediately to your family and your warm kitchen, or don't tell us, and it will be a long cold time before you see them again. We'll find the books, I assure you, even if we have to take this museum apart plank by plank and leave nothing but a heap of lumber and stones. And we'll begin that work right now."

No response from Bierens de Haan.

"And then we'll do the same to the house next door. And next your own house. We'll find the books—I assure you."

Bierens de Haan thought for a moment and then, unexpectedly, wheeled to Egmond and said, "Take them to the books."

"And I demand the poem also," added Alfred.

"There is no poem," Bierens de Haan barked back.

The caretaker led them next door to a concealed closet in the pantry, where the rest of the books were clumsily stored under a canvas wrap and covered with crockery and jars of preserves.

The troops efficiently packed the library and all other goods of value—portraits of Spinoza, a seventeenth-century landscape, a bronze bust of Spinoza, a small reading desk—into wooden crates and carried them to their truck. Two hours later, the plunderers and the treasures were on their way to Amsterdam.

"I've taken part in many such operations, Reichsleiter Rosenberg," said Schimmer during the drive back, "but never one handled more efficiently. It was a privilege to see you in action. How did you know that books were missing?"

"I know a lot about the library. It will be invaluable to the Hohe Schule. It will help us with the Spinoza problem."

"Spinoza problem?"

"Too complicated now to explain in detail. Let's just say it's a major Jewish hoax in philosophy that has gone on for centuries. I mean to give it my personal attention. Ship the books directly to the Berlin ERR office."

"And I was impressed with the way you handled the old man. Bloodlessly. Efficiently. He caved in so easily."

Alfred tapped his forehead. "Show your strength. Show your superior knowledge and your determination. They pretend at great thoughts but tremble at the thought of their home in rubble. As soon as I mentioned no more warm kitchen, the game was over. This is exactly why we shall easily prevail all over Europe."

"What about the poem?"

"It was of infinitely less value than the books. It was clear he was telling the truth: no one giving up this priceless library would place himself in jeopardy for some scribbled lines of doggerel on a sheet of paper. Most likely it didn't belong to the museum but was posted by a guard."

The two Dutchmen sat dejectedly in the caretaker's kitchen. Bierens de Haan moaned as he held his head. "We betrayed our trust. We were the guardians of the books."

"You had no choice," said Egmond. "First, they would have torn down the museum and then torn down this house and would have found not only the books but her as well."

Bierens de Haan continued to moan.

"What would Spinoza have done?" asked the caretaker.

"I can only imagine he would have chosen virtue. If it's a choice between saving valuable goods and saving a person, then we must save her."

"Yes, I agree. Well, they're gone. Shall I tell her it's over now?"

Bierens de Haan nodded. Egmond went upstairs and, using a long pole, tapped three times on the corner of the bedroom ceiling. In a couple of minutes the trapdoor opened, a ladder dropped, and a frightened middle-aged Jewish woman, Selma de Vries-Cohen, descended.

"Selma," said Egmond, "rest easy. They're gone. They've taken everything of value and now will turn to plundering the rest of our country."

"Why were they here? What did they want?" asked Selma.

"The entire Spinoza library. I have no idea why it was so important to them. It's a total mystery. They could have easily plucked one Rembrandt from the dozens at the Rijksmuseum in Amsterdam that would have far greater value than all those books together. But I have something for you. One book they missed. There was one Spinoza book in Dutch translation, called *Ethica*, which I hid separately in my son's home. They didn't know about that one, and I'll bring it to you tomorrow. It might be interesting for you to read it—it's his major book."

"Dutch translation? I always thought he *was* Dutch."

"He was, but in those days scholars wrote in Latin."

"Am I safe now?" asked Selma, still visibly trembling. "Is it safe to bring my mother here? Are you, yourself, safe?"

"No one is entirely safe with these beasts loose. But you're in the safest town in all of Holland. They've sealed the museum doors and windows with tape, they've abolished the Spinoza Association, and the German government has laid claim to this house. But I very much doubt they'll ever return to this empty museum. There is nothing else of importance here. Even so, to be entirely safe, I'd like to move you to another spot for a month. Several families in Rijnsburg have volunteered to hide you. You have many friends in Rijnsburg. Meanwhile I need to install a toilet in your room before your mother comes next month."

When the books arrived in Berlin, Alfred ordered his men to deliver them immediately to his home office. The next morning he took his coffee into his office, sat down, and stared at them, simply luxuriating in the presence and aroma of these precious works—books that Spinoza had held in his hands. For hours he caressed the books and scanned the titles. Some authors were familiar—Virgil, Homer, Ovid, Caesar, Aristotle, Tacitus, Petrarch, Pliny, Cicero, Livy, Horace, Aristotle, Epictetus, Seneca, and a five-volume set of the work of Machiavelli. *Oh, he lamented, if only I had gone to the gymnasium. I could have read these. No Latin or Greek—the tragedy of my life.* Then, with a sudden shock, he realized there was not a single book he could read: none were in German or Russian. There was Descartes' *Discours de la méthode*, but his French was only elementary.

And most were entirely unfamiliar: a great many Hebrew texts, probably Old Testaments and biblical commentary, and many authors he had never heard of, such as Nizolius, Josephus, and Pagninus. Some, judging from illustrations, were works on optics (Huygens, Longomontanus), others anatomical (Riolan) or mathematical. Alfred had expected there might be clues to Spinoza's sources from his bookmarks or marginalia, and he spent the rest of the day turning every page of every book. But in vain—there was nothing, not a trace of Spinoza. By the afternoon, the harsh reality set in: he lacked the knowledge to learn anything about Spinoza from the library. Obviously, his next step must be to seek consultation from classical scholars.

Hitler had other plans for him. Shortly after the library arrived in Rosenberg's home, four and a half million Nazi troops invaded Russia. Hitler appointed Rosenberg as the Reich minister for the occupied eastern territories and asked him to draw up a master plan for a large area of Western Russia, inhabited by thirty million Russians, to be repopulated by Germans. Fifteen million Russians were to be deported. The other fifteen million were allowed to stay but had to be "Germanized" within thirty years.

Alfred had strong opinions about Russia. He believed that Russia could be defeated only by Russians and that the Germans should strive to Balkanize the country and seek to build fighting forces composed of Ukrainians who would move against Bolshevists.

This high-profile appointment, at first a triumph for Rosenberg, soon turned into a disaster. He submitted his plans to Hitler, but military leaders—Göring, Himmler, and Erich Koch—vehemently disagreed and entirely ignored or undermined all his suggestions. They allowed tens of thousands of Ukrainian prisoners of war to die in the camps and millions of civilians to die of starvation by shipping all wheat and foodstuffs to Germany. Rosenberg continued complaining to Hitler, who eventually responded harshly:

"Stop meddling in military affairs. Your preoccupation with ideological issues has blocked you from contact with day-to-day affairs."

Million-book best seller. Editor-in-chief of major newspaper. One prestigious government post after another: head of Nazi ideology and education, head of the ERR, Reich minister of occupied eastern territories. Yet always disliked and ridiculed by the Nazi inner circle. How did Rosenberg accrue so many honors? Sometimes abstruse, convoluted, inscrutable prose elicits an unrealistically elevated appraisal of the author's intelligence. Perhaps that is why Hitler persisted in offering Rosenberg so many demanding assignments.

Eventually, as the Russians began to repel the German forces and regain their territory, Alfred's position as Reichsminister of the occupied East became irrelevant, and he tendered his resignation. Hitler was too busy to reply.

His hope of an in-depth study of Spinoza's library never materialized. Before long the Allies were bombing Berlin in force. When a house only two hundred meters from his own was destroyed, Alfred ordered the library shipped to Frankfurt for greater safety.

Alfred's *Völkischer Beobachter*, "the fighting newspaper of Nazi Germany," continued fighting till the end, and Alfred never stopped slavishly honoring Hitler in its pages. In one of its last editions (April 20, 1945) Rosenberg celebrated him on the occasion of his fifty-sixth birthday by hailing Adolf Hitler as the "Man of the Century." Ten days later, as the approaching Russian army was only a few blocks away from Hitler's underground bunker, the Führer married Eva Braun, distributed cyanide capsules to the wedding party, wrote his will, and shot himself after his wife swallowed cyanide. Twenty-four hours later, in the same bunker, Goebbels and his wife killed their six children with morphine and cyanide, and then he and his wife committed suicide together. Even so, the *Völkischer Beobachter* presses continued to roll until the German surrender on May 8, 1945. When its offices were overrun, the Russians found a couple of predated editions. The last undistributed issue, dated May 11, 1945, contained a survival guide entitled "Subsistence in German Fields and Forests."

After Hitler's death, Alfred, along with the other surviving Nazi leaders, fled to Flensburg, where Admiral Doenitz, the new head of state, assembled his government. Alfred hoped that he, the senior surviving Reichsleiter, would be asked to join the cabinet. But no one took any heed of his presence.

Finally, he sent a carefully worded letter of surrender to Field Marshall Montgomery. But even the British failed to fully appreciate his importance, and Reichsleiter Rosenberg waited impatiently at his hotel for six days before the British military police dropped by to arrest him. Shortly afterward he was placed under American control and was informed that he, along with a small group of major Nazi war criminals, had been singled out to be tried at the Nuremberg special international tribunal.

Major Nazi war criminals! Indeed. A smile flitted across Alfred's lips.

Meanwhile, in Rijnsburg on VE day, Selma de Vries-Cohen and her elderly mother, Sophie, climbed down the ladder of their tiny room and for the first time in years stepped outside into the sunlight. They walked around the side of the house to the Spinozahuis entrance, where they signed the guest registry—the first signature in four years: "In grateful remembrance of the time we were allowed to hide here. To the Spinozahuis and to those who cared so excellently for us and saved our lives from the German threat."

CHAPTER THIRTY-THREE

VOORBURG—DECEMBER 1666

B ento, shaking his head in astonishment, walked over to the *huishouder* and murmured in Dutch that they would not be having lunch after all.

After she had left, he exclaimed, "Kosher! You keep kosher?"

"Of course! Bento, what did you think? I'm a rabbi."

"And I'm a bewildered philosopher. You agree that there is no supernatural God who has wishes or makes demands or is pleased or vexed or even aware of our desires, our prayers, or our very existence?"

"Most certainly, I agree."

"And you agree that the entire Torah—including Leviticus with the Halakha and all its arcane dietary rules—is a collection of theological, legal, mythological, political writings compiled by Ezra two thousand years ago?"

"Indeed."

"And that you are going to create a new enlightened Judaism?"

"That is my hope."

"But because of laws that you know to be sheer invention you cannot take lunch with me?"

"Ah, there you are *not* right, Bento." Franco reached into his bag and extracted a packet. "The family I visited in The Hague has prepared food. Let us share a Jewish meal."

As Franco unwrapped smoked herring, bread, cheese, and two apples, Bento continued. "But, Franco, I ask again, why stay kosher? How can you switch off your rational mind? I can't. It pains me to see a man of such intelligence obediently bowing to such arbitrary laws. And Franco, please, I beg you, spare me the standard answer that you must keep the two-thousand-year tradition alive."

Franco swallowed a mouthful of herring, took a sip of water, and thought for a few moments. "I once again assure you that I, like you—like you, Bento—disapprove of the irrationality in our religion. Consider how I appealed to reason when I spoke to my congregation about the false Messiah. I, *like you*, want to change our religion, but *unlike you* I think it must be changed from the inside. In fact it is through witnessing what has happened to you that I have concluded it can be changed *only* from the inside. If I am to be effective in changing Judaism and move my congregation away from supernatural explanations, then I must first gain their confidence. They must view me as one of them and that includes keeping kosher. As a rabbi in my community, it is necessary—it is imperative—that any Jew in the world feel comfortable visiting me and eating in my home."

"And so you follow all the other laws and the ceremonial rituals?"

"I obey the Sabbath. I lay tefillin, I say prayers at meals, and, of course, I lead many of the services at the synagogue—that is, until recently. Bento, you know that the rabbi must immerse himself fully in the community religious life—"

"And," Bento interrupted, "you do this solely to gain the confidence of the people?"

Franco hesitated for a moment. "Not solely. It would be dishonest to say so. Many times, when performing my ceremonial duties, I overlook the content of the words and lose myself in the ritual and in the pleasant wave of feelings that sweep over me. The chants inspire and transport me. And I love the poetry of the psalms, of all the *piyyutim*. I love the cadence, the alliteration, and am much moved by the pathos about aging and facing death and yearning for salvation.

"But there's something even more important," Franco continued. "When I read and chant the Hebrew melodies together with the entire congregation, I feel safe; I feel at home, almost merged with my people. Knowing that everyone else there shares the same despair and the same yearning fills me with love for every person. Did you never have these experiences, Bento?"

"I'm sure I did when I was young. But not now. Not for many years. Unlike you, I'm not able to turn my attention away from the meaning of the words. My mind is always vigilant, and once I grew old enough to examine the actual meaning of the Torah, my connection to community began to fade."

"You see," Franco clasped Bento's arm, "right there, we have a fundamental difference. I don't agree that all feelings must be subservient to reason. There are some feelings that deserve equal status to reason. Take nostalgia, for example. When I lead prayers, I connect to my past, to my father and grandfather, and, yes, Bento, I dare to say it, I think of my ancestors who, for two thousand years, have been saying the same lines, chanting the same prayers, singing the same melodies. At those moments, I lose my self-importance, my separateness, and become a part, a very small part, of an unbroken stream of community. That thought offers me something invaluable—how to describe it?—a connection, a union with others that is vastly comforting. I need this. I imagine everyone does."

"But, Franco, what is the advantage of these feelings? What is the advantage in drawing further away from true understanding? Further from a true knowledge of God?"

"Advantage? How about survival? Hasn't man always lived in some kind of community, even if simply a family? How else could we survive? You have no joy in community at all? No sense of being a part of a group?"

Bento started to shake his head but quickly caught himself. "I experienced that, oddly enough, on the day before our last meeting. On the way to Amsterdam I saw a group of Ashkenazi Jews engaged in the Tashlich ceremony. I was on the *trekschuit* but quickly jumped off, followed them, and was welcomed and offered bread by an older woman named Rifke. I don't know why her name sticks in my mind. I listened to the ceremony, feeling pleasantly warm and unusually drawn to the whole community. Instead of tossing Rifke's bread in the water, I ate it. Slowly. And it was uncommonly good. But then, as I continued on my way, my warm nostalgic feeling soon faded. The whole experience was another reminder that my *cherem* affected me more than I had thought. But now, finally, the pain of expulsion has faded, and I experience no need, none whatsoever, for immersion in a community."

"But, Bento, explain to me: how can you, how do you, live in such solitude? You are not by nature a cold, distant person. I'm certain of that because, whenever we are together, I feel such a strong connection—on your part as well as mine. I know there is love between us."

"Yes, I too feel and treasure our love most keenly." Bento gazed into Franco's eyes just for a moment and then looked away. "Solitude. You ask about my solitude. There are times I suffer from it. And I so regret that I haven't been able to share my ideas with you. When I am trying to clarify my ideas, I often have daydreams of discussing them with you."

"Bento, who knows—this may be our last chance. Please talk about them now. At least, tell me of some of the major directions you've taken."

"Yes, I want to, but to start? I'll begin with my own starting point— what am I? What is my core, my essence? What is it that makes me what I am? What is it that results in my being *this* person rather than any other? When I think of *being*, a fundamental truth seems self-evident: I, like every living thing, strive to persevere in my own being. I would say that this *conatus*, the desire to continue to flourish, powers all of a person's endeavors."

"So you begin with the solitary individual rather than with the opposite pole of community, which I hold paramount?"

"But I don't envision man as a creature of solitude. It's just that I have a different perspective on the idea of connection. I seek the joyous experience that issues not so much from connection as from the loss of separateness."

Franco shook his head in puzzlement. "Here you are just beginning, and I'm already confused. Aren't connection and loss of separation the same?"

"There's a subtle but crucial difference. Let me try to explain. As you know, at the very foundation of my thinking is the idea that *through logic alone* we can comprehend some of the essence of Nature or God. I say 'some' because the actual being of God is a mystery over and beyond thinking. God is infinite, and since we are only finite creatures, our vision is limited. Am I being clear?"

"So far."

"Therefore," Bento continued, "to increase our understanding, we must try to view this world *sub specie aeternitatis*—from the aspect of eternity. In other words, we have to overcome the obstructions to our knowledge that result from our attachment to our own self." Bento paused. "Franco, you have such a quizzical look."

"I'm lost. You were going to explain your loss of separation. What happened to that?"

"Patience, Franco. That comes next. First I've got to provide the background. As I was saying, to view the world *sub species aeternitatis* I must

cast off my own identity—that is, my attachment to myself—and view everything from the absolute adequate and true perspective. When I can do that,
I cease to experience boundaries between myself and others. Once this happens, a great calmness floods in, and no event concerning me, even my
death, makes any difference. And when others achieve this perspective, we
will befriend one another, want for others what we want for ourselves, and
act with high-mindedness. This blessed and joyful experience is thus a consequence of *a loss of separation rather than a connection.* So you see there
is a difference—the difference between men huddling together for warmth
and safety versus men who together share an enlightened joyous view of
Nature or God."

Franco, still looking puzzled, said, "I'm trying to understand, but it's
not easy because I've never had that experience, Bento. To lose your own
identity—that is hard to imagine. It gives me a headache to think of it. And
it seems so solitary—and so cold."

"Solitary and yet, paradoxically, this idea can bind all men together—
it is being simultaneously *apart from* and *a part of.* I don't suggest or prefer
solitude. In fact I have no doubt that if you and I could meet for daily discussions, our strivings for understanding would be greatly augmented. It
seems paradoxical to say that men are most useful to one another when
each pursues his own advantage. But when they are men of reason, it is so.
Enlightened egoism leads to mutual utility. We all have in common our
ability to reason, and a true earthly paradise will occur when our commitment to understanding Nature, or God, replaces all other affiliations, be
they religious, cultural, or national."

"Bento, if I grasp your meaning, I fear this kind of paradise is still a
thousand years away. And I also wonder if I, or anyone who does not have
your type of mind and your breadth and depth, will have the ability to grasp
these ideas fully."

"I don't doubt it takes effort. All things excellent are as difficult as they
are rare. Yet I do have a community of Collegiants and other philosophers
who read and comprehend my words, though it is true that many of them
write me far too many letters asking for greater clarification. I don't expect
my ideas to be read and understood by the unprepared mind. On the contrary, many would be confused or unsettled, and I would advise them not
to read my work. I write in Latin for the philosophical mind, and I hope

only that some of the minds I influence will in turn influence others. For example, at present Johan De Witt, our grand pensionary, and Henry Oldenburg, secretary of the British Royal Society, are among my correspondents. But if you are thinking that my work may never be published for a greater audience, you may be right. It is very possible that my ideas will have to wait a thousand years."

The two men lapsed into silence until Bento added, "So, given all I have said about my reliance on reason, you see now why I oppose reading and speaking words and prayers without regard to their content? This internal cleavage cannot be good for the health of your mind. I don't believe that ritual can coexist with the alert reasoning mind. I believe they are sharp antagonists."

"I don't regard ritual as dangerous, Bento. Remember, I've been indoctrinated into the beliefs and rituals of both Catholicism and Judaism and in the past two years have been studying Islam as well. The more I read, the more I am struck by how every religion, without exception, inspires a sense of community, employs ritual and music, and develops a mythology full of stories of miraculous events. And every religion, without exception, promises everlasting life, providing one lives according to some prescribed manner. Isn't it remarkable that religions emerging independently in different parts of the world so resemble one another?"

"Your point being?"

"My point, Bento, is that if ritual, ceremony, and yes, superstition also are so deeply embedded in the very nature of human beings, then perhaps it is legitimate to conclude that we humans require them."

"*I* don't require them. Children require things that adults do not. The man of two thousand years ago required things that man today does not. I think the reason for superstition in all these cultures was that ancient man was terrified by the mysterious capriciousness of existence. He lacked the knowledge that might provide the one thing he needed most of all—explanations. And in those ancient days he grasped at the one available form of explanation—the supernatural—with prayer and sacrifice and kosher laws and—"

"And? Go further, Bento—what function does explanation serve?"

"Explanation soothes. It relieves the anguish of uncertainty. Ancient man wanted to persist, was fearful of death, helpless against much in his environment, and explanation provided the sense, or at least the illusion, of control. He concluded that if all that occurs is supernaturally caused, then perhaps a way might be found to placate the supernatural."

"Bento, it's not that we disagree on this; it's just that our methods are different. Changing age-old thinking is a slow process. You cannot do everything at once. Change, even from the inside, must be slow."

"I'm certain you are right, but I'm also certain that much of the slowness stems from the tenacity with which aging rabbis and priests cling to power. It was so with Rabbi Mortera, and it is so today with Rabbi Aboab. Earlier I shuddered as you described how he fanned the flames of belief in Sabbatai Zevi. I lived among the superstitious my entire youth; I am nonetheless shocked at this Zevi frenzy. How can Jews believe such nonsense? It seems impossible to overestimate their capacity for irrationality. Somewhere in this world, with every blink of the eye, a fool is born."

Franco took his final bite of apple, grinned, and asked, "Bento, may I make a Franco observation?"

"Ah, my dessert! What could be better. Let me prepare." Bento leaned back and settled himself into the bolster. "I think I'm about to learn something about myself."

"You've said that we must liberate ourselves from the bondage of passion, and yet, today, your own passion has broken through several times. Though you are entirely forgiving of a man who tried to kill you, you are full of passion about Rabbi Aboab and those who choose to accept the new Messiah."

Bento nodded, "Yes, that is true."

"I'll go further—you were also more understanding of the Jewish assassin than you were of my wife's viewpoints. Is that not so?"

Bento again nodded, this time more warily. "Continue, teacher."

"Once you told me that human emotions could be understood just as lines, planes, and bodies. Right?"

Another nod.

"Then shall we try to apply that very principle to your vituperative response to Rabbi Aboab and the gullible followers of Sabbatai Zevi? And to my wife, Sarah?"

Bento looked quizzical. "Where are you heading, Franco?"

"I'm asking you to turn your instruments of understanding onto your own emotions. Remember your words to me when I was so enraged at the assassin. 'Everything, every fact, *bar none*,' you said, 'has a cause, and we must understand that everything *necessarily* occurs.' Do I have that right?"

"Your memory is impeccable, Franco."

"Thank you. So let us apply the same reasoned approach today."

"You know I can't decline that invitation while at the same time claiming that the pursuit of reason is my raison d'être."

"Good. Do you remember the moral of the Talmudic tale about Rabbi Yohanon?"

Bento nodded. "The prisoner cannot free himself. No doubt you're suggesting I can free others but not myself?"

"Exactly. Perhaps I can see some things about Bento de Spinoza that he himself cannot."

Bento smiled. "And why is your vision sharper than his?"

"Just as you described a few minutes ago: your own self is in the way and obstructs your vision. Take, for example, your harsh comments about the gullible fools in Amsterdam taken in by the false Messiah. Your passionate vitriol and their gullibility are *necessarily* so. It could not have been different. And, Bento, I have some notions about the sources of their behavior and of yours."

"And? Go on."

"First of all, it's of interest that you and I witness the same events and we have different responses. To quote you, 'It's our mind that makes it so.' Right?"

"Again, right."

"I'm personally not surprised or perplexed by the gullibility of the Marrano populace." Franco now spoke with much ease and conviction. "They *necessarily* believe in the Messiah. *Of course* we Marranos are susceptible to messianic thinking! After all, in our Catholic indoctrination, weren't we constantly confronted by the idea of Jesus as a man who was more than mere man, as a man who was sent to Earth on a mission? And *of course* Marranos are not outraged by Sabbatai Zevi's conversion under duress. Did not we Marranos experience forced conversion firsthand? And, what's more, many of us have had the personal experience of reconversion as a better Jew."

"Right, right, and right, Franco. You see how much I will miss speaking to you! You're helping me identify my unfree areas. You are right: my words about Sabbatai Zevi, Rabbi Aboab, and gullible fools are not in accord with reason. A free man does not disturb his peace with such feelings of scorn or indignation. I still have work to do controlling my passions."

"Once you told me that reason is no match for passion and that our only way of freeing ourselves from passion is to turn reason into a passion."

"Aha, I think I know what you may be implying—that I have so transformed reason that it is at times indistinguishable from unreason."

"Exactly. I've noticed that your anger and ill-tempered accusations emerge *only* when reason is threatened."

"Reason and freedom both," added Bento.

Franco hesitated a moment, choosing his words carefully. "On second thought, there is one other time when I saw your passions arise: when we discussed the place and rights of women. I believe that your arguments proving women's inferior intelligence lack your usual rigor. For example, you stated that women did not share rulership, yet you neglected the existence of powerful queens—for example, Cleopatra of Egypt, Elizabeth of England, and Isabella of Spain and—"

"Yes, yes, but time is precious today, and we cannot cover all issues. Let's work on reason and freedom. I'm most disinclined to deal now with the issue of women."

"Will you not at least agree that this is another area to consider in the future?"

"Perhaps. I'm not certain."

"Then simply allow me one final comment, and we'll move on to other topics." Without waiting for a response Franco hurried on. "It is clear that you and I have very different attitudes toward women, and I think I have an idea of the causative network. Are you interested?"

"I should be, but I feel some reluctance to hear you out."

"I'll continue anyway—just for a minute. I think it stems from our different experiences with women. I've had a very loving relationship with my mother and now with my wife and daughter, and my guess is that your attitudes toward women are *necessarily* negative because of your previous contact with them. From what you've told me your experiences have been bleak: your mother died when you were a young child, and your subsequent mothers—your older sister and then your stepmother—also died. The whole community knows of your harsh rejection by your remaining sister, Rebekah. I've heard she filed suit contesting your father's will so that you wouldn't receive his estate. And then there is Clara Maria, the one woman you loved, and she wounded you by choosing another. Aside from her I've never heard you mention a single positive experience with a woman."

Bento remained silent, nodding for a few moments, slowly digesting Franco's words, and then said, "Now to the other topics. First, there's something I haven't said to you—and that is how much I admire your courage in speaking out to your congregation urging moderation. Your public opposition to Rabbi Aboab was based on what I call 'adequate' ideas—driven by reason rather then by passion. I'd also like to hear more about your vision of the new Judaism you hope to create. Earlier, I may have diverted the discussion."

Both knew their time was running out, and Franco spoke quickly. "I hope to create a different kind of Judaism based on our love for one another and our shared tradition. I plan to hold religious services that have no mention of the supernatural and that are based on our common humanity, drawing wisdom from Torah and Talmud that leads to a loving and moral life. And, yes, we will follow Jewish law but in the service of connection and moral life, *not* because it is divinely ordained. And pervading all of this there will be the spirit of my friend, Baruch Spinoza. As I plan for the future, I sometimes imagine you as a father. My dream is to build a synagogue to which you would send your own son."

Bento brushed away a tear running down his cheek. "Yes, we are of one mind if you believe we should use enough ceremony to appeal to that part of our nature that still requires it but not so much as to enslave us."

"That is indeed my position. And is it not ironic that, though you try to change Judaism from the outside and I from the inside, we both encounter *cherem*, you already and mine no doubt to come?"

"I agree with the second part of your statement—the irony of our both encountering *cherem*—but, lest you misunderstand, let me say yet once again that it is not my intent to change Judaism. It is my hope that a vital dedication to reason should eradicate *all* religions, including Judaism." Bento glances at the clock. "Alas, it is time, Franco—almost two o'clock—and the *trekschuit* will be here shortly."

As they strolled to the *trekschuit* landing, Franco said, "I have one final thing I must say to you—that book you are planning to write about your critique of the Bible?"

"Yes?"

"I love you for writing it, but please, my friend, be cautious. Do not put your name on this book. I believe what you say, but it will not be listened to in a reasonable way. Not now, not in our lifetime."

Franco boarded. The boatman loosened the moorings, the horses strained at their ropes, and the *trekschuit* pulled away from the dock. Bento gazed at the barge for a long while. The smaller it grew as it moved toward the horizon, the larger loomed his *cherem*. Finally, when no trace of Franco remained, Bento backed slowly away from the dock, back into the arms of solitude.

EPILOGUE

In 1670, Bento, age thirty-eight, finished his *Theological-Political Treatise*. His publisher, quite correctly, predicted that it would be deemed inflammatory. Thus it was published anonymously, under the imprimatur of fictitious publishers in fictitious cities. Its sale was quickly prohibited by both civil and religious authorities. Nonetheless, numerous underground copies circulated.

A few months later Spinoza moved from Voorburg to The Hague, where he lived the remainder of his life, first renting a modest attic room in the home of the Widow Van der Werve and then, a few months later, even less expensive quarters—a single large room in the house of Hendrik Van der Spyck, a master painter of home interiors. A life of tranquility—that's what Spinoza wanted and found in The Hague. There he spent his days reading the great works in his library, working on the *Ethics*, and grinding lenses. Evenings he smoked his pipe and chatted amiably with Van der Spyck, his wife, and their seven children, except for the times he was too engrossed in his writing to leave his room, often for days on end. On Sundays he sometimes accompanied the family to listen to the sermon at the nearby Nieuwe Kerk.

With a cough that never improved and often produced blood-flecked sputum, he grew noticeably weaker from year to year. Perhaps the inhalation of glass dust from optical work had compromised his lungs, but most likely he had tuberculosis, like his mother and other family members. On February 20, 1677, he felt so weak that he sent for a doctor, who instructed Mrs. Van der Spyck to cook an old cock and feed Spinoza the rich broth. She followed instructions, and he seemed better the next morning. The family attended church in the afternoon, but when they returned two hours later, Bento de Spinoza, at the age of forty-four, was dead.

Spinoza lived his philosophy: he attained *Amor dei intellectualis*, freed himself from the bondage of disturbing passions, and faced the end of his life with serenity. Yet this quiet life and death left in its wake a great turbulence that roils even to the present day, as many reach out to revere and reclaim him while others expel and excoriate him.

Though he left no will, he made a point of instructing his landlord, in the event of his death, to ship his writing desk and all its contents immediately to his publisher, Rieuwertsz, in Amsterdam. Van der Spyck honored Spinoza's wishes: he tightly secured the desk and shipped it to Amsterdam by *trekschuit*. It arrived safely, containing in its locked drawers the *Ethics* and other precious unpublished manuscripts and correspondence.

Bento's friends set to work immediately editing the manuscripts and letters. Following Spinoza's instructions, they removed all personal material from the letters, leaving only philosophic content.

A few months after his death, Spinoza's *Posthumous Works* (containing the *Ethics*, the unfinished *Tractatus politicus*, and *De Intellectus Emendatione*, a selection from Spinoza's correspondence, along with a *Compendium of Hebrew Grammar* and the *Treatise on the Rainbow*) was published in both Dutch and Latin, again with only the author's initials. As expected, the state of Holland quickly proscribed the book in an official edict, accusing it of profane blasphemies and atheist sentiments.

As word spread of Spinoza's death, his sister, Rebekah, who had shunned him for twenty-one years, reappeared and presented herself and her son, Daniel, as Bento's sole legal heirs. However, when Van der Spyck gave her an accounting of Spinoza's possessions and debts, she reconsidered: Bento's debts for past rent, for burial expenses, for barber and apothecary were probably greater than the value of his possessions. Eight months later, the auction of his possessions (primarily his library and lens-grinding equipment) was held, and, indeed, the proceeds fell short of what he owed. Rather then inherit debts, Rebekah legally renounced all claims to the estate and once again vanished from history. Bento's small outstanding obligations were met by the brother-in-law of Bento's friend Simon de Vries. (Simon, who had died ten years earlier, in 1667, had offered to leave Bento his entire estate. Bento had declined, saying that it was unfair to Simon's family and that, moreover, money would be only a distraction to him. Simon's family offered Bento an annual annuity of five hundred guilders. That, too, Spinoza declined, insisting it was more than he needed. He finally agreed to a small annuity of three hundred guilders.)

The auction of Spinoza's property was conducted by W. van den Hove, a conscientious notary who left a detailed inventory of the 159 books in Spinoza's library, with precise information about the date, publisher, and format of each book. In 1900 George Rosenthal, a Jewish-Dutch banker, used the notary's list to try to reassemble the philosopher's book collection for the Spinozahuis at Rijnsburg. Great care was taken to purchase the same editions, with the same dates and cities, but, of course, these were not the very same books that Spinoza had held in his hands. (In chapter 32 I imagine a scene in which Alfred Rosenberg is unaware of this fact.) Eventually George Rosenthal was able to collect 110 of the 159 books in Spinoza's original collection. He also donated another 35 pre-seventeenth-century books, as well as works on Spinoza's life and philosophy.

Spinoza was buried under the flagstones inside the Nieuwe Kerk, causing many to assume that he had undergone a late conversion to Christianity. Yet, given Spinoza's sentiment that "the notion that God took upon himself the nature of man seems as self-contradictory as would be the statement that the circle has taken on the nature of the square," a conversion seems highly unlikely. In liberal seventeenth-century Holland, the burial of non-Protestants inside churches was not rare. Even Catholics, who were far more disliked in Protestant Holland than Jews, were occasionally buried inside the church. (In the following century, policy changed, and only the very wealthy and prominent were buried there.) As was the custom, Spinoza's burial plot was rented for a limited number of years, and when there was no longer maintenance money available, probably after ten years, his bones were disinterred and scattered in the half-acre churchyard next to the church.

As the years passed, the Netherlands claimed him, and his prominence grew such that his portrait was featured on the Dutch thousand-guilder banknote until the euro was introduced in 2002. Like all portraits of Spinoza, the banknote portrait was based on scanty written descriptions; no likenesses of Spinoza from his lifetime have been preserved.

A plaque was placed in the Nieuwe Kerk churchyard in 1927 to commemorate the two-hundred-fiftieth anniversary of Spinoza's death. Several Jewish enthusiasts from Palestine, who wished to reclaim Baruch Spinoza as a Jew, were involved in the commemoration. The Latin inscription reads: "This earth covers the bones of Benedictus de Spinoza, once buried in the new church."

In Palestine, at about the same time as the unveiling of this plaque, Joseph Klausner, the renowned historian and later a candidate in Israel's first presidential election, delivered a speech at Hebrew University in which he declared that the Jewish people had committed a terrible sin in excommunicating Spinoza; he called for a repudiation of the idea that Spinoza was a heretic. He ended, "To Spinoza, the Jew, we call out . . . from atop Mount Scopus, out of our new sanctuary—the Hebrew University of Jerusalem—*the ban is rescinded!* Judaism's wrongdoing against you is hereby lifted, and whatever was your sin against her shall be forgiven. Our brother are you, our brother are you, our brother are you!"

In 1956, the three-hundredth anniversary of Spinoza's excommunication, Heer H. K. F. Douglas, one of Spinoza's Dutch admirers, conceived the idea of constructing an additional memorial next to the 1927 plaque. Knowing that Ben-Gurion, the prime minister of Israel, much admired Spinoza, Heer Douglas asked for his support. Ben-Gurion enthusiastically offered it, and when the word spread in Israel, members of a humanistic Jewish organization in Haifa, who considered Spinoza the progenitor of Jewish humanism, offered to contribute a black basalt stone as part of the memorial. The formal unveiling of the monument was well attended and included governmental representatives of both Holland and Israel. Ben-Gurion did not attend the unveiling but visited the memorial in an official ceremony three years later.

The new plaque, placed next to the 1927 plaque, contained a relief of Spinoza's head and the single word "*Caute*" (caution) found on Spinoza's ring seal, and, below that, the black Israeli basalt stone sealed to the plaque contains the Hebrew word עמך (*amcha*), meaning "Your People."

Some Israelis took issue with Ben-Gurion's attempts to reclaim Spinoza. Orthodox members of the Knesset were so outraged by the idea of Israel honoring Spinoza that they called for the censure of both Ben-Gurion and the foreign minister, Golda Meir, for instructing the Israeli ambassador in Holland to attend the unveiling.

Earlier, in an article, Ben-Gurion addressed the issue of Spinoza's excommunication. "It is difficult to blame the Jewish community in seventeenth century

Amsterdam. Their position was precarious . . . and the traumatized Jewish community had the right to defend their cohesion. But today the Jewish people do not have the right to forever exclude Spinoza the immortal from the Community of Israel." Ben-Gurion insisted that the Hebrew language is not complete without the works of Spinoza. And indeed, shortly after the publication of his article, the Hebrew University published the entire body of Spinoza's work in Hebrew.

Some Jews wished Ben-Gurion to appeal to the Amsterdam rabbinate for reversal of the excommunication, but he declined and wrote: "I did not seek to have the excommunication annulled, since I took it for granted that the excommunication is null and void. . . There is a street in Tel-Aviv bearing Spinoza's name, and there is not one single reasonable person in this country who thinks that the excommunication is still in force."

The Rijnsburg Spinoza library was confiscated by Rosenberg's ERR in 1942. Oberbereichsleiter Schimmer, the working head of the ERR in the Netherlands, described the seizure in his 1942 report (later to become an official Nuremburg document): "The libraries of the Societas Spinozana in Den Haag and of the Spinozahuis in Rijnsburg also were packed. Packed in eighteen cases, they, too, contain extremely valuable early works of great importance *for the exploration of the Spinoza problem*. Not without reason did the director of the Societas Spinozana try, under false pretenses which we uncovered, to withhold the library from us."

The stolen Rijnsburg library was housed in Frankfurt along with the greatest store of plunder in world history. Under Rosenberg's leadership, the ERR stole over three million books from a thousand libraries. When Frankfurt came under heavy allied bombardment in 1944, the Nazis hurriedly moved their plunder to underground storage sites. Spinoza's library, along with thousands of other uncatalogued books, were sent to a salt mine at Hungen, near Munich. At the war's end, all the

Hungen treasures were transferred to the American Offenbach central depot, where a small army of librarians and historians searched for their owners. Eventually Dirk Marius Graswinckel, a Dutch archivist, came upon Spinoza's books and transferred the entire collection (minus only a handful of books) to the Netherlands on the *Mary Rotterdam*, a Dutch ship. They arrived in Rijnsburg in March 1946 and were once again placed on display at the Spinoza Museum, where they may be viewed to this very day.

For the month awaiting trial, Alfred remained in solitary confinement in the Nuremberg prison, meeting only with the attorney preparing his defense, an American military physician, and a psychologist. It was not until November 20, 1945, the first day of the trial, that he saw the other Nazi defendants as they assembled before the presiding judicial body and the teams of prosecutors from the United States, Great Britain, Russia, and France. Over the next eleven months all would assemble in the same room 218 times.

There were twenty-four defendants, but only twenty-two were present for the trial. A twenty-third, Robert Ley, had hanged himself with a towel in his cell two weeks earlier, and the twenty-fourth, Martin Bormann, the "dictator of Hitler's antechamber," was to be tried in absentia, though it was widely believed that he had been killed as the Russians overran Berlin. The defendants were seated on four wooden benches arranged in two rows, with a row of armed soldiers standing at attention behind them. Alfred was seated second in the front right bench. On the front left bench were Göring; Hess; Joachim von Ribbentrop, Nazi minister of foreign affairs; and Field Marshal Wilhelm Keitel, supreme commander of the military. In the months of detention preceding the trial, Göring had been withdrawn from drugs, lost twenty-five pounds, and now appeared sleek and jovial.

On Alfred's right was Ernst Kaltenbrunner, highest surviving SS officer. On his left were Hans Frank, governor-general of occupied Poland; Wilhelm Frick, Reich protector of Bohemia-Moravia; and at the end of the bench, Julius Streicher, editor of *Der Stürmer*. Alfred must have been relieved he did not have to sit next to Streicher, whom he found particularly repulsive.

In the second row were such eminences as Admiral Dönitz, the Reich president after Hitler's suicide and the commander of the U-boat campaign, and Field Marshal Alfred Jodl. Both maintained a haughty military bearing. Next sat Fritz Sauckel, head of the Nazi slave labor program; Arthur Seyss-Inquart, Reich commissioner of the Netherlands; and then Albert Speer, Hitler's close friend and architect—a man whom Alfred hated almost as much as Goebbels. Next there were Walther Funk, who turned the Reichsbank into a depository for gold teeth and other valuables seized from concentration camp victims, and Baldur von Schirach, head of the Nazi youth program. The two other defendants in the back row were lesser known Nazi businessmen.

The selection of the major Nazi war criminals had taken months. They were, of course, not the original inner circle, but with the suicides of Hitler, Goebbels, and Himmler, these men represented the best-known Nazis. Finally, finally, Alfred Rosenberg had entered the inner circle. True to character, Göring, Hitler's second

Image copyright Omer Tamir. Permission granted under Creative Commons/ No Derivative Works license.

in command, tried to take control of the group, using a seductive twinkle or a bullying glare, and soon many deferred to him. The prosecuting team, disturbed by the prospect of Göring influencing the testimony of the other defendants, quickly took steps to separate Göring from them. First, they ordered Göring to eat alone during lunch breaks on trial days, while the other defendants sat at tables of three. Later, to minimize Göring's influence even more, they enforced stricter solitary confinement for all defendants. Alfred, as always, declined to participate in the few remaining social opportunities available—during meals, on the walks to the courtroom, or whispered comments during proceedings. The others did not conceal their dislike of him, and he reciprocated fully: these were the men he considered responsible for the failure of the noble ideological foundation he and the Führer had so carefully fashioned.

A few days into the trial the entire court viewed a powerful film made by American troops when they had liberated concentration camps. Nothing, not a gruesome detail, was omitted: the entire court was stunned and revolted by the screen images of gas chambers, the crematorium ovens crammed with half-burned bodies, mountains of decaying corpses, huge mounds of articles taken from the dead—spectacles, baby shoes, human hair. An American cameraman trained his lens on the faces of the defendants as they watched the film. Rosenberg's white face registered horror, and he immediately looked away. After the film, he insisted, in concert with all of the Nazi defendants, that he had had absolutely no idea of the existence of such things.

Was that true? How much did he know about the mass executions of the Jews in Eastern Europe? What did he know of the death camps? Rosenberg took that secret to the grave. He left no paper trail, no definitive proof. (Even Hitler's signature never appeared on a document related to the camps.) And, of course, Alfred never wrote about the camps in the *Beobachter*, since explicit Nazi policy forbade *any* public discussion of the camps. Rosenberg was quick to point out to the court that he had declined to attend the momentous Wannsee Conference in January 1942, attended by top Nazi bureaucrats, during which Reinhard Heydrich vividly described the plans for the Final Solution. Rosenberg sent his assistant, Alfred Meyer, in his stead. But Meyer was his close associate for many years and it is inconceivable that the two never spoke of Wannsee.

On the trial's seventeenth day, the prosecution presented as evidence a four-hour movie, *The Nazi Plan*, compiled from various Nazi propaganda films and newsreels. The film began with clips from the Leni Riefenstahl film *The Triumph of the Will*, in which Rosenberg, preening in his elaborate party uniform, provided pompous narration. Alfred and the defendants did not conceal their enjoyment of this brief trip back to their time of glory.

When other defendants were being cross-examined in the courtroom, Alfred was inattentive. Sometimes he sketched faces of courtroom figures; sometimes he turned his earphones to the Russian translation of the proceedings, smirking and shaking his head at the plethora of errors. Even during his own examination, he listened to the Russian translation and publicly protested the many mistakes of interpretation.

Throughout the trial Rosenberg was taken far more seriously by the court than he ever had been by the Nazis themselves. Many times the court described him as the leading ideologue of the Nazi Party, the man who drew the blueprint of European destruction, and Rosenberg never once denied these charges. One may imagine Göring's mixed responses: scoffing at Rosenberg's presumed importance in the Third Reich and, on the other hand, snickering at Rosenberg's obliviousness to the fact he was driving nails into his own coffin.

During his long defense testimony, Rosenberg's evasiveness, pedantic tone, and complex language greatly irritated the prosecutors. Unlike Hitler, they were not taken in by his pretense at profundity, perhaps because the Nuremberg lawyers had the advantage of IQ test results administered by the American psychologist Lieutenant G. M. Gilbert. Rosenberg's 124 IQ placed him at the median of the twenty-two defendants. (Julius Streicher, editor in chief of Hitler's favorite newspaper, placed dead last at 106.) Though Rosenberg maintained his well-practiced superior smirk, he no longer fooled anyone into thinking that he thought deeper thoughts than they could comprehend.

The chief American counsel, U.S. Supreme Court Justice Robert J. Jackson, wrote, "It was Rosenberg, the intellectual high priest of the 'master race,' who provided the doctrine of hatred which gave the impetus for the annihilation of Jewry, and who put his infidel theories into practice against the Eastern Occupied Territories. His woolly philosophy also added boredom to the long list of Nazi atrocities."

In his collected letters Thomas Dodd, American executive trial counsel (and father of Senator Christopher Dodd), bared his feelings about Rosenberg: "Two more days are gone. I cross-examined Alfred Rosenberg this morning and think I did an adequate job. . . . He was most difficult to examine—an evasive lying rogue, if ever I saw one. I actually dislike him—he is such a faker, such a complete hypocrite."

Sir David Maxwell, the chief British prosecutor, commented, "The only evidence presented is the claim that Rosenberg wouldn't hurt a fly and that the witnesses have seen him not hurting flies. Rosenberg was a master of euphemism, a bureaucratic pedant, whose seemingly endless sentences snaked about, intertwined, and stuck to each other like overboiled spaghetti."

And the closing statement of the Russian chief prosecutor, General Rudenko, ended with these words: "In spite of Rosenberg's efforts to juggle with historical facts and events, he cannot deny that he was the official ideologist of the Nazi Party; that already a quarter of a century ago, he had laid the 'theoretical' foundations of the fascist Hitlerite State, which during this whole period morally corrupted millions of Germans, preparing them 'ideologically' for the monstrous crimes committed by the Hitlerites."

Rosenberg had only one possible effective defense—that his Nazi colleagues had never taken him seriously and that all the policies he proposed in the occupied eastern countries were entirely ignored. But he had too inflated an opinion of his worth to admit publicly his own insignificance. Instead, he chose to meander evasively hour after hour. As one Nuremberg observer put it, "It was no more possible to grasp what he was saying than to grab a handful of cloud."

Unlike the other defendants, Rosenberg never recanted. At the end he remained the sole true believer. He never repudiated Hitler and his racist ideology. "I did not see in Hitler a tyrant," Rosenberg told the court, "but like many millions of National Socialists, I trusted him personally on the strength of the experience of a fourteen-year-long struggle. I served Adolf Hitler loyally, and whatever the party may have done during those years, I supported that too." In a conversation with another defendant, he defended Hitler even more emphatically: "No matter how often I go over everything in my mind, I still cannot believe there was a single flaw in that man's character." He continued to insist on the correctness of his ideology: "What has motivated me the last twenty-five years was the idea of wanting to serve not only the German people, but the whole of Europe—in fact the whole white race." And shortly before his death, he expressed the hope that the idea of National Socialism would never be forgotten and would be "reborn from a new generation steeled by suffering."

October 1, 1946, was judgment day. The court had met 218 times and for the previous six weeks had been adjourned while the jurists engaged in prolonged deliberations. On the morning of October 1, each defendant learned, in order of their seating, the verdict of the court. Three defendants—Schacht, von Papen, and Fritzsche—were acquitted and offered immediate freedom. The rest were found guilty of some or all of the charges.

That afternoon each defendant learned his fate. Alfred was the sixth man to face the court: "Defendant Alfred Rosenberg, on the Counts of the Indictment on which you have been convicted, the Tribunal sentences you to death by hanging."

Ten other defendants heard the identical words: Göring, Von Ribbentrop, Keitel, Kaltenbrunner, Jodl, Frank, Frick, Streicher, Seyss-Inquart, and Sauckel.

Martin Bormann received his death sentence in absentia, and the remaining seven were sentenced to varying periods of imprisonment.

The executions were set for early morning on October 16, 1946. After the sentencing, a military guard stood outside each cell observing the prisoner around the clock through a small opening in the cell door. On the day before the executions the defendants could hear the sounds of hammering as three gallows were constructed in the prison courtyard.

At 11 PM on October 15, the night before the executions were scheduled to commence, the guard outside Göring's cell heard him groaning and saw him twitching in his bed. The prison commander and physician rushed into his cell, but Göring was already dead. Glass fragments in his mouth gave evidence that he had bitten into a cyanide capsule. Hundreds of such suicide capsules had been distributed to the Nazi leaders, but it has remained a mystery how Göring managed, despite multiple close searches of his self and property, to conceal the one that ended his life. The other defendants never learned of Göring's death. Von Ribbentrop would replace Göring as the first to be called. Guards entered each cell, one by one, called out the prisoner's name, and escorted the condemned man to the gymnasium, which only a couple days before had been used by American security officers for a basketball game. On October 16, it contained three black-painted wooden scaffolds. Two gallows were used alternately. The third one was unused, there only for insurance. Planks lined the base of the scaffold so that once the hanged man dropped, spectators could not see him struggling at the end of the rope.

Rosenberg, fourth in line, was handcuffed, brought to the base of the gallows, and asked his name. In a soft voice he replied, "Rosenberg," and, with a U.S. Army sergeant supporting him on each side, he ascended the thirteen steps of the gallows. When asked if he had any last words, his dark-circled eyes appeared bewildered as he looked at the hangman for a few moments and then shook his head vigorously. Each of the other nine Nazis made a final statement—Streicher shouted, "The Bolsheviks will hang you one day." But Rosenberg went to his death silently. Like a sphinx.

The bodies of Göring and the nine hanged men were placed in coffins and photographed to remove any doubt that they were, indeed, dead. By cover of night, the ten bodies were taken to Dachau, where the ovens were fired up one last time to incinerate their makers. Sixty pounds of ash, all that remained of the Nazi leaders, were scattered into a stream and soon drifted into the Isar River, which flows through Munich, where this saddest and darkest of all stories had begun.

FACT OR FICTION? SETTING
THE RECORD STRAIGHT

I've attempted to write a novel that *could* have happened. Remaining as close as possible to historical events, I've drawn on my professional background as a psychiatrist to imagine the inner worlds of my protagonists, Bento de Spinoza and Alfred Rosenberg. I've invented two characters, Franco Benitez and Friedrich Pfister, to serve as gateways to the psyche of my protagonists. All scenes involving them are, of course, fictional.

Perhaps because he chose to remain invisible, remarkably little is known with certainty about Spinoza's life. The story of the two Jewish visitors, Franco and Jacob, is based on a short account in the earliest biography of Spinoza that described two young, unnamed men who engaged Spinoza in conversation with the intent of encouraging him to reveal his heretical views. After a short while, Spinoza broke off contact with them, whereupon they denounced him to Rabbi Mortera and the Jewish community. Nothing else is known of these two men—not an unwelcome state of affairs for a novelist—and some Spinoza scholars question the veracity of the entire incident. However, it *could* have happened. The greedy Duarte Rodriguez, whom I portray as their uncle with a grievance against Spinoza, is indeed a historical figure.

Spinoza's words and ideas expressed in his disputation with Jacob and Franco are largely drawn from his *Theological-Political Treatise*. In fact, throughout the novel I draw many of his words from that text, from his *Ethics*, and from his correspondence. Spinoza as shopkeeper is imagined; it is doubtful that Spinoza ever operated a retail business. His father, Michael Spinoza, established a successful import-export business that, by the time Spinoza had entered adulthood, had run into hard times.

Spinoza's teacher Franciscus van den Enden was a remarkably engaging, energetic, free-thinking man who later moved to Paris and was ultimately executed by Louis XIV for plotting to overthrow the monarchy. His daughter, Clara Maria, is described by almost all Spinoza biographies as a fetching prodigy who ultimately married Dirk Kerckrinck, Spinoza's classmate in van den Enden's academy.

Of the few facts known about Spinoza, the most firmly established is his excommunication, and I have accurately reproduced the official text of the ban proclamation. Most likely Spinoza never again had further contact with a Jew, and of course his ongoing friendship with the Jew Franco is entirely invented. I have imagined Franco as a man far ahead of his time, a preincarnation of Mordecai Kaplan, a twentieth-century pioneer in the modernization and secularization of Judaism. Spinoza's two living siblings adhered to the ban and cut off all contact with their brother. Rebekah, as I have described, did resurface briefly after his death in an attempt to claim her brother's estate. Gabriel emigrated to a Caribbean island and died there of yellow fever. Rabbi Mortera was a towering figure in the seventeenth-century Jewish community, and many of his sermons still exist.

Virtually nothing is known of Spinoza's emotional response to being cast out of his community. My depiction of his reaction is entirely fictional but, in my view, a likely response to a radical separation from everyone he had ever known. The cities and houses that Spinoza inhabited, his lens grinding, his relationship to the Collegiants, his friendship with Simon de Vries, his anonymous publications, his library, and, finally, the circumstances of his death and funeral—all these are grounded in history.

There is more historical certainty in the twentieth-century portion of the novel. However, Friedrich Pfister is entirely fictional, and all the interactions between him and Alfred Rosenberg are imagined. Nonetheless, from my understanding of Rosenberg's character structure and the state of psychotherapy in the early twentieth century, all the Rosenberg-Pfister interactions *might* have happened. After all, as André Gide said, "History is fiction that did happen. Fiction is history that might have happened."

As indicated in the prologue, a document (17b-PS) written by Rosenberg's ERR officer (Oberbereichtsleiter Schimmer), who confiscated the Spinoza library, states that the library would help the Nazis explore the "Spinoza problem." I could find no other evidence linking Rosenberg and Spinoza. But it *could* have happened: Rosenberg fancied himself a philosopher, and he undoubtedly knew that many great German thinkers revered Spinoza. Hence every passage linking Spinoza and Rosenberg is fictional (including Rosenberg's two visits to the Rijnsburg Spinoza museum). In all other ways I have attempted to report the major details of Rosenberg's life accurately. We know from his memoirs (written while imprisoned during the Nuremberg trials) that he was indeed "set on fire" at the age of sixteen by the anti-Semitic writer Houston Stewart Chamberlain. This fact inspired the fictional meeting between the adolescent Rosenberg with Headmaster Epstein and Herr Schäfer.

The broad details of Rosenberg's subsequent life are based on historical record: his family, education, marriages, artistic aspirations, experience in Russia, attempt to enlist in the German army, escape from Estonia to Berlin and then Munich, apprenticeship with Dietrich Eckart, development as an editor, relationship with Hitler, role in the Munich putsch, three-way meeting with Hitler and Houston Stewart Chamberlain, various Nazi positions, writings, his National Prize, and experience at the Nuremberg trial.

I have more confidence in my presentation of Rosenberg's inner life than of Spinoza's because I have far more data culled from Rosenberg's speeches, his own autobiographical writings, and the observations of others. He was, indeed, hospitalized twice at the Hohenlychen Clinic, for three months in 1935 and six weeks in 1936, for what were, at least in part, psychiatric reasons. I have accurately reproduced the letter from psychiatrist Dr. Gebhardt to Hitler describing Rosenberg's personality problems (aside from the fictitious final paragraph dealing with Friedrich Pfister). Dr. Gebhardt, incidentally, was hanged in 1948 as a war criminal because of his medical experimentation in the concentration camps. The letter from Chamberlain to Hitler is cited verbatim. All newspaper headlines, edicts, and speeches are faithfully recorded. Friedrich's attempts at psychotherapy with Alfred Rosenberg are based on how I personally might have approached the task of working with a man such as Rosenberg.

Finally, though there were two Jewish women hidden in the attic of the Spinoza museum, I took the artistic liberty of placing them there during the Nazi confiscation of the library: in fact they arrived months later.

ACKNOWLEDGMENTS

I am grateful to many for reflections and suggestions after reading all or part of this text: Stephen Nadler, Van Harvey, Walter Sokel, the late Rudolph Binion, Rebecca Goldstein, Marianne Siroker, Alice van Harten, and members of the Pegasus writing group. My agent, Sandy Dijkstra, offered unflagging support and guidance. Many thanks to my research assistants, Kate McQueen, Moira van Dijk, Marcel Oden; to Maureen Lilla, who edited early versions of two chapters; and to a host of generous friends and colleagues who responded graciously to my many requests for consultation: Stephan Alder, Zachary Baker, Robert Berger, Daniel Edelstein, Lazar Fleishman, Dagfin Follesdal, Joseph Frank, Deborah Hayden, Lija Hirsch, Daan Jacobs, Ruthellen Josselson, Regina Kammerer, Jay Kaplan, Rabbi Patricia Karlin-Neumann, Molyn Leszcz, Pesach Lichtenberg, Miriam van Reijen, Aron Rodrigue, Abraham W. Rosenberg, Micha de Vries, Ori Soltes, David Spiegel, Daniel Spiro, Hans Steiner, Aivars Stranga, Carlo Strenger, Theo van der Werf, Hans van Wijngaarden, Simona van Wijngaarden-Bota, and Steven Zipperstein.

I am especially indebted to philosophers Rebecca Goldstein and Steven Nadler for their generous mentorship. My conversations with Rebecca and her remarkable work, *Betraying Spinoza,* were extraordinarily helpful in my understanding of Spinoza. Steven's biographical and other works on Spinoza were also indispensable.

I had the great good fortune to work with Daniel Menaker, an extraordinary editor who enabled me to write the book I wanted to write. As always, I had in-house support: my first editor was my wife, Marilyn, who is my most demanding critic and constant helpmeet; my son, Ben Yalom, a fine editor, added final polishing to the manuscript.